GRAPHITE AND TURBULENCE

THE ELEMENTAL ARTIST

JAMI FAIRLEIGH

Graphite And Turbulence

Published by Kitsune Publishing
23515 NE Novelty Hill Rd, STE B221-309
Redmond, WA 98058
www.kitsunepublishing.co

The Library of Congress has catalogued the hardcover edition as follows:

Fairleigh, Jami, author
Graphite and Turbulence / Jami Fairleigh - First edition
ISBN 9978-1-955428-08-8 (hardcover)
ISBN 978-1-955428-09-5 (paperback)
ISBN 978-1-955428-10-1 (lrg. print paperback)
ISBN 978-1-955428-05-7 (ebook)
ISBN 978-1-955428-11-8 (audiobook)

CONTENT WARNING

Graphite and Turbulence is an adult fantasy novel which contains violence and gore. A full list of warnings is available at:

https://jamifairleigh.com/cw-graphite-and-turbulence/

Or by scanning this QR code:

Dedicated to Mr. Onion
I love you, Dad.

Art is the lie that enables us to realize the truth.

— **PABLO PICASSO**

CHAPTER ONE

I sat on my horse at the crossroads, dreading what came next, but unable to put it off any longer. "Akiko, I'm sorry, but we're stopping in Whitehall before we travel to Saratoga Springs Depot."

Akiko's scowl deepened. "But you promised!"

I bit back my response because she was right; I *had* promised. Days earlier, in a moment of desperation, I'd dangled the lure of her own art supplies as a bribe. I swallowed, trying to ignore the guilt curdling in my gut, and the ever-increasing throb in my leg. "A quick detour, and then we'll continue to the depot. Bring Lady back, this is the turn."

When Akiko didn't move her horse, my remaining patience evaporated. "Fine. Enjoy your stay here on the road. I'm going to Whitehall." To prove it, I kicked Oxide and yanked on Magnesium's lead rope, turning them onto the narrow side route. My chest tightened, and shame flooded me as my horse grunted in discomfort, his ears twitching. My leg also protested the kick, sending waves of pain rolling up my calf.

This was not my finest moment.

As my horses clattered over the broken pavement, I tilted my head, listening for Lady's distinctive shuffling gait. If Akiko didn't follow, I'd have to turn back, and dusk was already approaching.

The road swept to the left, and I used the bend as an excuse to glance behind. Lady plodded after us, her rider drooping and tear-stained. I slumped as the tension drained from me, but even though Akiko had done what I wanted, this interaction dragged at me.

Each parental mistake I made stayed with me, coalescing into an ever-growing knot of remorse. It ate at my core, each memory a bruised apple with spots of rotten flesh for my fingers to sink into, leaving me hollow, a man-shaped husk of paternal failure.

Was this normal?

In life, I'd made mistakes, but out of all my misguided decisions, I had not expected to regret adopting Akiko. Even now, I dreaded facing her and her disappointment, hated causing the bruised look in her eyes. Would I return to make a different decision given the chance?

The trouble was, though I was barely twenty, I'd taken responsibility for the welfare and wellbeing of another *person*. And I'd done it with the same nonchalance I agreed to small improvements involving my art. But this time, instead of improving a life, I was tearing one apart. In the weeks since we'd left Wakefield, Akiko had transformed from a thoughtful, precocious eight-year-old into a sullen, scowling creature. Where had my sweet girl gone?

It galled me that I was failing at fathering Akiko.

In the past, I'd succeeded at everything I'd tried, and to nurture and protect a child had seemed a simple task. Yet despite my efforts, my best intentions fell flat again and again.

More than anything, I wished to be a good father, so this

time, like every time before, I promised I'd try harder to keep my patience. In time, with enough effort, I'd find the magic combination of words and actions, and Akiko would agree without an argument. But even as I resolved to do better, a tiny voice in my mind asked the question I hadn't wanted to consider when I'd adopted her.

What did I know about child-rearing?

My parents had abandoned me into the abbey system when I was four, to be raised by the masters at Popham Abbey.

My parents.

Would I finally find them when we reached Toronto Depot? Each year on family day at the abbey, I'd hoped they'd show up like the other boys' parents did, but no one ever came. Even when I graduated, there was no word, and the masters either couldn't, or wouldn't, tell me anything. It's why I'd set out on this journey after graduating from Popham Abbey. It was why I'd been traveling and met Josephine, Ben, Genevie, and Akiko... and it was why Akiko and I traveled together now.

I needed answers, and my birth parents could be in Toronto Depot.

Without warning, Akiko galloped her mare past us. Charcoal streaked after the girl, his face set and grim. Oxide shied to the side, cutting off Magnesium and nearly unseating me. By the time I'd balanced myself and settled the horses, my daughter, her horse, and my dog were out of sight.

"The masters would have never allowed behavior like that," I muttered. In truth, the masters had not dealt with a child such as Akiko—they only trained boys as artists.

Oxide's ear flicked backward toward me, and I patted his neck, my leg throbbing in protest as my weight shifted. My stomach knotted as I pictured her mutinous face, the outcome of yet another parental mistake.

Perhaps the larger mistake had been in leaving Wakefield

without the others. After learning my painting titled *Home* might depict Toronto Depot, I'd been eager to depart. I'd worried only about the weather and avoiding Talbot's next trap.

Talbot.

I still couldn't believe the community of Newfane had let Talbot walk away before we'd censured him for crimes committed under his watch.

Crimes like Whistler's death.

A lump grew in my throat, and I swallowed. After three weeks, the hurt was still too fresh, the loss too recent. It was unreal to think I'd never watch him tease his wife or pull a perfect pie from the oven again.

Worse, somehow, losing Whistler had morphed into a terror of losing Akiko too. Since the battle in Wakefield, whenever she was out of sight, gusts of guilt and fear blew through my core.

Like now.

Anxiety gnawed at me, and I urged Oxide to hasten. He quickened, his head nodding rhythmically as we flowed over the cracked pavement. The clatter of hoofbeats disturbed the birds flitting in the trees, and their songs turned to calls of alarm as we passed.

We rounded the next bend too quickly, and Oxide stopped hard to avoid colliding with Lady, who stood in the middle of the road. Our abrupt halt threw me over Oxide's neck, and although Akiko didn't appear to notice the near miss, her mouth twitched.

I gritted my teeth and pushed myself back into my saddle. "Nice riding."

Her lower lip poked out as she glared at me. "All we do is ride."

Since leaving Wakefield, I hadn't allowed either of us the

time to play or be creative. In the spirit of doing better, I reached for a compromise.

"Why don't we stop early today? If you'll work on your reading while I set up camp, I'll show you a new sketch technique."

She straightened, and though she feigned indifference, I could tell I had intrigued her. "Can we stop early enough for you to work on *Home*?"

"I haven't looked at it since we left Wakefield." The drive to work on the painting had faded after I'd learned it depicted Toronto Depot's skyline.

She watched me, her dark eyes wary. "If you finish it, we'll have someplace to go, and we can stop traveling."

I shifted, trying to ease the throbbing in my leg. "We'll see. The first one to find a campsite wins."

Her eyes narrowed. "Wins what?"

I dropped my reins, lifting my arms in a grand gesture. "Naming rights."

My attempt at humor worked, and though she sighed, she urged her mare forward.

"Naming rights *and* the best seat by the fire," I said in a tone of defeat.

Akiko flashed her gap-toothed grin, her disgruntlement falling away like dust. "I come up with better names."

My heart lightened at her change of attitude. "What? You didn't like Mud Pit?"

"Nope. Or Mosquito Pit, or Tree Pit, or—"

"Cherry Pit was a brilliant campsite, *and* we found cherries to eat."

Akiko rolled her eyes. "You put them on the tree!"

"Still counts." I grinned. "I hope we camp at Strawberry Pit tonight."

A warm breeze carrying the scent of wild roses and marshy

ground ruffled Oxide's mane as we continued down the empty road.

"I'd rather have Ben's Cooking Pit." Her shoulders drooped. "I miss them."

"Me too," I said, scanning the roadsides for a clearing. "I wish they were here."

Akiko sighed again. "Ben's stories. And his cooking."

Charcoal pounced on a green-and-brown mink frog, and though I winced at the squeak and slurping sounds that followed, my stomach growled too. "I long for Ben's cooking more than you do."

"I miss it more!" She toyed with Lady's mane. "They will come, right?"

Akiko's plaintive expression twisted my heart. "They will."

"How do you know?" Tears glimmered in her eyes.

I understood her worries—I'd grown up yearning for my birth family.

"They're coming because we're family. Even separated, family sticks together." Until I had met Ben, Josephine, and Genevie, I hadn't experienced the compassion, empathy, and emotional support a family could provide.

Spotting a suitable clearing, I cleared my throat. "Bet I'll find a campsite first."

Akiko squealed and trotted forward. "No, I found one first!"

I pretended I hadn't seen it and stared the wrong way. "Way too brushy."

She pointed. "No, the other side!"

I spun Oxide in a circle, lifting Magnesium's lead to keep it from wrapping around us. "This side is also too thick."

Akiko sighed. "You're thick. Come on, Charcoal."

I followed the girl and the dog off the road into a meadow, assessing the tree line for a suitable campsite. The mid-May grass was a lush blanket of emerald green with no hint yet of the seed pods and Magnesium knickered as he waded through the blades.

"Great find," I said, dismounting. The motion reignited the throbbing pain in my left calf, but I swallowed my groan before she noticed.

Akiko's brow wrinkled as she pointed. "Is that thing pretending to be a tree?"

The curious object *resembled* a tree. It had a trunk pieced together in sections, its seams made more obvious by rusting rivets. The lower branches stuck out about two meters from the trunk and incrementally shortened, giving it a conical shape. However, the metal spikes jutting from the top ruined the illusion.

I shrugged, tying Magnesium to a sturdy branch. "*Before the world died, people built a lot of strange things. Why did you notice it?"

"It's too regular." She turned toward me. "Trees don't look like that."

I glanced past her at the strange object. "Why not?"

She cocked her head. "Trees are full of happy mistakes."

I treasured these glimpses of how she observed the world. "Happy mistakes. I like that. I've made an unhappy mistake today, didn't I?"

Akiko bit her lip. "I want to go to the depot."

"I know, and I'm sorry about the delay. After Whitehall, we'll go straight there. One night here in Charcoalpitt, then onto Whitehall, then straight to the depot."

Her lips twitched. "This is Charcoal*ville*."

"Didn't we stay in Charcoalville last night?" I pulled the packsaddle from Magnesium.

Akiko dropped to the grass, giggling as Charcoal nuzzled her neck. "Yesterday we stayed in Charcoal*ton*."

"My mistake," I said, unsaddling Oxide. "Tell me, what lesson are you working on?"

She shrugged. "They're all the same. Squiggles and smudges."

I chuckled, taking Lady's reins from Akiko. "Letters and numbers. Tell you what, you come recite your letters while I set up, and I'll help with your reading."

Akiko sighed. "Do artists really need to learn how to read?"

"Yes," I lied.

After weeks of travel, the routine had become second nature again, so I listened with half an ear as I unsaddled Lady. I'd nearly finished before my mind registered the discrepancy. "Wait, what?"

Akiko shrugged. "What?"

I crossed my arms. "Repeat those last letters."

She rolled her eyes. "O, P, R, S, T, W, Y, Z."

"You're missing a few."

She rocked back and forth, hugging herself. "No one uses them, so I left them out."

I laughed. "How do you spell quiet?"

She stilled, staring left. "K-Y-E-T?"

"Q-U-I-E-T," I said, unfolding the tarpaulin.

She kicked a rock, frowning. "It's too hard for me. Maybe I'm dumb."

I glanced at her as I uncoiled the rope. "You're not dumb. It *is* hard, especially when you learn it later." I tossed the rope over a branch and pulled the canvas up to create a shelter. Akiko held one end while I tied off the other.

"How old were you?"

I shrugged, securing her end to an exposed root. "Five?"

Akiko played with the donkey's long ears. "See? Even a baby can learn it."

"You're not exactly elderly."

"Will you ever paint Sir Donkey? He's the only one without a name."

I winced as the heavy pannier banged against my injured calf. "If you tell me what pigments you'd use, we can name him right now and I won't even need to paint him."

Akiko wrinkled her forehead. "*That's* why Genevie calls him brownishgreyishyellowishblack?"

I laughed and carried the last of the tack under the shelter. Akiko hadn't moved, so I lay on the crushed grass next to her, my head pounding. "Let's watch clouds."

She wriggled closer to me. "I see a rabbit."

The cloud resembled a hare. "R-A-B-B-I-T."

"D-U-M," she said, showering me with dandelion fluff.

"D-U-M-B," I corrected.

The clouds formed and reformed shapes as they scudded across the cobalt sky. Dragon, waterfall, horseshoe.

Perhaps I had gone about this wrong. "Mouse, there are twenty-six letters in the alphabet."

"Only if you keep them all," she said in a matter-of-fact tone.

I grinned. "Twenty-six letters, *assuming* you keep each one. The letters get mixed into different combinations to make each word, like how we mix pigments to create an infinite rainbow of colors."

She rolled to her side and propped her head on her hand. "Letters are like pigments?"

"Sure. What happens if you put a smear of blue and a smear of yellow on a canvas?"

Her face tightened, as if the question was a trick. "You get a smear of yellow and a smear of blue."

"Correct. What about if you allow them to overlap?"

She sat up. "You get green where they touch."

"Why don't they stay blue and yellow?" I asked, turning toward her.

She chewed her lip before answering. "You said they bounce light different when they get mixed up."

I nodded. "Exactly right. We recognize green even though the pigments are still blue and yellow. Now, the letter T makes a 'teh' sound. What sound does an H make?"

Her eyes brightened. "Huh."

"And E?"

"Eee," she said, enjoying the game.

I picked a long stalk of grass and tickled her nose with it. "Put them together and you get the word 'the' even though it's spelled T-H-E."

She puffed out her cheeks. "Is there a color wheel for reading?"

I shook my head. "Nope, you learn it the hard way like I did, but once you get it, it sticks forever." To chase away her crestfallen expression, I stood, trying not to wince. "Let's be letters."

Akiko sprang up. "How?"

"*A*." I demonstrated, standing with my feet apart and my hands together above my head. She followed my lead, grinning.

"B!" I shouted.

She crooked one leg in a lowercase b before shouting, "C!"

We both bent, but where she bent forward, I tried curving sideways.

She scowled. "You're like a floppy *I*." When I copied her posture, she nodded. "*D*!"

We went through the rest, laughing. This time, she didn't skip any letters, shrieking with glee as I fell over while trying to contort into an S. After Z, we flopped on the grass. Blades poked through my hair, tickling my ears, but I ignored them, too lazy to move. The compromise had worked; not only had it avoided another squabble, but Akiko was more like her old self.

"I'm hungry," she said.

Charcoal squirmed between us, wedging himself upside down, panting happily.

"Me too. Your turn to cook," I said.

Akiko tried to poke me, but Charcoal's waving legs blocked her. "Get up, old man."

"Nope. I'll live right here."

She giggled. "On the ground?"

"On the ground." I settled deeper, breathing in the scent of crushed clover. "It's very comfortable."

"Get up!" Akiko panted as she pull my arm.

I sat up suddenly, tumbling her backward, my spirits rising as she collapsed into giggles. "You go pick our meal and find the pot."

She scrambled to her feet. "Okay."

Charcoal trotted after her, his eyes bright at the mention of food.

As soon as she was distracted, I lifted my trouser leg. The wound on my left calf was angry and raw, the white cut surrounded by swollen, red skin.

In moments of quiet, the hiss of the knife as its blade sliced through my leg echoed across my mind's canvas. Yet another reminder of what Talbot's people had done.

"Great," I muttered, gritting my teeth as I poked the wound. It oozed and the angry red lines extending laterally had deepened into a dioxazine purple. I'd clean it again after Akiko fell asleep, though I wasn't sure my ministrations were helping. I knew little of healing because they'd trained us in literature, philosophy, and art, but skipped the standard apprenticeship training most young people received.

"Hey Mouse, bring the map over?" I called, rolling my trouser leg down.

After we spread it on the grass, Akiko traced her finger down the route we'd followed. "We're here, right? All I could find for dinner was barley."

I groaned dramatically. "Only barley?"

Whitehall was the nearest community, and at least a day away. After what happened in Wakefield, it felt safer to detour around unknown communities, but I needed a healer. Plus, unless we wanted to eat unadorned grain for a week, we needed supplies. Last, although I had misgivings, Akiko needed a break from traveling. "We'll be there tomorrow," I said, pointing at the map.

She frowned. "Whit- Whit-e-hall. Whit-e-hall?"

"Whitehall," I said, sitting back.

Akiko's eyes sparkled. "That's how you spell white?"

"Mm."

Her brow furrowed. "Always?"

I grinned. "Yes, always."

"W-H-I-T-E," she murmured, her expression pleased.

Charcoal put one foot on the map, and Akiko batted it away, giggling. "You can't read."

He glanced at me and I smiled with sympathy. "Even if you *can* read, you can't read out loud, so she has you there."

After they scampered off to find firewood, I stared at the map, uneasy. If the community of Whitehall refused to help us, we would be on our own. There were no other farmsteads or communities on the map between Whitehall and Saratoga Springs Depot.

CHAPTER TWO

I retched over Oxide's left shoulder, hoping Akiko wouldn't notice. I didn't want to alarm her, but the dull pain I'd been ignoring had grown to a roar. Not much came up; it had been hours since breakfast, and the sun was high in the sky. I spat and rinsed my bitter mouth.

Akiko, riding lead, continued to chatter. "The colors between the horizons are strange. Don't you think it should be more gray than green?"

I shook my head to clear it. "What?"

Akiko twisted in her saddle. "Are you listening to me?"

"Yup." I tried to smile.

She spun around to ride backward. "Are the flashes a memory, or is someone pushing the picture into your brain?"

I blinked. "Pushing the picture?"

Akiko sighed. "Are you remembering or being shown the picture?"

This conversation again.

I shrugged, naming pigments to marshal my patience. "When a flash comes, I add it to the painting."

Akiko wrinkled her brow. "But you named the painting '*Home*,' so it must be where you're from."

"Maybe. Or perhaps I'm seeing a vision of the future," I said, shifting.

She nodded. "That would be nice. I've never had a home."

Her words squeezed my heart. "Never?"

She shook her head. "My parents followed preacher after preacher, so my whole life has been on the road." She sighed, turning around.

My shoulders drooped, head pounding and ears hot, so when Oxide moved to the left and bumped my calf, I groaned. My leg was so swollen I couldn't even lace my boot this morning.

Akiko turned her head. "Did you say something?"

"No." We needed to reach Whitehall before the infection in my leg spread any further.

When the road widened, Akiko made a kissing noise, loping her mare in a graceful circle before falling alongside me. "When are we stopping for lunch?"

I didn't want to stop because I wasn't sure I'd be able to get back on my horse if we did. "Don't you want to reach Whitehall first?" I asked through gritted teeth. "We'd get a better lunch there."

Her lower lip poked out. "I'm hungry now."

I dug through my pommel bag, fishing out a small sack of roasted sunflower seeds. "Here, try these."

She took the sack from me and peered inside. "What are they?"

"Sunflower seeds," I said, swallowing my nausea. "They're delicious."

She put one in her mouth and crunched it tentatively.

I attempted a grin. "Split the seed open with your teeth and eat the middle."

Akiko's nose wrinkled. "What do I do with the shell?"

"Spit it out."

She beamed, spitting the shell in my direction. "These are good."

"Nice try." My vision grayed, and I shook my head to clear it, then caught her expression. I needed to distract her. "Let's play a spelling game."

She frowned, squirming in her saddle.

To ease her worry, I explained the rules. "I'll say a word and spell it. You rhyme my word, then spell yours."

She pressed her lips together. "You start."

Head pounding, I said, "Mop. M-O-P."

Akiko frowned. "Top?"

I nodded. "Spell it."

"T-O-P," she said in a small voice.

I shifted. "Correct. Stop, S-T-O-P."

"Crop! K-R-O-P," she countered.

I made a buzzing noise. "Nope, crop starts with a C."

Akiko slapped her forehead. "Fine, smarty pants. New word."

"Cat. C-A-T."

She brightened. "Bat. Same as cat with a B."

"Brat. Same as bat with an R," I said, chuckling.

Akiko rolled her eyes. "Fat. F-A-T."

I opened my mouth, but no words came. Head pounding, I shook my head.

"Gnat, at, hat, that, flat, chat. I win," she crowed.

I tried to smile, focusing on the rhythmic *clip-clip-clop* of the horse's hooves striking the ancient pavement.

"Are you okay? Your forehead is wet." Akiko's voice sounded far away.

My vision grayed again. "I'm not well."

She quieted. "Then... we're traveling to Whitehall for a healer?"

There was no point in keeping the truth from her now. I nodded, fighting to keep my gorge from rising.

"Good, because your face is the color of a tube of yellow-gray." She clucked to her mare, and the horses quickened. "What do you think? About an hour?"

"I hope so." My voice was thin, and heat poured from my ears.

She stared at me. "Can we fix you with art? Like how you healed Josephine's arm?"

"No, this is more than skin deep."

She evaluated me, her face serious. "I'm taking your reins. You concentrate on staying on." Before I could protest, she reached down for Oxide's rein. "Tie Magnesium to your saddle."

As soon as I'd complied, she moved to the lead, squeezing her mare into a slow jog. Oxide quickened, Magnesium's lead tightening across my thigh until he matched our pace.

"Wow," Akiko said, as we passed an ancient farmhouse.

A tree had, long ago, broken through the dwelling's roof, so it appeared as though someone had built the structure around the tree. As the smaller buildings from *Before* had long since rotted and collapsed, we rarely found such reminders outside of filling stations and depots. Why had they used such flimsy materials to build their dwellings?

"Matthew? Matthew," Akiko repeated in an urgent voice.

We'd stopped moving. Confused, I shook my head, peering around. "Is this Whitehall?"

She smoothed her hair. "Sit up. They're coming."

A man with close-cropped hair reached us first. "Heya, Travelers. Welcome to Whitehall. I'm Atticus Rush, the administrator. How can we help you?"

Akiko jerked her thumb at me. "This is Matthew, and I'm Akiko, his wart."

"Ward," I corrected, my voice hoarse. I coughed to clear it. "Can we see your healer?"

"Ah." The administrator stepped backward. "Are you ill?"

I shook my head. "Leg infection."

Rush's expression cleared. "Wait here, and I'll get someone to help you down."

I nodded gratefully. When he left, I slumped forward, resting my chest against Oxide's neck. "Thank you, Mouse."

She dropped to the ground, stretching. "You fell asleep hours ago."

Hours? "You must be hungry," I said, glancing at her.

She shook her head. "I ate all the sun seeds."

"Sunflower." Several people approached, so I straightened. "Remember, don't let anyone see you sketching while we're here."

She rolled her eyes. "I *know*. You tell me every time."

With help, I dismounted, but my left leg nearly buckled when it touched the ground. Supported between two women, I hopped toward a faded red dwelling with a deep, covered porch. We struggled onto the porch, sapping my strength. Exhausted, I leaned against the door frame while they knocked.

An older man dressed entirely in black opened the door. "Yes?"

"Tuckett, Administrator Rush asked us to bring this man to you," said a woman.

Tuckett stared at me, unsmiling. "Put him in there," he said, pointing to a door on the left.

I hopped into the room and leaned against a long table, nodding my thanks to the women. They scurried out of the dwelling, closing the door behind them.

Tuckett crossed his arms. "What's wrong with you?"

Where was Akiko? Distracted, I peered through the windows. "My leg."

He didn't move. "Where are you from?"

I wasn't sure how to answer his question. "Where am I coming from, or where did I grow up?"

He blinked, waiting.

I shivered. "I grew up in Popham Abbey, but we've come from Wakefield."

His posture softened. "You're an artist? Give me your leg."

I tried to roll my trouser leg up, but it snagged on my swollen calf. "I'll have to take them down." With difficulty, I stood and unbuckled my trousers, sliding them to the floor. I kicked off my left boot and slid my pant leg over my foot. My calf throbbed as another wave of exhaustion slid over me.

Tuckett brought a tray to the table. "Sit back."

As I slid backward on the table, Charcoal streaked past the window, a stick in his mouth.

"Nasty. Did someone take a saw to your leg?" Tuckett poured a clear liquid into a ceramic dish and the scent of alcohol filled the room, stinging my nose.

"I..." I stopped. Should I admit I injured my leg during a battle?

He dabbed at the wound with the saturated cloth. "Go on."

I hissed, gritting my teeth. "People attacked the community we were in."

His expression remained unchanged, so I shook my head and chewed on my cheek until his lips flattened. "You should have kept it cleaner."

My eyes watered. "We've been traveling."

"We?"

"My ward and me. She's—" I craned my neck, but she wasn't visible. Unease flickered through me. "She's outside."

Tuckett shrugged. "She'll be fine. They like kids, these people." His words spiked my adrenaline.

These people. *They* like kids. Was he trying to tell me something?

When Tuckett pressed a square of linen near the swelling at the top of my calf, I groaned.

His eyes flickered with sympathy. "I'll need to drain this abscess."

I nodded miserably.

He patted my shoulder. "Lay back. It's better if you don't watch."

I complied, shivering as Tuckett moved around the room, gathering supplies. The cleaning had set my leg on fire; how much worse could it get? "Have you lived here long?"

"In Whitehall? Yes, though most here are new." He laid a blanket over me, leaving only my infected leg uncovered.

"Where did everyone else go?" I asked, propping myself up on one elbow.

Tuckett shrugged. "Some left to live with family. Some left in the middle of the night, saying nothing. These people didn't bring a healer when they arrived, so they've largely left me alone and have pushed none of their nonsense toward me. Here we go," he said. "On three."

I lay back again as something cold touched my leg.

Tuckett gripped my ankle with his left hand. "One, two—"

A searing pain shot down my leg, followed by the sensation of hot liquid running over my skin.

His grip tightened. "One more time. One—"

This time, he cut on one. I convulsed, but relief immediately followed the pain, tempering the hurt. A putrid stench, like sweaty feet bathed in rotten egg, filled the room.

I gagged, but Tuckett appeared pleased. "Good, you came in. You only had a day or two left to keep the leg."

Nausea roiled my stomach. "I want to keep my leg!"

"And so you shall." He peered at me. "Not the fainting sort, are you?"

My teeth chattered. "Why? Is there more?"

Mirthless, he grinned. "I'm packing the leg. Squeal if you must."

This time, I closed my eyes. Tears leaked from the corners, and I focused on my breathing while he pushed and prodded at the wound.

"There, done. And not one prayer uttered," he said, winding something around my calf.

My eyes shot open. "Prayer?"

He nodded, his jaw set. "You know religious followers appropriated Whitehall, right?"

The hairs along the back of my neck rose as I searched his face for the strange fire, which burned in Cara's eyes. If Tuckett wanted information, admitting I knew about the rise of religion could put us in danger... but nothing about Tuckett appeared false.

My head hit the table with a *thud*. "No, I didn't. This is the first community we've stopped in."

Tuckett relaxed, patting my shoulder. "Not the first religious folks you've run across though, by the look of your leg."

I squinted at him. "No."

"Good, then stay here until your fever drops and you regain your strength. I have room for your ward too. How old is she?"

I sat up. "Eight. I'm Matthew Sugiyama, artist. Thank you for your hospitality."

He nodded. "Well met. I'm Eliot Tuckett, healer. I have not been saved, nor am I likely to be so."

CHAPTER THREE

I leaned heavily against Eliot as we approached the chair. The morning dew soaked my boots, and I shivered.

"You shouldn't be taking part in this circus," he muttered. "You're still unwell."

"I owe the community for our keep," I said, wincing. He helped me sit, and I stifled my groan.

Tucket leaned forward to tuck a blanket around me. "If you need me to intervene, say you're having trouble breathing."

I nodded and attempted a smile, then faced the administrator. "What can I paint for you?"

Administrator Rush stepped forward and cleared his throat. "We'd like you to change the appearance of this building."

"The pub?"

The building was square and squat with a flat roof and too few windows. Crooked stairs led to a sagging porch.

"Our *meeting hall*," Rush said, taking a leather-bound portfolio from a teenager with a terrible case of acne. "We've collected these with great effort," he said, before handing me the portfolio.

I looked through the collection of records, turning each page with care as I scanned the drawings and printed images of buildings. The theme was clear; the buildings were white and featured ornamental windows made of colored glass, and many included a pointed tower on the front facade. "What do you intend it to be?"

Rush brightened at my question. "A beacon for the weary."

I kept my face neutral and played along. "Do you want a lamp in the tower?"

Rush's brow furrowed, but Preacher Saget smiled at me. "I believe Artist Sugiyama is referring to the towers standing along the coastline." Her expression remained warm, but a cold, yellow haze flickered around her.

Although I blinked several times, the blur didn't return.

"We'd prefer a bell in the tower," Saget continued. "But are you capable? Tuckett believes you need more rest."

I squared my shoulders. "Yes, with Akiko's help."

Saget nodded. "Children *should* build a work ethic while young. Please proceed."

Akiko had already clipped a sheet of watercolor paper to the easel and waited with a jar of water in her hand. I'd planned to paint in oils but didn't have the energy to argue with her, so I took the jar. "The square hog bristle, please."

Her eyes widened. "Which one?"

My lips twitched as she pretended ignorance. With the entire community watching us—their faces alight with anticipation—it was a smart move. "The square brush with the cream-colored hairs."

Akiko feigned rummaging through the supplies and straightened, holding two brushes. One, as she well knew, was ox hair and the other the hog bristle.

She held both toward me, and I pointed at the hog bristle. "I'll use this brush to dampen the paper."

The crowd murmured, their voices an excited hum. I wetted the paper and returned the brush to Akiko. She exchanged it for my palette, then held the tray of pigments for me.

After I'd collected what I needed, I said, "I'd like the round sable brush now. It has a red handle."

Akiko handed me my favorite paintbrush, and I blended the pigments to create the colors I needed.

"When I work, I first paint what I see," I explained. "Luckily, your pu—I mean *meeting hall* is already white, so I won't need to pull pigment off the paper when I make the modifications."

I handed the round brush to Akiko. "The square ox hair, please."

Akiko held out four square brushes, and I picked the one I often used for applying the background. After checking the paper for dampness, I lay down the background colors and glanced at the building while the pigments melded.

"The sable spotter brush next."

When Akiko stared at me with exaggerated confusion, I played along. "It has a very pointy tip with short fibers. I believe the handle is pale blue."

She handed it to me, and I said, "I'll use this brush to add the building's details." I swirled the brush in undiluted Payne's Gray pigment. "I work from the inside out to give the background drying time. If I started at the edges of the building, the water from the background color would blur the lines of the building."

I worked swiftly, evaluating the building with glances as I painted. From the corner of my eye, I watched Akiko absorb my technique. She'd seen me sketch and paint with oils, but watercolor was new to her, which explained why she'd chosen to set up the easel as she had.

Sneaky Mouse.

When I'd captured the building, I rinsed my brushes and instructed Akiko to let them air dry.

She grinned at me and flicked the brushes, spraying the people sitting closest to us.

Stretching my left leg, I groaned. The pain was less than it had been before Eliot lanced it, but my leg was stiff, and movement pulled at the stitches. Eliot leaned forward, but I shook my head.

"Help me stand?" I asked Akiko, gathering the blanket from my lap.

She nodded and shooed Charcoal from my feet before steadying me.

Saget glanced from me to the easel. "Artist Sugiyama?"

"This is part of the normal process." I massaged my hand, fighting the urge to rub my wrist. "I usually stand when I paint, and I'm letting the pigments dry before I continue."

She smiled. "I see. Would you like to break for lunch? Will the painting be safe?"

My stomach rumbled, but I put my hand over it. "The painting will be fine, but I'll finish the work first."

She beamed. "We're eager to witness what you can do."

What I could do. If she only knew.

The changes they asked for were simple, needing little effort or time. However, what they *wanted* was a show.

My earlier conversations with Tuckett had rattled me, and I wanted no excuse for Whitehall to delay our departure, so a show was what I endeavored to provide.

I tilted my head, letting the sun warm my face. Its light glowed red-orange through my closed eyelids. I raised my arms to stretch upward. None of this was necessary, but the movement improved my mood. Once I'd stalled enough, I dropped my arms, recentering.

With my eyes closed, I pictured the finished building on my mind's canvas. When it appeared, I rotated it, examining it from all sides, changing minor details. It was the tiny details which impressed people the most, as though large, structural changes were too big to comprehend.

I opened my eyes, accepting the palette and selecting a brush from Akiko. After a theatrical breath, I limped forward. With the wetted brush, I painted the areas I wanted to change with clean water. "Cloth please."

Akiko handed me a square of absorbent linen, and I dabbed at my painting, lifting the pigments from the paper.

Time for art.

Once ready, I worked quickly, the familiar tingle zinging through my fingers. The building groaned as I lifted the walls and steepened the roofs. Wood snapped with a sharp *crack* as I altered the structure's facade, adding arched doors and windows.

The gasps and murmurs around me rose in volume, and I let the crowd's excitement feed energy into my work.

With the foundational work done, I turned my attention to the bell tower. Crows erupted from nearby buildings, their caws alarmed, as the tower rose. Satisfied with the tower, I added a large circular window with a geometric flower design to balance and anchor the improvements. The bell's low tone reverberated in my chest as I painted its glint.

Saget's eyes shone. "Can we go inside?"

I inclined my head, finishing the stone patio. "Please."

She climbed the steps onto the new stone patio, then hesitated. When I waved her forward, she raised her chin and flung the doors open.

As the crowd surged forward, I sank into my chair, hands

shaking and stomach queasy. The colored glass window threw shards of jewel-toned light over the people crowded inside.

"You didn't have enough energy to paint." Akiko's tone was reproachful.

Exhausted, I nodded. "I know, but I needed to buy us a little time. Good show, by the way."

"Show?" she asked, cleaning the palette.

"Pretending not to know which brushes were which."

She grinned at me. "You could've used the ox hair to wet *and* cover the paper."

I chuckled. "Finishing too fast would have disappointed them."

As Saget reappeared, Akiko stiffened, so I pushed the satchel of art supplies into her arms and jerked my head at Eliot's dwelling. "Go."

Saget strode toward me with her face set in a hard smile. "Artist Sugiyama, the meeting hall is a marvel. May I escort you to lunch?"

"Yes, thank you."

"I hear you're traveling to Toronto Depot," she said, as we shuffled toward the far end of the green. "But we invite you to settle here with us."

I smiled at her, hoping to cover my dismay. "You flatter me."

"Good." She beamed. "Whitehall is small, but not without friends."

"Oh?" I asked, keeping my tone interested, but my gut twisted at the strange light burning in her eyes.

She took my arm, her grip too tight. "We're in regular communication with communities like ours."

My pulse quickened. If true, news of the battle at Wakefield could arrive at any moment. We needed to leave as soon as possible. "Like the Avalon Society?"

Saget stiffened. "I wasn't aware you'd dealt with them."

The scent of fried food wafted toward us. "They've offered several commissions."

She cocked her head. "You haven't accepted?"

I shook my head. She waited, but I volunteered nothing else.

When we reached the tables, I sank to a bench, levering my injured leg under the table. "Akiko?"

Saget gestured. "The children sit over there. They enjoy keeping their own company."

Though I smiled, I knew Akiko would later complain about being lumped in with the children.

Saget turned toward me, crackling with energy. "You didn't accept the society's commission?"

"No," I said, reaching for my glass. The water had a strong mineral flavor, unfamiliar and unwelcome. I grimaced and set it down, the odd taste lingering.

"Like them, we are a network of resourceful, connected communities," Saget said, her words chosen carefully.

She paused, drumming her fingers as a red-haired woman set down a tray, unloading a platter of fried patties, a bowl of potato salad, and small bowls of sliced strawberries. "Good afternoon, Preacher, Artist. Timothy will bring bread."

After the woman left, Saget bent her head and closed her eyes. Stretched and brittle, my nerves made my fingers twitch as I waited for her to finish.

When her eyes opened, she appeared pleased by my empty plate. "May I?" Without waiting, Saget set several patties and a scoop of potatoes on my plate. "We have resources and add more all the time. Strawberries?"

"Please." This wasn't the Strawberry Pit I'd envisioned for us.

"We also have an advantage over the Avalon Society," she said, handing me the plate.

"Oh?" I pushed the potatoes around my plate, expecting her to mention her faith or her god.

She smiled, smug. "We are a loving people. We live to be in service of others and what we hold dearest."

This, I *knew*, was untrue. The zealots who'd attacked New London, Brookfield, and Wakefield had shown no love or care for the people they'd slaughtered.

A boy carried a basket of sliced bread to our table, but the warm and yeasty scent of the fresh bread mingled with my memories: blood and screams, the *snick* of steel sliding through my flesh, the smell of Whistler's protruding brain—pink-gray and glistening—on the *wrong side* of his skull. My vision narrowed, the mealy potatoes souring in my mouth as I struggled to keep my face neutral. My fork clattered onto my plate as I dropped my hand to prevent Saget from seeing it tremble.

She didn't appear to notice my discomfiture and continued. "Finally, *unlike* the Avalon Society, we welcome everyone to join our communities."

CHAPTER FOUR

Pamela Saget rounded a corner and headed toward Eliot's dwelling before I could bolt inside. "Preacher Saget," I said, in a flat tone as the porridge I'd eaten for breakfast churned in my gut.

She held her palms up. "I'm told you're leaving at week's end."

I scanned her face as jitters spread through my belly. Had she received news about Wakefield? "Yes. Is there something else you'd like me to improve before I go?"

She sat on the bench beside me. "No, we're grateful for what you've done here."

After making the improvements to their meeting hall, I'd altered her dwelling to match in tone and style. The two buildings now had similar doors, windows, and roof lines, setting them apart from the other structures and dwellings in Whitehall.

"What have you come to discuss?" I asked, trying to keep the edge from my voice. We'd already argued several times over my refusal of her offer.

She plucked at her skirt. "Akiko."

I stiffened. "Akiko? What about her?"

Saget bit her lip. "Matthew, while it's clear you're fond of each other, we've noticed she is withdrawn, and either unwilling or unable to engage with her peers."

This wasn't what I'd expected. "Peers?"

"The other children." Saget glanced at me. "Akiko doesn't know how to play."

I frowned. "She plays."

Saget folded her arms. "She plays with the dog and you, but not the other children."

I scrambled for an explanation. "Our stay here is temporary. Perhaps she's kept herself apart on purpose."

"There's also the matter of her schoolwork," Saget continued.

I had pressured Akiko into attending lessons with the other children while I recuperated. Although she'd pleaded for me to reconsider, I'd been adamant. It was safer if we appeared like any other traveling family.

"She's behind," I said, "but we are working on it."

"Yes, well, many of our five-year-olds eclipse her. What kind of life are you setting her up for?"

To reassure Saget, I said, "Before we leave, I'll speak to the instructor and ask for suggestions." Saget didn't respond, so I tried again. "Thank you for seeing me about this, Pamela. I appreciate you taking the time to visit."

Saget arched her thin eyebrow. "You're not her natural father."

"No." Where was she going with this?

"Matthew..." Her lips pursed before she continued. "It may not be appropriate for you to continue traveling with Akiko."

I blinked. "What? Why?"

"You're a young man, and you've traveled since graduating from the abbey."

I nodded, unsoothed by her warm tone.

"Travel isn't good for a child."

The truth of Saget's words pierced me. Akiko had traveled her entire life because her parents traveled with revivalists, but admitting it could open the door to a conversation best avoided. Worse, Saget's invitation could change into a demand.

"Why not?" I asked, stalling.

Saget leaned forward, her gaze intent. "Akiko must be allowed to be a *child*. She needs to play games, make mistakes, experience the censure of her peers. Children yearn for familiar surroundings, stability, and structure."

Although I agreed in principle, I squirmed. "Akiko is special and unlike other children."

"I agree." Saget sat back. "Which is why we'd like her to remain here, with us."

I straightened, blinking. "Stay in Whitehall?"

Saget nodded. "We provide a loving community. We'll protect and educate her."

My heart thundered and nostrils flared. "*I* protect her. *I* love and care for her." Ignoring the pain shrieking up my leg, I stood. "We leave at week's end. I appreciate your concern, but I consider the matter closed."

Saget's eyes cooled. "You are not her father."

"I am," I said, lifting my chin.

She rose and moved toward me. "You are not her *natural* father and have no more claim over her than I do."

Chills tracked down my spine, and I licked my lips. I had no way to prove Akiko belonged with me, but shook my head, mustering all my authority. "I appreciate your concern, Preacher Saget, but we leave at week's end."

Her eyes narrowed. "Consider my offer. We'll talk again."

"I have—"

"She is not your child nor a puppy to drag around for your amusement," she snapped. "You haven't set clear expectations or provided her with any kind of structure. Furthermore, she will become a young woman soon. Are you equipped to handle that?"

"She's eight," I protested.

Saget's words picked up a shrill edge. "She has four to seven years of childhood left. It is not appropriate for a man —*an unattached man*—to have unfettered access to a defenseless girl."

Staggered by her implication, my gut churned. "Preacher Saget—*Pamela*, I hear your concerns and thank you for expressing them. While Akiko and I travel alone now, we are joining our family in Toronto Depot. The women in my family will help Akiko as she matures."

As Saget's certainty faded, I pressed on. "My sister, Josephine, is a scholar and will take over Akiko's education, but you've opened my eyes and I'll seek opportunities for Akiko to spend time with other children." This wasn't entirely a lie. I'd toyed with finding an abbey to foster Akiko.

I opened the door and stood on the threshold. "Thank you, Preacher Saget, and good day," I said, stepping into Tuckett's dwelling and closing the door behind me. I waited, worried she'd batter it down, but after a pause, she descended from the porch. I sagged against the door. That anyone would challenge my guardianship of Akiko hadn't occurred to me.

"We better get you out of here before week's end," Eliot said. He sat on the staircase with Akiko, who appeared frightened, her eyes huge.

Eliot's words were like a cold-water dowsing and I swallowed. "You heard?"

He nodded, hard-eyed. "Yes, but I don't think Pamela Saget did."

I shook my head. "Mouse, you don't want to stay, do you?"

"Please don't leave me here," she said, tightening her arms around Charcoal.

I studied Eliot. "They won't be happy if we slip away. Will this blow back on you?"

He frowned. "I'm not staying to find out."

"You're leaving? Because of us?" I glanced around the dwelling he had lived in for so many years.

Eliot shrugged. "I only stayed because I didn't have anywhere to go."

"Want to come to Saratoga Springs Depot?" Akiko asked.

He smiled at her. "No, little one. I'm traveling to Wakefield."

I gaped at him. "Wakefield?"

"Akiko told me they need a healer."

Akiko grinned and patted Eliot's head. "Even an old healer is better than no healer."

"Akiko!"

She giggled. "Eliot is even older than you. I drew a map for him."

Ice slid down my spine as she admitted she'd drawn something, but Eliot caught my expression. "Our secret, I promise."

I chewed on my lip. "I'll write a letter of introduction—Nicole will be wary of strangers."

"Thanks. Help me sort kitchen supplies?" he asked Akiko.

She nodded, taking his hand. "Take nothing easily spoiled, too heavy, or squishy."

Eliot pretended astonishment. "No raw fish?"

Akiko's nose wrinkled. "They'll track you by smell alone."

"I packed your things earlier," he called, as Akiko led him

into the kitchen. "Everything is in the cabinet at the top of the stairs."

While I wrote the letter for Eliot, my mind whirled through worst-case scenarios. From now on, we'd need to minimize our interactions with strangers, and I could no longer claim Akiko as my ward. This would make traveling more difficult, but I couldn't risk another community arriving at the same conclusions as Saget.

ONCE I'D FINISHED ELIOT'S LETTER, I STEPPED ONTO THE porch to take stock of our situation. The people of Whitehall bustled around like normal with several waving at me, so I adopted the air of someone strolling for leisure, ambling along the flagstone path I'd painted along the edge of the community's green. It was wide and graceful, shaded by the flowering fruit trees I'd added. Apple blossoms perfumed the air, alive with the buzzing of mason bees.

As I walked, I evaluated the livery where we'd boarded our stock. To sneak away at night would be difficult because of the time and effort required to catch, brush, saddle, and outfit the horses and donkey. If we left tonight, Eliot would also need a horse, further complicating things.

"Matthew! Well met," called Bert Moore, the hostler, as he crossed the green toward me.

I must have stared at the livery for too long.

"May I join you?" he asked, gesturing at the path.

Though anxiety prickled along my spine, I nodded, trying not to stare at his fingers. He'd bitten his nails to the quick, and his cuticles appeared red and raw. We wandered together, saying nothing, until my nerves shrieked.

"Lovely day," I said, unable to stand the quiet any longer.

"Yes," he agreed, but after a minute, he sighed. "Did Eliot tell you he's lived here longer than almost everyone?"

I nodded. "You've had quite a turnover in Whitehall."

Bert picked at his left thumbnail. "I grew up here. Eliot delivered me and later my three children, but we're all that's left of the Whitehall I grew up in."

I processed his words. "Your wife?"

Bert waved his hand. "She died three years ago, when my youngest was born."

"Oh, sorry."

He gave me a sideways look. "My oldest is ten, and in the same class as your girl. I hear your daughter is struggling with her lessons. I work with my kids on their studies every night. You must keep on them or they'll get behind."

I nodded, clenching my jaw. Had Saget sent him to convince me to let Akiko stay?

After a pause, Bert murmured, "In truth, I'm not wild about the lessons they are teaching our kids." His hands clenched. "Politics, Money, Power, Religion, and Greed."

"These are the things we never again need," I replied automatically. Adrenaline shot through me, and I froze, staring at Bert.

"Let's keep walking," he said. "The kids... I ask them about their lessons. Every night, I ask." He released his breath. "They are not learning what they should."

"No?" My pulse jumped again. Could I trust him? Bert could solve my problem... or warn the community about my plans.

"They're focusing on religious parables and morality."

No wonder Akiko had protested the lessons. To bribe her into attending, I'd improved rusty bicycles the children discovered in a ramshackle building, painting them a garish, bright pink at her insistence.

I studied Bert, searching for any trace of deception, but finding none. This was it. If I wanted to build trust, I needed to admit what I knew. "From the Bible," I murmured.

Relief flickered across his face. "I need to get my children away from here."

We'd almost finished the circuit. "Another lap?" I suggested. "If anyone asks, I can say you're helping me recover the strength in my leg."

Bert relaxed. "Why not?"

We turned, sauntering back the way we'd come, nodding at the others strolling on the green. When out of earshot, I asked, "What's your plan?"

Burt glanced at me. "There's an old wagon behind the livery, but it needs work. I tried to repair it, but the axle is cracked, and our metalsmith arrived with *them*."

Hope quickened my step. "I could repair it."

"Yes, but I have nothing to trade."

"Can you have my horses saddled and ready to leave tonight?"

"Certainly."

Trusting Bert was our best option. "Then do so, and we have a bargain. Come, I'll sketch it now."

Bert stared at me. "You don't need your paints? Your easel?"

I shook my head. "For this, a pencil sketch will suffice."

<hr>

BERT HAD HIDDEN THE WAGON BEHIND A STACK OF MOLDY straw bales. Upon reaching it, I dropped to one knee, ignoring the sting in my calf. A crack split the axel from the left wheel to where it intersected the frame on the far side. I eyed Bert. "Can you leave tonight?"

He nodded. "The sooner the better."

"Good." I pulled out my sketchbook and captured the scene, the damp from the ground soaking my trouser leg and chilling my knee. The iron sang as I repaired it, the wagon groaning as its frame straightened.

When I'd finished, Bert whistled, helping me up. "Thank you, Artist. On the road by myself with three children..." He shook his head. "But when it's time to go, it's time to go."

I nodded as I brushed at my trousers. It was time to go.

CHAPTER FIVE

In the dark, my fingers fumbled over the oiled leather, testing every buckle and fastener on our saddles again. Even though every second we delayed increased our chances of getting caught, I compulsively checked and rechecked our tack while waiting for the perfect moment to depart.

The night air was alive, its humidity malevolent. When the cicadas' song intensified, I froze, wondering if their music would wake the community and betray us.

Akiko stuffed something into her saddlebag. "You've checked everything three times."

I winced at the noise and drew in a deep breath, heavy with the scents of hay and leather and linseed oil. "You're right. Ready?"

Across the green, a light flickered. We froze as a figure passed in front of a window several times. A light in another dwelling turned on, sending gooseflesh up my arms.

Oxide tossed his head and snorted, jingling his bit.

My heart thudded as we waited, and I pondered the wisdom of leaving my sword in Magnesium's pack saddle. At any moment, an alarm could sound, rousing the very people intent on keeping us here. If the worst happened, we'd need to flee without the encumbrance of Magnesium and the donkey, so I unsnapped Magnesium's lead and severed the loop connecting them together.

The donkey wiggled his lips, and I watched his ears swivel, hoping they wouldn't lock onto the sound of someone creeping toward us through the thin moonlight.

The lights extinguished.

"Time?" Akiko whispered, pantomiming the motion of mounting.

I nodded, climbing onto Oxide. "Quietly now." I nudged Oxide out the livery door, directing him into the soft dirt at the side of the road. My nerves screamed, ears stretching for sounds of discovery. Beneath me, Oxide quivered, his skin shuddering, but the dirt muffled our footfalls, and we reached the road without an outcry.

"We made it," Akiko whispered.

"Shhh." I turned Oxide north and froze. A rectangular object lurked in the road.

What is that?

For a moment, nothing moved. Then, a whispered voice. *"Matthew?"*

I glanced at Charcoal, who appeared alert but relaxed. "Who's there?"

A man appeared out of the gloom. "It's us," he said. "Bert and Eliot."

They had left hours ago, their wagon creaking from the livery's yard well before midnight.

My eyes widened. "What happened? Why are you here?"

Eliot sighed. "We automatically turned north toward the depot. It's the only way we've ever seen people travel—we've never left Whitehall before. Is it safe to roll past the community?"

I hesitated, peering over my shoulder. It didn't appear that anyone had noticed our departure; the community buildings were dark and quiet, but I didn't want to check the map and chance someone from Whitehall seeing our light. I turned to Akiko. "You've been studying the map. Can they get to Wakefield without passing Whitehall?"

She bit her lip. "Only by going around the top of Lake George and down the other side."

"How much longer would it take us?" Eliot asked.

Akiko hesitated. "Three or four days?"

Eliot shook his head. "And we don't know what we might run into if we skirt the lake."

I shrugged. "If the route is even passable."

"We must chance traveling past Whitehall then." Eliot rubbed his jaw as Bert nodded.

Akiko tugged on my sleeve. "Can you use art to help?"

The wall I'd drawn around Brookfield popped onto my mind's canvas, squeezing my heart. After what had happened there, I would never wall another community again. "Not art, but" –I dug through my pommel bag, handing a thick graphite crayon to Bert– "rub this over anything that spins, to mute the noise."

Eliot squeezed my hand. "Remember us in your travels."

Akiko waved to the Moore children, and they waved back, their eyes gleaming in the moonlight.

Although my nerves screamed for us to flee, we crept down the road in silence. When the wagon groaned, we halted to listen. Through the trees, lights flickered on, followed by shouting. Akiko gasped and peered at me, her face frightened.

"Let's go." I made a kissing noise and Oxide sprang forward into a gallop.

"Charcoal, stay with Donkey!" I ordered, as we thundered past the dog. It was fortunate I'd released the donkey from Magnesium; the horse would've dragged the smaller animal off his feet.

"Wait, help!" Akiko cried.

My heart twisted; she was nearly out of her saddle, clinging to the horn as her mare galloped beside us.

"Whoa," I said, slowing Oxide. I moved him sideways and hauled Akiko back into her saddle. "Good?"

Her teeth flashed in the dark. "Good. Let's go!"

Again, I urged Oxide forward, and we clattered down the road. This time, Akiko rode easily—centered and balanced.

When Oxide's gait roughened, I slowed. The horses were breathing hard, their sides heaving, but I couldn't risk a rest. "Keep her at a quick walk. I don't want them cramping up in case we need to run again."

Akiko nodded, patting her mare's neck. "I don't see them."

The road behind us remained dark. "Good. With luck, no one will follow us."

Akiko shook her head. "No, I meant Sir Donkey and Charcoal."

I twisted to scan the road. "They'll catch up when they can. Come on." We quickened the horses and rode through the dark, my mind racing. To be safe, we needed to get as far from Whitehall as possible, but neither of us had slept, and the horses were tired. In case they pursued us, we also couldn't camp on the roadside.

In a small voice, Akiko asked, "Did Eliot and the others get away?"

My worry made it difficult to swallow. "I don't know. I hope so." If their luck had held, they were on their way to Wakefield. If it hadn't... what would Whitehall do? Saget's focus on Akiko suggested they valued children, but why? To what purpose? I shivered, pushing away my suspicions.

"Akiko, as we travel, we need to continue to work on your letters."

Her pale hand flashed in the moonlight. "*A* before *E* except after *C* or when sounding like *A* like neighbors or hay."

I sighed. "*I*."

She twisted toward me. "*I*?"

"*I* before *E*."

She scowled. "*I* for what?"

"For..." My stomach churned. "*I* for indoctrination."

"What's doctrination?"

Indoctrination.

Saget's people valued children, and spreading their religion via the young would take less effort. Moreover, the children would continue to disperse learned ideas as they matured. I hoped I wasn't correct, but if I was... we needed to be even more careful with what we told people in the future.

Akiko eyed me. "What's doctor nation? Something Eliot does?"

"Mouse, from now on, we're traveling at night. If people ask, we'll say we're traveling to Toronto Depot to meet family."

"Family? You know where my family is?" she asked in a thin voice.

"No, I—what? I meant Josephine, Ben, and Genevie." I shivered as a chill ran down my spine.

"You want me to lie?"

I winced. Some parental role model I was. "I want to... obfuscate the truth."

"What's ovensgate?" she asked.

"Obfuscate means to muddy or cloud the facts and is not lying exactly. It's more like..."

Akiko's voice brightened. "Like letting pigments wash together?"

I grinned as the moon popped out from behind the clouds, painting the fractured pavement silver. "Yes, like when painted objects blur and smudge into each other."

"We tell people we're traveling to meet family because Ben and Josephine and Genevie *are* family. Obfuscate."

My shoulders relaxed. "Quite. Can you do it?"

Silence.

If she didn't agree, we'd have to avoid all communities, which would make traveling nearly impossible. "Akiko?"

"Good plan, but can you learn me to spell it?"

"Teach not learn," I said, my chest loosening. "And yes, but let's start with easier words."

Akiko sighed. "Fine. Start with doctor nation."

Before I could respond, she cried out and turned toward me; her smile gleaming in the dark. "They're here."

Slivers of moonlight illuminated bobbing, black-tufted ears on the other side of Lady, and when I whistled, Charcoal trotted from around them and smiled, his tongue lolling, but the bands around my chest tightened. We had escaped—*this time*— but in the future, it would be better to evade than escape traps.

CHAPTER SIX

My plan to travel by night worked, and though we heard horses thunder past us several times, we reached Saratoga Springs Depot safely. After spotting its outskirts, we'd slept a few hours, anticipating we'd wake early and find an inn for breakfast. However, I'd misjudged how weary we were, so by the time we stepped into an inn, it was after midday.

"Welcome, welcome. You've missed my lunch rush, so take any table anywhere you like." The keeper bustled around, wiping tables and removing used crockery.

Akiko climbed into a booth near the front window, patting the bench beside her for Charcoal.

I slid onto the bench across from them, glancing through the window. After days of traveling at night and camping by day, I itched for news and adult conversation. This depot was large enough to keep us anonymous, and with luck, we'd only need a few days to resupply and pay for our keep. In case Saget had posted people here, the fewer who learned I was an artist, the better. With luck, I'd only need to tell the keeper and whichever librarian I found to work with.

I'd chosen this filling station because it wasn't in the central depot where most travelers would congregate. Even so, the street hummed with voices, their shouts punctuated by wagons rumbling over cracked pavement and the percussion of construction.

Akiko kneeled on the bench, her face pressed into the window, watching the bustle outside with rapt attention.

I poked her shoulder. "Have you been to a depot before?"

She shook her head, her breath fogging the glass.

"After we eat, we'll find the warehouse to resupply. I don't want you wandering off and getting lost, so stick close."

She nodded, her eyes wide.

"Good afternoon," said the keeper, a plump, middle-aged woman with a mop of ginger curls tied back haphazardly with a dish towel.

"Heya, Keeper, I'm Matthew Sugiyama, artist. We've come to resupply and hope you have room for us."

"Of course, sugar. You two get my last room. Are you hungry?"

Akiko nodded vigorously.

"I've got sandwich makings now, but there's stew on the stove, or I can make a salad if you like eating grass."

Akiko giggled. "Sandwich."

The keeper smiled. "Toasted?"

Akiko nodded, beaming.

The keeper turned to me. "What about you, handsome?"

Not wanting to risk discovery, we'd been eating cold, uncooked meals for days forgoing a fire. "Stew sounds wonderful," I said, my neck flushing under her scrutiny.

She nodded and winked at Akiko before squatting to peer at Charcoal. He gazed at her, then raised his paw.

The keeper shook it. "Bones it is."

Charcoal smiled.

Akiko glanced from him to the keeper with wide eyes. "Did you talk to him?"

The woman raised her eyebrow. "Certainly. What kind of keeper would I be if I didn't attend to all my guests?"

Akiko watched her leave, then whispered, "She can talk to dogs?"

"It appears so," I said, fighting to keep the smile from my face.

Akiko studied Charcoal. "Should I offer something to the keeper for my stay?"

I scratched my beard. "What did you have in mind?"

"Well," she said, tugging on Charcoal's ear, "you'll probably update the map, so that's out."

"Mm." My lips twitched.

"I could do chores or something."

I nodded. "Why don't you ask her?"

When the keeper returned, she set a large tray on the table next to ours, then placed a golden toasted sandwich in front of Akiko. Steam rose from the edges and melting cheese leaked from the corners.

My mouth watered as I eyed it, but Akiko glared at me. "Hands off."

The keeper smirked, setting a bowl of stew in front of me and thick, marrow-filled bones before Charcoal. Wisps of basil-scented steam rose from my bowl.

Akiko extended her hand. "Thank you, Keeper. I'm Akiko."

The keeper beamed as she shook it. "Susannah."

"Well met, Susannah. What can I trade for this sandwich?" Akiko asked, her face solemn.

Susannah's lips twitched. "Why don't you eat first? We can work something out afterward," she said, setting two bowls of fruit on the table.

"Done," said Akiko, picking up the sandwich.

Charcoal watched Susannah leave and waited for me to pick up my spoon before eating.

"Of the three of us, you have the best table manners," I told him.

Akiko's cheeks bulged with sandwich. "Mmm!"

I laughed, digging into my stew. It was delicious—salty and rich with generous chunks of potato and carrot. "Mmm," I agreed. I scooped a second spoonful but paused with it halfway to my mouth.

"What?" mumbled Akiko.

I tilted the spoon, examining the cube of beef. A jolt hit my stomach as a memory of perfectly cubed venison drifted across my mind's canvas. Setting the spoon down, I stared at the kitchen door. "I wonder..."

"What?" Akiko set her sandwich down. "It can't be as bad as your cooking."

I snorted. "Thanks for nothing." I dug through the stew, showing her a cube of beef. "I've only met one butcher who prepared meat this precisely."

Akiko shrugged. "Maybe there are two butchers."

There could be two butchers... or perhaps Earl was here. My heart hammered as I stood. "I'll be right back."

At the kitchen door, I hesitated before tapping on the door and poking my head in.

Susannah was elbow deep in sudsy water. "You finished already, little one? Oh, pardon—is everything all right with your meal, sugar?"

"Delicious, Susannah, thank you. Did you make the stew?"

She chuckled. "Of course! I'm known for it. Why do you ask?"

My face fell, and I shook my head ruefully. "The meat reminded me of... never mind."

"Ah," she said, nodding. "Yes, I see."

"Well, thanks," I said, opening the door.

"A butcher prepared the meat," Susannah called.

I spun. "Butcher?"

Susannah smiled. "Saved me a bunch of time, and I thought it a brilliant trade."

My heart soared. "Trade? She stayed here?"

Susannah raised her eyebrow. "I never said Earl was a *she*, but now I understand why she wanted to review my map before they stayed."

Earl *was* here.

A flush burned up my neck as Susannah's words danced across my mind's canvas. "They? She was with someone?" If Earl had left Star Creek with someone, did it mean she'd coupled? "Was it an older man, dark-skinned with a cap of white hair?"

"My name is still Bowman," said a voice behind me. "Well met, Artist."

I spun around and pulled him into a hug. "Bowman, you're here!"

"So I am." His chuckles rumbled against my chest.

I pulled back, squeezing his shoulders. "And Earl?"

"She'll be back shortly." Bowman glanced across the room. "You've picked up a traveling companion of your own."

"Yes, come meet Akiko," I said, clapping him on the shoulder. "Akiko, this is Bowman, an old friend."

"Hullo, child," said Bowman. "My man!" He held up his hand, and Charcoal gave him a high-five.

"Join us for lunch," I said, scooting onto the bench. My stew was nearly gone, the bread had disappeared, and the last of my fruit salad sat on Akiko's plate. "Well, I *had* a lunch..."

Susannah chuckled from behind Bowman. "I'll bring a refill. Engineer, what can I get you today?"

He eyed the empty plates and bowls in front of Akiko. "I'll have what she had."

Susannah raised her eyebrow. "Everything?"

Akiko cackled. "I was hungry!"

Bowman nodded as Susannah left. "If you're still hungry, I'll help you steal the rest of Matthew's lunch."

"Mouse, remember the flier I told you about? Bowman made it."

Akiko narrowed her eyes, as if trying to decide if I teased her.

"I did," Bowman confirmed. "I flew it here."

"Why are you traveling?" I asked. Memories of New London, Brookfield, and Wakefield flashed across my mind's canvas. "Did something happen to Star Creek?"

Bowman frowned. "No, why?"

"I remember you," murmured a low voice near my ear.

My head whipped around.

Earl.

She straightened, smiling. "Artist."

She looked exactly like I'd remembered, but better if possible. Her long, red-orange hair hung down in twin braids, and her deep-green eyes glowed. Outwardly, I grinned like an idiot while inwardly, my heart cartwheeled with delight as I fought the urge to pull her against me in an enormous embrace. "Butcher."

"Kid," said Akiko.

Earl laughed, the sound musical. "May I join you?"

Akiko moved over, pulling Charcoal with her.

Earl slid in and leaned back, appraising me. "So, you found me at last."

Akiko's brows knit. "We were looking for you?"

"Always," I said, grinning like a loon. Wild joy sparked through me, setting my blood singing.

Bowman snorted. "You go first. What's happened since we last met?"

I told them what had happened after I'd left them in Star Creek: rescuing Josephine, the accident leading us to Brookfield, the time spent in Rochester Depot, the invitations from the Avalon Society, and the trip to New London where I'd found Akiko. I didn't tell them about Talbot, how he had tried to prevent me from traveling, or the painting I called *Home*.

Based on the careful look she gave me, Akiko noticed my omissions, but also excluded them from her version of our story, picking up the narrative from where I'd rescued her. She told them about the bridge and about Ben and me rescuing Cara from the floating debris. I winced at the mention of Cara's name but focused on Akiko, they didn't notice.

"Ben sounds like a swell guy," said Bowman, after Akiko explained he was also an engineer.

"And Josephine?" Earl asked Akiko, though her eyes never left me.

Akiko waved her hands. "She's a scholar with a twisted face who loves Ben."

I nodded. "She may not know it, though."

Akiko grinned. "What a dumb-dumb."

I gazed at Earl as Akiko relayed the rest—the bodies we'd found stacked in the cellars of New London and racing back to Brookfield to find it destroyed.

Even though Akiko didn't mention how the wall I'd drawn around the town for protection had trapped and killed the murderers, my guilt roared. Art was about creation, but in this case, I'd brought death. The murderers had died horribly, trapped by my wall, burned by the fires they had set.

"More died in Wakefield," confirmed Akiko.

Earl and Bowman listened silently, their faces shocked while I told them, in faltering sentences, about the revivalists attacking Wakefield. But when Whistler's face flickered on my mind's canvas, my throat tightened. Unable to speak, I nodded at Akiko, who told them about our escape from Whitehall.

"Wow," said Bowman when we'd finished.

I laughed, the lump in my throat easing.

Earl's smile soothed me. "What now?" she asked.

I settled back to listen. "Your turn."

Susannah entered the room with their lunch, setting plates and bowls on the table.

Bowman picked up his spoon and pretended to sword fight with Akiko, sending the girl into a fit of giggles. "Star Creek is fine."

Earl brushed a strand of her red hair from her cheek. It fell back to the same spot, and my fingers itched to stroke it.

"Or was when we left it," said Earl, frowning. "We've been gone nearly a month now." She pulled the band from the bottom of her braid and raked out her hair.

"Since last we met, I finished my computer," said Bowman, picking up his sandwich, "and added a second seat. Then we tested the flier in different conditions so I could fine-tune the gearing."

I nodded, watching Earl re-braid her hair, mesmerized by the colors weaving back and forth.

"He wanted to put it to a proper test," said Earl, wrapping a leather lace around the end of the braid.

I waited, but neither of them spoke. Charcoal, finished with his meal, nosed Akiko.

"And?" I prodded.

"I wanted to observe how it would do in a storm," Bowman admitted.

"A storm? You flew the flier in a storm *on purpose*?" I shook my head, remembering the single flight I'd taken in the flimsy machine. "That's brave."

Earl grinned. "*I'm* brave for accompanying him. *He's* plain foolish."

"What happened?" Akiko asked.

Bowman chuckled, finishing his sandwich. "We got blown a little off course."

"About three hundred kilometers," Earl agreed.

Akiko's eyes widened. "You landed here?"

Bowman sighed. "No, child. The storm's pressure broke our computer, and I couldn't salvage what I needed from the nearest depot, so we flew here."

"Have you found what you needed?" I asked, hoping the answer was no.

Earl set her spoon down. "Nope. Not here either."

"You should come to Toronto Depot with us," said Akiko.

"You're heading to Toronto?" asked Bowman, as his gaze flicked to Earl.

If I played this right, I might get a second chance with Earl. Leaving Star Creek—*and Earl*—was one of my strongest regrets, but if we traveled together to Toronto Depot, perhaps we'd get another chance to begin again.

I nodded, attempting to appear neutral even as my pulse leaped. "After we resupply, we're Toronto Depot bound, and we'd welcome your company."

CHAPTER SEVEN

A rush of fresh air roused me from my work on Susannah's map, and I blinked at Bowman, back lit by the late afternoon sun. Where had the day gone?

He dropped into a chair at the next table over. "It's rare to find you alone, Artist. Where are the little ones?"

I stretched my hand, rubbing the cramp out of it. "Akiko's around—somewhere. She's helping Susannah, and Charcoal has appointed himself supervisor, so if you find one, you'll find the other. What are you up to?"

Bowman sighed. "Asking about the feasibility of finding the parts I need."

My pulse jumped, but I tried to keep my voice casual. "No luck?"

Bowman shook his head.

This was what I'd hoped for, and I'd slowed our departure in case they traveled with us to Toronto Depot. The prospect left me breathless. "You could come to Toronto."

Bowman grunted, scratching his head. "Might have to."

I bent back to my work. "Try to contain your glee, Bowman."

"Not *my* glee that needs tamping down my friend," he said, and cleared his throat.

My head snapped up. "It's that obvious?"

"Only to them who has eyes, but she's a looker, our Earl." Bowman chuckled and folded his arms.

I tapped my pencil against the table. "You two aren't..."

He shook his head. "No. She's my best friend, my heart, but my tastes run more to—"

Susannah walked into the room and spotted Bowman. "Hullo, sugar. Need anything from the kitchen?"

He brightened. "I'm peckish if you've been experimenting again."

"Sure have. Tea, Matthew?"

"Please." I lowered my voice. "Akiko isn't getting in your way, is she?"

Susannah patted my hand. "No, the girl is a hoot and is proving quite useful, since she can squeeze into the tiny spaces I no longer visit. Besides, children thrive when assigned chores. Be right back."

I twirled my pencil. Occasionally, I'd asked Akiko for help with minor tasks, but it hadn't occurred to me to assign her permanent chores. "Susannah is good with kids, isn't she?"

"Very. As a keeper, she's probably raised a passel between her own and the kids traveling through. She is a force of nature," said Bowman, watching her leave.

I jerked my chin in her direction and raised my eyebrows. "Is *she* your type?"

Bowman shook his head and leaned back. "No, but you are."

My pencil clattered onto the map. Was he serious? "I... uh...."

Bowman smirked, his eyes pinning me to my seat and his silence adding to the pressure.

I scrambled to say something, but my brain manufactured nothing but a buzzing roar. No one had ever overtly declared they liked me... like *this*. "Susannah!" I announced in a too-loud voice when the keeper reentered the room.

She responded by pointing at Bowman's table.

I hesitated but complied, dropping into a chair across from him. "My, this looks delicious." I scanned the tray, desperate to talk about something, *anything* else. "Honey! I love honey. I once met a man who kept bees. He was a keeper, too. Do you keep bees, Susannah?" By the way they stared at me, I knew I was babbling, but continued to chatter anyway.

"He let me try a range of honeys and the difference in flavors shocked me. I learned the flavor of honey is based on which plants the bees harvest. The flower type even changes the color of the honey..." My sudden silence added to my awkwardness, but I'd run out of words.

"I love honey," said Earl, her voice sardonic and amused.

Earl.

How much of my desperate patter had she overheard? My heart quickened as she slipped into the chair beside me, smelling like a summer's morning.

Earl nodded at Bowman. "Any luck?"

"No." Bowman picked up a brown cookie, watching me.

Unnerved by his scrutiny, I grabbed for a mug of tea, wincing as the hot liquid sloshed over my hand and onto the table. Words continued to fail me, so I wiped off my hand, hoping I didn't appear *too* pathetic.

Earl glanced from me to Bowman. "What's up with you two?" We shook our heads, so she turned to Susannah. "Are they behaving?"

"Who? These scamps?" Susannah eyed the spilled tea. "I'll get a rag."

Earl pushed her cup toward Bowman. "I had a chat with an administrator today. She asked if we are staying through the solstice."

Bowman filled her cup and asked, "Are we?"

Earl shrugged without glancing at me.

The solstice was weeks away, and I couldn't manufacture any legitimate reason to delay our travels any longer than I already had. A pang stabbed my chest at the possibility of leaving Earl behind again, so I shoved a green cookie into my mouth.

The cookie's floral flavor flooded my senses, and my eyes widened as the smooth, sweet outer shell gave way to a soft, chewy interior and creamy center. I closed my eyes and rolled the cookie around in my mouth, enjoying the dynamic contrast of sweet and tart flavors.

When I opened my eyes, Susannah stood before the table, watching me with a strange look on her face. Bowman and Earl sported identical expressions.

"My," said Susannah, fanning herself. "It's warm in here."

"What are these?" I asked. "They're marvelous."

"Macarons," she said, sinking into the last chair and pushing the plate toward me. "They're French cookies from *Before*."

I examined the plate of green, brown, and pink cookies. "You're a baker too?"

She shook her head. "Hobbyist only. I like to experiment with old cookie recipes and have been on a macaron kick for a spell now. I trade them with the local baker for bread and pastries."

"What's in them?" asked Earl, selecting a pink cookie and nibbling on the edge.

My groin tightened, and I shifted. It *was* warm in here.

Susannah picked up a cookie and peered at it. "Oh, egg whites, sugar, and ground hazelnuts. The recipe calls for almonds, but I've never seen one. You can put anything you want in the middle. Jam, cremes, paste. The green ones are melon, the brown ones are plum, and the pink ones are strawberry."

"Early in the year for melons, isn't it?" asked Bowman, sipping his tea.

"I made these from preserves I made last summer," said Susannah. "They prize my forsythia honeydew jam around here. In fact, use my account at the warehouse, and you can settle up with me later."

"Thanks, Susannah. Makes it simpler for me." Her offer would enable us to keep a low profile. Pleased, I bit into a pink cookie and beamed as its strawberry flavor burst over my tongue. Like the melon cookie, the delicate, sweet shell nicely balanced the tart jam filling.

Susannah laughed. "Akiko warned me you had a sweet tooth, but I've never seen my cookies have such an effect before."

Earl grinned at her mug. "Where is Akiko?"

"Hard at work," answered Susannah. "She's an industrious little thing."

My chest swelled at Susannah's praise. "I'm done with the map, but I owe you more work now, so what else can I do?"

Susannah bit her lip. "I'm not sure it's worthy of art, but I need a new coop for my hens. The old one is about to come down on top of me."

"Done." I half-expected Bowman to object since a coop was more in line with engineering than art, but I was eager to repay Susannah. Besides, the time alone would help me to recenter.

"Can I watch?" asked Earl.

I glanced from her to Susannah, noting their eager expressions. They expected me to do it *now*. My knees knocked, loose and weak, as I stood. I nodded, saying nothing, but my neck burned as I gathered my things.

"Bowman, you busy?" asked Earl.

He smiled. "No, honey. I'll watch, too."

Hyperaware of their eyes on me, I swallowed. "Ready," I said to Susannah.

She sashayed through the inn, leading us into a small, walled courtyard behind the kitchen. In one corner, the coop sagged, its small run draped with poultry netting. Raised garden beds bursting with flowering plants occupied the other corner.

Susannah sat at a small, iron table in the shade near the door, gesturing for Bowman and Earl to join her. The scraping of the metal chairs against the patio stones sent shudders down my spine.

I assembled my easel, considering what I could do with the structure. "What do you like about your current coop?"

Susannah crossed her arms. "That you're about to repair it."

When everyone laughed, my tension drained away. "What don't you like about it?"

Susannah pursed her lips as she studied the coop. "It's too short to stand in, making it a real pain to clean."

I nodded. "Sure, easy. What else?"

She snapped her fingers. "I'd like a second door so my girls can't bolt out when I feed them."

I secured the paper to the easel. "Good. What else?"

She squinted, her eyes unfocused. "I'd like to collect eggs without having to get into the pen. Oh, and could it be bigger? I'm about ten hens short between summer travelers and my cookie experiments."

I glanced at the building, nodding. "Any particular color you'd like?"

Susannah shook her head, examining the others. "Suggestions?"

Bowman leaned forward, resting his forearms on the table. "Not about color, but a steeper roof would shed snow better. Also, add gutters to the roof to capture runoff to water the hens."

"Good," I said, roughing in the sketch. "What else?"

"Put in large windows. Light improves laying productivity," said Earl, flashing her lopsided grin.

Time slowed, and I memorized the moment—texture, shadow, composition—and *her*. I ached to paint her, but with effort, I dragged my eyes away to refocus on my task.

The coop was a simple, boxy structure, and I captured it without trouble. As I worked, my ever-present worry eased, my shoulders relaxing. Art soothed me—the process, the techniques, the rituals. When I focused on improving a subject, everything else fell away, leaving me calm and peaceful.

As I added the last minor details, Earl murmured near my ear, "I almost want the old coop to remain. You've drawn it too beautifully."

Startled, my hand jerked, leaving a smudge on the page. When had she moved so close?

Earl gasped. "Sorry."

"No, it's fine," I said, blending the graphite into the shadow. "See? No damage done."

"Have you started the art?" asked Bowman from the other side of me.

I flinched a second time but hid it by brushing back a loose strand of hair, tucking it behind my ear. "No. I capture what is before starting the improvements."

"Art time?" asked Akiko, her hair covered in brown dust.

"Hullo, Mouse. Where have you two been?" I leaned down, pulling cobwebs from Charcoal's ears. He too was coated in the dust, dulling his blue-gray coat.

"Eating cheese." Akiko grinned as she studied my sketch. "It looks sad."

"Mm." I turned toward Susannah, but she wasn't at the table. "Where did she go?"

"Customers," said Akiko before catching my glance. "No one from Whitehall."

Earl frowned. "I can't believe their temerity. To attempt separating you…"

Akiko's brows knit. "Timareity?"

I sharpened my pencil, my gaze flicking back and forth from the coop to my sketch. "Temerity. It's another word for impudence or nerve."

Akiko brightened. "Like Sally! T-I-M—"

"T-E-M," I corrected.

"T-E-M" –her brow wrinkled– "E-R-ITY?"

Bowman handed a macaron to Akiko. "A five-cookie word."

"Temerity," said Akiko. "What color will the coop be?"

"Great question," said Susannah, reentering the courtyard. "No one here had a suggestion."

"Well," said Akiko, her tone serious, "How do you want to feel when you visit it?"

Susannah paused. "Feel?"

"Blue calms, but yellow makes me energetic," Akiko said.

Susannah flung her arms up, as if embracing the sun. "Then what is the color of enthusiasm? I come out here for a pick-me-up."

"Orange," said Akiko.

"Orange," repeated Susannah. "Like a good egg yolk."

"Or a pumpkin," said Earl.

"Or a butterfly," Bowman added.

"Or an orange," I said, blowing the graphite from my pencil.

Akiko giggled. "What's an orange? Do you mean the pigment benzimida orange?"

While on the road, Akiko had taken to memorizing pigment names. I hadn't minded then, but now, her knowledge of art materials could expose her secret. I shrugged, hoping no one had noticed her slip. "It's a fruit."

They watched me as if waiting for the punchline. I focused on the coop. "No, really. There's a fruit called an orange. It grows in the south."

"Is there a fruit called a white?" asked Akiko, her eyes dancing.

"Oranges exist," I muttered. "Maybe I'll find one for you in Toronto Depot."

Akiko skipped around me. "How about a purple? What's a purple taste like?"

I ignored her, closing my eyes to let the image of the new coop solidify. It had a steep roof, a gutter system, and large windows to which I mentally added shutters and window boxes. An orange swirled around the coop like a moon.

My eyes snapped open.

That never happened before.

Akiko stopped skipping. "What?"

Only Akiko would understand, but I didn't want to further risk her secret in front of the others. Rattled by the odd experience, I shook my head, reaching for my artist's objectivity. To make the coop larger, I'd either need to use more of the courtyard or push the stone wall back. "What's on the other side of the garden wall?"

Susannah shrugged. "A weedy patch of ground. I tried growing strawberries there, but people pilfered what little grew before I could pick them."

I glanced around the garden for a gate. "How do you get back there?"

Susannah snorted. "To water, I had to carry a bucket out the front door and around the side. A real chore, and another reason the berries didn't grow. The wall keeps the courtyard warm and out of the wind, but it is too small."

"Stone walls are difficult," said Bowman.

I smiled. Here was a task worthy of art. "I'll look."

"Me too," said Akiko.

⁂

ONCE OUTSIDE, AKIKO GRABBED MY HAND, SWINGING MY arm and bouncing beside me. Weeds decorated the three-meter-wide patch between the garden wall and alley. While Charcoal snuffled through the weeds, I sketched the scene for reference.

The murmur of voices floated over the wall, and Akiko stopped skipping. "Did he say Toronto?" Akiko whispered.

My pencil paused, and I listened, catching a few indistinct words.

She squinted at me. "Do we trust them?"

Her doubt plucked at my heart, and I squatted to face her. "We trust them."

She poked my chest. "But you didn't tell them about *Home* or Talbot."

I snapped my sketchbook shut in her face, making her giggle. "You're right. Should we?"

She tilted her head, spinning. "If they come to Toronto Depot, we should."

"Did someone mention Toronto?" I asked, as we reentered the courtyard.

Earl bit her lip. "The administrator said the southern route to the depot is impassable."

The news was a blow. "What? Why?"

Earl shrugged. "It flooded, saturating the route over twenty kilometers."

I groaned. Although I *might* find a way through it for Akiko and myself, the ground wouldn't be safe for our horses. Worse, now there was no way I could further delay our departure. Eight was too young to expect Akiko to travel the longer days an adult could endure.

Akiko tugged on my tunic, looking puzzled.

There was no helping it, so I shrugged and walked to the easel. "We leave the day after tomorrow, Mouse. The detour around the north end of the Ontario Sea will take us an additional month."

CHAPTER EIGHT

Bowman's eyes widened when he stuck his head into our room.

Surrounded by a pile of art supplies, I glanced up while unscrewing a jar of turpentine. The acrid pine odor hit my nose, and I winced. "Is it supper time?"

Speechless, Bowman shook his head.

Akiko sat cross-legged on her trundle bed. "We're organizing."

Earl peeked around Bowman and laughed. She slipped past him, moving a stack of sketchbooks to sit. "You packed all this into your panniers?"

I glanced around, tightening the jar. "Panniers, two sets of saddlebags, and our pommel bags."

"I use my pommel bag for snacks," Akiko reported. "So, it's usually empty."

The room was a mess. Stacks of supplies and our traveling equipment covered every surface so I could review it. The longer northern route required additional supplies, but once we'd laid everything out, I wasn't sure how to pack it together again. I'd even toyed with postponing our departure until Ben and the others arrived, since together, we could transport more.

"This isn't a good idea," Bowman said to Earl.

"What isn't?" I leaned against the bed, the frame biting into my mid-back.

Bowman sighed, opening the door wider.

"Careful!" My warning came too late, and the door struck a gigantic stack of dried foodstuffs. It teetered before crashing to the floor and scattering the surrounding stacks, the linen-wrapped parcels rasping as they slithered past each other.

Charcoal barked once before setting his head down with a disapproving grumble.

When the avalanche subsided, Akiko sighed. "You broke our Tower of Power." She picked her way through the debris field and cleared a space to kneel.

"Tower of Power, take two," I said, as she restacked the parcels. "What's the bad idea? Other than destroying our tower."

"Tower of Power," corrected Akiko.

Bowman bowed. "Deepest apologies, Ms.—"

"Sugiyama," said Akiko, intent on her task.

Tingles fluttered through me as she took my name, like the tiny bubbles in effervescent water.

"Ms. Sugiyama," Bowman finished.

"Hey, it's Bowman what?" Akiko asked.

He cleared his throat. "Bowman Jack."

Akiko narrowed her eyes. "Are you sure your name isn't Jack Bowman?"

Bowman chuckled. "That would make more sense, wouldn't it?"

"What isn't a good idea?" I asked for the third time.

Earl grinned. "Other than this conversation?"

"And Bowman Jack knocking over the Tower of Power," Akiko muttered.

Bowman sighed, backing through the door. Moments later, a light knock sounded on it.

"Who is it?" Akiko asked.

Bowman cracked the door. "May I come in?"

Akiko shielded the restacked pile. "Yes, all right."

Bowman stepped inside and shut the door behind him. "Good afternoon, Mr. Sugiyama. Ms. Sugiyama."

I hugged my knees, enjoying the show.

"Good afternoon, Bowman Jack," said Akiko, without looking up. "What can we do for you today?"

"Would you like to take the flier to Toronto Depot? In return, we'll bring your horses on the northern route around the sea."

"What?" Akiko twitched and knocked her pile over again.

Earl nodded. "Without the computer, we're too heavy together. Now, if Bowman had built it to let the pilot and passenger *both* pedal..."

Bowman grunted. "Version three."

"I'll be the pilot," said Akiko immediately.

"*I'll* be the pilot," I corrected, "*if* we take the flier."

Her dark eyes pleaded with me. "Why if? Don't you want to fly?"

I studied Bowman. "You said it might not be a good idea. Is the flier unsafe?"

He shook his head. "No, but you can't take much with you."

"You'd have to leave some of this behind," agreed Earl.

"No." Akiko shook her head. "We need everything here."

I gazed around the room. "We could pare back a bit."

"I don't pack like Ben," argued Akiko. "*He* brings a lot of stuff."

Ben.

I'd need to get word to him and the others. "You'd bring the horses around the north end?"

Bowman nodded.

I turned to Akiko. "We'd still have our things in Toronto Depot, but we couldn't take them with us on the flier. How much space do we have?"

Earl eyed our belongings. "We carry two small canvas sacks which together are roughly the size of your pannier."

"Oh boy," Akiko muttered, shoving items into her pockets.

"Mouse, we're not leaving this afternoon," I said.

She sighed, unloading her pockets.

I tapped my fingers along my jaw as I eyed the pannier. "Our friends will meet us in Toronto, so we'd need to leave word for them."

Earl turned toward me. "Would they mind if we traveled with them?"

"They won't mind," said Akiko. "But you'll bring Sir Donkey too, right? You only mentioned the horses."

Bowman nodded.

I glanced at the dog. "What about Charcoal?"

"He can sit with me," said Akiko.

I pictured the first time I'd pedaled Bowman's flier. "I don't know, Mouse. How big is the passenger seat?"

Bowman shrugged and pointed at Earl.

"Why don't we go see?" said Earl, standing.

"Sounds sensible," Akiko and I chorused. We glanced at each other and laughed.

"I see the family resemblance now," said Bowman.

***

"Are we ready?" I asked.

"Check."

I squinted in the afternoon sunshine as I circled the flier to check I'd lashed everything securely again.

"You've checked a bazillion times already," said Akiko, rolling her eyes. She and Charcoal sat side by side on the rear seat, and he wiggled as she slung her arm around him.

When I tugged on the harness I'd added to her seat, she groaned. "It's tight enough!"

I ignored her, checking Charcoal's harness again. He grinned at me, and I chuckled at the dog's appearance. "You are both mighty cute in your goggles. Now if I could only get you to act more like him," I said, tickling the girl under her chin.

She giggled. "Let's go, Aviator!"

"Check, Navigator."

I studied the flier. Even pared down, the stack of equipment I'd amassed wouldn't fit in the canvas sacks Bowman had installed as flier storage. To accommodate our equipment, I'd painted improvements to the flier. Widening the back seat had allowed the girl and dog to sit side by side. Beneath the seat, I'd created a hidden compartment no one knew about. At Bowman's direction, I'd lengthened the flier's nose and changed the design of the canard to balance the modifications I'd made.

As a defense against weather, I'd added a leather lap blanket to both seats. The blankets buckled to our seats and featured zippered pouches to store small items close at hand. In one of the storage bags, we'd each stored a change of clothing and art supplies. In the other, we'd packed our favorite traveling foods, a pot, a few small tools, and the canvas tarpaulin and cords we'd need to make camp. Susannah had manufactured slipcovers for our seats, which held our bedrolls and provided padding.

Earl shook her head. "You will travel in style." She

punched Bowman's shoulder. "You could have provided creature comforts."

"When we get the flier back, you can pedal me home," he said, his smile broad. "I'll lounge on the back seat and enjoy the ride."

I laughed, pulling Bowman into a quick hug. Earl's hug lasted longer, my skin thrilling at the contact. Her hair smelled of sunshine and chamomile, and I longed to melt into her. "Take care of yourselves."

"And the horses and Sir Donkey!" Akiko called from the flier.

"You got it," said Bowman. He patted his chest pocket. "I have the portraits you drew of your friends, so we'll find them."

I nodded, releasing Earl. She gave my hand an extra squeeze before stepping back.

Buckled into the front seat, I paused with my hands on the bars. "I haven't prepared a farewell, so I will now pedal away in my most majestic manner."

They nodded, then laughed when I struggled to move the flier. It creaked as it inched forward, but was soon rolling, the pedaling easier as we picked up speed.

My heart fluttered and my palms dampened. "Ready?"

"Check!" Akiko called.

I pedaled toward the small drop-off, and as the front wheel reached the edge, pulled the lever to change the wing angle. The flier's nose tilted up as my stomach dropped away.

"We did it!" Akiko cheered, Charcoal barking with excitement.

We climbed in a spiral, waving at Bowman and Earl. "You doing okay back there?"

"Charcoal loves it up here. Me too."

"Me three." I grinned, my heart soaring. The blue sky beckoned as I trimmed the wings to cruise. We banked one last time before flying west toward Toronto and my birth family. Somewhere ahead of me were the answers I sought, and now nothing stood between me and the end of my quest but the clear blue skies. Clear blue skies and a *lot* of pedaling.

"Springs is so tiny now. Why is it called Springs?" she asked.

I settled back and sipped from my canteen. "It's actually called Saratoga Springs."

"But why Springs?"

"Why do you think?"

The flier wobbled as Akiko squirmed. "It could have been a bouncy place."

I laughed. "Like walking on a mattress from *Before*?"

"Yup!"

Up here, the air was cooler and less humid. I smiled, breathing deeply. "It wasn't bouncy at all, was it?"

"No. Very disappointing."

"Did you try the bubbly water Susannah brought to the inn? They named the depot after the mineral springs that create the water."

"The bubbles tickled my nose."

I chuckled, remembering Charcoal's sneezing fit. "Mine too. I liked it better when she added strawberries."

"Oh, brother, you and your strawberries. This depot looks like a spider web."

The old routes below us resembled a spider's web, radiating from the center and disappearing under the deep-green forest canopy at the edges of the depot. "Keep us on track, Navigator."

"Check!"

"Is Route 29 below us?"

"Check!"

"Good, we'll follow it west."

The map rustled as Akiko refold it. "Ferris Lake Wilds, Silver Lake Wilds, Pigeon Lake Wilds... sure are a lot of wilds here."

I grinned. "Perhaps they're infested with pirates."

"Or creepy bugs that ate the people from *Before*."

"Spooky." I scanned the ground, catching flickers of cracked pavement through the thinner patches of the tree canopy.

We flew west for several hours before the sparkle of blue water glinted to our north.

The map rustled again. "Hmm. The Great Sack-and-ah-ga Lake."

I pictured the map. "It's pronounced 'sac-can-dog-a,' but your reading has improved."

"It made sense when Bowman showed me," she said.

Although there was no malice behind her statement, the words stung, another reminder of my inadequacy.

Charcoal barked, and I glanced left but saw nothing.

"Oh, look!" Akiko exclaimed.

To our right, a flock of geese rose in a v formation, leveling out above us. I trimmed the nose, and we climbed until the geese were at eye level with us.

Akiko sighed. "Beautiful. I wish we could paint them."

The geese, sleek and confident, flapped next to us, unconcerned by our presence, but Charcoal whined.

"Keep him calm, Mouse."

"He's fine, aren't you, Char—"

But Charcoal wasn't fine and barked when the edge goose drifted too close.

Alarmed, the goose honked and swerved *into* us.

Akiko shrieked, and I reflexively jerked the handlebars to the left, banking the flier steeply.

"Hold on!" I pedaled furiously, trying to wrestle the bars

straight as Bowman's warnings of a wing stall echoed through my mind. If we stalled, we could induce a spin, the force of which could tear through the gossamer material covering our wings.

While I struggled to pull the nose up, the fabric above my head luffed, and Akiko shrieked again. "We're flying too slow!"

Speed.

The way to prevent a stall was to pick up speed. "Hang on!" The nose dropped when I pushed the bars forward and the flier lurched, diving toward the ground.

My eyes watered from the wind, and my stomach jumped into my throat as I struggled with the controls.

Breathe, Artist.

The wings leveled as I hauled on the bars, slowing our dive. The extra speed helped, but I over-corrected and almost tipped us to the right. We were still dropping, but with the wings level, I no longer feared I'd fall off the flier. I pedaled as fast as I could, my lungs on fire and mouth sour with fear.

Our dive shallowed, but Akiko shrieked a third time. "Trees!"

I yanked back the bars, the veins in my arms popping out from the effort. "Working on it!"

We leveled too slowly, and the tips of the conifers slapped against our landing wheels. Charcoal barked maniacally as birds flushed from the canopy.

My legs burned, and my chest heaved, but if I slowed my pedaling, we would sink into the canopy. I gathered my remaining energy and pedaled faster. By the time we cleared the treetops, I was wheezing. "We need a place to land," I said, between gasps.

"Check."

CHAPTER NINE

My legs, sore from yesterday's punishment, shrieked as I reached for the rope's loose end. The sandy gravel shifted beneath my feet as I snatched at the flapping rope, but it struck my face before flipping up, out of reach. Stung, my eyes watered. "Blast."

Akiko extended her hand. "Here, eat a pink cookie."

I eyed the macaron. "Where did those come from?"

"Susannah."

"But where did they come from?"

Akiko shrugged. "The seat."

I opened the rear seat and frowned. When I'd loaded the flier, the hidden space had contained *Home*, the letters I'd found on the dead minstrel, and the sword they had given me as a lad at Popham Abbey. Now it also held trinkets, socks, and several satchels.

"Akiko, this must weigh a ton!"

She squinted at me. "I didn't want to hurt Susannah's feelings."

I stared at her. "Susannah gave you all this?"

Akiko squirmed, then scowled. "She gave me the cookies. But it's not like Bowman could wear my socks!"

I closed my eyes, naming twenty of my favorite pigments. "Akiko—"

"Sally gave them to me before she left," she interrupted, sounding miserable.

It wouldn't serve either of us to argue again, so I closed the seat cover and sat down, staring at the flapping tarpaulin. "I should break down camp."

Akiko shrugged and picked up the stick Charcoal had brought. "We're sploring."

They raced down the beach together, her laughter and his barks reminding me of my carefree youth.

Why had I agreed to *fly* to Toronto Depot? I'd waited nearly two decades for answers about my family already, so what would an extra month have mattered? The wing's fabric flapped in response to a powerful gust but didn't answer my questions. As Akiko's peals of laughter floated on the wind, I sighed.

Done is done.

I hauled myself up, opened the seat, and found three satchels of macarons. I took a pink cookie before limping back to the shelter.

Could we take another day off? My legs could use the break, but the blue sky was cloudless. "Blast." To console myself, I bit into the cookie and the strawberry flavor burst forward, more vibrant than the actual fruit.

"Hey, you're eating my cookies."

I froze, caught. "*Our* cookies."

She grinned. "So, we can keep them? And my socks?"

I grunted. "We'll see. Roll up the bedding and stow it on the flier, please." Susannah's words echoed in my memory. "From now on, this will be one of your chores."

Akiko crossed her arms as if to argue over it. "We're not staying?"

"Staying?" I scanned the campsite. "Here?"

She nodded. "It's okay to be scared."

"I'm not scared," I lied. "My legs were sore, so I took a break."

But Akiko was right; I was terrified. The flight yesterday had gone from pleasure to horror in a blink. Or more accurately, in a bark. What if I hadn't righted the flier in time?

She stared at me without expression. "Okay."

The wind died, and I snatched the rope as a powerful gust hit the shelter. The rope slid through my hand, burning my palm, but I yanked on the knot, collapsing the shelter.

Two lumps squirmed under the canvas. "Hey!"

"Whoops. Here, let me help you," I said, but each time the lumps moved to an edge, I held it down. "No, move to your left!"

"We did!" Giggling, Akiko fumbled toward another edge.

I flipped up the tarpaulin, laughing. "There you are!"

They crawled out, wriggling with delight.

Akiko stuck her tongue through the gaps in her teeth. "I won't get the bedrolls until you fold the canvas."

"Okay." I clowned around, pretending to struggle with it, but the wind picked up again, nearly ripping it from my hands. "Whoa." I gathered the canvas and held it until the gust subsided. After Akiko helped me fold it, I sat back on my heels. "I *am* scared, Mouse."

"We know," she said.

"We?"

She poked my hand. "Me and Charcoal."

"Charcoal and I."

"No, Charcoal and me."

I chuckled. "Never mind. I'll make lunch before we go. Are you finished packing?"

"Yup."

I pulled out cheese and bread to assemble sandwiches. When Akiko giggled, I glanced up in time to watch her slide Charcoal's goggles over his eyes. I smiled, slicing an apple. "Lunch!"

Akiko trotted over. "Where's Charcoal's sandwich?"

The goggles magnified Charcoal's eyes, but I shook my head. "He doesn't get lunch."

"But he's hungry."

To confirm, Charcoal glanced at Akiko and wiggled.

"Hungry?" she repeated.

Charcoal wiggled harder, smiling.

I sighed. "Here, have mine. I'll make another." I gave it to Akiko, then caught her handing Charcoal the entire sandwich. "Akiko! Tear it into pieces for him. I don't want him sick while we're in the air."

She exhaled in an exaggerated sigh. "*Okay.*"

After assembling two more sandwiches, I wrapped one for Akiko for later. She was always hungry now.

"I made you this," I said, setting the wrapped sandwich in front of her.

She pulled a pair of goggles from behind her back. "I made you this."

"Those are yours."

She pulled another set of goggles from her pocket. "Nope, mine has stars on the straps."

I glanced at the two pairs of goggles in her hands, then at the pair on the dog. Three pairs of goggles. "Where did those come from?"

She blinked. "I *drew* them."

I choked down the rest of my sandwich, mumbling,

"Show me."

On the fourth page of her sketchbook, she'd drawn many sets of goggles. I picked up the pair she'd handed me and compared them to the sketches, spotting a match. They were like hers, though larger and devoid of stars.

"You drew these," I said, studying them. A buzzing filled my ears as I held them to my eyes and peered through. They had a slight tint which blocked the sun's glare.

Akiko turned her palms up. "What?"

Dry-mouthed, I shrugged, unsure of what to say. "Thank you."

She nodded, stowing her extra sandwich. "I'm keeping this as a snack."

I nodded, watching her skip around the flier.

No one could create from nothing... but Akiko could.

I stared at the goggles, then pulled them on.

"They look great!" said Akiko, buckling Charcoal into his harness.

My mind reeling, I finished stowing the last of our things in the canvas sack, lashing it to the wing.

Akiko's lips compressed. "Can you make sure our harnesses are tight?"

Subdued by her request, I took my time, checking each buckle and latch. When I'd finished, Charcoal licked my hand. I scratched him behind his ears before sliding into my seat. My breath came in small gasps as I buckled my harness and fastened my lap blanket. "Ready?"

"Check."

My legs protested when I lifted them onto the pedals. This wouldn't be fun.

I turned us in a wide circle, trying not to groan at the effort. We stopped, facing into the wind, the gusts pushing me against my seat.

"Is it too windy?" Akiko asked in a small voice.

I adopted a false cheer. "Nope. Bowman told me it's easier to launch into the wind."

My legs shook as the flier lurched forward, but once the flier rolled easily, I trimmed the wings, and we immediately climbed.

"That *was* easy!" called Akiko.

I grunted. My legs burned, and though I was already gasping, I wanted to climb a hundred meters above the tallest trees. The air warmed as we rose, scented with pine and dust.

"This little lie of mine, I'm gonna let it shine," sang Akiko. Charcoal yipped, and she sighed. "New song? Okay. Ring around the poles, your eyes shine with holes, ashes, ashes, we all fall down!"

"New song!" I called.

Akiko cackled, then hummed the tune again.

I pedaled without stopping through the unrelenting wind, my legs as heavy as iron. The hours passed slowly, giving me plenty of time to think.

Akiko could *create*. At the abbey, it took years to teach students to manipulate energy. The energy work was how we made changes, or what we referred to as improvements, to physical objects. The complexity of creating something from nothing was incomprehensible, yet somehow Akiko had done it. Even after all my success at school, I had attempted nothing like this. The most I'd accomplished to date was when I constructed the wall around Brookfield, but I'd done so by manipulating the energy of the stone and earth in the community.

I glanced down to ensure we followed Route 29 and made a minor correction. After studying the map last night, I remembered the road would merge with Route 90 south of the Shaker Mountain Wild Forest.

As a distraction, we'd manufactured ghoulish and silly reasons they'd named the lakes and forests 'wild.' Cannibals, robots, aliens, radioactive tar pits, great hordes of groping zombies. My favorite had been a purple mist Akiko had theorized would make one lose all ability to speak, leaving the afflicted to grunt, groan, or gesticulate.

Perhaps her creativity fed her artistic abilities. Without training, Akiko had developed her own style of art. In Wakefield, her serialized, interrelated sketches illustrated the narrative of the battle as it unfolded. She'd used her art to alter the course of the fight, like when she'd opened a gap in a stone wall so Genevie and I could escape attackers. Akiko had also created a rock fall, killing several of our captors and allowing the people of Wakefield to escape a trap I'd inadvertently created with *my* art.

Even though I was an artist of exceptional skill, Akiko's abilities bewildered me. Where I had honed and perfected my skills over the sixteen years I was at the abbey, her talent was innate, intuitive.

I sighed as I glanced down at the rolling green canopy. Although the facing wind had helped us launch, it hadn't allowed us to travel far over the last hours. At least my rubbery legs no longer burned.

A strange noise caught my attention. "What was that?"

"Charcoal snored, but it's a good thing."

"Why?"

Akiko sighed. "Because they fly faster than us."

I blanched as a flight of swallows passed us as though we stood still. "This wind is brutal. We'll stop soon and make it an early night."

From the back seat, something rustled. "Good. We could have *walked* farther today," she mumbled, her mouth full.

She was right. Again.

CHAPTER TEN

The sounds of a pencil scratching roused my attention. "You better not be drawing my head."

Akiko giggled. "Big ears or another eye?"

I chuckled. She wouldn't dare... would she? When I ran my hand over my head, Akiko laughed, so I shook my fist at her.

Akiko spotted a herd of cows and chortled. "From up here, they look like bugs!"

"Maybe up close, bugs resemble cows."

She scoffed at my suggestion. "Up close, ants look like monsters."

"How do you know what a monster looks like?"

"Want me to draw one for you?"

I shivered, a part of me afraid she could create one. "How about you describe it with words? Bonus points for five-cookie words."

She clapped her hands at the game. "The monster has slimy spikes instead of hair and a lugubrious expression."

I shouted with laughter. "Lugubrious? Where did you hear that?"

"Earl said Bowman had a lugubrious expression when she suggested they trade their flier for our horses."

"Oh?"

"Yup. Five cookies for me. Bespattered with rainbow-colored freckles, the monster has seven eyes. *And* he has knives for fingers."

My stomach growled again, and I scanned the ground. We'd covered a lot of ground today—the pedaling easier when not fighting a headwind. "Please never draw it. You'll give me nightmares."

"What are you looking for?"

"It's lunchtime, but there's nowhere to land."

"I'm hungry too, and I ate my snacks *hours* ago."

My stomach rumbled as I searched the horizon. "Check your pocket."

The zipper slid with a *thwip*. "Nope."

I rummaged through my lap blanket, too. "Me neither. If we're lucky, a big bug will fly by." I waited but got no response. "A nice, juicy bug with a crunchy shell and squishy guts."

"I've eaten bugs but they're not too bad," she said, her voice drowsy.

Akiko had slumped to the side, her head resting on Charcoal, who was fast asleep. The flier wobbled, so I whipped my head back to front.

Kilometers of forest unrolled beneath us without a break as they slept. If I'd known the monotony of the undulating green carpet and silent hours, I would have stowed extra food within reach. Perhaps I'd make a modification to the flier tonight, after we landed.

If we landed.

Bored, I squinted at the sun. Though it was still high in the sky, it had traveled toward the west. "I'd guess three o'clock."

There was no response.

Through thin patches of the tree canopy, Route 90 continued westward. If the weather held and the winds were favorable, the glimmer of the Ontario Sea would soon break the horizon. It wasn't much, but the last thing of interest we'd passed was Utica Depot, hours ago.

It had been eerie to view a depot from the air. The fractured towers had risen over thirty meters into the air, and I'd allowed the flier to descend lower to better observe it.

A hawk's scream caught my attention. It circled far below us. "He's probably also hungry."

"Huh?"

"Welcome back, Mouse."

"We're *still* flying?" The flier wobbled as she fidgeted and moments later, her pencil resumed its scratching.

"What are you drawing?"

No answer.

"Entertain me. What are you sketching?" It had better not be the monster.

"Look at your—she paused—six o'clock."

My lip twitched. "That's behind us."

"Um, your nine. Or eight-thirty."

A bare patch of ground had appeared in the middle of the vast forest.

I swallowed. "Akiko, did you—"

"Yay, some dirt! Let's have lunch," she interrupted.

The clearing appeared large enough to land in. "Okay, I'll circle and land facing north."

"Check!"

The flier sank toward the ground, but without warning, we dropped a meter, then popped up again.

My stomach flipped.

"Matthew?" Akiko sounded frightened.

I gripped the bars—my knuckles white—and glanced up,

expecting a rip in the fabric above us, but the wings appeared fine.

My gut churned as I scanned the area again. We'd descended to about sixty meters but were still well clear of the trees at the edges of the field. Without warning, the flier surged and dropped twice in quick succession. Akiko shrieked, and my grip on the bars tightened as the flier bounced in the air. During one jarring drop, my teeth snapped on my tongue, flooding my mouth with blood.

Twice, a wing dipped as the air beneath it collapsed. Though I'd lined us up for landing, the flier continued to buck, its movements unpredictable and wild, as the wall of trees at the far end of the clearing appeared to grow taller.

Charcoal whined as we slipped and bumped sideways, and Akiko wailed. "Something's wrong!"

"Mission aborted. Sorry, Mouse, but this field doesn't want us here." I pedaled hard, trimming the wings to climb. We rose in a slow spiral, widening our circumference with each loop. Once we were over the trees, the air evened out, and the flier stopped shaking.

Akiko sobbed while we continued to climb, shrieking as the odd air pocket collapsed or pushed us to the right or left.

"You okay?" I asked, banking west.

"I lost my sketchbook in the bumps," she said, her voice thick with tears.

"We have one more."

She hiccuped. "What happened? Did I do the field wrong?"

To admit the truth wouldn't help, so I shook my head. "We hit chaotic air."

She sniffled. "What's that?"

"Bowman called it turbulence. He warned me we could hit turbulence over mountains or during storms."

"But the field was flat, so what made the crazy air?"

I hated not having a confident answer for her. "Perhaps a change in temperature?" Though my heart resumed its normal rate, I remained alert, ready for the next catastrophe.

"Could changing from a forest to a field affect the temperature?"

I trimmed the wings again and settled back. "Sure. Sunlight bounces back from grass or trees differently than from rock or water. Perhaps creating a new surface caused a temperature difference between the field and the forest."

"Oh." Akiko sobbed again.

"What now?"

"I'm hungry."

"Me too. Keep watch for somewhere to land." To distract us, I started a game. "I spy with my little eye something starting with a *B*."

"Blue sky," she said, her voice bored. "Blue sky, green trees, brown head. All day there's only blue sky, green trees, and a brown head."

"What shade of blue?"

"Antwerp," she said immediately. "The trees are a mix of cobalt and emerald green. Not mixed up, but trees of each color standing together."

"And the brown head?" I asked.

"Sepia with streaks of indigo. Although in the sun, it looks more like raw umber with Pozzuoli Earth and Indian red."

"At least you didn't say Davy's gray," I muttered.

"You're old, but you're not *that* old."

I snorted. "Can you hear me rolling my eyes, wretched child?"

"I spy with my little eye something starting with an *S*!"

I glanced around. "*S*?"

"Sparkle! Is that the Ontario Sea?"

I squinted into the falling sun. "No, we're not far enough west. Want to pull out the map?"

Paper rustled.

"Don't drop it," I warned.

"Don't fly bumpy," she retorted.

The sparkle *was* water, but from a smallish lake, nowhere near as large as the Ontario Sea. Thirst plucked at the back of my throat, and I sped up my pedaling.

"It might be Oneida Lake," she said, her voice muffled.

I scanned the nearest shoreline. "Any communities on the lake?"

"No." She sighed. "Nothing."

"Shall we try it, anyway?"

"Can we stay the night?"

It was only late afternoon, but I was exhausted too. "I suppose. Are you all right?"

"I'm thirsty."

Neither of us had been drinking much because we couldn't easily stop to relieve ourselves. "Looks like there is a sandy beach."

"Check, but let's go lower."

I trimmed the plane, and we slowed. "Any obstacles?"

"No. Will it be bumpy?" Her voice caught.

"Nope!" I said, mustering as much confidence as I could.

Charcoal whined, but Akiko said nothing as we circled again, now thirty meters from the ground.

"Okay, we're going in." I pressed my lips together as I slowed my pedaling. The beach was approximately fifteen meters wide, stretching in a gentle curve for more than a hundred meters, and the flier sank toward it, needing few corrections. When the rear tires bounced, Akiko gasped, but the flier settled back to the ground, rolling forward smoothly.

"Nothing to it," I said, my hands shaking as I unbuckled myself. I groaned as I stood. "My legs are like jelly."

Akiko was almost out of her harness, so I shuffled around the flier to unbuckle Charcoal. He jumped down gracefully, stretched, and rolled on the sand.

"Be right back," I said, heading toward the trees.

"Be right in front," she said, sprinting ahead of me.

The shade was cool and smelled of ferns and moss, and my bladder ached with relief as I stepped behind a tree. When finished, I evaluated the area, calmed by the chirp of frogs and the steady lap of wavelets against the pebble-strewn sand. A faint gurgle told me fresh water flowed somewhere in the forest. Why were we flying? I was much happier on the ground.

"Let's set up camp here," Akiko called.

"Check, but help me push the flier up near the trees first."

"I'll pedal it," she said bossily. She sat in the front seat, her tiptoes barely reaching the pedals. "Give me a boost."

I leaned my shoulder into the frame and pushed, grinning as my toes dug into the pebbled beach and Charcoal zoomed around us, his eyes wild and ears flat against his head.

"I'm doing it," Akiko called in a cheerful voice as I pushed the flier toward the edge of the woods.

Under my direction, Akiko steered the flier, parking it with the nose pointing toward the water. After I unhooked the canvas sacks, I used our spare cords to tie the flier to a tree.

Akiko watched, her eyes curious. "Why are you putting it on a leash?"

I shook my head. "I don't know. Weather?"

"With Antwerp blue skies?"

I winced at her correct use of a pigment name. "Just a feeling. Akiko, when we're in a community, you need to be more careful about what you say."

She stared at me. "Huh?"

I unrolled the canvas. "At Susannah's, you mentioned benzimida orange."

Her eyes narrowed. "So? I didn't sketch or paint or anything."

"I know, but remember how you pretended you didn't know the different paintbrushes in Whitehall? It's the same with pigment names."

Akiko's eyes flashed. "So, I can't draw, know about paintbrushes, *or* use pigment names?"

My shoulders relaxed. "Exactly."

"That's not fair!" She crossed her arms and stamped her foot, glaring at me.

I blinked. "Fair? Akiko, you're a girl."

Her arms dropped and her hands clenched into fists as she scowled. Without a word, she whirled and dug through the canvas sack.

I bit my lip. "What are you digging for?"

"The sketchbook you *said* I could have."

I flapped the tarpaulin open. "Be careful with it. It's the last one."

Her eyes filled with tears. "I'm sorry!"

A pang of guilt speared me, and I kneeled to hug her, but she pushed me away. I sat back on my heels. "It's okay. We'll get more in Toronto Depot. Help me set up camp?"

Her eyes narrowed as she wiped the snot from her nose with the back of her arm. "Why should I? I'm just a *girl*."

I stood, frowning. "Take Charcoal to collect firewood, then get our bedrolls from the flier. From now on, you're responsible for creating a fire ring too."

She rolled her eyes. "Check, Aviator."

"Roger that, Navigator," I said, matching her sarcasm.

"Charcoal, give stick!" Akiko ordered.

I hauled the canvas over the nearest limbs, fuming while I

lashed it into place, and secured it with stress knots. Though gentle waves lapped at the beach and the sky remained serene, I draped the spare canvas sheet from our shelter to the flier, creating a sort of sloped wall.

"You wrecked our view," said Akiko, returning with an armload of sticks.

"Make the fire over there," I said, pointing.

Akiko huffed and dropped the wood. "Anything else, *sir*?"

I ignored her surly tone and glanced at the sky again, but nothing appeared amiss. "You decide."

The small fire crackled as I lay on my bedroll, eating my meal and staring at the canvas above my head. Despite my best intentions, I'd let her needle me into losing my temper again. Worse, now I'd have to monitor her constantly, in communities *and* when we were on our own. Although things had turned out fine, the danger she'd put us in had shaken me, and I needed to corral her enthusiastic art.

Out of nowhere, an image bloomed on my mind's canvas, the shape and hue fleeting. I sprang to my feet, retrieving *Home* from the flier. Even though we knew my family was somewhere in Toronto Depot, the more I could finish the painting, the easier it would be to search for my family.

"Did you have a flash?"

I nodded. "Bring the art supplies to the shore?"

She wavered like she wanted to argue, but nodded. "Only because I want to see what's next."

CHAPTER ELEVEN

Akiko poked my cheek. "You awake?"

I said nothing.

She poked me again. "It's raining, so you can keep sleeping."

I cracked my eye open. "Then why did you wake me?"

"So you could keep sleeping," she whispered.

I nodded, closing my eyes.

"We're going to go play," she whispered, then raised her voice. "Come on, Charcoal."

When Charcoal grumbled and clambered up, she scolded him, "Hush now, don't wake him."

After she tiptoed away, I cracked an eye and rolled onto my side. Predawn mists drifted across the lake, and Akiko giggled as she played with the dog under the dense tree canopy.

My gaze drifted through the gloom to the painting I'd propped on the easel. Though I'd been working on *Home* for months, I still didn't understand where the images came from. Without warning, a shape would flash onto my mind's canvas, and I'd rush to capture it. As far as I knew, this wasn't a typical artist thing, but I didn't know it for certain since I had told no one about *Home* until Josephine and I stayed in Brookfield.

Brookfield.

My breath caught at the memory of the damage, death, and needless destruction I'd caused. Swallowing, I sat up to check on Akiko, but the forest was empty. I scrambled to my feet. "Akiko?"

"Here." She stood at the lake's edge, struggling to skip a rock.

"Mouse, get back here—you're getting soaked."

I stepped back under the canvas and shook out our bedrolls until they trotted in. "Where's the firewood?"

She pointed at Charcoal. "He has it."

I cocked my head and raised my eyebrows. When Akiko mimicked my facial expression, I stared at her, unwilling to blink first.

But when my lips twitched, she bounced up and down. "Saw that! Goody, I win again."

I had yet to win a staring contest. "If you get firewood, I'll cook breakfast."

She stopped bouncing. "If *you* get firewood, I'll cook our breakfast."

"You can't cook."

"So? You can't either." She waited with her hands on her hips.

Should I insist? I didn't want to provoke another outburst from her or invite the reappearance of the *other* Akiko. "Point taken. What would you make?"

Her face twisted while she thought, then smoothed. "Noodles with sauce."

"For breakfast?"

She nodded, her eyes bright.

"Okay. I'll get the firewood. You make the noodles and

sauce. Good luck." We had neither pasta nor the ingredients needed to make any sort of sauce.

She beamed and pointed at the heavy, gray skies. "Get a lot, because we'll be here until the rain stops."

I nodded, whistling for Charcoal. The forest's dense canopy muffled the patter of rain, and my hand trailed through a fluffy bush, releasing a spicy fragrance that mingled with the scents of moss and damp bark. I stopped to breathe deeply, my heart gladdened by the memory of its fragrance, roaring fires, and carols sung at the abbey. I snapped two branches off the shrub and tucked them through my belt. We wandered on in search of firewood through bunches of red columbines which waved as raindrops hit their foliage.

The ground was free of downed branches, and the logs I found were rotted and friable, so I whistled for Charcoal. "Give stick."

He spun in a circle, then gazed at me with a furrowed brow.

My shoulders slumped. "Let's check the trees along the beach."

Charcoal padded after me as I moved toward the edge of the woods. Here, the ground sported masses of wintergreen with delicate, pinkish-white flowers.

When a twig snapped underfoot, I bent down to pick it up. "See? Give stick."

Charcoal promptly dipped his head and pulled up a stick. He wiggled at me, his eyes shining with hope.

"One time," I said, and tossed it to him.

He brought it back and dropped it at my feet, dancing.

"I'm keeping this one, but if you get another, I'll toss it, too." I played fetch with the dog until we'd gathered enough wood to keep the fire fed for several hours. "It's been too long since we played, eh, boy?"

"Perfect timing," said Akiko, when we entered the shelter.

"For?" I asked, dropping the wood near our fire. I stirred the coals, gratified when embers winked at me.

"Breakfast."

I laid a cradle of sticks on the embers, blowing on the base until several flames licked up. When I sat back on my heels, Akiko shoved a bowl of pasta into my hands and pulled the branches from my belt.

I stared at the bowl and the odd, irregular pasta. "We didn't have any noodles."

"Nope. Want sauce?" She sniffed at the spice bush branches I'd brought.

I dangled a triangular piece of pasta that had a long, spiraling tail.

"It's good," she mumbled, her mouth full. When I didn't move, she lowered her bowl, an expectant expression on her face. Charcoal also stared at me, a line of drool spilling from his mouth.

I put the noodle in my mouth and chewed. It was softer than usual, but it had the same flavor as any pasta I'd eaten. After swallowing, I waited. For what, I don't know—heartburn, gut cramps, or to turn to stone—but nothing happened.

"Sauce?" she asked again.

I nodded, holding my bowl out. She carefully poured a vibrant red sauce into my bowl, then set a pot I didn't recognize near the rekindled flames. I watched it as I ate, the tang of the tomato sauce rich and jarring.

"It won't burn up—it's a metal pot," she said, her face covered with sauce.

I fought the urge to wipe her face clean. "Where did the pot come from? And the noodles?"

She looked bewildered. "From my art."

I lowered the bowl, peering at my meal. "I suspected you'd say that."

"Is something wrong with it?" Her eyes glinted.

Helpless, I shrugged. "I don't know."

When a teardrop tracked down her cheek, I beckoned for her to come to me.

She circled the fire, her tears spilling as she sat next to me. "I wanted to make a nice b-breakfast," she sobbed.

"I know," I murmured into her hair. "Delicious. Best noodle breakfast I ever had."

She hiccuped, squirming closer, feverishly hot.

"Hey, even Charcoal likes it." The dog had finished our meals and flashed us a guilty expression.

Akiko's chin trembled. "He's picky."

I laughed. "He is. Did I ever tell you about how he refused to eat the first breakfast Josephine made for us?"

Akiko chuckled and wiped her eyes with the back of her hand. "No. But poor Charcoal, having to travel with you two."

I kissed the top of her head. "You *create* things—from nothing—with art."

She nodded, her face tear-stained.

"It's not something we do."

Her eyes widened. "Like erase?"

"No, we don't erase because we shouldn't. Art is about creation, not destruction. What I meant is they don't teach artists to create."

She pulled back, looking surprised. "You didn't learn how to do it?"

I shook my head.

"But I bet you can." She retrieved her sketchbook, pulling the pencil from the pot of tomato sauce. "Here."

I accepted the sketchbook but squinted at her sauce-covered pencil. "I'll use mine."

She nodded and licked her pencil as I pulled another from my coat pocket. "Draw an apple."

"Sure." I complied and showed her my sketch.

She frowned. "No, draw an apple so it's *real*."

When I improved things, I locked the mental image of the changes I wanted to effect on my mind's canvas. Perhaps it would work for creations, too.

The fire popped and crackled as I closed my eyes to picture an apple. Once it was solid, I mentally rotated it and considered it from all sides. I set the glossy texture, the rough stem, even the bumps near the core on the bottom of the fruit. "Got it." I sketched the fruit I'd locked onto my mind's canvas.

"Beautiful," Akiko said, when I finished.

I glanced around. No apple. "You do it."

She took the sketch pad from me and sat cross-legged on the ground. Charcoal moved between us, watching the fire as Akiko drew the basic shape of an apple and defined the shape before adding shading and anchoring the apple onto a flat surface. When finished, she gazed at me.

I shrugged. "What?"

She lay down her pencil and picked up an apple I hadn't seen from the ground next to her knee.

I scrambled to my feet, breathing heavily.

She creates.

Until she'd held the apple out to me, I hadn't truly believed it was possible no matter what I'd seen. Akiko bit into the fruit, and the resulting *crunch* stopped my pacing. "May I have a bite?"

She nodded, handing me the apple.

I closed my eyes and took a bite. The apple had the correct texture, crunch, and sweetness, and juice beaded the skin next to where I'd bitten. This was a real apple. "Delicious."

Her face broke into a broad smile as she reclaimed the fruit.

If anyone found out, they'd come for her.

The notion nearly stopped my heart. At the abbey, the masters began our combat training at six years of age. At first, the skill sessions were a fun way to exercise, but as we grew in strength, the lessons turned serious and included fencing, strategy, and grappling. One master had scared us with anecdotes of artists forced into directed artwork, but we never knew if the stories were true, or merely meant to scare us into taking the lessons seriously. Whatever the truth, we learned to fight, but we were boys and Akiko was a small, defenseless girl.

"Mouse, this gift you have is truly marvelous. I want to learn more about it, and I won't ask you to stop creating."

She grinned. "Okay." She tossed the apple core into the fire, and Charcoal whined, his eyes locked on the fruit.

"I'm not done." I kneeled before her, taking her chin in my hand. "You cannot tell anyone about this. No one."

She nodded, a serious expression on her face.

"I mean it. No one."

Akiko made a face. "No one. Got it."

"Good." I dropped my hand and sat back on my heels. "Including Ben, Josephine, and Genevie."

Her head whipped up. "Not even them?"

"Knowing could put them in danger."

Akiko shrank. "Is it bad?"

I hesitated before answering. "Remember when I trained Wakefield for combat?"

She nodded.

"The masters trained us to fight at the abbey so we could defend ourselves."

Her shoulders squared. "So, teach me."

I rubbed my face with my palms. How could I make her understand? She was worth more than all the artists living, and her gift would make her the most sought-after prize in the world.

"I'll start your combat training today, but the *best* defense is to keep secret what you can do. Understand?"

"Yes, a defensive secret," she said, but her face remained devoid of expression.

Did she understand?

"Our secret," I agreed, desperate to convince us both.

CHAPTER TWELVE

Akiko snorted from the back seat of the flier. "The quick brown fox jumps over the lazy dog. But what does it mean?"

I shrugged as the afternoon sun beat on us, sapping my energy. "A fast brown fox jumped over a worthless dog?"

Akiko sighed. "This book is full of stupid sayings. I've had enough reading for today."

I scanned the sky and turned. "Maybe the sayings are from *Before*."

Charcoal's tongue flapped in the breeze, but when I made a kissing noise, the dog's shoulders wiggled happily in his harness, making me smile. I turned back around, scanning the air again. In the week since leaving Saratoga Springs Depot, I'd become more vigilant, hyperaware of how quickly things could go wrong. The pressure wore on me as my mind spun through scenarios meant to keep Akiko safe from people and the dangers of travel.

"Ooh," said Akiko as we approached the Ontario Sea.

Small clouds scudded overhead as I banked north. We'd

flown past the edge of our map and would have to follow the shoreline instead of staying overland. The land south of the sea was a giant bog, with clumps of dead trees standing in sluggish, brown water. Over the last several days, we'd spotted few signs of human occupation in the drowned lands, making the hours in the air tedious. Until I'd suggested Akiko work on her reading as we flew, she'd complained of boredom, periodically begging to fly over the swamps, so she'd have something to sketch. Though the diversity of the bird populations in flooded areas astounded me, after our experience with the startled goose, I'd taken to avoiding flocks when possible.

Akiko squirmed, rocking the flier. "Will the air be cooler over the sea?"

The air was heavy and oppressive, making breathing a struggle. It was like trying to draw air through a wet towel.

"I hope so. When we reach the shore, I'll fly over the water."

"Good," Akiko muttered. "I'm sticky."

I was sticky too. Between the pedaling, the constant sun, and the humidity of the June weather, I needed a bath.

After checking for birds, I slowed my pedaling, letting us sink. I groaned as my legs relaxed.

Akiko mimicked me. "Oh, nice."

"Cooler?"

"No. It's quieter when the propeller isn't turning."

My legs protested as I resumed pedaling, and the propeller moaned as it spun. "You're right—it's noisy. If you remind me tonight, I'll put graphite on the bearings."

"Graphite like our pencils? You gave some to Bert and Eliot."

"It's smooth and makes a good lubricant." I tugged at the collar of my shirt. We'd already shed our coats and long sleeves, opting to sit on our leather lap blankets instead of under them. "Water, please."

Akiko handed me the canteen over my shoulder. "Check. Can we practice my combats tonight?"

"If it's not too hot. Need some?" I asked, before taking a swig. With the amount I'd been sweating, I'd been able to drink frequently without worrying about my bladder.

"Nope. Still have the other one too."

Right. I'd forgotten she'd created another canteen.

The water tasted of the murky pond we'd taken it from and smelled of algae and mud. I poured the rest of the water over my head, which I shook like a dog, spraying them. Akiko squealed, and Charcoal yipped happily. I grinned, handing the empty canteen back.

The sound of Charcoal's lapping and her chortles made me smile. "What's going on back there?"

She giggled. "A little rain."

We'd nearly reached the edge of the plateau, and the ground dropped steeply away from us toward the lake, rocky and barren. I took advantage of the slope to stop pedaling and let the flier glide while I gazed at the sea. It spread before us, huge and sparkling. To the north were a handful of islands, while the drowned lands lay to the south. Somewhere beyond the western horizon lay Toronto Depot and the answers I sought.

The skies above us were azure, speckled with clouds. The cooler lake air was a shock, and the hairs on my arms rose while I stretched my neck. We weren't dropping as fast as I'd expected, so I took my feet off the pedals, rotating my ankles clockwise then counterclockwise, the sweat on my back cooling.

"We sure got high," said Akiko. She coughed.

"Mm," I said, gazing at the horizon. I shivered again.

"Really high," said Akiko, her voice sleepy.

I glanced down. Somehow, the shoreline had fallen far below. I giggled.

Charcoal, panting heavily, barked once.

I twisted in my seat to observe them. Akiko was asleep with her head lolled to one side and her skin tinted a cerulean blue. Charcoal gazed at me, and I giggled at his goggle-magnified eyes.

I turned back, and a chill nested between my shoulder blades.

Was I cold? I examined my arm, mesmerized by the way my skin rose in bumps, a hair waving on each bump like a flag on a hillside.

Odd.

A thump broke my reverie, but nothing appeared out of place. I gazed back at the horizon, but it had disappeared behind a bank of clouds. Had they lowered while we flew? I'd never been this close to clouds before. Everything above us was a dazzling silver-gray.

Maybe I could pedal up and touch them.

It took great concentration to get both my feet onto the pedals, and I giggled as my left foot slipped off several times. The clouds above me appeared sullen and mean, but I ignored them and focused on the friendly cloud in front of us. We'd visit the nice cloud, the puffy cloud. My legs jerked as I pedaled, and the flier wobbled, my fingers tingling on the handlebars. It was the same tingle as when I changed the physical world with my art.

Was I creating art?

The nice cloud drifted closer, and I grinned, pedaling faster. My feet appeared far away, and I laughed in a strange, gasping manner. Though I barely pedaled, I was already out of breath, but when I ceased pedaling, my breath didn't return. I exhaled forcefully, then laughed at the fog I'd created. Fog on a hot, humid day?

Bizarre.

Angered that I'd stopped pedaling, the friendly cloud I'd been chasing withdrew, soaring far above my head. I watched it retreat, my heart wrenching with sorrow, but shivered as my mind cleared enough to focus on the aching cold. The clouds rose with staggering speed, and I tilted my head to watch them fly away, then noticed the wing's fabric stretching upward, toward the sky.

The clouds weren't rising—we were dropping.

I pedaled faster as icy water dripped from the gossamer fabric above us. "Akiko?"

"Just here," she said, her words slurring. "Cold."

"Me too." Even though I pedaled, we continued to drop. The air was easier to breathe, and I reached up to trim the flier, but we were still in a cruising configuration.

"Ugh, the air got wet again," Akiko complained from the back seat. "It's sticky."

As the air grew heavy and warm, our descent slowed, and I glanced at Akiko.

Her skin no longer held a blue tint as she frowned. "My head hurts. Want a snack?"

I shook my head. "My stomach is too unsettled." Our ascent into the clouds rattled me. We must have caught an updraft from the exposed rock on the edge of the plateau. Bowman had warned me of hypoxia, but I hadn't paid attention, never dreaming we would ever fly high enough to be in danger. My head pounded as I gazed at the clouds.

I checked our surroundings while allowing the flier to descend toward the water. "Keep watch, and with luck, we'll find a community or someplace nice to stop."

We followed the shoreline, watching the water change

colors, shifting from blue to gray to green as we passed under clouds. When the sea's edge bent toward the south, we followed the curve, and the northern shore retreated into the horizon.

Akiko shrieked. "I ate a bug!"

Something struck my face before I could respond, and within seconds, a thick, dark cloud of insects enveloped us. Insects pelted us, the sheer number of them darkening the surrounding air. Akiko squealed, and I trimmed the flier, pedaling faster. As we climbed higher, the insects diminished, and we watched several more clouds of them fly beneath us as we continued west. "Sorry. Lesson learned."

"Don't do that again!" said Akiko. "The bugs get thick when the air gets smelly."

"They're from the drowned lands. Are you okay?"

"We're fine," she said, "but do better please."

I sighed. First, I'd nearly suffocated us by not recognizing the effects of hypoxia and then flown through a swarm of insects so thick it could have taken down the flier. I needed to do better. "Check."

The desolation of the drowned lands was eerie. As we flew over them, I tried to imagine people from *Before* living here. It was nearly beyond belief, but occasionally, I spotted remnants of the long-lost world in the murk, like a length of pavement, cracked and buckled, rising above the mire, or a metal tower standing alone—skeletal and spiny.

"The people from *Before* left a lot behind," said Akiko, as we passed the remains of a ruined depot.

"Like hopes, dreams, and family histories?"

Akiko snorted. "Junk, weird stuff, and backpacks."

I raised my eyebrows. "Weird stuff?"

"Yeah, they liked weird stuff."

My lips twitched. "Such as?"

"Oh, you know. Moldy pillows shaped like animals. Flat, round, sparkly things. Rubbish."

I grinned at the child's observations. "It might not have been rubbish to them."

"Still. What a waste. And why did they need so much glass?"

I shook my head. "They liked windows."

"And plates and cups and jars and bowls and sinks. They even hung glass from their *ceilings*. They didn't care about the people who would have to clean it up."

"It might have meant something to them."

"Special glass?" She was silent for a moment, then sighed. "It's all rubbish."

"It is now," I agreed.

I watched the shore for signs of people but found nothing. No waterfront communities, no docks, no boats bobbing on the shores of the great sea.

"Matthew?"

"Yes, Mouse?"

"The bag with the art supplies is missing."

I frowned, trying to make sense of her observation. Did we forget to pack it? No, I remembered hoisting it up and buckling the straps this morning. "Are the straps there?"

"Nope."

I groaned, remembering the odd thump, and mentally cataloged what we'd lost. The oil paints, watercolor pigments, my palette, and the easel. My favorite paintbrushes. The last of our watercolor paper, and our spare clothing.

"At least *Home* is safe," she said, "but now you can't work on it."

I sighed. "We better add art supplies to the list of things we need from Toronto Depot."

"Check."

CHAPTER THIRTEEN

I grimaced as the flier touched down with a squelching noise, our forward motion slowing too quickly. The abrupt change jerked me forward against the harness and, based on the groans from the back seat, I wasn't the only one. I'd left finding a campsite too late, forcing me to land somewhere—anywhere—before the sun set.

Not my finest decision.

Akiko grunted as the flier slid to a stop and we rocked backward. I squinted at the ground. From the air, it had appeared firm and studded with tufts of grass, but what I'd assumed was bare soil was instead several inches of mud.

Great.

Akiko made a disgusted noise. "Can you go forward? This is icky."

A tire spun as I strained against the pedals. "Nope."

A cloud of gnats enveloped my head as I unbuckled myself and slid from my seat. My feet sank into the muck, the damp seeping into my boots, and the stench of decay clogged my nose.

Akiko groaned. "This place stinks."

I ignored her as I scanned the area for solid ground. We couldn't sleep in the mud. "We may have to sleep on the flier."

"What? No way." Akiko fumbled with her buckles.

"Watch out. The mud could get deeper, so don't let it pull your boots off."

She scoffed, slipping from her seat. "Yeah, right. Mud can't do that."

The memory of traveling through a ravine with Josephine played across my mind's canvas. "Don't bet an egg on it."

Akiko watched the mud ooze over the toes of her boots. "Yuck."

Charcoal squirmed, clearly expecting to be released. He yipped once, struggling in his harness.

Against my better judgment, I freed the dog. He jumped down, trotting in wide circles around the flier, nose down and investigating. At least I'd made one passenger happy.

Akiko crossed her arms, scowling. "What did you do that for? His belly is now covered with mud."

"Yeah, but he's sleeping on *your* bedroll tonight."

The mud made a sucking noise as Akiko spun. "Where will we sleep?"

"Let's search for high ground, or at least something firm."

She stepped through the mud carefully, legs wide and arms stretched out for balance.

How badly were we stuck? Without our weight, the flier slid forward when I shoved it. So, it was possible, but by the time I got it moving, the sun would have set, and the dark would make finding a new landing site impossible. I rested my forehead against the flier's frame. The evening skies had cleared, and with luck, it wouldn't rain tonight, but we'd have to sleep here tonight.

The mud sucked at my boots, and I widened my stance like

Akiko as I trudged away from the flier. After about twenty meters, the ground hardened, the soil moist rather than mucky. Somehow, I'd found a berm or man-made structure roughly three and a half meters wide, appearing to run in an east-west direction. I wiped my mouth with my forearm to brush away a bug, leaving the mineral taste of mud in my mouth. I gagged and spat.

"Find anything?" Akiko yelled. She'd returned to the flier and perched on the rear seat, legs swinging.

"Yep." I struggled back to her to retrieve our things.

"Stay down, muddy dog," she ordered.

"You're almost as filthy as he is," I said, unbuckling our remaining bag.

Akiko perked up. "What did you find? Is it nice?"

"Sure is. A little cottage with a porch and a fireplace. We can bake cookies later."

Akiko rolled her eyes. "We're staying *here* tonight?"

"I'm afraid so. I dub it the Muck Pit."

Akiko slapped her arm. "This is stupid. The mosquitoes are almost as big as Charcoal."

As campsites went, it was terrible, but at least I'd kept us safe—finding landing sites was proving more difficult than I'd expected. I pulled my bedroll out, swatting at a mosquito whining near my ear, and folded her bedding in half.

"Leave it here and I'll come back for it."

"No. Give it to me." She held her arms out straight, so I draped her bedding over them.

I hoisted the remaining canvas bag over my shoulder, nearly dropping my bedroll. "We'll be lucky if any of us aren't sleeping in filth tonight. Come on."

We staggered back to the firmer ground, but when we reached it, Akiko scowled. "Is this *it?*"

I shrugged. "It was nicer the last time I visited."

She spun, scrutinizing the berm. "How will you tie the canopy up?"

Good question.

I spun and pointed. "There is a tall shrub or something over there."

Akiko rolled her eyes but accompanied me.

The ground rose as we walked west and what I'd assumed was a shrub turned out to be two short trees.

"I can barely see the flier from here," said Akiko, scowling and slumping against a tree.

I glanced at her as I tied the tarpaulin up. "Should we post a guard? We could rotate every two hours."

"You're not funny, and I'm too tired to do our combats tonight."

I tossed my bedding over a low branch and shrugged the canvas sack from my back.

"All right, I guess done is done. Here, I'll put your bedding over a branch to keep it clean. I'll choose a better campsite tomorrow."

Akiko pointed at the mud-covered dog. "Unless you can wash him, the bedding won't stay clean." Charcoal grinned, his teeth gleaming in his brown-black, mud-covered face.

Another parental win.

***

"Pull harder, Charcoal," Akiko muttered, grunting as she strained on her rope.

"Okay, take five everyone." I collapsed against the flier, panting. We wouldn't get far today. It had taken us hours to pull the flier to the berm, and we'd lost the morning already. I sighed, studying the flat, marshy ground. The skies remained overcast and dry, but the dampness in the air had grown, as had the swampy aroma of mud, vegetation, and rot.

Akiko groaned. "Five what?"

I straightened, my hands on my hips. "Five elephants with five hats topped with five golden rings."

Her eyes narrowed. "You've lost your last five marbles."

"Marbles? Why marbles?"

Akiko shrugged, twirling her rope. "Rudy used to say people who didn't believe in the Word had lost their marbles, but I don't remember losing mine."

"Me neither. Ready to pull?"

Akiko made a face. "Can't you improve the ground with art?"

"Sure, twenty meters ago, but we're nearly there."

She pouted. "Camp is way over there."

"I'll pedal once we get it on the berm," I said, slapping a mosquito on my neck.

"Oh. We're not pulling it all the way?"

"Nope, so pull on three. One, two, three!" I flung myself against my rope, straining with everything I had. Something popped in my left calf as the flier slid greasily onto the berm.

Akiko cheered, dropped her rope, and bent to pet Charcoal. While she was distracted, I glanced at my calf. My trouser leg had darkened, and my calf stung.

Wonderful.

"Let's get these ropes off."

Akiko tugged at the knots on Charcoal's harness, her tongue protruding as she struggled. "These got muddy."

Once freed, Charcoal danced around her, barking while I coiled the remaining ropes. "Time to go." They ignored me, so I pedaled the flier toward our campsite.

"Wait," Akiko squealed, running to catch up.

I slowed the flier until she'd almost reached her seat, then sped up before she could climb on. "Coming?"

She almost caught the flier several more times before feigning surrender, so I pretended I hadn't noticed and kept pedaling. She shrieked again and ran after me, laughing. By the time she'd caught up, we were in camp. She clambered into her seat, triumphant, until I pointed at her bedroll.

She sighed. "Why do *I* have to stow the bedrolls?"

I copied her sigh. "Because you get to laze away the day while *I* pedal."

"I'll pedal! Can I please?"

"Hm, let me think. How about... no? But you *may* stow my bedroll."

Her eyes danced as she pretended to pout. "Thanks. Real big of you, Artist."

While Akiko was occupied, I stepped behind the brush and pulled up my trouser leg. Blood leaked from incision sites. Although Eliot had stopped the infection, we'd snuck away from Whitehall before my leg had fully healed.

We hadn't brought sterile dressings or poultice materials, and we'd lost our spare clothing, so I could do nothing about my leg. I pulled my trouser leg down, hissing as the blood and mud-stiffened cloth scraped the open wound. If we continued to wallow in filth, I'd be lucky if the leg didn't rot off before we reached the depot.

Akiko had buckled herself and Charcoal into their harnesses and sat bouncing her legs up and down.

"Did you have a pee? Got your sketch book and snacks?"

"No and yes," she said, continuing to kick her legs.

I strapped the canvas sack into place and checked the buckles twice. We couldn't afford to lose anything else. After I tightened their harnesses, I stopped to glance around.

"What?"

"Are we forgetting something?"

"Did you pee? Do you have your snacks?" she asked, mimicking me.

I bit back my retort. "I'll check the landing site."

Nothing appeared out of place as I surveyed the mud where we'd pulled the flier onto the berm, so I sighed, retracing my steps. When I reached the flier, I climbed on and buckled my harness. "Ah-ha!"

"What?"

I unbuckled myself and pointed to a tree branch where her jacket fluttered. After retrieving it, I handed it to her. "Put it on."

"But I'm hot."

"Akiko."

She pulled her coat onto her arms backward and glared at me.

I waited, my face blank.

"Fine." She unbuckled, pulled on her coat, and re-buckled herself into her seat. I tightened her harness and strapped myself in.

"Matthew?"

"Yes, Mouse?"

She snorted. "Where's *your* coat?"

"What?" I scanned the trees, then twisted toward her.

She smirked, pointing at the wing onto which I'd earlier tossed my coat.

I unbuckled myself and lurched forward to grab the dangling sleeve. As I fell back into my seat, my jacket stuck before loosening with a horrendous ripping sound. I groaned as the flier's torn wing flapped in the breeze.

"Oh perfect," said Akiko. "Can we still fly?"

"Probably not." I gazed at the wing, trying to picture how

I'd repair the fabric. There weren't any seams in the left wing, so I didn't want to chance a patch.

"What kind of material is it?"

I shrugged. "I didn't ask Bowman."

She raised her palms. "Was it salvaged or manufactured?"

"Not sure."

I kneeled on my seat to get a closer view of the fabric. The material appeared woven, but I couldn't tell what they'd made the clear fiber from. I brushed it with my fingertips, thinking about its synthetic texture.

"What's wrong?"

I slumped into my seat. "I'm not sure how to sketch it."

"So, paint it."

"We've lost our paints, paper, *and* brushes."

"Oh. I'll make some more." Her pencil scratched, but after a while, she sighed. "Nothing is happening."

I shrugged. "I've tried to improve supplies in the past, and it never worked for me either."

The flier bounced as Akiko kicked her feet. "If I can't make paint, can I create a wing?"

I squinted at the tear. "How would we attach it?"

"Oh. Could I create new cloth?"

"I still don't know how we'd attach it."

Akiko huffed and unbuckled her harness.

"Where are you going?"

She shrugged, releasing Charcoal. "Seems like you'll be awhile, so we're going sploring." They skipped down the berm, heading west.

I studied the wing before closing my eyes to picture the wing as it had been, but the fabric on my mind's canvas remained torn.

"Witchcraft," I growled, opening my eyes. Using the other wing as a model, I tried sketching the flier, but the resulting drawing wasn't correct. Sighing, I closed my eyes to examine the torn wing with my mind's eye. As I studied it, the tear widened, and an orange dropped through it.

My eyes popped open.

No orange.

To remove the orange from my thoughts, I sketched it before attempting the wing again. And again. Each failure increased the pressure in my chest. If I didn't figure out how to fix it soon, we'd have to spend another night here.

While I'd struggled to repair the flier, the temperature had risen. Sweat ran down my face, and I licked it from my lip, grimacing at the bitter salt. A marsh wren trilled, competing with the bassy sound of a calling bullfrog.

"Nap time?"

I cracked my eyes, blinking at the glare. "No, I'm trying to figure out how to draw see-through fabric with a pencil. This would be easier if we hadn't lost our watercolors."

She glanced at my sketchbook. "How would watercolor be different?"

"I'd paint the wing and lift most of the pigment."

"Oh." She pointed at my sketch. "What's that?"

"An orange."

Her eyes sharpened. "Oranges exist?"

I snorted. "They do."

"What color are they?"

I raised my eyebrow until she giggled.

"Orange?"

"Good guess."

She climbed into her seat, and the air filled with familiar scratching sounds. When the sound ceased, she tapped me on the shoulder, holding an orange. It had a garish, unnatural shade, but otherwise appeared like the fruit I'd drawn.

"Let's open it." I slid my hand into my coat pocket and yelped.

"What?"

"Found the culprit," I said, pulling out my unsheathed knife.

Akiko glanced from the knife to the torn wing. "Oops."

"Oops," I agreed, sucking on my injured finger. I cut a wedge from the orange and examined it. The inside of the fruit mimicked the peel; it had the same pitted surface and garish shade.

"Interesting." I sniffed, but it had no aroma. "Sorry, kid. I guess you'll have to experience a real orange before you can create one." I handed it back, making a mental note to find an orange for Akiko. Perhaps I didn't have to worry about her creating monsters after all.

She examined the fruit, then tossed it toward Charcoal. "Can you draw the wing like water?"

"Water?"

"It's clear, but you can draw it with pencils."

The tear on my mind's canvas closed neatly. "Mouse, you're a genius. We'll leave shortly."

CHAPTER FOURTEEN

I pedaled on, hollow and glassy-eyed. The pain in my leg had subsided to a dull ache, but I wasn't sure it was an improvement.

"A boat! I win."

The afternoon sun dazzled my eyes, but I squinted through the glare to scan the shore. Several times we'd believed we'd spotted a boat only to find a mirage of our reflection or floating debris. But this time, it *was* a boat.

"You win." I searched the shore, but there wasn't anywhere for a boat to dock.

"Why are we climbing?"

"I want to find where the boat came from."

"Why?"

"I'd like to check in with a healer, so I don't get sick again."

The answer seemed to satisfy her. "Oh. We need to look at a new map, too."

"Good thinking. Keep your eyes peeled."

"Huh?"

"It means to keep them open." I pedaled with renewed

vigor as we climbed, willing a wisp of smoke, a dock, or a community green to appear.

There was only forest—the tree-covered hills rising steeply from the shore; nowhere for a boat to beach, or for us to land.

Akiko sighed. "Maybe the community is on the other side of the sea."

The far shores of the great lake weren't visible, so what would we do if there was no community on this side? We couldn't land on the water, and I wouldn't risk setting down in the drowned lands again. We'd gotten lucky last night at the Muck Pit, but my leg couldn't handle another mishap.

As we passed a bend in the shoreline, my heart quickened at the sight of a second boat. Around the next ridge, a bay opened in front of us, and a cluster of buildings hugged the shore.

Sweat dripped as I slowed my pedaling, letting the flier descend as I assessed the community. The boardwalk and buildings along the shore appeared to be in good repair. As we sank, the flier shook. Alarmed, I glanced over my shoulder, but this time it was Akiko waving, not turbulence. When someone on the boat waved back, Akiko waved harder.

The community's green sat at the top of the hill, and I banked toward it, my leg throbbing.

"I'll pedal past the green to make sure it's safe to land."

"Check! I hope they have a filling station or a pub because I'm hungry."

The green appeared clear to me, and Akiko clapped. "No fences or 'lectric lines. We're good to land, Aviator."

"Check, Navigator. Here we go."

I banked and adjusted our trim, hoping to use the wind coming off the lake to our advantage. The breeze was stronger than I'd expected, and I held my breath, willing the flier to land and not pop back up into the air. As we crossed the midpoint of the field, the breeze died, allowing us to roll to a smooth stop with ten meters to spare.

"Navigator, I promote you to Flight Ambassador." I slid my goggles up and waved at the assembling crowd before fumbling with my harness. "Here they come."

The men stopped several meters away, and a cluster of women held children back at the edge of the green.

"Roger, Aviator." Akiko sounded cheerful, and the flier rocked as she released her harness. "Let's go, Charcoal."

The men visibly relaxed as Akiko and Charcoal jumped off their seats, and the cavorting, goggle-clad dog broke the children's restraint. They rushed toward Akiko, giggling and jabbering.

I groaned as I stretched, lifting my hand in greeting. The men waved in response and approached the flier, their eyes bright.

"Heya, Traveler," said a man.

"Heya. I'm Matthew Sugiyama, and that was my daughter, Akiko. Well met."

After we shook hands and exchanged pleasantries, they asked questions about the flier and escorted me to a faded yellow dwelling.

"A boat's coming," shouted a boy.

Akiko ran to me. "They're going to the shore. Can I go, too?"

"Yes, but keep Charcoal with you. I'm meeting with the healer over there."

"Check!"

Before we reached the dwelling, a young, blonde woman opened the door. "Is there a boat?"

"Aye," said an older man.

Focused on the lake, she ignored me and brushed past us.

When she reached the hill, she made a skipping step and trotted after the children.

"Was she the healer?" I asked, cocking my thumb toward the lake.

"No, I am." An enormous woman with a florid face stood in the doorway. "Are you the fool who arrived in a mechanical bird?"

"I am," I said, my neck heating.

"Come on in—I saw you limping. Ted, send word if the boat is from Milford. Coming, duckie?"

I nodded, clambering up the stairs.

She waited for me in a kitchen paneled with darkened wood. "Welcome to Pultney. Come, sit on the table."

I cocked my hip, sliding onto the table, but when I leaned over to pull up my trouser leg, she put a hand on my arm.

"Have you noticed how filthy your trousers are? Sorry duckie, but they have to go." She produced a giant pair of shears and cut along the inside seam. "I'm Freda Melonie."

"Matthew Sugiyama. Well met, Freda."

She raised an eyebrow, glancing at me.

"Artist."

She nodded, cutting my trouser leg off at the knee. "There. Now let's see what we have."

She grasped my ankle and motioned me to scoot back. Setting my leg on the table, she prodded it. I groaned when she pressed near my kneecap.

"You've seen a healer for this already."

"I have. How could you tell?"

She pointed to the slim cuts flanking the original wound. "They made these cuts to relieve pressure. Did you have an infection?"

I nodded. "Will I develop another?"

Freda moved to a cupboard, pulling out a manganese-blue, enameled bowl and several white cloths.

"You've re-injured the leg, but there's no sign of infection. It needs cleaning though," she said, "and it won't be pleasant."

She was right. I gritted my teeth and dug my nails into my palms as she worked. Freda hummed a familiar tune but asked no further questions, and I kept my eyes averted as the water in the bowl turned from clear to a deep chestnut.

"There, done."

"Thank you, Freda," I said, after releasing a shaky breath.

"Stay put, duckie, and I'll dress it," she said, as she rummaged in a cupboard.

I glanced around the room, noticing fish nets, jars of preserves, and a weather chart. "Do you get many travelers?"

"Oh, a fair few, but we're primarily a mariner's trading post."

"Trading post? Pultney appeared relatively small from the air."

"Pultney is," she agreed. She set a brown bottle down on the table. "We have about twenty-five full-time residents and another fifteen mariners who spend a few months a year here."

"Ah."

She poured a foul-smelling, brown liquid on a clean cloth and considered me. "This will be worse than the cleaning."

I yelped as she pressed the cloth against my wound.

"We have about fifty homesteaders here, too."

"Homesteaders?" I asked, through gritted teeth.

My eyes teared. I wasn't sure if it was from the sting on my leg or the pungent scent of the liquid—somewhere between turpentine and peroxide.

"Aye. They trap, fish, and bring their wares to trade. Many live by themselves... somewhere out there." She shook her head.

"They get peculiar but are harmless enough. There, done. Now, can I ask for an improvement to our community?"

"Certainly—I'm grateful for your aid. I'll need trousers too, but if you'll point me toward your administrator, I'll negotiate services."

She set her hands on her ample hips and tilted her head. "Unless you fancy wearing a cast-off dress, I'll have to ask the men for spare trousers. I'm the administrator."

I blinked. "You're the administrator and the healer?"

She nodded.

"All right," I said, sorting through what we needed. "I'd like to review your map. We could also use fresh supplies, and I'll need trousers."

Freda beamed. "Done, done, and done. I'll throw in a bottle of disinfectant, too."

"What can I help Pultney with, Freda?"

"We'd like a dock."

My brow furrowed. "A dock?"

She dropped the soiled rags into a bucket by the door and beckoned. I eased to my feet, expecting my leg to complain. It appeared atrocious, but the pain had diminished. "It doesn't hurt as much."

Freda nodded. "My gran's secret recipe. Stings like the dickens but also numbs and disinfects. I'll send you with a bottle *if* you'll use it." She eyed me as we stepped onto her porch. "Come."

Self-conscious in my mutilated trousers, I followed her down the hill to where Akiko and the other children scrambled over the shore.

The boat had anchored in the bay and small crafts rowed to it. Beyond the boardwalk, large cobbles covered the shore. The rocks nearest the water's edge were slick with algae. Towering trees flanked the community, and I eyed them as I rubbed my jaw. "Why don't you have a dock? You have plenty of lumber."

Freda chuckled. "Since I've been an administrator, we've built seventeen docks. It's difficult to drive pilings here because the ground is rocky and dense, so we haven't gotten them deep enough to withstand the pressure."

Placid waves sighed as they lapped the shore, and a black-headed tern squawked a shrill *meep-meep* as Charcoal raced toward it. "Pressure?"

"Our winters are harsh, and storms blow in with four-meter waves. Our last dock took out our cannery after a storm smashed it to bits."

I watched several boats row toward shore. "You unload all boats like this?"

"Yes, the ones who will still come. In years past, Pultney was popular with the mariners, but few tolerate the delay required to load and off-load cargo. If we had a dock capable of withstanding the winter and spring storms, I could entice new people to settle here and retire one of my roles, which would give me more time with my granddaughter. Can you help?"

Since they had removed the debris from the last dock, I had nothing to improve, but if the ground was as stony as Freda said, I could build a new stone pier by raising the ground and then improving it into a solid structure. "With pleasure. I'll retrieve my things from the flier."

She clapped me on the back with a broad smile. "Eat first. Your leg needs feeding, and I bet your girl is the type to devour everything in sight."

I laughed as we ambled up the hill. "She's become voracious."

"She's at that age, that's for sure."

"Akiko," I called, "You hungry?"

The girl scrambled toward us, beaming, and Charcoal followed her, his eyes nearly as bright.

Where most filling stations featured large bays to board horses and mules, they filled this one with piles of ropes, nets, and fishing gear. On one side of the room, plastic buckets from *Before* labeled 'Tar' and 'Epoxy' sat stacked against a scuffed wooden wall.

Freda pointed to a table overlooking the bay. "Sit here, and I'll ask the keeper for a meal."

Akiko burst into the room, skidding to a stop. She examined me with narrowed eyes. "You've lost your leg."

I glanced at my exposed calf. "Breezy."

Akiko rolled her eyes and pointed. "Their map."

Pultney, marked with a blue star, centered the map, which included the entire lake. The cliffs where we'd gotten stuck in the updraft were labeled Oswego.

Akiko jabbed her finger at a location at the far end of the lake. "An abbey!"

I craned my neck. "Niagara Abbey." It was on the southern shore of the sea, almost directly south of our target.

"Look here's another." Akiko's eyes widened. "Two abbeys so close together?"

I whistled. "Niagara *and* Erie Abbey. How odd."

"Can we visit one?" Akiko's face was wistful, as though doubtful I'd agree.

My heart twisted—I'd disappointed her too many times. Although I ached to reach the depot, if we continued to follow the southern shoreline, we'd pass directly over Niagara Abbey. The delay would give us the opportunity to restock our art supplies and perhaps find a master willing to answer my questions about why women weren't artists. "Yes, we can stop at Niagara Abbey."

Akiko grinned, hugging Charcoal. "Goody! What's for lunch?"

"Fish," said Freda, reentering the room. "Every day is fish day in Pultney. Come, child. Let's get you washed up."

While waiting for them to return, I studied the map. My finger tapped Niagara Abbey's location as I surveyed Toronto Depot. With luck, we'd reach the abbey in a day or two, and Toronto Depot the day afterward. Ever since the scholar from Newfane had mentioned the skyline suggested in *Home* might fit the abandoned buildings in the depot, I'd been wild to reach it. Even though I'd waited my entire life to learn about my family, if a quick detour could make Akiko happy, it was worth the delay.

CHAPTER FIFTEEN

Three days later, we flew a circle around Niagara Abbey.
"I'll land over there."

"It looks weird."

"Agreed." I'd grown up in Popham Abbey, an imposing, crescent-shaped, stone building built at the edge of the great Atlantic. I spent my childhood listening to waves crashing on the rocks and gulls swooping overhead, so I'd assumed all abbeys enjoyed a similar status and setting.

In contrast, Niagara Abbey perched on a flat hilltop overlooking the Ontario Sea. Instead of the crescent-shaped building I'd expected, they had built the abbey like a five-pointed star with a circular ring cut from its center. Four stone buildings defined the center ring, and the roofs of the outer, star-shaped perimeter walls were green with vegetation. A graveled road surrounded the compound.

The flier landed on the road with a gentle bump; gravel crunched beneath the tires as we rolled to a stop.

"Are artists wizards?" Akiko asked.

I twisted and raised my eyebrow. "Am I a wizard? Are you?"

She grinned. "I'm not an *artist*. Only men are artists."

I chuckled, unfastening my harness. She was right, and this was my chance to find out *why*.

Large, wooden doors creaked open as I unbuckled Charcoal.

"Say nothing of your art, your sketching, or anything else. Check?"

"Roger. Should we get down?"

I tried to ignore the worry in her tone. If they didn't let her stay, we'd have to find somewhere to camp before the sun set, but we still had time. I tried to play it off. "Charcoal grew up in an abbey and knows how to behave."

Akiko gazed at me. "I don't."

My heart ached for her, but I winked. "Mind your manners, Princess Mouse, or they'll lock you in the dungeon."

"There's a dungeon?" Her eyes widened.

"Most likely. Besides, if they don't have one yet, a quick sketch will rectify it."

She grinned. "Now I'm sure you're teasing. Here they come."

I turned, raising my hand. "Good afternoon, Masters."

They inclined their heads but said nothing until I bowed. "*Ego autem* Popham."

Their faces broke into broad smiles, and an older man stepped forward. "Well met, Brother. I'm Rufus Bower."

"Well met, Master Bower. I'm Matthew Sugiyama."

Bower turned to Akiko. "Miss?"

"Sugiyama," she replied. "Ago out them, too."

My heart swelled. She was adorable. How could they turn us away?

"Miss Sugiyama," he said, bowing. "I think you meant *ego sum*." He turned to me. "Conjugation is important."

I laughed. "I'll remember if I attempt to teach her Latin."

"How can we be of aid, Brother Sugiyama?"

"We've had some mishaps and need respite and supplies. May we stay?"

They exchanged a look, but the youngest man nodded. "We always welcome artists."

"Miss Sugiyama is welcome at Niagara Abbey, too," said Bower.

Akiko relaxed. "Thank you, Master Bower."

Bower folded his arms. "Nothing comes for free, young lady, so we expect a service from you."

Akiko's brow furrowed. "What?"

"Your presence as a model," he said, raising his eyes to me. "You and Brother Sugiyama will occupy the small dwelling we keep for visiting guests and studio models."

She stilled. "What does a model do?"

I grinned. "Pretend to be a statue. May I sit in on the class?"

"I insist on it," Bower said. "Come, let's get you settled." He turned, holding out his hand. Akiko took it, skipping beside him as they disappeared through the wooden doors. Charcoal trailed behind the girl, glancing at me over his shoulder.

"Can I help carry anything? I'm Tom Staker, first-year master."

I unbuckled the canvas bag from the flier and opened the hidden compartment to remove *Home* and my sword. "This is all we have."

"Traveling light. Brother Sugiyama, I'm Elwin Robbert," murmured the other man.

"Well met, Master Robbert. Please, call me Matthew."

He smiled, gesturing toward the wooden doors. "Well met, Matthew. This way."

I followed them through the doors, nodding to the boys who pushed the doors closed behind us. The security bar dropped with a *thud.*

"Headmaster McCully will want a word," said Bower, as we joined them. "Staker, please escort Miss Sugiyama to the auberge. Master Sugiyama, come with me?"

I winked at Akiko. "Watch Charcoal. I'll collect you for dinner."

She lowered her voice. "Can I take a bath?"

I glanced at the others. "Does the auberge have a bathtub?" They nodded.

"Give Charcoal a scrub too," I called, joining Bower.

THE HEADMASTER'S OFFICE REMINDED ME OF POPHAM Abbey. Sunlight streamed through a gridded glass wall where a half-finished canvas sat on an easel. A massive bookshelf occupied the far wall, showcasing books, elegant pots, and small statuary. But where Headmaster Sinclair had an oversized mahogany desk, Headmaster McCully had a cozy seating area.

Bower gestured to an armchair, but I crossed the room to examine the canvas. The detail on the painting was exquisite. The artist had attempted to capture the view from the window in a pearly gray light that reminded me of dawn, and the wave pattern attempted to convey a swelling movement instead of the more traditional breaking waves. My eyes focused on a blank section of water, and for a moment, I imagined a face beneath the waves. Eyes narrowed, I stepped backward.

"I've been working on capturing water for nearly sixty years."

"As a boy, the patterns made by light reflecting off the water fascinated me." I turned, studying the man now sitting opposite Bower. "I'd lay in a sea cave for hours trying to capture it, but I haven't gotten it right yet."

He was thin, with hollow eyes and cheeks, and exuded calming energy. He gestured toward the empty chair. "Please join us, Brother Sugiyama."

"Thank you, Headmaster." I settled into the chair facing the windows.

Headmaster McCully patted the arms of his chair. "They informed me you arrived on a flying contraption."

"Yes."

"Is the machine a result of your art?"

My eyebrows raised, and I sat back. "No, an engineer built it. I'm flying it to Toronto Depot for him, and he's meeting me there."

"Ah."

Headmaster McCully templed his fingers, and I sensed he waited for an opportunity.

"Why do you ask?"

He leaned forward, his eyes crackling with energy. "It's the answer to a question we have wrestled with. We've lost touch with Erie Abbey."

My gaze flicked from McCully to Bower. "Has something happened?"

Bower shrugged. "We couldn't spare a master to investigate."

"No, I suppose not." I studied them. "You'd like me to fly to the abbey."

Headmaster McCully nodded, leaning forward. "It is an imposition, but we'd be in your debt."

That could prove useful. "Will they welcome me?"

"We don't know," said Bower. "But our abbeys enjoy a cordial relationship, and we share masters. It typically takes two weeks to travel between us. We send a master to them, and they send one of theirs back. The partnership has allowed us to expand what we can offer our pupils since we have so few resident masters."

I swallowed. "How long has it been since the last master traveled to them?"

Headmaster McCully cleared his throat. "Over five weeks."

Their worry concerned me. Had someone attacked the abbey? Popham's masters had provided us with combat training for this very reason.

It would cost several days for me to fly to the abbey and investigate, further delaying our arrival in Toronto Depot. Doubt flickered inside me. If it was dangerous, I couldn't take Akiko. The child had seen enough death and destruction to last a lifetime.

They built abbeys like fortresses, and the masters in the abbey system raised hundreds of children, so she would be safe here with the masters and other students... if they would let her stay without me. "I'd require Akiko and my dog to stay here. I cannot risk their safety."

Headmaster McCully nodded. "Should you not return, we'd ensure her safety and happiness. You have my word."

A shiver crawled down my spine. "Depending on what I see, I may not land," I warned. "I'll make a judgment based on what I can observe from the air."

"That's our preference, too. If something has happened... we won't risk losing another artist."

Refusal sat on the tip of my tongue. My priorities were to keep Akiko safe and find my family in that order. But if brother artists were in peril and I declined to help... I sat back. Perhaps I could turn this to my advantage.

"I have questions—things they didn't share with me as a

student. If I do this, I'd like a frank conversation with you about the abbey system."

McCully nodded once. "I'll answer what I can."

"I also need art supplies. We lost a case containing my charcoal, pigments, brushes, and palette." Bower's lips tightened, and a flush crept up my neck.

They glanced at each other, and my stomach twisted.

Calm down, Artist.

I was no longer a student to be chastised and had lost the supplies because of an accident, not negligence. If they wanted my help, they'd need to negotiate in good faith. I lifted my chin, meeting Bower's eyes. "I'll procure much of what I want at Toronto Depot, but to be prudent, I'll need the basics from you before I can agree."

It worked, and Headmaster McCully stood. "Rufus can help you find what you require. Will you go?"

I stood and bowed, making my decision. "Thank you, Headmaster. I can leave after dinner if needed."

"No, please stay the night. Tomorrow morning is soon enough."

"Very well. Shall we?" I asked Bower.

He nodded, telegraphing his irritation. "Follow me."

I trailed Bower down several richly appointed corridors before descending into a subbasement. The stone steps appeared ancient; hundreds of footfalls had worn the center of each tread, creating a dip.

"I cannot relinquish any of our unused brushes," Bower muttered. "We keep those for students, so they start with an identical set of tools." He paused and unlocked a heavy wooden door. "But when a master dies, we don't throw away their things. This is our vault."

I stepped into a small room, and Bower latched the door behind us.

Handsome wooden shelves held rows of palette knives and other tools. The polished wood gleamed in the dim light, the air scented with beeswax and mineral spirits. Beneath the shelves were narrow drawers. "What a treasure."

Bower's face softened. "Many of these are from brothers long gone. They're organized alphabetically by fur or bristle first, then by type."

I ran my fingertips along the polished wooden drawers, sliding several open. They had laid the brushes on velvet runners. I selected a round sable brush inscribed with a name and a set of dates.

"Jared Dewing." I picked up another. "Monty Handal." A lump rose in my throat as I set the brushes down. I'd never considered what happened when an artist died; death had appeared too distant. "Do all abbeys have vaults?"

Bower nodded, grief deepening the lines along his cheeks. "This is what happens when we die. Please, gather what you need, but treat them with care."

CHAPTER SIXTEEN

Soaked and shivering, I pedaled through the misty morning, peering through the gloom for the stream. Tom Staker had assured me I couldn't get lost if I followed its path toward Erie Abbey. The trouble was, Staker and the stream traveled *beneath* the tree canopy, not above. Even without the fog, it would have been difficult to make out the small waterway as it twisted and wound through the forest.

Earlier, I'd tried flying just above the canopy but had encountered turbulence and brushed several trees tops as unseen air currents pushed the flier around. After a conifer had flashed out of the gloom, I'd climbed higher, trading visibility for safety.

The deep clouds had subdued the sun, so I couldn't check my bearings. Was I even following the right stream anymore? If I missed the abbey, it could take me days to get back to Akiko.

My stomach churned as I scanned the dense canopy. Akiko had warned me not to overindulge at breakfast while trying to convince me she should accompany me to Erie Abbey. I wished

I had let her come; an extra set of eyes would be helpful in this fog.

Had I made the right decision about leaving her behind? Neither option reassured me. If I'd brought her with me and Erie was unsafe, I'd have delivered her into danger, but leaving her and her astonishing talent behind also felt unwise. I'd warned her not to show too much interest, but wasn't sure she'd be able to help herself. The first class she would model for was a beginning sculpture lesson. She had only asked me questions related to drawing and painting, but I hadn't exposed her to sculpture.

A cedar waxwing squealed a high-pitched warning, flushing several birds. They wheeled around me, alarmed. As the birds exploded away from me, I jerked the bars to the right, gulping air. When calmer, I searched for a shimmer or glint through the canopy to correct my course.

Droplets of water beaded against the metal handle bars, soaking me as the wind blew them onto my sodden coat. I shivered, increasing my speed to keep warm.

By mid afternoon, the fog thinned. Based on the sun's position, I'd been pedaling for over seven hours. I welcomed the sunlight's warmth, though the air was thick with damp. Clouds of insects rose from the dripping canopy, tickling my eyelashes as I pedaled. The stream had broadened, making it easier to follow.

Assuming I followed the right stream.

My stomach growled, and I pulled out the second to last ham sandwich. Why had I told Brother Robbert I only needed four? Eating more than half my food was probably a mistake, given the uncertainty of the situation. With luck, there was a simple explanation and the masters at Erie Abbey would provision me for my return trip. If not... grim images of what I could find crossed my mind's canvas and the sandwich turned to dust in my mouth. I spat out granules of salty ham and bitter rye, my stomach lurching. To calm it, I focused on the colors in the tree canopy, the occasional perylene maroon of a wild plum breaking the monotony of emerald, helios, and chromium oxide greens.

This was the first time I'd ever traveled by myself, and it unsettled me. The trouble was, horseless, dogless, childless, and friendless, I had nothing to distract me from my worries about Akiko... or how to find and then approach my family.

"Worry not, pretty boy. The world spins on regardless," Genevie's voice chuckled in my mind.

The sun's light faded as a fat drop of water hit my cheek. I peered at the gathering clouds, purple and ominous. That they had obscured the sun so quickly raised gooseflesh along my arms.

Great.

A jarring clap shook the air as rain smashed against the flier. Alarm snaked through me when a second thunderclap boomed. Bowman had warned me thunderstorms could generate unstable air currents which could flip the flier or smash it down. My heart pounded as I increased my speed, searching for a place to land.

I pedaled faster, my breathing ragged, but the endless canopy undulated without pause. A sudden, powerful gust caught my left wing, lifting it and sending me into a right turn. I rode out the turn and corrected my direction when the gust died.

Sheets of rain blew across my path, the deluge impenetrable.

I glanced at the gossamer material above me. What happened if the wings became saturated? Another gust sent me careening left. I fought the flier for control; if the pitch steepened, the wing would stall.

The curtain of rain parted long enough to present a patch of viridian: the hue lighter and more vibrant than the canopy's deep tones.

Could it be grass?

I swiped at my goggles as the flier bounced through the sky, shouting when the next clap of thunder boomed, the *crack* so loud it slapped my chest. The air smelled strange, pungent with a chlorine tang. Hairs on the back of my neck stood—I was flying a metal-framed vehicle through a thunderstorm.

I'm going to be struck by lightning.

I leaned forward, pedaling faster, seeking the grass-like green. Even landing in a field of low shrubs would be better than flying through the storm... assuming lightning didn't strike me first.

A bolt of lightning sizzled with a *crackle-snap* to my left. For a heartbeat, time and sound ceased. Two more forks of lightning knifed through the air, brilliant white against the gloom, and I screamed, but their flashes illuminated a large clearing centered by a star-shaped structure. I thrust the handlebars forward, the flier diving toward the ground. The rain flayed my uncovered skin, but I hunched my shoulders and pedaled forward, my teeth chattering.

The flier bumped toward the clearing, crabbing sideways in the heaving winds. Five meters above the ground, a gust hit, and I threw my weight to the opposite side to keep my wings level; if one wingtip hit the ground, the flier would cartwheel.

The flier straightened and bounced hard enough to snap my head back before we settled on the grass. My head bobbled on my weak, floppy neck as another gust hit the flier and the tires left the ground. Panic drove me toward the star-shaped wall, and I pedaled on, searching for an entrance. So much for cautious reconnoitering.

The tires slipped over the wet grass, and winds continued

to buffet me as I circled the compound. Around the last corner, I spotted an arched entryway a few meters from where I'd touched down.

Of course.

I turned the flier toward the doors, willing someone to open them for me. Surely an alarm had gone up as I'd pedaled around the compound. When the doors flew open, I'd never been more thankful for my brother artists.

Inside the abbey's perimeter wall, the wind's power dimmed but didn't stop. I climbed off the flier on shaky legs, stumbling in the gusts blowing through the doors. There was no one to help me close them; perhaps they'd ducked back inside to escape the weather.

The massive doors were slow to close, the wind battering against them as I strained to push them shut. When the lock bar dropped into place, I sagged against them, panting.

In the open courtyard, the flier shuddered and rolled forward; the nose bouncing as the front tire lifted from the ground. If I lost it, it would take me weeks to walk back to Niagara Abbey. The rain lashed my face as I raced to it and leaped into my seat. Even with my weight, the storm tried to lift it as I backed it under the arched entryway.

Once under cover, the storm's violence dulled, and I took a deep, bracing breath. While I waited for someone to greet me, I scrutinized the buildings, hoping to catch a flicker of light or a wisp of smoke through the near-impenetrable deluge. When no one came, I retrieved my sword from the hidden compartment and peered through the rain.

What next?

Before me sat two elongated buildings connected by a gallery of windows set over an arched passageway. If Erie was like Niagara Abbey, the hallways and bed chambers would be in the star-shaped walls, and the courtyard buildings would house the lesson rooms, the dining hall, and the master's chambers.

I sprinted through the rain with my teeth bared toward the central arch, cringing as the dead artists' brushes tumbled in my bag. My legs and lungs on fire, I reached the arch and bent over, gasping. Identical wooden doors sat on each side of the arch, so, after straightening my sodden coat, I knocked on the first.

No answer.

I crossed to the second door, pressing my ear against it, but hearing nothing, I rapped on it hard enough to make my knuckles smart. The door moved, so I pushed it in. It opened into an antechamber of sorts, festooned with coats, boots, gardening tools, and baskets. I crossed the room to the second door and knocked again. Perhaps they were in the other building.

I retraced my steps, opening the first door I'd tried. This antechamber was like the other but neater, organized, the shoes and boots tidy on wooden shelves beneath the long benches.

The master's quarters.

I rapped on the interior door.

No answer.

I shivered, my coat dripping on the floor. "Blast protocol." Like the first, this door opened when I tried the knob.

"Hullo?" My call echoed through the hall. I stepped inside, closing the door behind me, waiting in still air redolent with dust and mildewed wood. Meager light trickled through the windows, illuminating the hall and central staircase. Two immense doors flanked the stairs.

I crossed to the first and opened it, stepping into the dining hall where long tables and benches gleamed in the dim room. The second door opened into a room filled with empty easels along a windowed wall, a massive fireplace dominating the far end. My footsteps echoed as I crossed the room and held my hand over the ashes, then touched the mantle stones.

Cold.

I retreated, peering up the staircase. "Hullo?"

The stairs led to a long hallway with facing doors, the energy strange and unharmonious. As a boy, I'd noticed unaligned doors in every Popham hallway. Perhaps this was why. The first two doors opened into large bed chambers. I walked to the far end, knocking on each door as I went and opening several.

Nothing.

I retraced my path and sat on the top step of the stairway. I could search the second building or the hallways within the star-shaped walls, but I wouldn't find anyone. No one had been here for a long time, perhaps even longer than the five weeks Niagara Abbey had waited, so the storm must have blown the doors open for me.

A gust of rain pelted the windows, and I shivered. The light was already fading. With my luck, the wind would blow me kilometers off course in the dark, so I couldn't fly through this gale back to Niagara Abbey. Better to stay here tonight and reassess in the morning.

The mournful wind howled around the master's lodge, and the building creaked.

Ears alert, I waited. After a while, I called "Hullo?" but the building's quiet sucked up my voice like I'd said nothing.

CHAPTER SEVENTEEN

By mid-morning, I'd explored every room in the master's lodge and moved to the boys' dormitory. They used the lower hall for training; it featured classrooms for art, letters, and combat. A large dormitory full of bunk beds occupied one side of the upper hall, and single and double-occupancy rooms filled the other. These would be for older boys, students with only five to six years of training remaining.

I sat on a bed, staring at the rain, stumped. The violence of the previous day's storm had abated, but the driving rain had delayed my departure. If it didn't let up soon, I'd be forced to leave and chance flying through it, or stay, which would worry Akiko and the masters. They'd already be anxious after yesterday's storm—for all they knew, I could have crashed the flier.

I leaned back on the bed, studying the room. There was a single wooden chair, several hooks on the back of the door, and a small dresser I'd already searched.

The narrow bed creaked as I twisted to peer out the window. From here, the entire courtyard was visible.

Nothing.

This room, like the others I'd searched, provided no clues as to its former occupant. There was not a scrap of paper, clay figurine, or sketch on a wall, in a drawer, or propped up on a windowsill.

On a whim, I stood and flipped the mattress, but found nothing beneath the bed. The springs of the bed frame twanged as I let the mattress fall. I coughed as a cloud of dust erupted from the bed, chasing me from the room.

What next?

I could either search for access to the basement or explore the abbey's fortified walls, but I didn't want to do either. Why had I agreed to come? If I hadn't, Akiko and I might have reached Toronto Depot by now.

"This much quiet could drive a man mad." As I left, I kicked a small object. Instead of the rock I'd expected, I found a geometric shape roughly the size of a pebble. I turned the object and counted its faces.

"Sixteen."

My geometry lessons at Popham Abbey had primarily focused on capturing natural angles, but I remembered deltahedron was the name of any object with equilateral triangular faces. One boy had fired an eight-sided deltahedron in our pottery class, each face carved with unique symbols. We used it to bet on the outcomes of things—which boy would receive the top marks on a live portrait or be selected to sit at the headmaster's side at the solstice feast or watch our bad-tempered acrylics master shred their painting.

The deltahedron I held was unmarked, and I couldn't detect any sort of pattern in the glaze. It told me nothing, but it was the first personal thing I'd found in the compound—the first link between me and the boys who had lived here, so I pocketed it. As I descended to the ground level, I slapped my feet against the stair treads, delighting in the hollow booms.

Hollow.

Both doors at the bottom of the stairs opened into large rooms, so I examined the interior walls for seams or panels but found nothing. No rugs hid trapdoors, and there wasn't any furniture to hide a passage behind. My curiosity grew as I examined each stair tread and riser face and then scrutinized the walls along the stairway. I even peered behind the faded portraits and paintings, but finding nothing, I leaned against the banister, tumbling the little deltahedron in my pocket. If I wanted to reach Niagara Abbey today, I needed to leave now. Outside, the rain continued to fall in sheets, which meant I'd have little visibility. Inside, I had an abbey to explore and no one to scold me for snooping. I estimated the stairs covered an area roughly eighteen meters long and four meters wide. Why would they ignore a space as large as this?

"I'll be back tomorrow, Akiko," I said, as I pushed away from the banister.

The staircase on the master's side of the complex was a duplicate, so I thumped down the stairs and trotted from the boys' hall to the masters' lodge, to see if the other building could shed light on the mystery.

I tapped the first two stair risers, disappointed by their solid sound, but the stairs rang hollow from the third riser up. With great care, I checked the dining hall and the windowed classroom, but found no obvious means of entry. Running my fingertips down the long tables, I sighed as I drifted through the dining hall. When I reached the far end, I surveyed the room. There were only two doors: the one I had entered through from the entry hall and a door I assumed led into the kitchen.

Last night, I'd gnawed on strips of dried meat and fallen

asleep without exploring, and this morning, I'd finished the apples and the last sandwich, so I hadn't investigated the kitchens. The hinges shrieked as I pushed the door open to peer into the dark, windowless room. When I let go of the door to drag a bench over, it complained noisily as it swung back and forth. Again, I waited for someone to investigate, but no one did.

I propped open the noisy door to brighten the gloom, then opened the next door. Light spilled into the kitchen from the small, walled garden. Through the sheeting rain, I could make out brushy herbs, greens, and a large strawberry patch. I propped the garden door open for the fresh air and light and unlatched the last door.

It opened into musty darkness, my grasping hand finding nothing. The light in the kitchen wasn't sufficient to illuminate the dark beyond the doorsill, so I rummaged through the drawers for something to light, finding a flint and steel in the last one.

"This won't help much." The sound of my voice disturbed the abbey's quiet and startled me. "I'll make a torch," I said, raising my voice. "I'm using a towel to do so," I shouted as I yanked drawers open. When I pulled out a cotton towel, I dumped the drawer onto the slate floor with a *bang* and cocked my head to listen for a response.

The rain sighed.

After wrapping the towel around a long-handled, wooden spoon, I dipped it into a pot of lard sitting near the stove. I struck the flint, raining sparks onto twists of paper from my sketchbook. Once they caught, I used them to light the torch. It flared brightly, but I pocketed the flint and steel, and tucked a second towel into my pocket in case the torch burned out.

Stone steps led into inky blackness. The guttering torch

provided light enough to walk but not enough to show the entire staircase. At the T-shaped intersection at the bottom of the stairs, my torch illuminated little, so I turned left into a spacious hallway and stopped at the first door. My nostrils flared as I poked my head in the abbey's cold room. Spices, sausage, and cheese. At least I wouldn't starve.

I passed several more doors before reaching another intersecting hallway. Now what? I spun in a slow circle and noticed a torch in a sconce on the wall. I lit it and turned left.

As I explored, I continued to light each torch I found. All the doors were closed, and none were marked. Many of the rooms were empty—the darkness echoing my calls. I counted between eight and ten doors in each section of the hallway, but soon lost track of how many sections I'd passed. At yet another intersection, I stopped. If I continued, I could spend days exploring the warren of tunnels.

I retraced my path to the kitchen, extinguishing the hallway torches as I went. The kitchen smelled of rain and wet herbs, a welcome respite from damp stone and scorched cotton. I leaned against the doorframe, watching the rain and the hissing steam billowing from the torch I tossed onto the saturated soil. The clouds were low, barely clearing the sodden treetops. I plucked a mint leaf from a patch next to the door frame and shivered as a fat drop of rain hit the back of my neck. Flying back would be unpleasant.

I chewed on the mint as I counted the paces needed to reach the staircase. With a fresh towel, I made a new torch, lit it, and descended the stairs again.

This time, I turned right and measured my steps. My paces brought me between two doors, so I opened the first.

"Hullo?"

Nothing answered from the dark as I stepped inside. It held crates and plaster-molded holiday decorations. The flickering torchlight illuminated grinning elves and sinister, smiling animals so unsettling I backed out and closed the door. In the second, larger room, the torchlight failed to illuminate the far walls or ceiling.

"Hullo, hullo." My voice and footsteps echoed as I roved through the room in a counterclockwise direction. They had outfitted the walls with desk-like workstations, but based on the equipment on the desks, they hadn't used this room to teach art. I picked up a set of something shaped like earmuffs, tethered to a panel festooned with dials and knobs and held them to my ear. Nothing.

"Next time, I'll bring Ben. Come on, torch, let's keep exploring."

The remaining workstations contained similar equipment, and I skirted the room, arriving at the door with no better idea of the room's purpose. A round metal tower occupied the middle of the room, so I circled it, seeking a hatch or door, and found a ladder attached to the far side.

"What's up there?" Switching the torch to my left hand, I climbed the ladder. A meter above the top of the door, the ladder bent inward toward the center of the cylinder. I continued to climb until I reached the top but found nothing but metal poles stretching up into the gloom.

"Mystery solved." Metal poles attached to a giant metal cylinder occupied the space under the stairs. Finding the answer to my question had provided no clarity, nor was it as satisfying as I'd hoped.

I closed the door behind me, strangely deflated.

What had I expected? Bodies stacked in the cellars?

I could keep exploring, but I'd found no evidence to suggest anything untoward had happened. While it was possible something sinister had occurred here, I couldn't envision marauders packing and storing everyone's belongings. More likely, the masters and boys had packed their things and departed en masse, not notifying Niagara Abbey on their way out.

My shoulders slumped as my hand brushed the deltahedron in my pocket. I may have failed the masters at Niagara Abbey, but I had my own mysteries to solve. Even if the rain continued tomorrow, it was time to go.

CHAPTER EIGHTEEN

I followed a river north, munching on a piece of cheese sandwiched between two slabs of salami. The tang of the cheese was almost painful, but the combination of salt and fat was oddly comforting. Although I hadn't found bread or crackers in Erie Abbey's larder, I'd discovered several wheels of cheese and cured meats. I'd packed everything I could carry onto the flier to take back to Niagara Abbey. Perhaps the offering would mollify the masters; I had nothing else to offer. If not... I shrugged. I wanted answers from the masters, but I needed to reach Toronto Depot.

After two days of rain, the air sparkled, scented with spicy pine. The day was mercifully cool with virtually no headwind, so I would make good time. With luck, I'd arrive at the abbey before noon. Assuming I could debrief with Headmaster McCully this afternoon, Akiko and I would arrive in Toronto Depot sometime tomorrow. While this delay had frayed my nerves, it had also renewed my eagerness to search for my birth family, or at least the location depicted by *Home*.

I unfastened another button on my coat and ate the last bite of my meat and cheese, wiping my greasy hand on my trousers, filthy from the dust and grime I gained by exploring the abandoned abbey.

The river's noise grew to a crescendo as I flew around the next bend. The water was turbulent; slashes of white broke the Monastral blue water as its speed increased. Without warning, the river dropped away, the noise of it roaring from the sheer stone walls. The deafening thunder of the plummeting water reverberated in my chest. Eyes wide, I pedaled the flier in a circle to study the massive waterfall.

The canyon was carved like an enormous animal had slashed out the riverbed, its claws raking deep gouges into the rock. The water fell nearly seventy meters and disappeared into a dense mist. Turning around, I flew at the falls, washed by icy spray. The sheer walls rose around me, culminating in a deep V at the center. As I neared the waterfall, the flier bucked in a powerful downdraft. I trimmed it to climb, awestruck by the volume of water sheeting over the edges. As I rose, I marveled at the waterfall's enormity before following the serene river north toward the Ontario Sea.

"How big was it?" Akiko skipped in a circle around the flier as I unbuckled my bag. Charcoal cavorted on the other side, delighted to be together again.

"Massive." I'd distracted her with the details of the waterfall as a defensive act, and once her imagination had taken hold, she had forgotten she was angry with me for leaving her behind. Even though I'd prevented one confrontation, the knot in my stomach grew heavier. How would the masters take my news? I dreaded disappointing them. Leaving Popham under strained circumstances had troubled my dreams for months, an experience I was not keen to repeat.

Akiko's eyes sparkled. "How massive?"

I stretched my arms wide. "This whole abbey could fit into the plunge pool at the base of the falls. The strength of the rushing water has carved a deep canyon, almost as wide as it is tall."

"Wow. It wasn't labeled on Pultney's map! How tall was it?"

"From the crest to the base is almost 70 meters. How was it here?"

Akiko shrugged. "Boring."

"Oh?"

She nodded. "I couldn't ask questions, and I have so many! When in the process does the energy work begin? Why doesn't every artist make sculptures? How can you tell what's a 'right' change?"

"Okay, enough." I faced her.

Akiko stopped skipping.

"I'll answer your questions when we're in the air, but not before."

She brightened. "When can we go?"

"I've just landed, so I've earned a rest and a meal. Afterward, I report to the headmaster, so we'll leave this afternoon."

Akiko's face fell. "It will take *ages*."

I glanced around, then whispered, "Question."

Akiko leaned in. "What?"

"What's for lunch?"

Akiko smirked. "That's for me to know and you to find out."

"Oh." I slapped my forehead and straightened. "I haven't fallen for that one since I was twelve."

She skipped toward the master's lodge, turning as she reached the door. "Lunch is now, Brother Sugiyama."

My lips twitched. "Beg your pardon, Brother Sugiyama."

"I'm not your brother!"

"Nor am I yours." I stuck out my tongue at her as we entered the dining hall.

Heads swiveled toward us, and Headmaster McCully beckoned to me. "Matthew, I was pleased to hear you'd arrived safely. Let's speak after lunch."

"Thank you, Headmaster."

He nodded and waved me away.

"Dismissed," I murmured, as Akiko pulled me toward a table.

She grinned. "Like any boy here."

I poked her side, and she smothered a giggle, giving me a stern look. She guided me to two empty seats and made the introductions. She'd made friends with several boys her age and led the lively conversation. I listened to their chatter as I dug into the creamy potato salad, feeling old.

After lunch, I followed Headmaster McCully to his study. Bower and a master I didn't recognize were already there waiting for us.

"I've asked them to join us for your report," said McCully.

I relayed what I'd found, or hadn't found, at Erie Abbey and they groaned.

Bower's brow furrowed. "No signs of violence?"

"None, and no indications of a quick escape. They left little behind—furniture and a few portraits hanging near the central staircases. I brought back several wheels of cheese and cured meats." My hand patted the deltahedron in my pocket, the lump comforting.

"What about art supplies?"

I shook my head. "The abbey is massive, and none of the

doors were marked. I didn't find a map, directory, their vault, or even their headmaster's office."

McCully sighed. "Thank you, Matthew. It's less than we'd hoped but better than we feared. If you'll excuse us, brothers?" After Bower and the other man exited, McCully settled into his chair.

"I promised you answers. What would you like to know?"

Questions sprang forth, tumbling over each other. I plucked the easiest from the list. "Are abbeys usually located so closely together?"

He didn't appear surprised by my question. "No, but we enjoyed the proximity to Erie Abbey."

What he hadn't said sparked my curiosity. "Did you consider combining the two?"

He pursed his lips. "It would have made sense to occupy a single location, but neither abbey is supported by a community. Although Erie Abbey is larger and would have easily fit us all, we can get resources from the mariners. In contrast, Erie Abbey had to grow, harvest, and store what they could."

"Yes, I see. What a shame."

McCully nodded. "Between you and me, they took great pride in being self-sufficient and treated us as their inferiors, making any real talk of combining the abbeys impossible."

I tried a more sensitive question next. "Master Bower showed me your vault. Do all abbeys have such a room?"

"Yes. What else?"

I rubbed my beard. "What if an artist dies outside of an abbey?"

McCully frowned. "Then the community must return the artist's belongings. It's written into the commission agreement."

I couldn't help myself and kept pushing. "What if the artist has no community? What if they're traveling?"

McCully's frown deepened. "Artists don't travel. I assume the masters at Popham told you this."

I swallowed, the hairs on my arms standing. "Why aren't women trained to be artists?"

McCully's eyebrows rose. "They'd be too old to learn."

My palms wetted. "Forgive me, but why aren't *girls* invited into the abbeys? Are there female-only abbeys?"

McCully's manner changed, his voice hardening. "What an absurd notion. Women are not artists, so we do not need to train girls."

It was clear from his demeanor I wouldn't learn anything more by pressing him further. Worse, if other headmasters agreed with McCully, there was little chance I could find an abbey who would foster Akiko. My shoulders sank, but I changed the subject. "What do you think happened to the masters and pupils of Erie Abbey?"

McCully relaxed, steepling his fingers. "My primary worry was they'd been invaded or overrun. However, it sounds as though they departed voluntarily."

"Is there another abbey near here?"

"No."

If there was no other abbey nearby, and the masters and students of Erie Abbey hadn't come here, where had they gone?

A deep weariness settled over me as I cast around for another question. "May we stay another night?"

McCully smiled. "Yes. Will you depart tomorrow?"

"Yes, assuming the weather holds. Where can I find Akiko?"

"If I'm not mistaken, she's modeling for a plein air water-color class on the north lawn. Come, I'll take you." He led me through a door hidden behind a tapestry, into a long stone corridor with a rounded ceiling.

I squinted as we stepped outside, the afternoon light

dazzling. The students painted on the lawn, facing the sweeping view of the lake. Lavender tumbled along the edge of the lawn, perfuming the air. They'd dressed Akiko in a fabric that floated in the breeze. She faced the water, holding a bunch of flowers in one hand and a kite's string in the other. The kite's tail fluttered and snapped in the wind.

The master teaching the class bowed to us and gestured toward two empty easels. I took my place and smiled with pleasure at the materials brought to me. After wetting my paper and mixing pigments, I half listened to the master who spoke about the flow of the fabric draped over Akiko, the sunlight sparkling on the water, and providing the impression of wispy clouds though there were none in the sky.

I relaxed into the moment, allowing my worries about Akiko to drift away. What to do about her was a problem for future Matthew.

The knots in my neck released as I painted. I loved watercolors, watching the colors blend and furl as inferred edges met. That I could create deep vivid colors and pair them with muted pastels by moderating the water on my brush pleased me.

The sun's heat warmed my chest, but the landward breeze kept me cool. The sound of the other students blended with the lap of waves, birdsong, and buzzing insects.

"Very nice," said Headmaster McCully over my shoulder. The abbey's masters flanked McCully, their eyes curious. Gratified by his praise, I set my brush down and stepped back.

The master teaching the class joined us. He frowned as he studied my painting, then asked. "May I?"

I nodded. "Please."

"Class, come gather."

The students crowded around the easel to examine my painting, and Akiko pushed through them, craning her neck as the master pointed out details with his paintbrush.

"Brother Sugiyama is an exceptional watercolorist. Notice how he's captured the movement of the kite's tail and matched it to the flow of the dress? In the background, he's added more movement, mirroring the snap of a wave to the cresting clouds. You can tell a storm is coming."

"Is it moving?" a small boy whispered.

His fellows pushed his shoulder with a jeer.

McCully settled the scuffle by frowning at the boys. Once they had quieted, he turned to me. "Would you permit us to keep your painting as a teaching aid for future classes?"

"Yes, Headmaster," I said, my spirits lifting, the head boy once again.

McCully's smile warmed further. "Why don't you join us at the masters' table for dinner?"

Pleasure bubbled in my chest. Here again was a chance to learn a little more about the abbey system, but as an equal, not a student. "Thank you, Headmaster. I'd like that very much."

CHAPTER NINETEEN

My legs burned as I pedaled into the headwind. "You guys are too heavy."

"Be nice, fathead."

"Fathead?" I grinned. Akiko had gotten along well with the lads at Niagara Abbey. So much for Preacher Saget's worries about Akiko not relating to her peer group. Akiko's peer group was art students, not zealots-in-training.

"The boys said it. When will we hear the water?"

I checked the horizon. Akiko had begged to visit the falls, so instead of heading north across the lake, I'd agreed to another detour. Now that our destination was within reach, I was strangely reluctant to arrive at the depot. The detour would only add a few hours to our trip, and besides, I wanted to witness her reaction.

"We might see the spray cloud before we hear the falls, but I'm not sure because last time, I flew in the other direction."

As we flew, I scanned the riverbanks for signs of a ford or a trail. Last night during dinner at the master's table, I'd learned over one hundred boys and masters had occupied Erie Abbey, but none had passed Niagara Abbey when they had abandoned Erie, so perhaps they had traveled north along the river to… wherever they had gone.

White mists rose above the treetops ahead. Akiko was busy chatting with Charcoal, so I dropped into the river canyon and pedaled upstream. The trees muffled the sound, and Akiko didn't hear the falls until we rounded the last bend.

"Oh, look!"

From this height, the falls were even more impressive. An astonishing volume of water gushed over the edge, falling into the basin pool with tremendous force. The icy spray dampened us in an instant.

"Let's go closer!"

"For safety, we're staying back." I trimmed the nose to climb and pedaled faster toward the falls. Not only did we need to clear the onslaught of water for safety reasons, but the sound and sight of the falls were a painful reminder of my overfull bladder. "I remember a beach on the other side of the falls," I shouted over the roar of the water. "We can take a break there, then fly back over the falls on our way north."

We cleared the point of the falls with fifteen meters to spare, and I pedaled us to the beach. The water's roar rumbled in my chest as the flier bumped down, jolting along the cobble-strewn beach. My teeth clacked hard, the shock spreading through my neck and sparking a dull ache in my head, but Akiko laughed.

"Boing, boing! Is this a long break?"

I rubbed my neck. "No, so use the facilities. It will be a long flight to Toronto Depot."

The flier bounced as she kicked her legs. "You hear that, Charcoal? Use the facilities."

"Forthwith," I said, as the flier rolled to a stop. "Last one back is the fathead."

I bolted toward the tree line, followed by her peals of laughter as she struggled to unbuckle herself and the dog. Charcoal waited by the flier when I returned, and I buckled him in before checking the straps securing the bags again.

"You're the fathead," I called, as Akiko trotted back to the flier.

"It's easier when you're a boy."

I smirked. "Or a dog. Come on, let's go."

The flight back over the falls was no less impressive. Since we were higher, I flew two full turns over the spectacle before flying north.

"It was massive. This is the land of the massive."

I stretched my neck. "Oh?"

"Vast lakes, enormous waterfalls."

Huge, empty abbeys.

The kilometers passed quickly, with Akiko recounting her time in Niagara Abbey and peppering me with art-related questions. The winds helped, and we reached the sea before the sun hit its zenith.

Akiko rustled behind me. "Isn't Toronto Depot northwest?"

"Mm."

"Then why are we flying north?"

I released the handlebars, and the flier immediately turned west. "That's why."

"The wind is pushing us?"

I nodded. "Your colossal head is like a sail."

She chortled. "I'll give you massive ears if you're not careful."

"I'll confiscate your sketchbook if *you're* not careful."

"Oh. Did you get more?"

I glanced over my shoulder. "One, but we'll pick up another in the depot."

The sun warmed as we flew north, and despite the steady

westward wind, I dripped with sweat, the water in my canteen turning tepid and sulfurous. When familiar snores rumbled from the back seat, I turned. Akiko had twisted in her seat and slept with her cheek against the backrest and her legs curled sideways. Charcoal's hind legs jutted out, and his head lolled behind him, his tongue flapping in the wind.

I snickered and faced front to scan the horizon. By squinting, I could just make out the start of a skyline. Crossing the open water had been a gamble, but one I was now glad we'd taken, as it appeared we'd arrive by early evening.

The prospect of finding my birth family filled me with wild energy. I had so many questions to ask, so many doubts about myself to assuage. Why had they abandoned me into the abbey system with no contact?

I also wanted information about Talbot. Since meeting him, I'd wondered why we appeared so similar, why he knew more about my family than me, and why he'd done everything in his power to prevent me from finding them. It was only by sheer luck I'd slipped past the obstacles he'd put in my way.

My friends had encouraged me, but no one else had supported my search. The masters at Popham Abbey, the Avalon Society members, and even *Talbot* had said my quest was self-serving, but the society had made multiple offers to me, and even Preacher Saget had tried to guilt me into staying in Whitehall, so perhaps they were the ones who were greedy in desiring my skills for themselves.

I tapped my fingers along my jaw. An artist's skill set was always in demand, so perhaps some community had even come and offered commissions to Erie Abbey's masters and students. I wouldn't put it past the Avalon Society to engineer a merger... if it benefited them, but since they only extended invitations to 'the best', the lesser students and masters would eventually end up in smaller, more remote communities.

Akiko yawned. "Look, the tower! But the buildings are too tiny. Is this really a depot?"

"I bet the buildings are between sixty and one hundred meters tall," I said, as I checked our trim.

"No way!"

My estimates proved accurate, and we flew north along the shore, gaping. Toronto Depot was massive, and the skyline stretched to the northern horizon. Beyond the towers were kilometers of buildings stretching as far as we could see. Patches of trees had sprouted in places, but other than where nature had reclaimed the land, the depot appeared entirely artificial.

"How will we find somewhere to land?"

"Good question." Open land surrounded every depot I had visited before, so I hadn't expected this to be an issue. A massive road ran along the waterfront, but too many bridges and lines crossed it for us to attempt a landing. There was no shore at all; the water met the built environment squarely. Although several of the docks protruding into the lake could be long enough to land on, I didn't trust their structural integrity.

As we flew, gulls screeched and wheeled below us, their cries comforting and familiar, but my stomach sank with each kilometer of the depot we passed. Most of the roads appeared to have evenly spaced posts along their edges, and from this height, I couldn't estimate if they were wide enough for the flier. Many appeared to be cluttered with debris or crisscrossed with cables and lines. The roadways that seemed the most open were often too short or appeared hilly—while we might land, taking off again could be a problem.

The tall buildings fell away as we continued north, but a second set of structures loomed ahead of us, this group even larger than the last. I shook my head. Even if we found a place to land the flier, how would we find my family in a depot of this size? Unstable air swirled around the structures, flinging the scent of dust and hot pavement high into the air, causing minor pockets of turbulence.

Above everything stood the white tower, its apex two hundred meters above the nearest buildings. The tower rose like an elongated pyramid from an impossibly narrow base, its smooth white walls unblemished. A window-covered bulb bulged two-thirds of the way up.

Akiko gasped as we passed it. "Windows! Was that for *people*?"

The astonishing scale of the depot left me hollow as, for the first time, I truly understood the magnitude of technology we'd lost after the world died. How people had built something so massive with *tools* instead of art staggered me.

"Can we splore the tower?"

"Yes, after we find somewhere to land."

"I'm peeling my eyes, but I really only see *that*."

She wasn't alone. The tower had dominated *Home* and long captivated my dreams, and I couldn't keep my eyes off it.

CHAPTER TWENTY

Twilight had descended into dusk by the time we found a place to land. Our landing didn't go well, and I cursed as my head snapped back on the second bounce. "You guys okay, Mouse?"

"Check," she said, her voice weary. "But..."

"Yes?"

"Do we have to find it tonight?"

"Tonight?" I twisted to face her and Charcoal. "Of course not. We may not even reach the tower tomorrow."

It was hard to judge how far we'd flown from the tower. When we hadn't found a suitable landing area near the waterfront, we'd taken to flying in semicircles with increasing radiuses as we searched. We had flown countless arcs before spotting this odd, rectangular field.

Akiko squatted to touch the ground. "It's not real grass."

Its individual blades resembled grass, but they yielded little, like a paintbrush left to stiffen, and rasped as I brushed my fingertips across them. "It's authentic enough to sleep on, I suppose. I have jerky if you're hungry."

Akiko yawned. "I'm not hungry, but can you put up the roof before you eat?"

"Too late." I tore into a chunk of dried meat, my mouth flooding at the spice and salt. Though structures surrounded the artificial field, I wasn't enthused to explore them in the dark. We'd seen no one so far, but I had a strong sense someone watched us and although it would take less effort to camp next to the flier, the idea of sleeping in the open field raised the hairs on the back of my neck.

Charcoal lifted his nose, his brow furrowing, but all I could detect in the evening air was hot pavement.

"Instead of camping here in the open, I'll search for somewhere to park the flier under cover."

Akiko groaned, flinging herself over the back seats. She cracked an eye to ensure I watched, then made exaggerated snoring sounds.

"Charcoal, let's go. Her snores will chase away any curious neighbors."

The corner of her lip twitched, but she continued to feign sleep.

I jogged toward the end of the field but nearly ran headlong into a black-tinted chain fence. By following it, I found an opening and approached the nearest set of buildings. I poked my head into the first one, but only the facade was intact; the rest of the structure was rubble.

The second building appeared whole, but my senses screamed it was... occupied. I waited at the gaping threshold. Nothing moved, but when Charcoal's hackles raised, I backed out of the open door in small, slow steps. Once clear, I bolted away.

Charcoal raced beside me, glancing back at the building.

The next two structures were too small to house the flier. By the time we'd reached the far end of the field, I'd exhausted my remaining reserves. I stopped, hands on my knees, gasping as I surveyed what had appeared as a natural hill. Although shrubs and grasses grew on it, upon closer inspection, I noticed the mound was man made. It had a tall arch dug into it like a shallow cave, so with my arms outstretched, I stepped into the gloom, moving forward at a snail's pace until my knuckles hit the back wall with a muffled, metallic *clang*. "Perfect. We'll camp here."

We trotted toward the flier, but this time, I ran face-first into another black chain fence. The fence twanged but luckily for my face, it had some give to it. Blinking, I skirted the edge and trotted back across the field to the flier.

Once there, Charcoal circled it, whining.

Akiko was gone.

"Akiko?" I called, my voice low. My gaze flicked toward the ominous building, and I turned in a slow circle, squinting into the dark. "Akiko?"

Charcoal whimpered, his cries raising the hairs on my arms.

"Find her!"

Nose down, the dog circled the flier, then trotted toward the buildings we'd explored. I jogged after him, lungs burning, careful this time to avoid the fence. He trotted past the first building and sniffed the doorway of the second.

My heart in my throat, I willed him not to enter. He turned, tracing the girl's scent toward the far end of the field. Even after more than a week of pedaling the blasted flier, my legs were leaden as I hurried after him. In the gloom, I lost sight of the dog, so I stopped at the entry to the artificial cave. "Akiko?"

No answer.

My stomach churned, but something gleamed white on the field. My breathing ragged, I circled the invisible chain fence, giving it what I assumed was plenty of room before sprinting toward the flier. Again, I misjudged it and my foot caught on a metal post at the end of the fence, sending me sprawling on the artificial grass.

"What are you doing?" Akiko whispered.

I rolled over. "Where were you?"

"I tried following, but you were too fast. I ran across the field, but you left again." She burrowed into me, hot and trembling. "I'm scared."

"I know. We'll camp here tonight, so I'll get the flier."

Her arms tightened around me. "Don't go near the buildings."

"Check. Stay with Charcoal; I'll be right back."

Upon reaching the flier, I froze at a small sound and scanned the field.

Nothing.

I tried to swallow, but my throat was too dry as I pedaled the flier toward the artificial hill. Even with my head on a swivel, I saw nothing, but the hair on my arms and neck continued to stand under the pressure of the invisible eyes.

With Akiko's help, we pushed the flier under the archway. At least I'd have only one direction to watch. As I tugged a tarpaulin over the flier, I said, "Lay your bedroll here under the canvas."

She lifted the canvas, then paused, yawning. "Where will you sleep?"

"I'll keep watch for a while, so get your bed set up for sleep."

She disappeared and rustled under the canvas, then pushed the tarpaulin up and handed me my sword. "Just in case. I'm staying up with you 'cause I'm too scared to sleep."

I took the sword. "Great idea, but first, can you lay down and pet Charcoal? He's anxious too."

"Okay," she said, retreating.

Minutes later, her breathing deepened, turning rhythmic. I settled in front of the flier, leaning my head against the frame. My hearing sharpened as my eyes raked the gloom, but other than the breeze and the sighs of the girl and dog, there was little sound.

No birds, no insects. No stealthy footsteps.

The depot's quiet was eerie, like when the forest falls silent as a cougar pads through a woodland. At Popham, the crashing waves had lulled me to sleep, and I'd woken to shorebird cries each morning. When traveling, I'd had the horses with me but besides them, the woods were full of sounds—falling leaves, wind-rustled branches, birds, the creak of a trunk, squirrel chatter. In my life, I'd never experienced this type of prolonged quiet, but why was I so alarmed? I never worried about safety in a depot before.

The canvas rustled as Akiko rolled over, and in a heartbeat, I knew. I was afraid for *her*. The prospect of losing her made it hard to breathe. If something happened to Akiko... I couldn't even finish the thought. Even if no one learned about her uncanny, artistic abilities, what if another person here questioned my fitness or suitability as a father? Worse, what if I found my family... but they didn't welcome Akiko?

The glimmer of stars brightened as the night deepened. The new moon was halfway toward a waxing crescent, but I was grateful for its scant light. As my eyes adjusted, I could discern the outline of the chain fence. What was the purpose of a fence ten meters long? It would neither keep livestock in nor deer out. Not that the people from *Before* could have farmed with the artificial turf covering the land.

Something drew my attention, and my eyes snapped back toward the field. I scanned it, my eyes pausing at a dark spot. Had it been there before? I watched it for several breaths, a chill descending my spine. I rose, my eyes glued to the spot.

Was it a trick of the light or debris I hadn't noticed while crossing the field?

The spot shimmered.

Had it moved… or was my imagination playing tricks? My eyes watered and I blinked several times, but when they cleared, the spot was gone.

My heart jolted as I stared at the location, and icy sweat broke out across my chest. Every bit of me itched to explore the field, to stalk the watcher, but moving would break my cover. Deep in the shadows, they wouldn't be able to distinguish me from the shape of the flier… unless I moved.

I listened for the scrape of a shoe or whisper of cloth as I scanned the area. Again and again, the spot drew my eyes, my neck aching and entire body stiff and tense from the effort of holding still. My nerves jangled as I swallowed the urge to giggle or shout. Even charging onto the field would be a release and a relief, but when Akiko murmured in her sleep, I marshaled my self-control and crouched, resuming my seat. Someone, or something, knew we were here, so there was no question of sleep now.

CHAPTER TWENTY-ONE

After our tense and restless night resulted in nothing, my fears faded under the morning sun. I made a cursory search of the area but found no answers and returned to our campsite. Unsettled by my thoughts and sleepless night, I tried to focus on our preparations. Perhaps I had imagined the unseen eyes.

After transferring our supplies and ensuring the flier was adequately hidden, we headed east, toward the rising sun and the tower. Even though we started out in good spirits, tedium soon replaced the novelty of traveling by foot as we passed kilometers of abandoned structures. While Akiko chattered, I made mental notes of odd structures, topography, and other landmarks I could use to navigate back to the flier.

As I climbed over a low wall bewhiskered with a bird's nest of metal bars, the sound of my trousers tearing registered before the pain hit my leg. "Whoring foot fondler!"

Akiko giggled. "I miss Sally."

"Her... *colorful* technique doesn't help much with the

ouch." I winced as I pulled my trouser leg up. The wound had reopened, and I'd ripped several of Freda's stitches. Eliot's incisions had knitted, but the original wound oozed, as raw as dinner. I scowled at my leg; if I didn't take better care, it would never heal.

Akiko dropped her pack near me. "What's whoring?"

My face contorted. "Ask me in seven years." I dragged my trouser leg higher. "Did we bring Freda's brown bottle?"

Akiko wrinkled her nose. "The smelly one? Should be in my bag." She skipped a circle around me. "I'm going sploring."

"Exploring."

"Yup."

My chin snapped up. "Stay within eyesight."

She pouted, her hands on her hips.

After the scare last night, a sharp fear gnawed my belly each time she disappeared from view. "I'm serious. This place is vast, and I can't spend hours tracking you down."

Akiko scowled. "Charcoal can find me."

"Keep Charcoal with you." I matched her stare until she rolled her eyes and nodded, whistling for Charcoal.

Once they left, I rummaged through our bags to find Freda's brown bottle. After I'd sketched the basic designs, Akiko had created packs for each of us. With all three, we'd been able to carry all our supplies. I'd even hidden both *Home* and my sword within the frame of my pack.

The wicked solution burned like a branding when I pressed the saturated cloth to my leg. My eyes watered, and I gulped air as the medicinal scent seared my nose, but when the burn faded, the numbing compound kicked in, so I reset three stitches across the widest gap. Although I couldn't feel it, my stomach lurched as the needle's sharp, cruel point popped through my skin. After I tied the last knot, I unrolled a linen bandage and looked up.

Akiko was gone.

In my haste to stand, I nearly dropped the uncapped bottle. "Akiko!"

"What?" she asked from behind me.

"Sorry. Find anything interesting?" I asked, patting my leg dry and binding it with the linen.

"The tower is visible from the top of the hill. We're not far now."

"Wonderful. Let's go." I held her pack while she shrugged on the shoulder straps.

She swung one leg back and forth, waiting for me. "Maybe we'll find the warehouse today."

"Right." I tried not to wince as I settled my pack. We'd only walked a day and already my shoulders had rubbed raw, the straps chafing like sand across a sunburn.

Akiko and Charcoal scampered up the hill, fueled by boundless energy, while I trudged after them. My footfalls echoed off the rusting metal wrecks and ghostly structures as I scanned the buildings for signs of life. We'd seen no one since arriving and the near silence of the depot continued to rattle me. Surely, we'd find directions to a warehouse, or an operating fueling station as we traversed the depot, but the loneliness of the wrecked and abandoned city ate at my hope. Several times, I'd imagined eyes tracking our progress, but never with the same malevolence as last night.

Akiko and Charcoal squatted in a patch of shade as I clambered to the top of the hill. The view was incredible; as promised, the tower dominated the skyline. A breeze blew from the sea, ruffling the sweaty hair on my neck and bringing the cool, green scent of water. I skirted the remains of a concrete wall bristling with another tangle of braided metal stakes and helped Akiko climb past the rubble.

The urge to reach the tower dragged at me, but Charcoal

yipped as his pack snagged on one of the rusty bars. By the time I'd freed the wiggling animal, Akiko had dropped her pack and pulled out sandwiches.

At this rate, we'd run out of food before we reached the tower. I sighed, setting aside my tower fever. "Lunchtime, I guess."

She grinned. "Let's study the painting again."

Dust kicked up as I set my pack next to hers. "Picture it on your mind's canvas or enjoy the real thing. Removing the painting from my pack is a bear."

"You're the bear."

Perhaps, but I was also sick of studying my painting. Based on the shapes we assumed were a skyline, the angles in *Home* made no sense.

Akiko wiped her mouth with the back of her arm, dragging a smear of dirt across her face. "What's next?"

When I bit into my cheese sandwich, Charcoal whined. I tossed a piece to him, but after he snapped it up, he continued to stare at my meal. "You never ask for Akiko's share."

Charcoal drooled, his eyes fixed on my food. I tore off another piece and moved it to the side. Charcoal's head followed the morsel.

"Do you think we should explore the waterfront north of the tower before we head south?"

His eyes flicked to me before refocusing on the sandwich. I moved it up and down, smiling as the dog nodded in response.

"Am I the handsomest man in this depot?"

Again, Charcoal nodded, following the food.

Akiko squirmed, looking delighted. "Do you think Matthew's ears are so big he could fly if he flapped them?"

The dog glanced at the girl and smiled, panting.

She laughed, throwing her hands up. "No bribe!"

I tossed the bite to the dog and stuffed the rest of my meal in my mouth, wincing at the dry, bitter rye and sharp cheese.

Akiko unwrapped a third sandwich and fed it to the dog in dainty pieces.

"If he had his own lunch, why did you let him guilt me out of mine?"

Akiko gave me a pained look. "Be nice."

"I'm always nice. Too nice." Drowsy from the food, long walk, and sun-warmed pavement, I leaned against my pack and turned my face to the sun. I closed my eyes as Akiko chattered to the dog.

"We're going sploring again."

"Exploring. Stay within eyesight." The sun warmed my face, burning red-orange through my eyelids as I considered the best way to begin our search.

Ever since the scholar had told me the skyline could depict Toronto Depot, my sole focus had been getting here, on reaching the tower. But now that we were near, the enormity of our task dragged at me. Why had I believed finding my childhood home would be easy? The hilt of my sword dug into my back, and I shifted as Akiko continued to chatter.

"And now we're looking for the house."

"He knows," I said, my eyes still closed.

"Do I?" asked a voice I didn't recognize.

My eyes popped open, and I squinted into the sun, my heart thumping. "Akiko?"

"Welcome back. This is Olen."

Olen? I sat up, shielding my eyes. "Sorry, I thought she was talking to the dog."

"They have called me worse. I'm Olen Ash. Well met, Matthew Sugiyama."

I scrambled to my feet, meeting him eye to eye. "Matthew Sugiyama."

Akiko rolled her eyes. "He just said that."

"Howdy," Olen said, extending his hand. He was rangy, with a mop of russet-colored hair. He seemed a little older than me, but his face was weathered and tanned, making it hard to judge.

I stared at him before remembering my manners and shaking his hand.

He grinned, patting Akiko on the head. "I understand you're sploring the depot."

"Exploring," I corrected automatically. "Sorry. You understand what?"

Akiko squatted to pet Charcoal. "Olen is *exploring* too."

"Mm. For records," said Olen, stretching his neck.

I blinked. "Records. You're a scholar."

"Got it in one." Olen smiled at Akiko. "You were right. He catches on quick."

My neck flushed. "Where's the warehouse?"

Olen shrugged. "I hoped you could tell me. You're the first folks I've seen in days."

"We haven't found warehouse markers either, but we didn't travel in on the primary route." My mind groped for something else to say, but my mental canvas remained blank.

"Akiko tells me you're heading to the tower. May I join you? My brother's place is somewhere near there."

Even though meeting Olen had knocked me off balance, with the three of us, we were more likely to spot warehouse markers, so I had no reason to say no.

"Sure, but if we find nothing, can your brother point us toward the warehouse?"

Olen raised his palms but smiled. "Perhaps. Shall we go now... or do you need to finish your nap?"

"I wasn't napping." To hide my scowl, I stooped, then hoisted my pack.

Olen whistled. "Nice. It reminds me of equipment from *Before*."

"Really?" asked Akiko, struggling into her pack. "They carried their campsites too?"

Olen nodded as he helped her. "According to the stories I've read."

The idea was absurd. Why would the people from *Before* need to camp? "To what purpose?"

Olen shrugged. "Fun."

Fun?

"They enjoyed communing with nature," said Olen. He slung a small bag across his back, not even large enough to hold a bedroll.

"Nature is far away when you live in a depot like *this*. Let's go this way," said Akiko, skipping to the crest of the hill. When the pack on her back bounced, she stopped to tighten her hip belt.

A hip belt that hadn't existed before lunch.

I hoped Olen hadn't seen her sketching and eyed his small bag. "Are you from around here?"

Olen shook his head as we started down the hill. "No, I've just arrived to visit family and evaluate a potential move. I've traveled from the southwest."

"The *actual* southwest? Where cowboys live?" Akiko's eyes widened.

"Why yes, ma'am. We cowpokes are often homebodies, but some of us wander a mite farther."

"Did you ride a cow here? Where is it now?"

Olen laughed. "I rode a painted horse, but he's stabled in a livery I found on the outskirts. Not much grazing in a depot."

The Ontario Sea sparkled in the midday sun, and I squinted from it to the dazzling tower. "Why so far? There must be depots in the Southwest."

"Yes, but I fancied an excuse to visit my brother, and a nearby community offered a commission."

"Are scholars courted with commissions like artists?"

Olen's eyes slid to me. "Not typically, but this community is different."

I studied him as he helped Akiko climb over a rusted metal barricade. "The Avalon Society?"

Olen arched his eyebrow. "Yes."

Akiko said, "They've invited Matthew a bunch of times, but he keeps putting them off."

When Olen's gaze sharpened, I made a mental note to remind Akiko about private information. We stopped at the top of a steep hill to evaluate our options. Brush dotted the slope, but it appeared passable. At the base of the hill, a large, open plaza led to the tower.

"Down or around?" Olen asked, turning to me.

His question felt like a challenge, but before I could study his body language for clues, movement on the slope drew my attention.

"She's already almost down," I said, gesturing toward the bottom of the hill where Akiko and Charcoal raced toward the tower.

"Right." Olen vaulted the fence and trotted down the slope, raising little puffs of dust.

Mindful of my fresh stitches, I picked my way down the hill with cautious footsteps. When I joined them at the base of the tower, I craned my neck. From this vantage, the windowed bulb was so far above us, it made me dizzy.

"I wish we could go up there," Akiko sighed.

"Me too," said Olen. "Can you imagine the view?"

Akiko and I glanced at each other. Did Olen know about the flier?

She hopped from foot to foot. "Can we walk around it?"

"Why not?" Checking to make sure we were out of earshot, I beckoned her to come closer. "Did you tell him about the flier or *Home*?"

Akiko narrowed her eyes. "I'm not dumb."

"No, you're not. Sorry." I ruffled her hair, relieved.

Charcoal followed as she trotted the rest of the way around the base, and I ambled after them, my fingertips brushing the smooth white wall. The tower was pristine, as though only built last year.

For so long, I'd fixated on reaching this spot, thinking once we did, everything would click into place. But now that we were here, nothing had changed. I had no sense of completion, no spark of recognition, and I gazed at the sea with no idea of what to do next.

Akiko scampered to me, her eyes glowing. "We did it!"

I pasted a broad smile onto my face. "We sure did! Next, we establish a base camp. Let's go to the waterfront."

"Great! I'll tell Olen."

While I watched her skip away, I tried to order the tasks ahead. Although I wanted to jump into the search, we first needed to find a place to stay, negotiate for art supplies, and develop a methodical search plan.

In the distance, a three-masted sloop crossed the horizon. I imagined approaching Toronto Depot by ship, the wonder of the astonishing skyline rising like the teeth of a great beast. A heartbeat later, icy doubt cascaded over me, compressing my chest, and stealing my breath. Ever since Alma Sanu had suggested *Home* depicted Toronto Depot, I'd clung to the idea my family, or at least my family home, was here. Time and again, I'd pushed away the worry flaying the edges of my mind's canvas.

The angles on *Home* made little sense... so what if my assumptions were wrong and there had never *been* a family home? My stomach roiled. If my family had been mariners —*travelers*—there may not be a permanent home for me to find.

CHAPTER TWENTY-TWO

The third time Akiko pointed out a ladder, I sighed, shaking my head. "Akiko, *no*. We need to find an inn or a place to camp, and we're running out of daylight." The afternoon shadows had lengthened, and I wasn't sure we had enough food left to put together a reasonable dinner. After learning Olen was in the Avalon Society, I'd made excuses to stay behind when he'd left to find his brother. I wanted to put distance between him and us, and with luck, I'd remain unnoticed by the local society members. But now, we needed to hustle to find a place to sleep before dusk.

Akiko scowled at me, her chin rising. "How can we decide where to go without information? From up there, we'll have a better view."

"It may not be safe, Mouse. Besides, you can't climb with a pack on your back."

She dropped her pack and leaned it against the building's footing. "Problem solved!" She crossed her arms, her posture warning that we neared another tantrum.

I scrutinized the building, trying to find another excuse, but it looked sturdy enough, and the ladder appeared solid. If we *wanted* to scale a building, this wasn't a terrible choice.

Akiko pleaded for me to agree with her eyes, her expression not unlike Charcoal's when he wanted my meal. The bottom rung was almost two meters above the ground, but I could lift her to it. Not only would climbing the building satisfy Akiko, we'd also increase the distance between us and Olen. Any information we gleaned from the top would be a bonus.

"Okay, I'll test it." I shrugged off my pack and stretched, the breeze cool against my sweaty back. I jumped to the bottom rung and shook the ladder with my full body weight.

No wobble.

I dropped to the ground, my leg protesting the impact, and exhaled. "Okay, you go first."

Akiko squealed as I lifted her, then clambered up the metal ladder without hesitation.

Charcoal whined, but leaned down and scratched his ear. "We'll be right back." I jumped to grasp the bottom rung, wincing at the sharp pain in my calf.

Charcoal barked and spun.

Akiko peered down. "He wants to come."

After pulling myself onto the first rung, I glanced at him. "He can't climb a ladder."

When Charcoal continued to bark, her lip poked out. "Carry him up?"

"What? How?" I thumped the rusted iron ladder with my hand, wincing at the resounding *clang*.

Akiko narrowed her eyes and cocked her head. "Clip him onto your pack?"

I sighed. "Not a good idea."

Her eyes flashed as she tried again. "It won't take long, and *you* said family sticks together."

I glanced from the dog to the girl, prepared to argue, before remembering my resolve to do better at keeping my temper. I sighed and dropped to the ground. "You're a spoiled mutt."

Charcoal leaned against my good leg, smiling, so I patted him before unbuckling the canvas bag from my pack's frame.

"You won't like this," I warned, clipping Charcoal's pack to my frame. We groaned in unison as I picked up the frame with the dog attached. After shrugging the pack on, I waited to make sure he wouldn't struggle before I approached the ladder.

"You can do it, easy," Akiko called down.

Right, easy.

Taking a deep breath, I crouched and sprang up to grasp the lowest rung. This time, it was much harder to haul myself up. I panted as I got my foot onto the rung. "You've fed him too many sandwiches."

Akiko cackled. "Climb, Artist!"

We reached the top of the building without incident, and Akiko helped me lower Charcoal to the ground.

"Stay here while I check it out." With cautious steps, I crossed the flat roof. The building appeared sound; I found no cracking, depressions, or other sign the structure was in danger of collapsing. "It seems fine but, to be safe, stay away from the edges."

She nodded, following me to the far side. "Look! What's that?"

I shielded my eyes and squinted at the sparkling water. "Islands, several of them."

"Think your house is there?"

I pressed my hand against my stomach as it fluttered. "Could be. Look, a boat is crossing the water."

"Can we go visit? I want to ride the boat!"

Of course she did. "This *is* a splendid view." I scanned the waterfront, mapping it on my mind's canvas. "That may be a warehouse sign," I said, pointing north.

Charcoal barked once, peering down.

"Where?" Akiko asked. "I don't see it."

I lifted her, pointing again, and she pressed her cheek against my arm. "Oh! But let's do the boat ride first."

Charcoal lay next to the ladder with his paws curled over the edge, intent on the ground. As we approached, he gazed at us with his brow furrowed.

"I have to clip you in again." He didn't protest until I lifted him, but then scrabbled, his claws scraping my arm. "Blast. Settle!"

"Shh, little brother, shh," Akiko crooned. "You okay?"

"Fine," I said, checking the back of my arm

"I asked *him*."

"Let me go first," I said, backing over the edge. Charcoal continued to squirm as we descended and when I stopped to gauge our progress, Akiko stepped hard on my left hand, pinching my fingers between her foot and the metal rung. "Akiko! My hand!"

She squeaked, clinging to the ladder. "Sorry."

I flexed my hand several times. My knuckles ached, and hot, coppery blood dripped from my lacerated palm.

"Are you okay?"

"I'll be fine, but there's blood on the rung," I warned. "Don't slip in it—try to move to your right if you can."

Akiko's foot descended toward my right hand.

"Stop!"

She froze, her foot hovering scant centimeters above my good hand.

"Go up one rung and wait."

"Okay."

I tucked my injured hand to my chest, descending the last three rungs. "Ready, chap?" I dropped as lightly as I could, but the shock of impact moved painfully through my feet, ankles, and calves. I winced, gritting my teeth. "Okay, Mouse, come down."

Charcoal whined again, squirming as I reached for her.

Together, we lowered the dog, releasing him. Charcoal cavorted around us, racing circles with his nose to the ground, a smear of red on the side of his pack from my injured hand.

The sharp rung had slashed my palm just below the base of my middle and pointer fingers. The bleeding had slowed, and while the cut didn't appear deep, it gaped each time I flexed it. "I need the brown bottle."

Akiko caught the racing dog and pulled it from Charcoal's pack. "Here."

"Thanks." I unwrapped the cloth and dabbed the pungent tincture on the cut.

"Matthew?"

I scowled at the sting. "It's fine, but stings a little."

"Matthew."

"Don't worry, Mouse. It was an accident." I blew on the laceration, waiting for the pain to abate.

"Matthew!"

Something in her tone caught my attention, and I looked up.

"Our bags are gone."

"What?" I glanced around. "Where did we put them?"

"There," she pointed. "What do we do now? They took everything."

I stared at the spot we had left them and groaned. "Our bedrolls, our food, our art supplies."

"Not your brushes or pencils. They're in Charcoal's pack."

I patted my coat pocket. "I still have my sketchbook."

"Me too."

I sighed. "I guess there's nothing we can't replace."

"Who would take our bags? And why?"

I shook my head. "I don't know."

"What do we do now?"

I scanned the surrounding area as if the bags had accidentally rolled a short distance. Akiko's face was already a mask of worry and alarming her wouldn't help. "Let's go to the boat. A ride and a meal are exactly what we need. Come on."

We followed the road closest to the shore and scanned the open water for the yellow boat we'd seen. Alarmed shorebirds warned each other as we passed, their screeches soothing to me. "I grew up with gray gulls like these."

"At Popham?"

"Mm."

"Maybe here too."

Home.

I froze, gut-punched. "We have to go back." I spun, sprinting back the way we'd come. When I reached the ladder, I turned, searching for something, anything.

"M—Matthew," Akiko sobbed, trotting up. "Wait for me. Don't leave me behind."

What would we do now? My mouth dry and metallic, I stalked to where our bags had been and scrutinized the ground for signs.

"What are you looking for?"

"Clues."

Akiko remained silent.

I stared at the ladder. "Stay here with Charcoal while I climb up."

"But your hand!"

I wrapped cloth around it before jumping up to grab the bottom rung. I climbed as quickly as I could and ran to each side of the roof, scanning the surrounding area. In the distance, the yellow boat crossed from the island to the shore.

"Blast!" I shouted. I slumped down to the roof, leaning my

back against the wall, ignoring how my pack frame poked me. How could I have lost *Home*? Charcoal had tried to warn me, but I'd ignored him. I was good at ignoring advice because I *always* knew better... except that I didn't. I wanted to scream, but it would frighten Akiko, so I thumped my fist on the roof. The impact wakened the cut on my palm, but Freda's numbing bottle was with Akiko.

Akiko.

I jumped to my feet and ran to the edge of the building, expecting not to find her. She huddled in a corner with Charcoal, and seeing me, waved.

My heart thumped as I climbed back down.

"Did you see anything?"

I shook my head as I dabbed disinfectant into the bleeding cut. "Nothing," I said, winding the cloth around my palm again

"We lost *Home*, didn't we?"

I nodded.

Her lip trembled. "Let's go find it."

I stared at her. "How?"

A single tear tracked down her face. "It's my fault."

"No," I said, as Charcoal licked her cheek. "Done is done."

She climbed to her feet. "Let's look, anyway."

I shook my head. "Whoever took the bags is gone, but the boat has crossed back toward the shore. Let's go meet the boatman."

"It could be a boat lady," she said in a thin voice.

I reached out my good hand, and she took it, her small hand hot in mine. "Could be."

We retraced our steps, heading toward the yellow boat, but as we walked, I scanned every open window and doorway, hoping to spot our things.

"I looked through Charcoal's pack while you were up top."

"Good thinking. What do we still have?"

"Some cord, the mink tail we got from Freda, and the brushes and pencils."

My lips tightened. "That's all?"

"Yup."

I sighed. "Better than a poke in the eye."

"Sorry," she said, her chin trembling again.

"I'm not, because we still have the most important thing."

She gazed at me, puzzled.

"The mink tail," I said, reaching over to tweak her nose.

She gave me a watery smile. "*Why* do we have it?"

I shrugged. "No clue."

She wrinkled her nose. "Who wants an old tail?"

"Other than the mink?" I shrugged. "Brush makers use the hairs. Truly. Here's the boat."

Akiko narrowed her eyes. "And the boat *lady*."

It *was* a boat lady. A beautiful boat lady.

"Heya, Travelers," she called. She was tall and willowy, a few years my senior, with long dark hair which swirled around her. "Going to the island?"

Akiko nodded, her eyes eager. "Can we ride in your yellow boat?"

The woman looked stern. "Please."

Akiko glanced at me, confused.

"Can we ride in your yellow boat, *please*?" I asked.

The woman laughed. "Climb aboard."

I hesitated. "What can I offer you in return?"

"Take it up with my mother. She's the keeper on the island."

"Perfect, a ride and a meal." At least *something* had gone right.

She unshipped long oars attached on swivel pins to each side of the boat. "Coming?"

"Check! I mean, please." Akiko scrambled into the boat and

made her way to the bow. Charcoal followed, his tail stub wiggling.

"I'm Matthew."

"Rebecca, but everyone calls me Beck. Take your seats, Mr. Matthew, Miss Matthew, and Doggie Matthew. Here we go." Beck rowed with long, even strokes, breathing easily.

I sat facing her, growing more and more uncomfortable. "Can I help?" I asked finally.

Beck eyed me without breaking her rhythm. "Why? Because I'm a woman?"

"Yes." I squirmed and hid my bandaged hand beneath my thigh.

Beck tossed her head back and laughed. "Five points for honesty. Well, let's see. Did you bring your own oars?"

"No." I frowned.

"Then I guess you can't help."

Akiko snickered from the bow of the boat.

CHAPTER TWENTY-THREE

Beck steadied the boat as Akiko and I clambered onto the dock. "The inn is up the stairs."

I examined the building, but the afternoon sun reflected on the inn's windows, obscuring the interior. During the boat ride over, I'd wrestled with how to sweet-talk the keeper. If there wasn't room for us in the inn, perhaps she'd let us camp on the island, although it would be a hard night without a shelter or our bedrolls. After the last several days, I didn't want another sleepless night in a wrecked building, watched and exposed. I tugged Charcoal onto the dock. "Thanks, Beck. You're available if we need to get back over?"

"It's what I do. Back and forth, at your 'Beck' and call." She pushed off and waved before swinging the boat around and rowing toward the other side.

Akiko's eyes were full of admiration as she watched Beck row away. "Her arms are as strong as your legs. Maybe stronger."

I snorted, but Akiko wasn't wrong.

"Heya, Travelers, welcome to Hanlan's Island." A tall

woman approached us, tossing a towel over her shoulder. "You must be Matthew and Akiko."

Akiko slid behind me to peek at the woman. "You know us?"

"Freda sent word warning of a handsome, albeit clumsy, man traveling with his daughter, and your limp gave you away. I'm Rebecca."

I hooked my thumb toward the departing boat. "Like her?"

The woman laughed. "Well, I suppose you could say she's Rebecca, like me."

I grinned. "You named your daughter Rebecca."

She shrugged. "Men do it, so why can't I? Besides, everyone calls me Mama."

"Well... Mama," The word stuck in my throat, unfamiliar and unnatural. Heat crawled up my neck. "We're hoping for a room."

"And a meal," said Akiko. "Please."

"I hoped you'd ask," said Mama. "Follow me."

My heart gladdened and, based on Akiko's relieved expression, I wasn't the only one dreading another night in the depot. We followed Mama up the path and around the corner of the inn, into an attached boathouse. Water rippled inside the wooden structure.

"I need this fixed," said Mama, pointing at the ceiling.

Clouds danced across the blue sky through the hole. "What caused it?"

"Years of neglect, a wayward branch, and a dreadful storm. Freda's note praised your artwork."

My face turned as red as my neck, but Freda's recommendation lifted my spirits. "Done."

Mama beamed. "I'll prepare a meal and a room."

I released my breath, and my chest loosened. This was an

easy trade. "I'll fix this now if you can point me toward a vantage where I can view the entire structure."

"There's a schooner on the deep pier. They'll let you come aboard." Mama turned to Akiko. "Freda's note mentioned you like maps."

Akiko's eyes brightened.

"Come with me, girl." Mama held her hand out. Akiko's smile turned bashful, and she glanced at me. When I nodded, she brightened and took Mama's hand. Charcoal threw me a look of apology, but followed them into the inn.

The deep pier stretched thirty meters east, and a three-masted wooden ship bobbed at the far end.

"Ahoy," called a man as I approached. He had a shaggy, gray mane that curled into his beard.

I raised my hand. "Heya, Mariner. Can I climb up?"

"Are you asking permission to come aboard, landlubber?"

I blinked. "Yes? I need a higher vantage to view the boathouse."

"Then ye be the artist, sent to patch the great hole."

I laughed. "You must have brought Freda's message from Pultney."

The man winked. "Permission granted. Climb aboard."

The rope ladder stretched and shifted as I attempted to climb, my injured hand protesting. By the time I hauled myself over the railing, I was out of breath.

The man crossed his arms and watched me slither over the railing, falling in a heap onto the floor. His boat was beautiful; the wood polished to a high sheen.

I stumbled as the boat shifted. "Nice floor."

"It would be if 'twere in a house," the man agreed. "But here on *Marybelle*, 'tis a deck. I'm Gunther."

"Matthew."

"Aye. Now, what can I get ye, Matthew?"

"Get? Oh, nothing." I patted my chest pocket. "I have what I need."

Gunther nodded and settled himself against a short, wooden wall, clearly intending to watch me work.

The unfamiliar rocking motion sparked my nausea whenever I focused on my drawing, but I sketched the boathouse despite my stomach's lurching. When finished, I examined the building to ensure I'd captured it correctly.

Gunther pulled on his pipe before speaking. "Still and all, 'twill be a shame to lose the light."

I glanced at him. "Light?"

"Aye. From the great hole," he said, waving his pipe toward the boathouse.

I studied my sketch. "I could put in a window."

Gunther's feet clomped across the deck toward me. "A window in the roof? Aye, 'twould be exactly the thing."

I eyed the building. "Will Mama approve of the changes?"

Gunther chuckled. "I'm in charge of boat repair, so leave Mama to me."

His homespun clothing and massive, gray beard told a different tale. "Aren't you a mariner?"

"Aye, so I am. But I only sail the great sea four times a year. The rest of me days, I'm Mama's dogsbody."

I must have conveyed my confusion, because he chuckled. "I'm her husband."

My forehead relaxed. "She's your wife."

"No sir, *I'm her husband.* She's married to me, but she's no one's wife." Gunther chuckled again.

I sketched the skylight into the roof, then added a second skylight to balance the building.

"Aye, 'twere a good trade," said Gunther, after I finished altering the building.

He smiled as Akiko and Charcoal raced down the pier toward us. "The wee ones are yours?"

I tucked my sketchbook into my pocket and shook Gunther's hand. "Yes, they're mine. See you at supper?"

"Aye." Gunther stuck the pipe back in his mouth. "Bring your biggest belly. Mama can cook."

Akiko skidded to a stop in front of the sloop, her eyes glowing as Charcoal danced around her. "Come see!"

"Stay there, I'm coming down." I half-climbed, half-fell down the rope netting, acutely aware of Gunther's amused gaze. By the time I reached the dock, the bandage on my lacerated hand had stained oxide red. "What is it?"

"Dragons! Come see!" Bouncing with excitement, Akiko led me around the north side of the inn. "Look!"

A herd of rainbow-colored dragons wheeled and flapped above us, their long tails streaming behind them. We sank into the ankle-deep grass, watching the handful of people fly the enormous creatures.

Akiko kneeled next to me, her face filled with wonder. "What are they?"

Her expression lifted my heart, making me doubly glad we'd chosen to stay on the island. "Kites."

"Kites? But I thought the little square thing I flew at Niagara Abbey was a kite."

The nearest flier grinned at us, a smile flashing on his freckled face. "Wonderful day for a flight."

"Wonderful," repeated Akiko.

Beck, flying a large purple dragon with an orange and black striped tail, waved. "Welcome, Miss Matthew. Come over... if you dare."

Akiko bounded to her.

"Would you like to help me fly my dragon?" asked Beck, her eyes fixed on the flapping creature.

Akiko shivered. "Yes, please!"

"Here, Mr. Matthew, hold this."

I grasped the primary control, my grip tightening as the kite fought for its freedom. Beck untied a line from a ground stake and attached the line to a horizontal bar. "Here, Miss Matthew."

Akiko froze, her hands white on the bar.

Beck clucked her tongue. "If you hold my dragon too tightly, she won't fly. Here, let me show you. You're flying her head, so if you swoop this way..." Beck raised her hands in an arc, and the dragon's head snaked in response, following the direction of the bar. "Want another go?"

"Yes, please!" This time, Akiko played with the controls, nodding the dragon's head while Charcoal barked and leaped into the air, trying to snatch the bar from her.

"Great wind today," said Beck, taking the primary control from me.

The dragons soared above us like magic. They wheeled and dove, eliciting shouts of delight from the fliers. The fabric snapped and rustled in the wind, the largest creatures even generating a low, roaring sound. Enchanted, I dropped to the ground to watch the firedrakes dance on the wind. Charcoal climbed into my lap, his claws scrabbling against my thighs as he monitored Akiko.

As the wind slowed, Beck's queen slumped, its tail drooping toward the ground. Beck's shoulders squared, and she spun the primary control while shouting instructions to the other fliers. "Roll your controls, or your creatures will crash!"

Her face a mask of concentration, Akiko followed Beck's directions exactly, and I cheered for her when the purple dragon landed gracefully on the grass. Charcoal leaped off me to investigate, and I stood, brushing dog hair from my chest and legs. "Nice flying, dragon tamers," I said, admiring the exquisite workmanship, earning a smile from Beck.

Under her supervision, we stored the kites in a shed. "Thanks for the help," she said, latching the shed door. "Mama will hold dinner until after I row my students back, but while you're waiting, let her change the bandage on your hand."

AKIKO COULDN'T STOP TALKING ABOUT BECK ALL THE WAY to the inn.

"Did you fly a dragon?" asked Mama, after we entered the common room.

Akiko nodded, her eyes wide. "The purple one."

"You flew Beck's queen. That's *quite* an honor, young lady."

I tousled Akiko's hair, grinning as she slapped at my hand. "Beck is rowing the others over. Where can we wash up?"

"Use the sink in the kitchen, and when you're done, carry this to the table. We'll eat when Beck gets back," said Mama, loading plates onto a wooden tray.

After supervising Akiko, I washed the cut in my hand, wincing at the water's sting. Akiko continued to chatter about the dragon kites as she followed me back into the common room, but stopped when she spotted Gunther and slid behind me.

I nodded to him as I carried the tray of plates to the table. "Who makes the kites?"

"Beck," he said, digging into a basket of rolls. "I taught her how sails work when she was a girl, but she took the knowledge to another level entirely." He tossed a roll to each of us.

Charcoal leaped up to catch a roll, then carried it to Akiko. When she shook her head, he dropped to the ground to gnaw on it, his tail stub wiggling. My stomach growled at the yeasty scent as I caught mine, and this time, when Whistler's face flashed onto my mind's canvas, a bittersweet wave followed it instead of the clawing nausea I'd experienced in Whitehall.

Over dinner, I asked questions about the warehouse and the makeup of the communities supporting the depot, but the careful way they answered my questions gave me pause. There was obviously more going on in Toronto Depot than I'd expected, and I made a note to find out why this gregarious group was circumspect about the depot they lived in. I learned theirs was not the only deep-water pier, which made sense since most goods transported to and from Toronto Depot came by ship.

Beck sighed at the meal. "Delicious Mama, thanks. Matthew, tomorrow is market day, and I'm taking several kites to trade, so if you want a lift to shore, rise early."

"People trade for your kites?" Akiko asked, her eyes large.

Beck's smile split her face. "You bet. I also take custom orders to build over the winter."

I mopped my plate with a roll, the peppered gravy rich and savory. "Who trades for kites?"

Gunther's chest swelled. "Near all the waterfront communities. Them dock-mounted kites are about the one thing everyone agrees on, and they entice mariners. Beck has traded to the Avalon Society too."

"They invited her," said Mama, rising to take the empty platter to the kitchen.

Eyebrow raised, I glanced at Beck.

She returned my gaze and shrugged. "Who would row the boat? Anyway, Akiko tells me you've lost your belongings. Want to come to the market tomorrow?"

Akiko squirmed when I frowned at her, but lit up when I said, "Yes, thanks."

Gunther's brows knit. "The world has changed. Theft, 'twas unthinkable ten years ago, even here."

Mama returned from the kitchen with a second platter of fried chicken. "Nice and hot, help yourselves. What are we talking about?"

Beck pulled a drumstick from the platter. "Someone stole their bags, Mama."

Mama shook her head. "The world has lost its manners."

Charcoal's brows furrowed as he watched Mama fill a plate, cutting the meat into small bites. He stared at her with pleading eyes as she set the dish before him.

Mama winked and nodded at the dog. "Good boy, you have pleasant manners. If we're not careful, we'll find ourselves like the people from *Before*, which is why manners are so important, young lady."

I caught Beck mouthing her mother's speech word for word and smothered my smile behind my napkin. "Have you lived here long?"

Gunther nodded. "Aye. Mama's father ran the inn before her."

"And my grandfather before him," Mama agreed.

I studied the depot's broken skyline through the window. The tower pulled my gaze and again, I mentally compared it to my memory of *Home*. "Was there ever another house here?"

Mama wiped her hands on a napkin. "On this island? No, not within my family's history."

Her words dashed my remaining hopes. Although the angle of the view had seemed off from my painting, I'd still believed I'd find something of my family. "Are there any houseboats in the harbor?"

"Nope," said Beck, her expression curious. "Boats on water, houses on land. Can you be up early tomorrow? I'll need to set up my stall before the market opens."

"Yes, please," said Akiko.

I nodded. "We'll give you a hand and go to the warehouse afterward."

Gunther crossed his arms. "Good luck. We have too many librarians, and they don't work well together. 'Tis easier to procure things at the market."

Tension coiled in my overfull stomach. I'd been counting on the warehouse to replace what they had stolen.

"Did Freda send you with a mink tail?" asked Gunther. He leaned back, cradling a steaming mug.

Akiko rolled her eyes. "Yes, but why?"

"Well, 'tis the fashion here and means she liked you," he said, winking.

"Fashion?" Akiko wrinkled her nose.

"Aye. Many at the market will kit you in exchange." He pulled out a pipe, filling it.

I sighed. "Then it's lucky we didn't lose it, too." I'd worry about the warehouse tomorrow.

"Aye."

"We better turn in," I said, as Akiko's yawn nearly split her face. "Thank you for the meal, Mama."

Mama smiled. "Breakfast will be ready as early as you are."

THE WINDOW IN OUR ROOM WAS OPEN, BRINGING THE rhythmic lap of the waves and scent of water.

"Can we keep the window open?" asked Akiko, her voice sleepy.

"Yes, I prefer it, too."

"Tonight, we both sleep." She snuggled under the covers. "No eyes in the dark."

Charcoal jumped onto her bed and stretched out next to her.

"No," I said, kissing her forehead while patting my dog. "Sleep well, Miss Matthew, Doggie Matthew."

I sank onto my bed and listened to the murmur of the waves. Tomorrow, we'd work on establishing a semi-permanent base and getting resupplied. For now, all I wanted was a moment of peace and safety with no eyes in the dark.

CHAPTER TWENTY-FOUR

y heart thrummed as my eyes swiveled; market day in Toronto Depot was a revelation. Even though the market wasn't officially open, crowds had already arrived. A woman wearing a swirling, red cloak caught my eye, but she disappeared into the throng, reminding me to keep a watchful eye on Akiko.

The vendors nearest Beck's stall offered everything from saddles to jars of preserves, and Akiko admired a table of silver wrist cuffs while I helped Beck assemble her stall.

"I've seen nothing like this during my travels." With clumsy hands, I unfurled the tarpaulin cover for her stall. I needed to learn how things worked here; if I had to strike a bargain with each vendor, replacing our lost things would take forever. It might be better to chance the warehouse.

Beck raised her eyebrow as she unpacked her queen from a crate. "Really? Other depots don't have market days?"

I glanced at the myriad of boats bobbing at the edge of the boardwalk. They'd been streaming across the lake all morning.

"Not like this." I pulled the lines tight and unfolded the table I'd carried up from the yellow boat. "Here?"

"Yes, thank you. Stick around; you're useful. Miss Matthew, would you like to help me set up the queen?"

"Yes!"

"Please," I mouthed from behind Beck.

Akiko's eyes widened, and she tried again. "Yes, please. What should I do?"

"If Mr. Matthew will set a tail stake, you and I can work on the liftoff."

Akiko brightened. "What's a liftoff?" Beck stared at Akiko until the child giggled and slapped her forehead. "Like it sounds?"

Beck's lips curved. "Yes. Now, to get liftoff, we'll need about twelve meters of line spooled out. Then, when I give the signal, we run toward the lake and release the queen."

Akiko's head bobbed. "Then what?"

"She'll do what she does best. Mr. Matthew, do you have the stake set?"

I nodded, my spine popping as I straightened.

"Excellent. Now, I'll take the controls. Miss Matthew, take her head, and Mr. Matthew, take her chest. A firm grasp works best."

Beck's grin was wicked, and I tried not to flush.

"Steady, steady..."

When several leaves rose from the ground in a swirling motion, Beck shouted, "Now!"

Together, we sprinted toward the lake, and Charcoal chased us, barking happily.

"Release!"

We let go and whooped in unison as the dragon soared into the sky, its purple tail snapping in the wind.

"Very nice," said Beck, spooling out line. "You Matthews make an excellent team." Under Beck's hands, the dragon came alive and flew through a series of loops, dives, and curves. The demonstration attracted a small crowd, and they applauded as Beck bowed before attaching the controls to the stake I'd set.

"You don't have to fly her?" Akiko asked, as Beck rejoined us.

"No, a kite needs only wind and tension to fly. We work the controls to make them *dance*. Come, time to unpack the rest of the herd and meet my customers."

While we were outdoors, Gunther had arrived and finished unpacking the kites. A crowd of children and adults clustered around Beck, asking questions about her kites. Akiko slipped between them, working her way to the front.

Gunther sidled next to me. "Beck make you hold the chest?"

This time, the flush crept past my neck, into my face.

Gunther chuckled. "She's Mama's girl, all right."

"Not yours?"

Gunther shook his head. "I was there for her birth, but I didn't sire her. Still, 'tis not biology that makes a father, and once they're in your life, you're helpless. Fatherhood changes things."

Gunther was right. I'd not planned to adopt Akiko, but now I couldn't imagine not having her in my life, even when we were at odds. Surrounded by other children, my girl's energy and intelligence shone, and once again, I mentally promised to improve my parenting skills.

Gunther clapped my shoulder. "What's next for you two?"

"We're meeting the rest of our family here, but they're traveling around the north side of the sea and may be weeks away. Does the warehouse have living quarters?"

Gunther nodded. "Aye, though the librarians will demand too much labor, and you will get caught in the middle between the factions. Better to reserve a cottage from a dock administrator."

"Dock administrator? I thought they only existed in small communities like Pultney."

Gunther tugged on his beard. "Aye, 'twas so, but the depot kept growing. The harbormaster tracks the boats, the administrators organize the depot, and the librarians catalog the supplies in the warehouse. Even so, we needed *more* management, since no one could get along. The dock administrators handle the transfer of cargo and the transient folks. Besides the dock administrators, keepers like Mama also hold dual roles."

"What else does Mama do?"

"She's a healer." He eyed my hand. "She's waiting for you to ask for help."

I flexed my stiff hand with a rueful smile. "Noted. Which dock administrator should I work with?"

Gunther cast me a shrewd look. "Kelly Potter is scrupulous. He'll set a fair bargain and hold to it."

I clapped him on the back. "Thank you, friend."

Gunther grinned, revealing several gold teeth. "You got a mink tail from Freda and built her a fine stone pier, so you have integrity."

I beckoned to Akiko, but she pretended not to see me. "What if Freda hadn't sent us with a tail?"

Gunther shrugged. "We have five dock administrators I would have sent you to. Each one runs their domain like a mini-community because they don't get along with each other either, so once you choose one, you best act as if the others don't exist."

I laughed. "How do I find Kelly?"

Gunther squinted at the sun. "He'll be busy until noon, but

afterward, you'll find him drinking mead in the pub. Buy him a pint and he'll sweeten."

Mead. I hadn't indulged since the night I'd spent in Chester before the attack on Wakefield. "I will, and one for you, if you're around."

"Thank ye. If I'm around, I'll take it. If not, tell him Mama Rebecca sent you."

"Not you?"

Gunther tugged his beard again. "Mama is the one with the pull."

After I pried Akiko away from the booth, we wandered through the market, speaking with vendors and making notes of which stalls to visit after lunch. The aroma of pastries and roasted nuts teased my stomach as we strolled through the aisles to admire the wild abundance of goods. Throughout the crowded market, I marveled at the diversity in clothing and hairstyle among the patrons. As we walked, the chatter of the shoppers and patter of vendors swirled around us in the music of commerce. I kept a surreptitious eye out for our bags, appraising each vendor and everyone who passed by, but when surrounded by so many beautiful things, it was clear the theft of our meager possessions had been an absurd act.

Who would take our things in a *depot* of all places?

"Do we make bargains with everyone?" Akiko asked, after we left a vendor specializing in custom leather goods.

I shook my head. "Gunther said to set up an account with the dock administrator. They will evaluate our asks and set a fair bargain to cover our supplies and a temporary dwelling."

"Can we stay in a cottage near the water?"

I ruffled her hair. "I hope so."

"Good. I like sleeping with lake sounds."

"Me too. Let's go find this Kelly."

AFTER THE SIGHTS AND SOUNDS OF THE MARKET, IT WAS A relief to step into the dim quiet of the pub. The keeper, an ugly man with a scar crossing from his left jaw to his right ear, nodded when we told him we wanted to meet with Potter. He handed me a pint of chilled mead and a half-pint of brown liquid to Akiko. She took careful steps as she carried it and beamed when we arrived at a table without mishap. "I have cider," she said, climbing onto a bench.

"Let me try it." The unfermented cider was sweet-tart and cold, the apple scent invigorating. It was too early in the year for apples, so the depot must boast cold storage. "Father approved, Miss Matthew."

Akiko giggled and took a careful sip. "Yummy. I feel grown-up."

I grinned. "You look grown-up, especially with the mustache."

We passed the time eating sour pickled eggs with coarse brown bread, making up stories about the other patrons, and arguing over how many children an impressively rotund man had.

When the tiny man with a tidy haircut stepped inside, I first took him to be a child, then realized by his beard he was a dwarf. I watched with interest as the keeper directed him to our table but muttered, "Manners, Mouse," as I stood and waved.

He stopped at our table with his hands clasped behind his back. "Matthew Sugiyama?"

Akiko straightened, her eyes alert and interested, but I hoped she'd say nothing. I nodded at the man. "Administrator Potter?"

He nodded in return, his gaze cool. "At your service."

Gunther's words rose onto my mind's canvas. "Please, join us. Mama Rebecca advised us to work with you."

Potter relaxed, pulled out a heavy chair, and laboriously climbed into it. Once he had, the keeper set down fresh drinks for us and a bowl of water for Charcoal.

When Akiko opened her mouth, I shot her a warning look, but she ignored me. "Hullo, Administrator Potter. I'm Akiko."

I mouthed *'No!'* but she either didn't see me or pretended she hadn't.

"We'd like a cottage near the water, and I'm taller than you."

Kelly set his glass down and gazed at her.

Akiko's eyes widened. "Oops. I mean, please. A cottage near the sea, *please.*"

I wanted to crawl under the table. If she had insulted Potter, we'd be forced to work with a less-reputable dock administrator. There was a long and awkward silence, and I took several quick breaths before clearing my throat.

Kelly ignored me and took a long pull from his mug. "Well met, Akiko. I have exactly the cottage for you."

"Oh, good. We're waiting for family to arrive, so we may live here a while. Do you have one for them, too?"

Kelly raised his eyebrow. "How many?"

"Five. All *well-behaved* adults," I said, glancing at Akiko.

She licked her upper lip, looking pleased with herself.

"I have a four-bedroom cottage and a two-bedroom next door for you. Both face the water," he said preemptively when Akiko opened her mouth. "You can sleep in either while you wait."

"Thank you, Administrator Potter," I said, wiping my damp palms on my trousers.

He nodded, finished his pint. "Your profession?"

I quickly downed mine, gesturing for another round. "Artist."

Potter's eyes gleamed. "An artist! You're very welcome, indeed."

"We've had a slight setback and will need to set up an account to resupply."

The keeper set down the fresh drinks, and Kelly nodded at him. "Certainly. Use my name at the market or in the warehouse, and I'll take care of it. I could use improvements more than the labor hours, if you don't mind?"

My shoulders relaxed. "Not at all."

"We have a mink tail, too," said Akiko. "Do we give it to you?"

Kelly leaned back and smiled. "So, you've met Freda, and Mama referred you to me. Even if you weren't an artist, you'd be welcome, Matthew and Akiko. Most welcome. Now, young miss, a mink tail is a special thing, not to be traded for eggs and bedding."

Her eyes brightened. "What's it for?"

"Something special. Something to make you smile each time you see it."

Akiko leaned forward and nearly knocked over her cider. "What do they do with the tails?"

Kelly leaned closer and lowered his voice. "They trade them for something that makes them smile."

Akiko eyed him. "The tails just go round and round?"

Kelly wriggled off his chair and straightened his vest. "And around. We don't have many, and each one is special, so use it wisely." He turned to me. "When you're ready, find me in the blue and white tower on the boardwalk."

I straightened. "A lighthouse?"

Kelly smiled. "You must have grown up on water."

Akiko's eyebrows shot up. "What's a lighthouse?"

"I'll explain it later," I promised.

"Does it float in the air?"

I grinned. "That would be a trick."

Potter rapped on the table. "I'll be off now. See you soon, Matthew, Akiko. You're both very welcome, even if you *are* taller than me."

CHAPTER TWENTY-FIVE

The girl was gone.

Again.

We had wandered for hours, trying to make heads or tails of the warehouse signs. In every depot I'd visited, the warehouse was well marked. Here, there was a jumble of signs in a riot of colors and shapes. The people we'd asked along the way had further confused us, contradicting each other *and* the signs.

"Akiko!"

"Here!" she shouted from behind me.

I spun, irritation and relief flowing through me in equal measures. "Where were you? I told you to stick close."

She glared at me. "But I'm tired!"

"Me too. Now, we've tried following a particular color and the newest-looking signs. What should we try next?"

Instead of responding, Akiko stamped her foot. Charcoal's brows furrowed, and he swung his head back and forth between us.

I scowled and mentally rattled off my favorite pigments to calm myself, then attempted to soften my voice. "We must find the warehouse. Right now, I don't have enough materials to make the improvements we owe for the supplies we've collected."

Akiko frowned, her lips compressing into a tight line. "But I want *my* stuff."

I attempted a cheerful tone that jarred with the swirling energy inside me. "Let's try following the circles this time."

She crossed her arms. "Why?"

I sighed. "Follow me." I walked away, listening for her footfalls. After a moment, she followed, and we walked for some time without speaking.

The sun had set before I turned a corner and found the warehouse's entrance. Waves of fatigue washed over me, and I hoped the warehouse's kitchens hadn't closed. I lifted my nose but could detect nothing but dust. "It was the circles, after all."

Silence.

I turned, but the girl wasn't behind me. Closing my eyes, I listed every green pigment I'd ever used because losing my temper wouldn't help. "Akiko?"

No response.

I walked back to the intersection and scanned the empty roads. I stared at the dog. "Where is she?"

Charcoal whined, sitting.

I scowled at the warehouse's entrance. "Go get her."

Charcoal circled me, then sat again.

"Find Akiko."

When the dog scanned me without moving, icy sweat sprang down my back. "Akiko! Mouse, where are you?"

My question echoed eerily off the buildings as I waited for a response.

None came.

"Akiko!" I shouted again.

Now what?

My heart thudded, and I fought to keep my churning stomach. I paced a tight circle, and Charcoal whined, dropping to his belly.

Once she realized she was lost, would she search for us, or sit down and wait for us to find her? I glanced at the warehouse entrance again, but she couldn't have arrived here before us.

My mind raced, and I struggled to swallow.

Think, Artist.

Would she try to find Kelly Potter? We hadn't checked in with him, so she didn't know where the cottages were. Maybe she'd returned to Beck's yellow boat. Either option meant returning to the waterfront. After hours of wandering through the wrecked and abandoned buildings, I wasn't sure in which direction the waterfront lay. Disoriented, I spun and scanned the sky. Wispy clouds had rolled in as the day had waned and now obscured the stars. The moon hadn't yet risen, and surrounded by buildings, I couldn't check the horizon to find my bearings. I needed a landmark.

The tower.

The white tower gleamed, visible even at night. Would Akiko think about going there?

I tried again. "Akiko!"

Charcoal lifted his head from his paws and whined.

"I know, boy. We—*I*—must do something. Come on." My stomach growled, and I squeezed my eyes shut. We hadn't eaten supper, and my mind spun with visions of Akiko lost, scared, and hungry in the dark. Taking a last glance at the warehouse entrance, I turned toward the tower. Charcoal trotted next to me, his nails clicking on the pavement. My footsteps ricocheted off the buildings, the echoes eerie, as if someone followed us.

The depot was difficult to navigate in the dark, and we repeatedly arrived at dead ends, the routes blocked by rubble, a wall, or once, a dense thicket of holly which slashed at my face. I kicked unseen obstacles, stubbed my toes, and even gave myself a hard crack on the head, moaning at the hurt as stars burst in my periphery. My thirst turned aggressive, the back of my throat aching for relief as my mouth filled with chalk.

The moon had long passed its zenith by the time we reached the tower. "Akiko?" My throat tightened. "Mouse?"

There was no answer.

I balled my hands and leaned against the tower, waves of fatigue and worry washing over me.

Now what?

Charcoal huffed, and I sighed, pushing away from the tower. "Let's check the docks."

No lights glimmered from Mama's inn, and the yellow boat bobbed at the short dock on the island.

Charcoal whined as he gazed at the lake, licking his muzzle. The wall between the boardwalk and lake was sheer; there was no way for him to reach the water.

"I'm thirsty too, boy." I spun, searching for something, anything.

Down the boardwalk, a light flashed.

Potter.

"Come on, perhaps she's there." When I reach the lighthouse, I hesitated. Based on the moon, it was after two in the morning and Potter wouldn't appreciate being woken, but I was out of options.

I raised my hand to knock on his door, but spotted the piece of paper tucked into the doorframe. I slid it out and turned it to capture the moonlight.

Sugiyama, to reach the cottages, walk north to the second set of stairs. The cottages are on the right side of the third landing. Use either. Potter.

Had Akiko seen the note?

I hurried up the boardwalk, tucking the note in my pocket. When I spotted the stairs, I bounded up them two at a time. On the landing, I found benches and a narrow trail, but no cottages.

Stymied, I pulled out the note and reread it. "Second staircase, Sugiyama."

As the moon disappeared behind drifting clouds, I shook my head and hurried back down the steps. At what I assumed was the bottom stair, I turned left, stepping onto nothing. My arms windmilled as I fell hard onto my right shoulder. I lay on the rough wood, my head swimming with the pungent, greasy scent of creosote until Charcoal swiped my cheek with his tongue.

"Thanks for warning me about the last step."

He pressed his cold nose into my neck, and I sighed. "I'm getting up."

I climbed to my feet, rubbing my bruised shoulder. "The other staircase should be farther down, but this time warn me if I'm about to step off a cliff or down a hole."

We reached the second staircase without further mishap and climbed to the third landing. There were two dwellings on one side of the stairs. Both were dark, and the moon popped out in time to glint off the glass, giving them an odd, soulless leer.

I climbed onto the first porch, wincing at the hollow boom of my footsteps. I twisted the knob and opened the door. "Hullo?"

No answer.

Moonlight flooded through the windows, illuminating a counter on the back wall. "Water!" I trotted across the room and turned on the tap, slurping from the faucet.

Charcoal yipped.

"Sorry, chap." I rummaged through the cabinets until I found a bowl. "Here," I said, filling it and setting it down for him. While he drank, I searched the drawers for candles but found nothing. Still, I opened the remaining doors, peering into the bedrooms, pantry, and toilet. All were empty. "Let's try the other one."

The second dwelling was also vacant. I stood on its porch with my fists clenched as I stared at the lake. In the moonlight, the jagged waves resembled knife serrations, but to the south, the tower gleamed like a beacon.

Maybe she'd arrived after me.

I considered my choices. If I went back down to the shore, I'd have to climb the hill to the tower, and I was already halfway up the hill. With luck, if I climbed up, the stairs would intersect with a road or walkway, shortening the distance to the tower.

"Let's go, boy." We continued climbing and found a north–south oriented road at the top of the stairway. "Perhaps our luck is changing."

I rested for a moment at the top, my vision graying as Charcoal gazed at me, his stomach growling audibly. "Sorry, chap, I have nothing for either of us."

We made it to the tower without incident, and I circled its base, calling softly for Akiko.

What now? I'd searched everywhere she might have gone. For all I knew, she'd curled up in a dark corner to wait for sunrise.

A glimmer of gold grazed the horizon as dawn approached. I yawned, worn out. I wanted to leave her a message but had nothing to anchor a note so it wouldn't fall or blow away. As I trudged around the tower, my fingertips skimmed its smooth surface.

Could I sketch on the tower itself?

I pulled out my pencil and scribbled a line. The graphite stood out against the stark surface. My thoughts foggy, I sketched the view from the porch of the cottage, wincing as I defaced the pristine structure. Within my sketch, I incorporated the water, the staircases, and the boardwalk below the porch.

Akiko would understand. She had to understand.

We retraced our steps toward the cottages and had nearly reached the staircase when a figure approached from the north.

I paused, unsure if I should duck down the stairs or wait and greet the person. It could be Akiko—who else would be out wandering in the predawn hours?

My hesitation lasted too long, and a man arrived. His shuffling footfalls stopped several meters away. "Heya?" he called in a wavering voice; his breathing labored.

"Heya."

"What are you doing?"

"Searching for my daughter. You haven't seen a young girl, have you?" Hope brightened my words.

The man shuffled closer. "I know your voice."

Eyes cloudy with fatigue, I shook my head. "Unlikely. I arrived a week ago."

"I *do* know you. Matthew Sugiyama. It is, isn't it?" the man asked, poking me in the chest.

My eyes widened, trying to read his face in the gloom. Was he a vendor I'd met in the market? "Yes, but—"

"It's me. Robin Pritchard."

I searched my memories, but the only Pritchard I remembered was a master at Popham. "Master Pritchard?"

He chuckled. "My eyes have faded, but my ears are sharp as a Nitram pencil. How are you, my boy?"

"I'm well, Master Pritchard. Relatively."

"You were one of the finest students I ever had. What are you doing here in Toronto Depot?"

"I'm looking for a girl."

"So you said. Your daughter? How is that possible?"

Guilt stabbed my heart several times. For all my success as a student at Popham, I was the poorest excuse for a father there could be. Not only had I lost my child, I'd also planned to catch several hours of sleep before resuming the search. "She's my ward, Master Pritchard. We were on our way to the warehouse when we got separated."

"Poor child. When you find her, come visit me. I'm the administrator of the Coldwater Dock. Follow the shoreline north, and I'm the last large pier before you reach the swamp."

"An administrator? But you're an *artist.*"

Pritchard raised his hand and ducked his head. "Hush, son."

"Why?" I asked in a lower voice.

His voice was thick with sorrow. "I'm not what I was, young Matthew."

"Master Pritchard?"

He clapped me on the shoulder. "Another time. Come and find me when things calm down for you."

Pain lanced my heart as I watched him shuffle down the road. He'd been a great favorite at Popham Abbey, but the years hadn't been kind. I'd never heard why he'd left, but I'd assumed he'd gone to another abbey to teach. Why wasn't he in one now?

Questions swirled in my mind, but the sky had brightened. If a few hours of rest could help clarify my mental fog, I'd be faster and sharper tomorrow. My footsteps heavy with failure, I descended the stairs to the assigned dwellings.

"We'll find her tomorrow, Charcoal. I promise."

CHAPTER TWENTY-SIX

Once again, I climbed the steps, my legs like an over-cooked noodle. After many trips circling from the warehouse to the tower, Beck's boat, Kelly Potter's lighthouse, and our cottage, I still hadn't found any sign of Akiko. The constant worry dragged at my gut. Terrible imaginings plagued me as I circled the depot; a terrified Akiko dragged away by shadowy figures, a hurt Akiko trapped under rubble, a lonely Akiko, scared and lost in this massive depot. Each version of her trusted I'd find her, and the terrible visions tore at my heart.

After graduating from Popham, Portland Depot had been the first I'd encountered. Fascinated by the ruins, I'd wandered down the waterfront, imagining the people from *Before*. Drawn by the flickering oil lamps and organ music, I had found myself before a carousel. People rode the contraption with glee, the garish wooden figures heaving up and down as the carousel spun. The carved figures had terrified me; I'd found their gaping mouths and desperate eyes sinister.

Now, starting yet another compulsive circuit, I understood their silent dread. "This time, she'll be at the cottage."

The water's surface rippled and tore, its raw umber hue sullen.

Charcoal's stomach gurgled, and I rubbed mine, my mouth sour. "I'm hungry too, chap."

The sun was past its zenith. Lunch would have been hours ago if I could've allowed myself to suspend my search. I didn't want to admit it, but the day had slipped by. Shame and my lack of acquaintances here in the depot had kept me from asking for help earlier, a decision I now regretted. My spent legs protested as I climbed the last flight to our dwelling.

A figure sat on the bench on our porch.

"Matthew," said Talbot.

Talbot.

The stack of dead bodies in New London, the razing of Brookfield and murder of my friends, the violent battle we'd narrowly won in Wakefield—every grisly, blood-soaked image flashed across my mind's canvas in a heartbeat.

Here on the steps, I was vulnerable. There was nowhere to hide, no one to help me face him. My sword, hidden in the frame of my pack, was in the cottage behind Talbot.

"Matthew," he said again, rising.

I bolted.

The stairs flashed by in a blur as I hurtled up them two at a time, racing toward the road at the top.

"Stop!" Talbot shouted.

Heart thumping, I bounded across the street and sprinted up the hill.

Charcoal's nails scrabbled over the cracked pavement as we raced through twisting alleys. I turned right and narrowly missed a jumble of pipes and wires protruding from a decaying building. Blind fear fueling my flight, I ran without marking my path.

Had he followed?

I glanced back as we darted into a narrow passage between two buildings.

Talbot pursued us, his face set and hard, running with a loose, even stride.

The passageway twisted to the left and ended abruptly, depositing us in a blind alley.

No way out.

I moaned and spun, sprinting for a gash in the wall of a tall, derelict structure. Sunlight slanted through cracked panes, illuminating a staircase. I pounded up it, my breathing ragged. Up and up, we raced, leaping over the gaping holes in the rotten stairs.

We burst out a door, and I skidded to a stop, squinting in the blazing afternoon sun.

The roof was large and flat, with a waist-high wall on all four sides. The footsteps thudding on the staircase toward us told me we had little time.

I slammed the door shut, but there was no latch or lock on my side—no way to secure it. Nerves screaming, I galloped to the north side of the building, peering over the edge. Thirty meters below, the ground swam, the fractured pavement rippling.

Glancing at the door, I ran to the east edge. The gap to the neighboring building was smaller. If I could get a running start, I could probably jump it, but I'd have to throw Charcoal.

Time was running out.

My lungs were on fire as I raced to the south side, the door behind me flying open with a crash. Adrenaline flooded through me, and lightheaded, I slipped, smashing into the low wall with my shoulder.

The wall disintegrated, and my momentum carried me over the edge.

I twisted and caught the edge of the roof with my fingertips as the debris rained onto the pavement below with a clatter; the sound echoing off the myriad of abandoned buildings.

Talbot's footsteps crunched on the roof as he circled the access doorway. As soon as he turned the corner, he'd see me.

The cords in my neck popped out as I strained to pull myself back onto the roof. My forearm was on the decking when Talbot ran toward me.

As Talbot approached, Charcoal's bark grew ferocious, and he moved between us.

My feet scrabbled against the side of the building, trying to find a toehold to anchor against. If Talbot reached me before I was back on the roof, I'd have no chance.

Charcoal charged, howling with fury, his hackles raised.

Talbot spun to the side and kicked him, catching him in the ribs.

Charcoal's yelp fractured my heart.

It was over. I'd failed. Closing my eyes, I waited. After everything, Talbot had won. A simple kick to the face would be enough; I wouldn't survive the fall.

My skin crawled as Talbot grabbed my wrist, but I opened my eyes. I would face my death like a man, with the dignity and courage of an artist. "Goodbye," I said, hating the quaver in my voice.

"You fool," he growled, as he pulled my arm. "Help me!"

Instinct kicked in, and I reached for an exposed board. It broke as I tried to haul myself up, and I fell backward.

Talbot lunged forward, landing on his chest and catching my other wrist.

I hung over the alley, helpless. When Talbot let go, I'd plummet to my death.

"If you don't climb, we're both going over the edge. Help a fellow out, Artist." Sweat dripped from his forehead, and the vein in his neck throbbed.

Why hadn't he let me drop?

"Climb, Artist!"

Twisting my arms, I clung to his forearms, hard and slick, and pushed against the building.

He slipped forward, his face blanching, but I walked up the side of the building, leaning back, using his grip for leverage. As I climbed, he inched backward, his jaw clenched and face distorted.

Simultaneously, he gave one last heave as I threw myself forward. He landed on his back, and I lay with my torso on the roof, legs dangling over space.

Talbot chuckled.

Unnerved by the sound, I squirmed the rest of the way onto the roof, collapsing next to Charcoal. The dog whined once and licked my face, glaring at Talbot.

If Talbot came after me now, he'd win, no question. Whatever he'd saved me for was undoubtedly worse than falling from the roof. I'd utterly failed. I'd lost Akiko, allowed myself to be captured by Talbot, and hadn't even kept my dog safe.

Talbot's silhouette towered over me. "Come."

I squinted into the sun and didn't move, but before I could reply, Talbot hauled me to my feet, sending Charcoal into another barking frenzy.

Talbot ignored the enraged dog. "Let's go."

Charcoal leaped forward, but I caught his collar. We were too close to the edge, and I didn't trust Talbot not to boot him off the roof. "Leave it."

Talbot shoved my shoulder toward the exit.

My expression mulish, I clomped down the stairs, hoping they'd collapse behind me and drop him into a deadly void. Once on the ground, I considered sprinting away, but Talbot's hand gripped my shoulder as if he'd read my mind.

What was the point? He had proven he was faster than me.

As we emerged from the warren of derelict buildings, the waterfront spread before us. Talbot prodded me toward the stairs leading to my cottage, and my confusion turned to dread.

What was he planning?

My gut clenched as I climbed onto my porch. My throat impossibly dry, I entered the dwelling, expecting his followers to be waiting for us.

The room was empty.

Talbot crossed to the table and pulled out a chair. "Sit."

The chair's hard edge bit into the back of my thighs as I scanned his face for answers.

Charcoal crept under the table and pressed close to me, trembling. Without taking my eyes off Talbot, I palpated Charcoal's sides, searching his short coat for blood or cracked ribs. He flinched but didn't protest.

Talbot rummaged through the cabinets, returning to the table with a bowl of water and a towel. He slid another chair over. "Give me your foot."

"Why?"

His eyes flickered. "You've injured your leg. Give it to me."

My trouser leg had darkened with blood, but I pressed my foot into the floor. "No."

Talbot shoved me, catching my foot as I rocked backward. He pushed up my trouser leg, his face contorting as he examined my wound.

I glared at him but refused to yank it back. "It's been like this for a while." Since *his* soldiers attacked Wakefield.

Talbot dipped the towel in the water and swiped it across the wound.

The sensation was like getting kicked in the stomach, and I jerked my leg back. "What are you doing?"

Talbot tightened his grip but continued to clean my leg.

My pulse jumping, I barely registered the sting. "What are you planning to do to me?"

Talbot ignored my question. When finished, he released my ankle and rinsed the towel and bowl in the sink.

Would he ever say anything? "How did you find me?"

Talbot sighed. "The message on the tower."

"It wasn't for *you*."

"So I gather." He gestured at my leg. "Do you have antiseptic?"

My lips flattened. "The brown bottle on the counter."

Talbot squinted and made a face after sniffing the contents. "Better you than me," he muttered, handing me the bottle and a fresh towel.

The liquid stung, and my eyes welled at the sensation and the sharp pine scent.

"Sorry," said Talbot.

"I'm not—" I stopped, clearing my throat. Why bother explaining myself? "What now?"

"Now?" Talbot leaned against the counter as he dried his hands.

I glanced at the door. "Are they coming?"

"Who?"

"Your people." My pack's frame leaned against the wall next to the door. Could I get to my sword before they arrived?

Talbot followed my glance and picked up the frame. "Clever."

My hands tightened into fists, and I drew a breath to calm myself. "When are your people arriving?"

Talbot tossed the pack's frame into the larger bedroom and shut the door. "What people?"

I glared at him. Was he pushing my buttons on purpose?

He folded his arms and leaned against the counter. "I'm here alone."

"Yeah. Right." I snorted. "What happens next?"

Talbot shrugged, appearing unconcerned. "You tell me."

I blinked. "But I'm your prisoner."

Talbot chuckled. "Prisoner?"

"You made me come here with you."

"Because of your bleeding leg," he said.

Heat coiled in my gut. This was as infuriating as our conversation after the battle in Wakefield. "Why did you chase me?"

Talbot raised his eyebrow. "Because you ran." He turned to gaze through the window. "Beautiful view. Growing up on the ocean must have been a gift."

After my sleepless night, nothing made any sense, and Talbot's proximity left me unbalanced. I glanced at the bedroom door. Did I have enough time to go for my sword? Sweat prickled along my spine.

"Is it like Popham?" he asked.

"Pardon, what?"

Talbot joined me at the table. "Does the view remind you of Popham?"

"No, Popham was on the ocean." Although Talbot's expression was neutral, my eyes tightened under his scrutiny. "This is a sea," I said, "a large lake. Why are you *here*?"

"Here?" He shifted, frowning.

My chest heaved as I fought to control my breathing. "Be straight with me. Why are you in Toronto Depot?"

Surprise crossed Talbot's face. "Because you are."

What? "You're in Toronto Depot because I am?"

"Yes."

I tried again. "You're in this cottage because I am."

"Yes, certainly."

I rocked to my feet and, trying not to limp, stepped onto the porch. If I were a prisoner, he'd come after me. But when

Talbot remained in his seat, his posture relaxed—my shoulder slumped. I was too tired to test him.

A breeze ruffled my hair, bringing the scent of tar and creosote from the piers. The light was still strong, but the faint tinge of rose reminded me sunset wasn't far off. I still hadn't found Akiko, but with Talbot here, she was probably safer wherever she was.

Assuming his followers hadn't captured her already.

I faced him. "You kicked my dog."

Talbot cleared his throat. "Right. Sorry, but I needed to help you."

I scowled. "He's a *dog*."

"Not my finest hour."

Did he mean it, or was he being glib? I couldn't read him at all.

"Talbot," I said softly, "I don't understand why you're here in Toronto Depot. I don't understand why I matter to you." His expression didn't change, so I limped back to the table. "I... I cannot deal with this today. Right now, I need to find my missing ward, so what do you want?"

The open door slammed shut, and I jumped, knocking into Charcoal.

When he yelped, Talbot's face softened. He leaned back in his chair. "What I want—"

My heart hammered, and I held my breath, not daring to move. Would he finally explain who he was and why we resembled each other?

Would he tell me about my birth family?

Talbot's mouth tightened. "What I want is dinner, but I'll come back in the morning to help you search."

Before I could collect my wits and respond, Talbot left, leaving me dazed and alone with a vortex of questions and a fear-shattered heart.

CHAPTER TWENTY-SEVEN

Talbot was in Toronto Depot. He wasn't trying to kill or capture me, and he wanted to help me find Akiko.

These facts were bizarre, unreal.

Even more incredible, Talbot had offered to return this morning to help me search for Akiko. After he'd left, I'd slept poorly, waking at every small noise, expecting Talbot's people to storm through the door. Nothing happened, but I'd woken aching and nauseated hours before sunrise.

Where was Akiko... and what did Talbot want?

Despite my heartache, the sunrise was spectacular and the artist in me pushed away my turbulent emotions to witness the show. Wrapped in a quilt, I sipped lavender-chamomile tea and watched as gold glimmered where the lake met the sky, bursting into vivid vermilion bands. As it rose, the sun painted the dark water gold and the sky a riot of purples and pinks. Had Akiko seen dawn's magic?

Talbot appeared as sunrays fanned through the purple-tinged clouds. "Good morning. Where should we start?"

A buzzing roar filled my ears, but I pushed aside my anxiety. "The tower, I guess?"

Ears pricked and body taut, Charcoal monitored Talbot, placing himself between us. Somehow, his mistrust of Talbot reassured me.

The morning air was dense with humidity and rust as we climbed the stairs and turned south. My leg burned, but I tried not to limp as I scrambled for something to say. So far, I'd learned almost nothing by questioning him, and each question he'd deflected cost me points in this game I didn't understand. After the battle in Wakefield, we had one brief conversation where he'd admitted he'd tried to prevent me from traveling to keep me safe. After someone interrupted our conversation, Talbot had refused to say anything else, and before I could confront him, he'd escaped from Newfane.

What had he been doing since then? Would he tell me if I asked?

Perhaps I could learn more through indirect questions, but where to start? There was only one subject I truly cared about, and he'd already rebuffed my questions, so asking again would make me sound needy and weak.

I studied Talbot with furtive glances as we walked. Small talk was another skill I hadn't developed, but he didn't appear to be bothered by the silence. He strolled with his hands in his pockets, his brow smooth, eyes bright, and no flickers of uncertainty or anxiety crossed his face.

What did he see in mine?

"Here we are."

After our silent walk, Talbot's words released a spike of adrenaline. My armpits prickled as I scanned the empty plaza around the base. "I'll check the other side."

"Sure." He stretched and wandered toward the railing and the view.

I jogged around the base of the tower to search the far side, Charcoal trotting beside me.

Nothing.

When I circled the tower again, Talbot stood at the viewpoint with his back to me, so I examined the sketch I'd made to communicate with Akiko. The edge had smudged as though someone had traced their finger down the line of graphite. I scrutinized it, catching a faint figure in the smear, the lines only visible because the graphite used was denser than what I'd sketched with. The figure was of a girl flying a square kite.

This was a sketch of the watercolor I'd painted at Niagara Abbey.

Akiko.

Except for the students and masters at Niagara Abbey, only she would recognize it.

I glanced at Talbot, but he hadn't turned, so with my pencil, I lengthened the tail of the kite, making it snap in the wind. Would she understand I'd received her message? I wished she had come to the cottage, but at least she wasn't lost.

I walked to Talbot and sighed, trying to keep my relief from my face.

"Nothing?"

"No."

He nodded. "Where should we go next?"

I pretended to consider his question. "Akiko and I climbed a building to get our bearings when we first arrived. We could try there."

"Lead the way."

As we walked, I peered into doorways and alleys. Catching Talbot's quizzical expression, I shrugged. "Someone stole our bags while we were on the roof, but some part of me hoped they reconsidered and brought them back."

Blast.

Another point to him. I hadn't meant to volunteer *any* information., but before I could stop myself, I continued. "I suppose it was foolish to leave them unattended."

Talbot shrugged. "Theft makes no sense when supplies are plentiful."

"Exactly, but I won't make the same mistake again."

His face was neutral as he studied me. "You've had a rough time."

"I have, yes. My things were stolen, I lost my ward, and I nearly lost my life by fleeing from my enemy." There. I'd admitted what I'd been thinking this entire time. Score another point for Talbot.

Blast his game.

I turned and faced him. "Why didn't you let me fall?"

Time slowed as I waited for his answer, hardly daring to breathe. The moment dragged on for eternity as we stared at each other.

"Come," he said, walking to a low wall. He brushed it off, then sat, beckoning to me.

A breeze swirled around us, emitting an eerie *woo* as it blew through the rotting buildings.

Was his trap about to snap? My eyes darted around to make sure we were still alone, my ears filled with a strange roaring. My body tensed, ready to flee.

"I'm not your enemy, but I *did* try to stop you." Talbot leaned forward, his posture open and eyes warm.

I snorted. "Did?" He'd admitted this in Wakefield, but somehow, this confirmation boosted my confidence. "Why?"

He exhaled as his shoulders sagged. "To stop you from seeking your family."

I held my breath, my heart thudding in my chest. This was it. I'd finally learn my truths. "Why shouldn't I seek my family?"

Talbot stared at the ground and said, "Because of Reverend Carter. It's not safe."

I sank to the wall, trying to digest the information. Who was this Reverend Carter, and why was he dangerous to me?

Talbot chuckled and rubbed his palms over his face.

My hands balled, leaving me twitchy and unsettled. "Why is this funny?"

"It's not funny, but it's ironic." Talbot sighed and shook his head. "When your parents sent you to Popham, Carter was in the Southwest. With you in New England and him down there, you were safe. But somehow, despite all the planning and *my* efforts, you both ended up here."

I waited, picking at the crumbling concrete, but he volunteered nothing else, so I tried another tactic. "What did my parents want for me?"

His expression cleared. "To settle and accept a commission in a small community."

"Any specific community?"

He shook his head. "An unconnected community."

"Unconnected." My mind buzzed. "Unconnected... unlike the Avalon Society?"

"Yes."

Questions fell around me like rain. "How were you told?"

Talbot hesitated, then sighed. "I received a letter from my aunt."

Why would his aunt care what I did after I graduated? "Who's your aunt?"

He blinked several times, his face softening. "Your mother."

"My mother? She's alive? We're cousins?"

He pinched the bridge of his nose. "Yes, we're cousins."

I rocked onto my feet as his words thundered in my ears. *Cousins.*

Charcoal edged between us, focused on Talbot.

My stomach knotted. "I don't understand any of this."

"Tell me what you *do* know." He rose, moving closer to me, ignoring the warning growl from Charcoal.

I narrowed my eyes and stepped backward.

He sighed. "If you tell me, I can fill in the blanks where I'm able."

And we could keep spinning around and around the truth. "You tell *me* my story."

Talbot turned, staring at the water. "I can't. I've taken oaths."

My lips flattened, and I fought the urge to shake him until his teeth clacked, but even as I glared at him, the hairs on the back of my neck rose.

Someone watched us.

"I haven't had breakfast. Let's go find some," said Talbot in an unnatural voice. He pointed at Charcoal, who had raised his hackles.

My skin prickled and my breathing shallowed. "There's a pub by the docks I like."

This time, Talbot chattered about nothing as we walked.

I tried to pretend I was engaged in the conversation, but my head remained on a swivel until we neared the market stalls and the hunted sensation lessened. "Safety in numbers," I muttered.

"Privacy too," Talbot said, ceasing his small talk.

I opened the door to the pub, fighting the urge to slam it shut behind us.

The same ugly keeper bustled past us, carrying a tray of dirty bowls. "Table in the back is open. Just two?"

Talbot nodded.

"I'll bring meals."

I trailed Talbot to the corner table but took the bench along the back wall, leaving him to sit with his back to the pub.

Blast manners.

He pursed his lips but sat. "Tell me everything."

I hesitated, then sighed. "It's not much. One, they sent me a great distance to Popham Abbey when I was three. While I was there, I studied art from a place of privilege, even within the abbey. Two, I received no visitors, correspondence, or packages. When I asked about my family, the masters either didn't know or wouldn't tell me anything. Three, everyone urged me to accept a commission upon graduation, but I refused."

Talbot nodded, "Go on."

I held up my hand as the keeper trundled toward us with a tray. "Shall I add this to your tab?" He asked, setting a bowl of porridge in front of me.

"No, mine," said Talbot. "Talbot Santo. I'm staying in the armory."

"Good, good," said the keeper. "And you're contracted with?"

"Harper."

"Very well. Good morning, gentlemen."

My bowl steamed, its nutty aroma waking my stomach. Talbot's last name was Santo, which meant my mother and his were sisters. I had a mother, an aunt, *and* a cousin. I'd assumed finding answers about my family would fill the holes inside me. But instead of becoming whole, I was hollow... numb.

Talbot sprinkled his porridge with salt and added a pat of butter. "What else?"

What else?

I filed away the small pieces of information I'd learned for later and added sugar to my bowl. It melted in rivulets of brown ochre across the top of the oatmeal. I tasted it, the maple flavor sharp across my sour tongue, and smiled as childhood memories of the abbey flooded back. "The flavor of maple reminds me of boyhood."

Talbot glanced at my sugar-laden bowl and shook his head. "I didn't try it until I'd grown, but I find the flavor too strident."

My vision clouded, and my nerves jangled with disappointment. If he hadn't grown up in the northeast, my family probably wasn't here in Toronto Depot either.

I swallowed as my throat tightened. If they weren't here, I needed to learn everything I could from him, so I continued.

"Four, after I left the abbey, I met an administrator who believed I'd accepted a commission in Hamilton, her community. You played a nasty trick on her."

Talbot blinked.

"Five, I found the letters you wrote to the minstrel. Once I'd read them, I knew someone was actively trying to stop me."

Talbot's spoon clattered to the table. "You met Gabriel?"

The door opened, and I glanced up in time to glimpse Akiko scamper across the room, holding her finger to her lips.

My heart squeezed, and my breath quickened. She was fine, she was safe. She was *here*... and she knew Talbot was, too. Beside me, Charcoal tensed, so I put a hand on his rigid neck to still him.

My gaze flicked back to Talbot. Had he noticed our reactions?

Talbot waited, his eyes wide and hands splayed on the table.

To feign nonchalance, I swallowed another sticky-sweet bite of porridge. "I didn't meet him. I found him dead on the side of a road."

CHAPTER TWENTY-EIGHT

The morning sun streaked through the windows, illuminating the interior of the pub with a warm, golden glow. But even as my heart soared, Talbot slumped forward with a strangled cry, his face in his hands.

Startled, I spilled my hot tea as I jerked backward, hitting the back wall with a *thud*. Wiping my hands, I stared at Talbot. To have this kind of reaction, Gabriel must have meant something to him.

While Talbot was distracted, I scanned the room.

Akiko peeked at me over the back of a booth, and tiny wings fluttered in my stomach. Charcoal stiffened again, and I grabbed his ruff while making a small, shooing motion with my left hand. When she slid out of sight, Charcoal whined, straining for me to release him.

She's safe.

How long had she been nearby? She hadn't approached, so she probably had recognized Talbot. I needed to get rid of him, but if I excused myself, he might follow and see her. Even though I'd accepted Talbot's help to search for her, the picture of her within his grasp made my heart slam against my chest. But, without the excuse of searching for Akiko, did we have any reason to remain in contact? The longer we remained cordial, the more I could learn about him and my family.

The scent of maple tickled my nose, and my stomach growled. Once I finished my meal, I'd have an excuse to leave. I'd have to engineer some way to keep him from following me, but it would give me time to slip Akiko out the back.

I studied Talbot while I ate my porridge. The maple sugar had melted, leaving a cloying, over-rich syrup across the top. I stirred it, watching the ribbon of brown swirl.

The keeper approached with his kettle. "More hot water, gentlemen?"

I nodded to the keeper and slid my mug across the table. "Yes, thanks."

The keeper stared at Talbot but filled his mug and set it on the table without a word.

Talbot *still* hadn't moved, so I watched the keeper cross the room toward Akiko's booth, where I assumed he took her order. When he glanced back at me as if to ask permission, I nodded before turning back to Talbot. "You cared for him, this Gabriel," I said, warming my hands on my freshened mug.

Talbot raised his face and stared at me with haunted eyes. The set of his jaw told me my news had caused him pain.

My heart clenched; he was a person, my *cousin*, not an adversary. Family. My appetite fled, and lightheaded, I gripped my mug, the heat uncomfortable against my rigid hands.

Talbot swallowed twice, his throat convulsing, and shivered under my scrutiny.

A sympathetic lump rose in my throat. "I'm sorry." Now that my child was safe, I had warmth and caring to spare.

My change in attitude softened him, and he cleared his throat. "I had hoped... well, never mind."

I waited, sensing he had questions for me. If he asked, should I tell him what I knew? This reversal was strange, and the memory of confronting Talbot after the fight in Wakefield seeped like dark oil across my mind's canvas. In the battle's aftermath, I'd reeled with pain and sorrow, desperate for answers, and Talbot had wielded his knowledge like a weapon.

I would *not* be like Talbot.

"I found him on a side road while traveling. Jo—"

I stopped, not wanting to give him Josephine's name, but Talbot's eyes pleaded for more.

I cleared my throat while picturing the scene. "I found him seated next to a wooden donkey cart. The road's edge had collapsed, leaving the cart stuck on a stump. He clutched his fist near his heart."

Talbot released the breath he'd been holding. "Natural causes?"

My hands relaxed. "I think so. I dug a grave and buried him there."

"Thank you for that." Talbot blinked several times and shook his head.

"I found letters from you in his things, which is when I knew for sure someone was attempting to keep me from finding my family. *Our* family."

"My letters." Talbot picked up his spoon and set it in his uneaten porridge. "Gabriel is... or, rather, *was* a great minstrel and my mentor."

The news sent my nerves reeling. "You're a minstrel?" Although his followers had referred to him as Preacher Talbot, I couldn't imagine him entertaining a crowd.

Talbot tilted his head. "What else do you know?"

My leg itched like I was under attack from sand fleas, and I squirmed, crossing my arms to keep from scratching my injury or rubbing my wrist.

"That's it. I've told you everything." My gaze flickered toward Akiko's booth. "Why me? Why was it important to stop me?"

Talbot toyed with his porridge, then pushed it away, exhaling with a hiss. "I'll tell you what I can, so don't ask for more."

My heart hammered, and my mouth filled with a sour flavor.

"They sent you to the abbey because you come from a long line of artists, and they knew you'd be an artist, too."

The buzzing in my ears grew louder. "Why was I sent to Popham, and why did it take so long to travel there? Where am I from?"

Talbot's eyes softened. "Your parents sent you to Popham Abbey because they trusted Headmaster Sinclair to hide you from Reverend Carter."

Time slowed. "Why?"

Talbot shook his head. "I can't divulge."

The kernel of hope I'd carried within me sprouted, thrusting its roots into my core. My parents had sent me away to keep me safe and my father was an artist. "Are my parents alive?"

"Yes."

My fists clenched. "Can you tell me where or who they are?"

He shook his head again. "I'm sorry."

"Am I still in danger? Are you?"

Talbot's eyes tightened, and he shook his head a third time.

Did that mean yes or no? I pressed the heels of my palms into the table to keep from pounding my fists against it. If my father was an artist, was it possible I'd met him? There had been no other men with Japanese ancestry at the abbey, but perhaps I had my mother's surname, and Talbot had his father's.

"Do my parents live together?" I asked, hoping Talbot wouldn't recognize what I was attempting to learn through my questions.

The corner of his mouth lifted. "You haven't met your father."

Perhaps it had been a mistake to volunteer information about Gabriel. If I hadn't done so, I could have bartered fact for fact. It would have served Talbot right to withhold information from *him*. I glared at him and didn't bother to dull the edge in my voice. "Are you enjoying this?"

Talbot stiffened, setting his mug down and dabbing the corner of his mouth with his napkin. "Why would you ask me that?"

"Why are you stalling?" I countered.

A muscle flickered in his jaw. Finally, a point to me.

His gaze flattened. "Hasn't it occurred to you that you know so little by design?"

His question hit like a kick to the groin.

My parents had engineered my ignorance. They hadn't died or been imprisoned. They hadn't lost their memories or befallen any of the tragedies I had imagined as a boy. Instead, they had abandoned me at Popham with no information, no way to communicate with them, and no way to find them. My entire life, they'd known where I was, but they hadn't communicated or sent word to ensure I was well. Or visited to marvel at my skill or accomplishments.

My parents had deserted me into the abbey system. On *purpose*.

Old hurts bubbled forward, black and acidic, until I wanted to smash my fist into Talbot's smug face. "Why harm all those people?" I asked to needle him.

Talbot's head snapped up. "I never ordered violence," he said. "It was Rudy's doing."

"Rudy worked for you."

"Rudy worked for—" Talbot stopped, his eyes narrowing. "I can't discuss it."

"Blast your oath."

We glared at each other, neither willing to back down.

Charcoal sighed and laid his head on the table, breaking the moment. I pushed my half-eaten meal toward the dog and took some small pleasure in the disgust on Talbot's face as Charcoal slurped from my bowl.

"Now what?" I asked, pulling Talbot's attention back.

He rapped his knuckles on the table. "Right. I have contacts here, so I'll try to find your bags and ask about your ward."

"My ward," I repeated, struggling not to glance in Akiko's direction.

"It may take a day, but I'll leave a message at your dwelling." Talbot leaned back and sipped his tea.

Clearly, he was in no hurry, and the longer he lingered, the greater the chance he'd see Akiko. It was time for him to go. "I could come to the armory."

He reviewed me coolly. "You could, but I may move lodgings."

I used his statement as an excuse to feign offense and rose. "Thank you for the meal."

Talbot stood in response but appeared confused.

"Let me know what you find," I said, my tone cold. Let *him* feel dismissed.

Talbot stiffened, nodded curtly, and left without turning back.

CHAPTER TWENTY-NINE

I waited several minutes to ensure Talbot wouldn't return before crossing the room to Akiko. She saw me and grinned, her tongue poking through the gap in her teeth.

My fury, worry, and exhaustion dissolved in a flash as I pulled her toward me. She clung to me, fire-hot, her arms like steel bands around my waist. Her hair smelled of strawberries and tar.

Questions swirled, but I didn't want to take the chance of Talbot returning and finding us. I squeezed her once more. "Let's go."

Akiko squatted to hug Charcoal. "One more hug, first."

The dog wiggled and whined; his smile huge. Once released, he circled us repeatedly, as though to ensure we remained together.

We slipped into the alley behind the pub and worked our way through narrow passages toward the waterfront. Stepping out from between two crumbling brick buildings, I scanned the boardwalk.

The late morning sunshine was warm but not hot, and the

breeze from the lake kept the temperature pleasant. No one seemed suspicious—neither too still nor too interested in the people passing by.

My shoulders relaxed. "I think it's okay."

Akiko searched my face. "You're limping again. Did *he* do it?"

I shook my head. "Where in the blast have you been?"

Akiko squinted one eye and tilted her head.

I sighed and softened my tone. "I was worried."

"Me too."

I bit my lip. "What happened? Where did you go?"

Her gaze slid sideways as she mumbled something.

I stopped walking to tilt her chin up. "What?"

She sighed. "I wanted a break from you, but when I was ready to walk again, you were gone."

"Why didn't Charcoal stay with you?"

Akiko grinned at the dog who had backed into her legs. "I told him to go. He's a good boy."

"Mm, usually. Come on," I said, holding my hand out for her again. "Where did you sleep last night?"

"In the yellow boat."

"Beck's boat?"

"Uh, huh. I didn't know why Preacher Talbot was at the cottage. Did you find our stuff?"

Talbot.

I needed to hide Akiko, but I'd just found her. How could I let her go again? But if I didn't, and Talbot's people captured her... I refused to imagine it. If Talbot had been watching me, he'd know about Mama's, so Akiko wouldn't be safe there either.

Holding out my hand, I shook my head. "Come, I'm taking you to Master Pritchard."

"Who?" Akiko took my hand and skipped next to me.

"He was a master at Popham Abbey." Talbot's words whispered in my memory. My parents had sent me to Headmaster Sinclair to hide me, too.

Charcoal circled us as we walked, his ears perked and eyes watchful.

Akiko bounced alongside me. "Master Pritchard is an artist?"

"He was, but he's an administrator now."

She dropped my hand. "Why?"

"Let's find out." I rubbed my jaw. "He's on the last dock, near the swamp."

Akiko wrinkled her nose. "Swamp. Thwamp. Bwamp."

I bent, pretending to check my bootlace, using the movement to make sure we weren't being followed.

Akiko peered down the boardwalk. "He's not behind us."

So much for stealth. "It might not be him who is following us."

"Then how would you know, anyway?"

She had a point. "Mouse, we can't trust Talbot, so I want you to stay with Master Pritchard for now."

"For art?" she asked, brightening.

"No!"

Akiko blinked.

I kneeled before her. "Sorry, Mouse, but your art must stay our secret for now. Just you and me, okay?"

She patted my shoulder. "Okay."

We ambled down the boardwalk, enjoying each other's company and watching the bustle of activity. Although the sails were kept furled while the ships were in the marina, ropes slapped against metal masts with a rhythmic *cling-cling* as the boats groaned and squeaked in their moorage. The breeze ruffled the hair around my neck, and I tied it back with a spare leather lace.

Akiko patted her neck. "Do mine too. Look, more kites!"

I untied my hair, snapping the lace in two. "Did you find the kite tail I left?"

"On the tower? Yes, I watched you draw it."

I chuckled and finished tying her hair. "I sensed someone watching. Where were you?"

"Under the boardwalk."

I frowned, pulling my hair back. "Then how did you watch me? You can't see the tower's plaza from the boardwalk, let alone from under it."

Akiko winked and glanced around. "It's another secret."

"Let's go over there," I said, pointing at a bench.

Perched on the bench, Akiko pulled out her sketchbook and slid it toward me while she looked elsewhere.

I grinned. "Sneaky. I like it."

Her art fascinated me; I loved how she drew a story in a series of frames. I flipped to the next page and stopped at a frame of me drawing on the tower. "How did you draw this if you couldn't see me?"

Akiko tapped her head. "I watched you in here, in a drawing, so I drew what I saw. The backward of normal."

The backward of normal. Typically, I assessed a scene with my eyes, then changed it to match my mind's canvas. Could I reverse the process? I pulled out a pencil and sketched in Akiko's book.

"Hey!"

"I'll give it to you in a minute," I said. Finishing the sketch, I handed it to her.

She pouted, her lower lip stuck out, but glanced at it anyway. "It's me, holding my sketchbook!"

"Let me try something." I pulled out my sketchbook and visualized the change I wanted to make to Akiko's book. My fingers tingled as I drew the words 'Sneaky Mouse.'

Akiko squealed and flapped her book. "Look!" The cartoon version of her sketchbook now contained my message.

My pulse leaped. "Let me try another." This time, I drew a simple box on her page, then visualized the outcome, writing my message with exaggerated care in my book. I laughed as my fingers tingled again.

This worked.

"Practice your reading," Akiko read from her book. "Not as much fun."

"Mm, but it's important. The ignorant can't be artists. Now you try."

Akiko hunched over her sketchbook, tongue hanging from the corner of her mouth.

I watched my book as a caricature of myself appeared, with a speech bubble reading, "Matthew is the dumb-dumb."

I made a face at her. "You made my ears too big."

"Whatever, potato head."

"*Potato* head? Be nice."

Akiko sighed and squirmed out from under Charcoal. "Okay. But Preacher Talbot is the *real* potato head."

"His ears are bigger than mine," I said.

The dock bustled with activity, but after asking several people, we found our way to Master Pritchard. He was busy directing the loading of a ship, so I pulled out the sack of salt-water taffy I'd found at the market and shook it at Akiko.

She squealed and unwrapped a piece. "You're the best."

"I am," I agreed.

Akiko fed the first piece to Charcoal, who smiled, chewing loudly. When Akiko laughed, my heart lightened.

"One for you now," she said, handing me a piece.

I unwrapped it and popped it into my mouth, the raspberry flavor sticky-sweet. "Mmm."

She patted the dock next to her. "Sit."

Master Pritchard was still busy, so I sat on the sun-warmed wood and tried not to groan as I stretched my injured leg out. Gulls wheeled and called above us as the waves slapped the piers below. Their cries, combined with the squeak of stretching ropes and sweet candy, brought me back to my boyhood.

"So, you've found your wayward ward," Pritchard said. He bent down and peered at Akiko with filmy eyes.

"Hullo, sir. Would you like a taffy?"

"Why thank you, Miss...?"

"Akiko," I said, scrambling to my feet. "This is Akiko."

Akiko stood gracefully and bowed. "Master Pritchard."

He smiled at me. "Polite. Very nice."

I ruffled her hair. "She can be. Well met, Master Pritchard."

"Well met Matthew, and please, call me Robin. You're no longer my student." Robin's eyes twinkled as he unwrapped his candy. "How was dear Popham?"

"It wasn't the same after you left, Master—I mean, *Robin*. The new master was a stickler for precision."

"Oh, eh? I dare say you boys needed someone with a little more bite to sharpen you up! Now, I've finished here, so come with me and we'll have tea."

Even as an elder, Robin's energy exceeded mine. He marched up the hill chatting with Akiko, and I trailed them to a small dwelling perched above the pier, my leg protesting each step. I sank onto a cushioned chair on Robin's porch and groaned.

"Ouchie?" Akiko asked, after Robin had gone inside to make the tea.

"Mm. My fault this time."

"What happened?"

"Draw you later," I whispered.

Robin pushed open the door with his hip and set down a

tea tray. "This is the tea I like best. I make it from a combination of spearmint and mallow I pick myself."

"From the swamp?" asked Akiko, watching him pour.

Robin set her cup before her. "Yes, you clever girl. Here, have a sandwich. Young people are always hungry."

"We are," Akiko agreed.

The aroma of mint and something sweet tickled my nose. "Is the mallow leaf sweet?"

Robin sank into his chair and tapped his chest. "No, it's like any green. I harvest the roots to make marshmallows."

Akiko brightened. "Marshmallows?"

Robin picked up a square item from the plate and passed it to her. She pinched it several times, giggling as it sprang back to its original shape.

Robin laughed. "Taste it."

Akiko squinted at the brown lump but nibbled the edge. "Mmm!" she said, eyes widening.

"First, I grind the mallow root. Next, I boil water, dissolve a bit of maple sugar, and whisk in egg whites and the mallow powder. Et voilà, marshmallows."

I plucked one from the plate and sank my teeth into the corner. It was sweet and pillowy, with a sticky, airy structure.

"So good," said Akiko.

Robin chuckled and tapped her hand. "I'm pleased you enjoy it."

We chatted about the depot until I noticed Akiko had fallen asleep.

Master Pritchard put a finger to his lips and beckoned me into his cottage. "Now, my lad, what brings you to visit today?"

Although I wanted to ask why he'd left Popham, Akiko was my priority. If Talbot returned to my cottage with his followers, I didn't want her there. "A favor. My business here is incomplete, and I need to leave Akiko somewhere safe for several nights. I hate to ask, but I know so few people here. Can we impose on your hospitality? I'd happily trade or—"

"My boy, my boy." Robin shook his head. "We are *brothers* and the little one will be no trouble."

"Thank you, sir. I'm grateful. Please make sure she keeps up with her letters and reading. I've given her a sketchbook to practice in."

"Fine, fine. Perhaps we will make a batch of marshmallows while she's here. I could use a pair of young eyes to help find and dig up mallow roots. Go on, lad, we'll be fine."

After I finished my tea, I woke Akiko and gave her a hug. Before I could change my mind, I whistled for Charcoal. He followed, but stopped to gaze at Robin's cottage before trotting down the hill after me. I waved as I turned south and tried to ignore my heart's pangs. Now that Akiko was safe, I was free to dig into Talbot and his mysterious contacts.

CHAPTER THIRTY

Wind flicked my hair into my eyes, and I blinked to clear the sting. The heavy, gray skies had darkened as the day had worn on, and the humidity and heat were now oppressive. The breeze should have helped, but it was hot as it swirled around me, smelling of tar, creosote, and rot. I should have started my work earlier in the day.

I checked my drawing and scanned the dilapidated pier I would repair for Administrator Potter. It was in a sad state with leaning pilings and the decking slimy with rot. The ramshackle structure had been the perfect project for killing time, and I'd used my artwork to distract myself while I waited.

I was sick of waiting.

Waiting for Talbot to make his move. For my friends to arrive in Toronto Depot. Waiting for more flashes to fill in the gaps on my missing painting so I could continue my search.

My search.

If I couldn't discover more about my family, how would I find them? Was there a way to extract the answers I needed from Talbot? Did he even *have* any answers for me?

My gut twisted. This whole time, I'd assumed he knew everything, but what if he didn't?

Faithful Charcoal was good at listening to my litany of complaints but had little to offer in response. Perhaps hiding Akiko with Robin had been an overreaction.

"Matthew."

Talbot's voice cut through my trance-like state as though my thoughts had summoned him, and my heart jumped. "I'd nearly given up on you coming back," I said, pulling out my knife as I searched his face.

Charcoal stared at Talbot, ears pricked and body still. Talbot stiffened, his lips compressing and eyes darkening as he stared at my knife.

Talbot found *me* threatening? I raised an eyebrow, choosing a pencil from my case. "Well?"

The corner of Talbot's mouth lifted as he watched me sharpen my pencil. He glanced around. "Since we're alone..."

I didn't expect Talbot to tell me much, since our interactions left me with more questions than answers. "As alone as one can be in a depot," I said, stowing my knife and resuming my sketching. I'd been working on straightening the nearest piling.

The timber groaned as I adjusted it, and several gulls launched into the air, screeching. Waves smashed against the boardwalk's supports, the *thud* reverberating through the soles of my feet.

Talbot stepped closer; his breath catching as he watched the structure straighten. "It took a while to find answers."

"And?" I used the side of my finger to pull the charcoal into the water, adjusting the shadow.

"Reverend Carter's plans continue. Curiously, I heard mention of an artist who is recruiting talent for Carter. Will you be much longer?" Talbot stopped and whistled as I straightened the last two pilings and replaced the signal pole.

I glanced at the pier. "I'm nearly finished. An artist you said?" This wasn't the first time I'd learned of an artist working with the revivalists. I bent back to my sketch and continued my adjustments.

Talbot stepped closer. "How big of a change can you make?"

I shrugged as I repaired the rotted decking. "Not sure."

"What about many artists?"

The vertebrates in my neck popped as I stretched. "Working together?"

He nodded.

I stuck the pencil behind my ear and picked up my sketch. All the pier needed now was one of Beck's dragons flying at the end.

"Well?" he asked.

"Oh, it wasn't a rhetorical question? Come on."

Talbot followed me onto the pier, his steps light and hesitant. Charcoal maneuvered himself between us as we walked. Though the dog appeared to be gazing at the end of the pier, he'd swiveled his left ear toward Talbot. He clearly hadn't forgiven Talbot for kicking him.

"It depends, I suppose. On the skill of the artists, and if someone is overseeing the work to provide guidance and an overall perspective." At the far end, I turned back and examined the boardwalk. "Perhaps I should extend the pier or add a crane to aid with loading and unloading."

Talbot thumped his foot on the repaired decking. "Why? This is marvelous."

I shrugged. "To repair this pier was easy, perhaps too minor an improvement for the food, supplies, and lodging I've collected. Perhaps I'm used to things being harder to come by."

After I'd dropped Akiko off at Robin's dwelling, some part of me expected an ambush at my cottage, but nothing happened. In the two days since, I'd done my best to distract myself by working on Potter's projects, but my mind returned to Talbot and my family again and again.

Without warning, Talbot pulled me into a hug. I rocked onto my toes, my body rigid. We stood like statues—unmoving, unyielding, frozen together. Before my mind could process my swirling emotions, my unburdened arm snaked around him, surprising us both. He tightened his hold, and I let myself lean into him and into the embrace.

As I did, our energies synced, changing *everything* between us.

Talbot had told me the truth. His every action had been protective, an attempt to keep me from harm. He was honor-bound to keep information secret, but he held no malice or deceit toward me.

My heart swelled as though it would burst. Talbot was my family.

Blood family.

When Talbot stepped back, wiping his eyes, Charcoal sank with a groan, flopping onto his side. Talbot's eyes shone as he scanned the dog. "I guess I'm forgiven. Did you find your ward?"

"I did, thanks. It was a small misunderstanding."

He smiled at me. "We've synced, cousin, and I'm glad."

"Me too, and I'm pleased you're back." I meant it. What a strange world this was.

"Are you done here?"

"Mm. Why?"

"You should go through your bags and check if anything is missing."

I shouted with laughter. "You found our bags!"

"Yes, I left them at your cottage."

"You have better contacts here than I do." I shook my head.

His eyes warmed. "Happy to be of help. I *am* sorry for all the trouble I've caused you in the past."

"I believe you. How did you know they were our bags?" I asked, packing up my supplies.

Talbot shrugged. "I wouldn't have if I hadn't glimpsed your painting in Wakefield."

Home.

"Ah." I sat back on my heels.

A scholar had confirmed the tower-like structure on *Home* could be the tower in Toronto Depot after the battle in Wakefield. I remembered Talbot's face at the window, then his steadfast refusal to tell me anything about my family. I slapped my knee. "It's how you tracked me down."

Talbot shrugged, a small smile playing on his lips. "You followed *me*. I traveled here as soon as I left Newfane."

"Escaped Newfane, you mean. You should have seen their faces when they told me."

"I... walked away. It was simple." Talbot chuckled. "How did you beat me here?"

Charcoal jumped as I folded the easel with a *crack*, so I rubbed his shoulder with my toe while glancing around to see if I'd missed anything. "We flew."

Talbot stared at me. "You flew."

"Right. Why the interest in what artists can do?"

Talbot's eyes narrowed. "Because Reverend Carter is gathering artists."

Gathering?

I searched Talbot's face but found no hint of humor or sarcasm. Icy sweat prickled along my spine and in my armpits. "What do you mean gathering? Is this the same Reverend Carter you mentioned before?"

Talbot blinked. "Yes. He's also the man behind the revivals."

The news hit me like a gut punch. "Behind the revivals?" Bitter bile filled my mouth as I gazed across the slate-colored water. "I didn't know there was a *design* behind the revivals. I assumed they were a set of horrific coincidences, or a few larcenous men copying each other to exploit communities. Did he tell Rudy to—"

Memories of the charred remains in Brookfield, the stacked bodies in New London, and Whistler's lifeless eyes in Wakefield flashed onto my mind's canvas and I retched.

Talbot set his palm, light and warm, between my shoulder blades. "I'm sorry."

"Headmaster Sinclair tried to warn me before I left the abbey how little I knew of the world, but I didn't listen." Wiping my mouth on the back of my arm, I stood. "Why is this Carter gathering anyone?"

Talbot shrugged. "I'm not sure, and I haven't worked my way up high enough to ask those questions. Several people mentioned crusaders, but I didn't learn why."

Talbot's new openness would take some getting used to. His words tumbled through my buzzing brain, and I gave up trying to organize them. When Josephine arrived, I'd ask her about the crusaders. "You said you haven't worked your way up. You're in the organization for information?"

Talbot blanched and glanced around before leaning toward me, his voice low. "Yes, but keep it between us. Right now, they think I'm trying to recruit you for our side. When I found out Pritchard recruited for—"

My ears filled with a peculiar roaring as I sprinted toward the shore, leaving Talbot and my things behind. He shouted my name, but I didn't respond as I skidded onto the boardwalk, racing north.

CHAPTER THIRTY-ONE

I registered the cleat too late and tripped over it, landing on the boardwalk with a grunt. Splinters lanced through my cheek and the heel of my hand, the sharp pain muted compared to my fracturing heart. I rolled onto my back and drew my knees toward my chest, groaning. Ragged breaths tore at my chest, souring my tongue.

The steel-gray clouds overhead amplified the day's humidity, adding to the pressure Talbot's news had brought. My chest heaved as I struggled to breathe, panic rocketing my pulse.

"You okay?" asked Talbot, gasping.

I was *not* okay. Pritchard worked for Reverend Carter.

Charcoal panted in my face, his tongue swiping at my forehead.

I pushed him away and reached for Talbot. This delay —*any delay*—was perilous.

After he hauled me to my feet, Talbot thumped my back. "Where are we going? What's wrong?"

My heart screamed as I bent, my hands on my hips, words stuttering as I struggled to catch my breath. "I'm—an *idiot*."

Talbot pointed at my leg. "It's bleeding again."

My mind immediately labeled the hue—alizarin gold—of the stain spreading across my last pair of trousers. I swallowed and pushed away the thought of my dripping leg. "I'll deal with it later. Come, I left Akiko with Pritchard."

Air exploded from Talbot's nose like a pressure pot. "Blast! If only I'd found you sooner."

I skittered around a man rolling a barrel, then shook my head. "It wouldn't have mattered. I took her to Pritchard's as soon as you'd left the pub."

Talbot's jaw tightened. "Why?"

Why? Because I was a fool and a terrible father. "To hide her from you."

The hill to Pritchard's house was tortuous after our run, but I stumbled up it, clinging to the hope Talbot was mistaken. Or that a different Pritchard recruited artists for Reverend Carter. But when we found Pritchard's cottage empty, my hopes shattered. We searched the entire building and opened every cabinet and drawer, but found no traces of Pritchard or Akiko in the dwelling.

Ice snaked through my veins, and my body trembled as my vision went hazy before alighting on the small deltahedron on the windowsill. The deltahedron Akiko had taken from me. "This *is* the right house."

Talbot gripped my shoulder as though to steady me. "I believe you. It is too clean to have been long empty."

His support made my eyes sting. Once again, I'd trusted the wrong man and lost Akiko. Despite my warnings to keep her art a secret, had Pritchard learned about her unusual gift? If so, where would he have taken her? In a depot the size of Toronto, Pritchard could hide anywhere. My breath caught—what if he took her out of the depot?

Charcoal whined, sniffing at my leg.

I needed to search quickly, but after Pritchard's betrayal, I didn't trust any of the other acquaintances I'd met to help me. The fastest way to survey the depot by myself would be from the air. "I'll retrieve the flier."

Talbot straightened. "Should I come with you?"

I shook my head, blinking back tears. "Will you reach out to your network to learn where Pritchard has gone?"

Talbot bit his lip but nodded. "If I find anything, I'll come to your dwelling."

I clapped Talbot on the shoulder while whistling for Charcoal. "Be careful, cousin."

After checking Akiko hadn't left me a message in my sketchbook, Charcoal and I raced west toward the artificial field where I'd hidden the flier. As we stumbled along the routes, I used the tower as a landmark to stay oriented. The gleaming beacon was a constant, reassuring guide, even as fears and questions tumbled through my mind.

How could I have left Akiko with *Pritchard*?

I was a sham, a counterfeit parent, and Akiko deserved better. Although I'd wondered why Pritchard had left the abbey system, I hadn't bothered to verify his character. But just because he was an old acquaintance, and a fellow artist, didn't mean he was trustworthy.

Why had I believed I could adequately parent her? The throbbing in my leg and Charcoal's tummy rumbles proved I couldn't even take care of myself or my dog.

The sun set before I reached the strange, artificial field and the dusky light reminded me of the first, fear-soaked night we'd spent in Toronto Depot. When Charcoal sprinted ahead of me, my heart lifted and I trotted toward the artificial hill at the south end of the field, ignoring the protest from my leg. If Akiko escaped Pritchard, she may have come here too.

My chest loosened. "Akiko?"

No answer.

Charcoal disappeared behind the debris I'd leaned against the flier. I pushed it away, pulling the canvas tarpaulin toward me.

The flier was gone.

I blinked at the spot where I'd left it, the space now occupied by junk. The thief had been clever, stacking materials to make it look as though the flier was still under the tarpaulin.

"And then the world died!" I dropped to the ground, smashing my fist into the cracked pavement as I bellowed profanities.

Of *course* the flier was gone.

I lay back, spent, and stared at the rapidly darkening sky. Charcoal sighed as he leaned against me.

Tears leaked from the corners of my eyes. "I've lost her again, Charcoal. Now what?" He whined, laying his head across my chest, and I stroked him to comfort us both. "Worse, blast me, this is all my fault."

I was tired. Tired of making mistake after mistake. Of choosing the wrong people to trust. Weary of the ever-present pain in my leg. Of not understanding the undercurrents seething and swelling around me.

Like a cork, I bobbed in the sea, oblivious to the monsters swimming in the gloom below. Had the world always been this complicated? Or was the darkness, this ever-increasing sense of dread, new?

I groaned and rubbed my forehead, hissing as the motion drove a splinter deeper into my palm. I sat up, and Charcoal flopped onto his side, grumbling. My hand throbbed, and gingerly I explored my cheek, wincing when my fingers discovered the companion splinter. Without a mirror, I had no way of patching myself up.

It was time to ask for help.

"Come on," I said, as I staggered onto my feet. "Let's go."

Charcoal eyed me but didn't lift his head.

"I can at least feed *you* while trying to figure out what to do."

At the mention of a meal, Charcoal stood and shook. He took several steps and huffed, then trotted west. I followed, heartsick and weary.

Where was my girl?

AFTER NAVIGATING KILOMETERS THROUGH THE DARK, THE harbor's lights lifted my spirits. Ravenous, we hurried toward the pub.

When I pushed the door open, I found the room crowded and noisy despite the late hour. For once, I was glad for the throng. The abandoned streets of the depot had induced a craving for life, for laughter and noise. I pushed my way to the bar, searching for the keeper.

"You'll have to wait," he said brusquely as he carried a tray of empty mugs through the narrow galley. He set it down and glanced at me, wiping his hands on a towel. "Your face resembles raw sausage."

My hand flew to my face reflexively. The automatic gesture reminded me of Josephine, and another pang tore through me. My shoulders drooped, and to my embarrassment, my chin trembled.

The keeper sighed and shook his head. "Potter said you're to be given any aid you request. Come with me. My wife Matilda will help you and I'll bring a meal when I can."

"I don't have time," I protested, but the keeper had already stomped into the kitchen. Charcoal pleaded at me with his eyes, so I sighed and followed the keeper through the kitchen and up a staircase. "Thank you, Keeper. I'm Matthew."

He glared at me. "I'm charging you double. Matilda, this is Matthew, one of Potter's prizes. Can you tend his face?"

I blinked at the beautiful, blonde woman. "Hullo."

The keeper growled and slammed the door behind him.

Matilda laughed, her mass of golden ringlets bouncing. "Don't mind Aya. He gets like this when he's busy, but he loves it. Please," she said, pointing to a straight-backed chair.

I sank into it, trying not to groan. "Really, I don't have time for this. I came in for a quick meal, but I must get back to—" I stopped, unsure if I should confide in her.

Matilda surveyed me with her hands on her hips. "You're a right mess. Aya cooks everything to order, so we may as well get you patched up while you're waiting for supper. Any more splinters?"

I nodded, showing her my torn palm. Charcoal copied me, holding his paw up for inspection, too.

She took his paw and shook it with a serious expression. "Pleased to meet you, little chap." She turned to me. "I can pull your splinters and wash the wounds while you wait, but if you can spare another delay, visit Mama Rebecca after you eat. She's the best healer around."

Someone rapped on the door.

"It's open," Matilda called, while disappearing into the next room.

The door opened, and a man stepped in. "Matilda my love, let's run away together while your man is busy downstairs."

I straightened. "Olen Ash?"

He stared at me, then snapped his fingers. "Matthew Sugiyama, well met. What are you doing here, where's your sidekick, and what the blast have you done to your face?"

My heart sank; I had no answers to his questions.

Before I could stammer out an excuse, Matilda returned, setting down a bowl and a clean towel.

"Hullo, you scoundrel," she said to Olen, while tilting my chin up and to the side. "I'll try a warm compress first." Her grip on my chin tightened as she pushed a hot towel to my cheek.

I shrugged at Olen, unable to speak.

Olen chuckled and dropped into a fat armchair near the fire. "You have time for all the boys but me, my love."

Matilda checked beneath the towel and prodded my cheek. "Hush. Matthew will get the wrong idea."

"Matthew is confused," I said, through gritted teeth.

Matilda smiled. "There, got one. Hold this."

I pressed the towel to my cheek while she inspected my hand and glanced from her to Olen, raising my eyebrow.

"Matilda would have been my bride if she hadn't run off with my brother," he said.

She clucked her tongue at him but smiled.

I examined Olen's handsome face, searching for a resemblance. "The ugly keeper is your brother?"

"And my husband," said Matilda. "He may not be handsome, but Aya is a wonderful man."

"Beg pardon," I said. "I meant no offense."

"A cougar attacked my brother when he was little," said Olen. "He's lucky to have survived."

I nodded, hoping to distract Olen. "Your accents are different," I said, wincing as Matilda dug into my palm to drag out the splinter.

"Mother refused to live in the desert after what happened to Aya and moved here with him when I was a nipper. I stayed near my father until his death, then accepted the commission in Aurora so I could be nearer to Mother, Aya, *and* this angel."

Matilda raised her eyebrows, chuckling. "There, the best I can do."

The heavy door swung open, and Aya stomped into the room. "Steaks and spuds are what you get. I brought enough for you too, moron."

Olen grinned. "Hope the cow didn't spy your mug before it died. Hate me a terror-toughened steak."

Aya gave him a practiced sneer, but Olen only laughed and ruffled his brother's hair. Matilda angled her smooth cheek for a kiss, but Aya grabbed her chin and kissed her full lips. When she closed her eyes and leaned into the kiss, I glanced away, flushing.

Charcoal drooled as he stared at the platter of meat. Despite my worry and impatience to get back to my search, the intoxicating scent of the meat hit my nose. I flushed deeper when my stomach groaned; the noise interrupting the couple's embrace.

"Well said, Matthew." Olen chuckled and handed me a pint of ale from the tray. "Let's pretend they aren't snogging and see what damage we can do to this meal."

CHAPTER THIRTY-TWO

Tipsy, I stumbled through the dark. After the ales I'd consumed in Matilda's apartment, it was miraculous I hadn't tumbled down the stairs while climbing to my cottage. I crashed into the doorframe, accidentally kicking Charcoal.

He growled.

"Sorry, chap." I groped in the dark for the lantern I'd left on the table. My hand slid into something, and a heartbeat later, glass shattered. The smell of lamp oil spread, greasy and floral.

Someone coughed.

I whirled, my mind clearing. "Who's there?"

Alert, my ears rang with the silence. Backing, I swept my foot for the bags Talbot said he'd left along the front wall. Were they even here? If someone had gotten into the dwelling, they could have taken my things again. My hands tightened into fists. I'd lost enough—it was time to fight back.

My knees nearly buckled as my hand found and grasped my sword's handle, the grip solid, familiar, and comforting. I lifted it and straightened my shoulders. "Who's there?"

Nothing.

"Pritchard, is that you? I want a word," I said, "several, actually."

Sword before me, I stepped forward, ready. I couldn't make out anything in the gloom and waited, listening to the silence.

A whisper of movement flickered to my right, so I swung my sword in an upward arc, snarling as it connected with flesh.

Silence followed the single, sharp yelp.

My skin crawled and nerves jangled as I waited in the dark. The scent of blood strengthened, but no attack came.

Maybe I'd defeated the intruder with a single blow. On high alert, I crossed the kitchen and pulled a candle and flint from a drawer. My hands shook as I lit it, but the dim light illuminated nothing.

I turned slowly, my foot nudging Charcoal. "Move," I muttered in warning. If the intruder was still mobile, the flickering candle made me an easier target.

The dog was still.

I scanned the room, then peered through the gloom at the doorway at the far end.

Nothing.

I glanced down. Charcoal lay in a slowly spreading pool of black.

"Charcoal?"

His ear twitched.

My sword clattered as I dropped it, and buzzing filled my ears. "Charcoal? Blast, what have I done?"

Hot blood seeped into my shirt as I gathered my dog and lifted him, stumbling toward the door. I careened down the stairs toward the boardwalk and ran for the yellow boat.

"Beck! Rebecca!" I bellowed from the shore.

A lantern appeared on the far dock.

"Who is it?" called a voice across the water.

"I need Mama! *Please!*"

Oars splashed in the water as I sank to my knees, cradling my dog. "Hold on, little brother, hold on," I crooned, hot tears splashing his fur. "Don't you dare leave me. Hold on."

I glanced up, but the boat was impossibly far away.

"Hold on," I sobbed. "Please wait, I can't lose you too."

CHAPTER THIRTY-THREE

The yellow boat glided across the black water.

"*Hurry!*" I shouted.

"Matthew Sugiyama?"

"Beck, I need Mama, now!"

"Why?" Beck stopped rowing to crane her neck.

"Hurry! He's bleeding!"

Beck rowed faster. "Quickly now, ring the bell three times, then three times again."

I gaped at her.

What bell?

"On your right," she called, swinging the boat in an arc.

A rope hung from the post next to me. Shifting Charcoal's weight, I yanked the rope three times.

Clang, clang, clang.

"Again!"

I pulled three more times, my arm shaking.

"Come on!" She'd swung her boat parallel with the dock, ready to row back as soon as we were on board.

In my haste to clamber in, I nearly fell when the boat

rocked, but Beck grunted and pulled hard against the oars, knocking me backward into a seat. Charcoal lay heavy and hot in my arms as we skimmed across the inky water. On the island, windows lighted one by one.

The oars streaking through the water beat an ominous rhythm, but moved too slow. "A few moments more," she gasped.

I stared at the far dock, unable to speak.

Mama and Gunther waited on the dock, their faces set and serious. Before Mama had tied the boat, I'd handed Charcoal to Gunther. My arms shook as I hauled myself onto the dock, and I tripped, nearly falling backward into the boat.

"Steady," muttered Beck, pushing me forward.

My throat tight, I nodded my thanks and trotted after them.

Mama was packing Charcoal's shoulder with a green paste and shouting orders when I burst into the kitchen. I ran to the plank table. "What should I do?"

Mama glanced up and flinched. "Are you cut, too?"

When I shook my head, she jerked her chin toward the wall. "Go sit," she said. "Stay out of the way."

Perched on the edge of the stool, my heart thrummed as I craned my neck, but I couldn't observe much from my vantage.

Beck strode into the kitchen. "Will he make it?"

Mama muttered as she examined Charcoal. "What was he cut with?"

"A blade," I whispered.

"What?"

"A blade!"

Mama pursed her mouth. "Beck, heat the saline."

"Saline?" I asked, but no one answered me.

"What's saline?" I asked again.

Mama murmured something to Gunther, and he nodded.

He beckoned to me as he wiped his hands on a bloody towel. "Come, son."

I rose but didn't move. "I want to stay."

"You're doing more harm than good," Gunther said in a kind tone. "Come with me so they can work."

Gunther set two pints of ale on the table. "Have a drink."

The scent of hops nauseated me, and I shook my head. If I hadn't drunk so much earlier, none of this would have happened.

"Fine, more for me," he said. He took a long drink and set down his glass, wiping the table with a clean towel. "Saline is boiled seawater, diluted with purified water."

The chair leg screeched against the tile floor as I pulled it out to join him. "Why do they need saline?"

Gunther tugged at his beard. "To keep his heart from giving out."

My forehead hit the table with a *clunk,* and I sobbed until I could catch my breath. I looked up, wiping the snot and tears from my face with my sleeve.

Gunther eyed me. "You're a mess, son. Here."

I took the damp towel and wiped my face, but it came away red, and tears splashed down my cheeks again. "I'm sorry, I'm sorry." When the tears slowed, I hiccuped, wiping my face again with the soiled towel.

"Drink your ale," said Gunther.

Numb, I picked up the glass and took a slurp. It was cold and bitter; the sensation shocking my eyes dry. I gulped half of it.

Gunther nodded with approval. "What happened?"

My tears welled again, and Gunther sighed. "Little chap means a great deal to you, eh?"

I nodded, swallowing furiously.

"Where's the little miss?"

I lost it again, my body shaking with racking sobs.

"You'll need to stay here," said Gunther, pulling at his beard, "so I'll row you over at first light."

Would Charcoal make it to dawn?

Gunther cleared his throat. "I'll check their progress."

I rose, but Gunther motioned me back. "No lad, stay here."

I sank into my seat, hollow as memories of Charcoal as a pup sprang onto my mind's canvas. Every muffled sound from the kitchen made me jump to my feet, so to distract myself, I wandered around the room, examining their trinkets and treasures with little interest. After several circuits, I dropped into an upholstered chair near the fire and picked at the dried blood on my fingers.

What a mess I'd made.

With a glance at the door to the kitchen, I pulled out my sketchbook and wiped the smear of red staining the cover. I flipped through the pages, thumbing to the end.

Nothing.

Where were Akiko and Pritchard?

I cleared my throat, glancing at the kitchen door again and twirled a pencil in my fingers. Should I send a message to her? Perhaps it was better to wait until I knew more; she'd be heartbroken to learn of my mistake, and I didn't want to frighten her needlessly.

Besides, what if she was already frightened? Her parents had been revivalists, and she would recognize the customs and mannerisms if Pritchard had taken her into a ministry. Blast the man.

The light outside the window became tinged with gray as dawn approached.

My throat tightened, and I closed my eyes. Pritchard wasn't the cause of my troubles.

I was.

I'd hidden Akiko with Pritchard, I'd lost the flier, and I'd injured Charcoal.

Intent on escaping my guilt, I strode to the door, determined to demand an update. The polished wood was smooth against my palms, and I hesitated, remembering Gunther's words. If there was still hope for Charcoal, Mama didn't need me underfoot.

I returned to the table and finished my ale. Why couldn't I learn to reason things through like Ben or Talbot did?

My hand tightened around the empty glass, and I rolled it on its edge. What would Ben do in this situation? My nails were black with grime and dried blood, and as I stared at them, I knew.

Ben would wash his hands.

I stood to wash them in the kitchen, but hesitated again. Maybe Gunther hadn't come back yet because Charcoal had died. Perhaps they delayed as they discussed how to tell me.

My chest ached, and the worry, lack of sleep, and ale condensed into a thick, mental fog. To make coherent, *rational* plans, I needed a clear head. I stepped outside, the morning's chill chasing some of my fog away.

A thin vapor floated above the water, ghostly in the predawn light. From the end of the dock, I stared at the glassy water. The yellow boat bobbed gently, knocking against the dock with a rhythmic *thump-thump*.

As I dove in, the water broke across the crown of my head like a fractured peel from a boiled egg, the shock of cold evaporating the fog from my mind. Bubbles streamed from my nose, and I followed them to the surface. My head clear, I treaded water, observing the lights glimmering in the depot.

"I said I'd row you back at dawn," said Gunther. "No need to swim."

I turned. "Is—" I couldn't choke out the words.

"He's resting. Come."

I swam to the side of the dock, searching for a ladder.

"You'll have to swim ashore. We make a habit of not falling in."

Gunther's words couldn't dampen the joy swelling within me as I swam toward the house. Thick mud sucked at my clothes as I waded into the marshy grass at the water's edge, but mud was better than blood.

My heart was lighter as I followed Gunther to the inn. If Charcoal could pull through, I could do this—make changes, find Akiko, even nurse Charcoal back to health. We'd be together, and I'd even learn to cook.

When we stepped into the kitchen, the warm, steamy air made me shiver.

They'd covered Charcoal with a heavy quilt, but his eyes opened, and he licked my face as I bent over him.

I smiled and teared up again. "Thank you."

Mama frowned at me. "Sit. Let me examine you. Gunther, we need a towel and another quilt." Clucking her tongue, Mama removed my sodden coat and shirt. Gunther returned with a towel, which I wrapped around my waist before kicking off my muddy boots and dropping my trousers.

As I shuddered under Mama's attention, I kept my eyes locked on Charcoal.

Beck whisked my things away, and Mama dabbed at my face with a dampened rag.

Though I steeled myself, I flinched at her touch. "Matilda pulled a splinter."

"She's a good egg," Mama said. "What's wrong with your leg?"

I glanced down and winced. "It's been healing for months."

She snorted. "That's not how healing looks. Bring it here."

I lifted my leg, setting it on her lap.

She pursed her lips as she inspected it. "You've had several healers work on it."

"Yes, one drained it, and Freda patched me back up, but I keep re-injuring it."

Mama shook her head. "This isn't from injury. Your leg is necrotic. Until someone removes the dead skin, it will remain open and raw. It's prone to injury because you're *not* healing."

I frowned at my leg. "It's fine."

"We need to cut it."

I jumped to my feet, dropping my towel. Face flaming, I picked it up and backed away, trying to cover my nudity. "I'm fine; I don't need it cut off."

"I won't cut your leg *off*, silly boy." She chuckled. "The dead tissue needs to be cut away, or the rot will spread. Come, sit."

The memory of Eliot Tuckett slicing through my flesh made my heart thump against my chest as I shook my head. "No—I *can't*."

Mama rubbed her forehead. "Charcoal will need to rest for several days before you can move him. Why don't we bring your things and your daughter here, and I can attend to your leg while you wait."

Pain lanced through my heart at her words. If I agreed to let her heal my leg, how would I search for Akiko? "Are you sure it won't heal on its own?"

Mama folded her arms.

My eyes tightened. "Is there any other way other than cutting it?"

This time, she nodded, her eyes thoughtful. "I could pack and bind it. It would take an extra day, but it might work."

Without the flier, I couldn't search quickly, and if my leg continued to deteriorate, it would further hamper my search. Allowing my leg to heal while I waited for Charcoal to recover seemed like a prudent, Ben-type of thing to do. I'd use the time to draw up a plan.

"Thank you, Mama," I said, wrapping my arms around her.

"You've lost your towel again," she said, chuckling as she patted my arm.

CHAPTER THIRTY-FOUR

The moment Olen spotted me, he laughed. "Matthew, you pop up everywhere I am. Tell me your head aches as badly as mine."

I gritted my teeth; the last thing I wanted to do was chat with him. "Hullo, Olen. No, I didn't have the pleasure of waking with a headache."

"So I see," he said, eyeing my borrowed clothing.

"You coming to the island?" Gunther asked Olen.

Olen glanced at him, then back at me. "I planned to... Matilda advised me to meet Mama. Matthew, are you okay?"

I wasn't, but I nodded anyway. "I'm collecting my things, then returning to the island."

Olen seemed happy with my answer and clapped me on the shoulder before climbing into the boat. "See you soon."

Gunther picked up the oars. "Ring the bell once when you get back."

Waves of exhaustion swept over me as I limped up the boardwalk, the worry and lack of sleep dragging at me.

Gulls wheeled and screeched in the blue morning sky as they picked mussels from the pilings.

As I reached for the knob, it turned, and the door opened.

Akiko?

Talbot gaped at me, white-faced. "Matthew?"

"Talbot." I pushed past him, deflated.

"You weren't here. Nothing was here but that," he said, pointing at the bloodstained floor.

I swayed and willed my eyes to stay dry. "It's been a long night."

"Where were you? Did you move dwellings?"

"Move dwellings?" I glanced around the empty room. My bags were gone. I trotted into the bedroom, but it was empty, too. "Blast and blast!" I slumped against the wall, sliding to the floor. Without my art supplies... I was too tired for this.

Talbot's eyes flickered. "What happened?"

I sighed. "I sensed someone was here last night, but accidentally struck Charcoal with my sword."

My sword.

I sprang to my feet and scanned the room. "They took it *too!*"

"Took what? That's Charcoal's blood?"

I nodded tiredly.

"Thanks be," Talbot murmured.

I glared at him.

"Things are replaceable," said Talbot.

I named every pigment I'd ever used twice before answering. "It would be nice if they didn't force me to do so every few days."

Talbot nodded. "Maybe you should keep better track of your things."

I closed my eyes, trying to remember why I liked my cousin. "I'm going," I said, limping toward the door.

Talbot followed me. "Where?"

I hopped down the stairs, keeping as little weight on my bad leg as possible. "The island. I need sleep."

Talbot watched me ring the bell and waited with me as Beck rowed the yellow boat across the water.

Her eyes widened as her gaze flicked from me to him. "Are you twins?"

I grunted, clambering into the boat.

She recovered quickly, a speculative expression on her face as she eyed Talbot. "You coming, gorgeous?"

Talbot grinned. "Lovely lady, I believe I will."

I rolled my eyes but moved over, my mind drifting. I could replace my art supplies at the warehouse, but I suspected my sword and painting were gone for good this time.

Someone *had* been in, or near, the dwelling, after all. If someone had targeted me, had they also taken Akiko? At least the island offered a modicum of security. "Any strangers arrive today?" I asked.

Beck raised her eyebrow. "We run an inn."

Another wave of exhaustion threatened to swamp me, and I slumped in my seat. Let them stab me in my sleep—I was too tired to care. All I wanted now was a pillowy bed, but when I groaned in anticipation, Talbot's head whipped around.

"What's wrong?"

I scowled. "I. Need. Sleep."

He blinked and turned back to Beck, resuming their flirtation like I hadn't spoken. Upon reaching the island, I limped to the inn without a word to either of them.

Mama opened the door. "Oh, good, you're back. Gunther's taken Charcoal to your room. He's weak, but I think he'll pull through."

My throat thickened with gratitude. "Which way?"

She gripped my shoulder. "Not so fast. We need to pack your leg."

"Now?"

She tugged on my arm. "Come on."

I followed her into the kitchen and dropped onto the bench.

Mama gazed out the window as she washed her hands. "On the table this time."

I complied, eyeing the cloth-covered jar in her hand. "Will it sting?"

She smirked. "No, but it may tickle. First, we'll clean out the wound." Mama dabbed at my leg with a warm towel smelling of mint until she'd wiped the grime away. "Squeamish?"

"No, why?" I asked sharply.

She pulled the ribbon from the jar, removing the cloth. "Hold still."

Disbelief and horror crawled up my spine as she sprinkled maggots onto my leg. "Mama!"

"Hold still," she repeated, continuing to pour maggots. They squirmed over each other, their pink-tan bodies glistening.

My stomach lurched, and I gagged as I watched them writhe into my wound.

Mama tapped my leg as though testing its soundness. "Good. Now, we'll bind you and let them have at it."

My teeth chattered. "You're leaving them on me?"

She nodded. "Hungry buggers. They'll eat away the dead flesh, and when they're done, we'll pack your wound with a poultice and let you get on with the healing."

I turned my head away and closed my eyes while she wrapped my leg, trying not to picture them eating me alive. My nerves shrieked, and I fought the urge to slap my leg, to smash them.

Mama clucked her tongue. "Let's get you upstairs to bed."

Like I could sleep now.

My fists spasmed as I followed her upstairs to a bedroom facing the sea's empty expanse.

Charcoal lay on a cot, covered by a quilt.

I sat on the bed, watching the quilt rise and fall.

Hold on, little one.

Mama peeled back his upper lip to study his gums. "He's doing well. Do you want breakfast?"

I shook my head. "Just sleep."

She patted my shoulder. "Come down when you're ready, and we'll launder your clothes." She glanced around. "Is Beck bringing your things?"

"No, they walked away while I wasn't there."

Mama sighed. "Again? You'll have to start over. Where's Akiko?"

"I left her with my old mentor." It was true and kept me from having to explain how I'd lost her again, too.

Mama brushed my cheek. "Rest now and leave your leg be." She left, murmuring to someone outside my door.

The door opened, and Talbot and Olen entered, twin expressions of concern on their faces. To keep from disturbing Charcoal, I reined in my temper. "Fellows."

Talbot sat on the chair, crossing his arms. Olen stayed near the door, bouncing on the balls of his feet.

They obviously wanted something. "What?"

Olen eyed me. "Did Mama put maggots on your leg?"

I nodded.

Olen's smile flashed. "Sick. Can you feel them biting?"

"For pity's sake," said Talbot. He shot me a pointed look. "We should talk."

Olen crossed the room to peer at Charcoal. "He seems okay."

"Do you need to be here?" asked Talbot.

Olen snickered. "Who put you in charge?"

I flopped backward, flinging my arm over my eyes. "Why are you here? Either of you?"

"We need to make a plan," said Talbot.

"I have a plan," replied Olen.

I lifted my head. "Plan for what?"

"For what to do next," they said in unison.

The tension in the room escalated as the silence lengthened. They glared at each other, neither willing to back down.

All I wanted was for them to leave. "Listen, I appreciate—"

"Who is this person?" interrupted Talbot, his eyes locked on Olen.

"His friend," said Olen, standing.

"You're not a close friend." Talbot rose too. "You mistook me for Matthew downstairs."

Olen stepped closer. "Honest mistake. Who are *you*?"

"His cousin." Talbot's voice dripped with scorn.

"Quit it," I said.

Olen's voice deepened. "Cousin from where?"

"Friend from where?" Talbot countered.

"Aurora." Olen's teeth flashed.

Talbot snorted. "Avalon Society. I should have guessed."

Olen's energy rose. "Based on what?"

Talbot stilled. "Arrogance."

"Excuse me?" Olen stepped closer to Talbot.

In response, Talbot stepped toward Olen. "You society cowards think you're the best."

"We are the best," said Olen reflexively. He raised his chin. "Cowards?"

Talbot's smile thinned. "You wall yourselves from the world."

"The walls are to keep out the rabble," said Olen in a low voice.

"Afraid?" Talbot taunted.

Violence shimmered in the air. This could get out of hand.

"Enough," I said.

They ignored me, glaring at each other, nearly nose to nose.

I dragged myself off the bed and limped between them. Placing a hand on each of their chests, I pushed them away from each other. "I appreciate your concern. I do. But I'm too tired to deal with this, with you, with your plans. Please let me sleep."

I peered from Talbot to Olen. "Go."

The men moved toward the door, still holding eye contact, their movements stiff and unnatural. I snickered at the absurd picture they made; two roosters ready to jump and squawk. Two sets of narrowed eyes turned to me as I flopped onto the bed.

CHAPTER THIRTY-FIVE

O len scowled. "What a pile of horseshit."

Olen and Talbot had access to resources I couldn't tap into and were my best chance of finding where Pritchard had taken Akiko. But to make an effective plan, I needed them to work together. I set my mug down, pulling out a chair. "You two become friends yet?"

They glared at each other across the table without answering me. A fire crackled in the hearth, perfuming the common room with maple and applewood.

Talbot leaned back and folded his arms. "How's the dog?"

"How's *Charcoal*?" asked Olen, raising his eyebrow at Talbot.

Rain pelted the window. The storm's energetic gusts had roused me from a restless torpor. Though it wasn't yet noon, the dark skies outside gave the impression of evening.

"He's weak." I turned the mug in my hands and watched raindrops wiggle across the glass. Now that I'd lost the flier, I'd need help to find Akiko, but assuming I could trust them, how could I encourage their cooperation?

Talbot leaned forward and patted my shoulder. "You should eat. Want me to call Mama?"

Olen narrowed his eyes and opened his mouth, then glanced at me and shut it again.

I watched a muscle flicker in his jaw. "What?"

Olen cleared his throat. "Once you can move Charcoal, I can offer the services of a skilled healer."

I gulped my tea, burning my tongue. The tea sloshed over the rim as I set the mug down too fast, splashing my fingers. There was no napkin or towel, so I wiped the table with my sleeve.

Talbot's lips curved. "Matthew may not be society material."

"Shows what you know," retorted Olen.

"Hey, easy," I said. "There's an animal healer in Aurora?"

Talbot frowned, leaning forward.

I held up my hand to prevent Talbot's argument and focused on Olen. If his healer could help Charcoal, I wanted to hear about it. Besides, it couldn't hurt to curry favor within the Avalon Society.

Olen grinned. "What don't we have access to? Our administrator brought in an animal healer to tend to his prized sheep. I'm sure he'd work with Charcoal too if I asked."

Now the muscle in Talbot's jaw flickered.

Would Aurora attach strings to Charcoal's recovery? "Tell me about Aurora," I said.

Olen beamed. "It's spectacular. I took the commission because it was so near Aya, but also because it's fantastic."

"How did you hear about them?" I took a tentative sip of my tea, but the burned spot on my tongue dulled the raspberry flavor.

Olen brushed his hand over his head. "The society? My

master referred to them as a prize I could win if I was diligent in my studies."

"What did you specialize in?" asked Talbot.

Olen's gaze settled on him. "The economic systems from *Before*."

Money was the concept from *Before* I most struggled to understand. "Systems? Didn't they trade money for supplies?"

Olen brightened, eager to discuss it. "Yes, during basic transactions. For small purchases, they carried money, but also used electronic money to purchase goods and services."

My mind went blank. "Electronic money?"

Olen bounced to his feet, nodding. "More hot water?"

I shook my head but eyed Talbot's empty mug. Olen took my hint and held out his hand.

Still, Talbot hesitated before handing it to Olen. "Thanks."

"Imagine you had five pieces of money," said Olen, as he poured from the kettle by the fire. "You could carry it with you easily. But what if you had five hundred or five thousand pieces? Large quantities of physical cash were hard to carry and easy to steal."

I shook my head. "I don't understand theft."

Olen laughed. "So I've heard." He handed the mug to Talbot. "They've stolen your bags twice?"

Frustrated, I set my mug down with a *thunk*. "Yes, but why? My things are valuable to me alone, and the librarians at the warehouse can replace most of it."

Talbot stroked his jaw. "Perhaps they targeted your bags *because* they belong to you."

Olen nodded. "Exactly, to thwart or perplex you. You wouldn't have to worry about theft or resupplying if you'd join us."

"The society offered you membership?" asked Talbot, appearing surprised.

"Yes, several times apparently," said Olen.

Talbot scowled at him.

I shrugged, not wanting to spark another argument. I'd ask Olen more about Aurora later when we were alone. Why would someone target *me*? I'd recently arrived and knew almost no one. Only Talbot had known I planned to visit the depot, and in the past, Talbot *had* tried to prevent me from learning about my family. Could our reconciliation be false?

My gaze lingered on my cousin, and Talbot's eyes widened. He rocked his head as if reading my suspicions. Olen smirked as Talbot squirmed, and I turned my attention to him. Could I trust Olen? Though I appreciated his offer to help Charcoal, he'd befriended Akiko first...

These questions left me restless, and I sighed. "The more I live in the world, the less I understand it."

Talbot's eyes crinkled. "A common sentiment."

"Not for me. I believe in designing your reality," said Olen.

Talbot glared at Olen. "Cloistering yourself from the world is not living. Don't you feel imprisoned behind your gates?"

Olen smirked. "Imprisoned? I'm here, aren't I? Come to think of it... so are you."

Talbot's eyebrows raised. "Oh?"

Olen chuckled and leaned back. "They warned us all about *Preacher* Talbot. I'm a little surprised at you, Matthew," said Olen, without taking his eyes from Talbot.

"Me? Why?" Adrenaline spiked through me as my stomach twisted.

The smile dropped from Olen's voice. "You're the reason we held Talbot."

My nerves jangled. Olen could only know about Talbot if the society had some way to communicate quickly between themselves.

"A simple misunderstanding," said Talbot.

I pounced on his explanation, grateful for his quick thinking. "Yes, I believed Talbot led a group of religious extremists, but I was mistaken."

"Understandable," said Olen. "Especially since the violent people accompanied minstrels preaching the old Christian religion."

"I am a storyteller," said Talbot. "I entertain with a variety of stories."

Olen's smile was all teeth. "Care to explain why some of your stories are biblical?"

My pulse jumped. As a scholar, Olen would have examined the religious texts from *Before* as a part of his studies.

Talbot remained relaxed, unruffled. "One of Cedrick Jacobson's stories is also biblical."

It was Olen's turn to appear startled. "You know Cedrick?"

Score one for Talbot. "Who's Cedrick?"

"A minstrel I've swapped songs and stories with." Talbot glanced at me. "We learn stories from listening to each other. No one is born with every story or song in their head."

"You're truly a minstrel?" asked Olen, sounding uncertain.

Talbot rose. "Excuse me."

We watched him leave the room, then shrugged at each other.

Olen gnawed on his lip. "Is he really your cousin? I mean, you look alike, but..."

I nodded.

Olen swallowed. "And that's why he came for you? He wasn't directing anyone to attack you?"

I shook my head. "He tried to protect me."

Olen deflated, rubbing his hand over his head.

Talbot returned with a guitar in hand. He tuned it, then nodded to both of us. He strummed it softly, the lush chords filling the room with music. Talbot's voice, a sonorous tenor, soared, filled with emotion.

> Who is this? And what is here?
> And in the lighted palace near
> Died the sound of royal cheer;
> And they crossed themselves for fear,
> All the Knights at Camelot;
> But Lancelot mused a little space
> He said, "She has a lovely face;
> God in his mercy lend her grace,
> The Lady of Shalott."

When he finished, I longed for him to continue—longed for any kind of escape or distraction—and clapped. "Tennyson! I loved his poetry as a boy."

Talbot set the guitar on the table. "I judged *The Lady of Shalott* appropriate, considering the audience."

Olen rubbed his jaw. "Clever. Well done, Minstrel."

Perhaps Talbot's charm *would* work on Olen. If I could further ease the tension between them, could I enlist them both to help me find Akiko? Before I could ask, a gust of wind rattled the window, and I jumped. When Olen raised his eyebrow in question, I rubbed my arms. "I'm a little unsettled."

Olen patted my shoulder. "Relax. Crossing the water in a gale like this would be suicidal."

Talbot strummed his guitar with a light hand. "You're safe enough for now, cousin."

They were right. Not only could no one cross to the island, there was no way for me to reach the mainland to resume my search. I stared out the rain-streaked windows, hoping Akiko was safe and out of the storm.

Olen and Talbot continued to snipe and pick at each other,

but thankfully, their posturing had assumed a friendly tone. Behind them, a door opened silently, and Beck stepped into the room.

Talbot set his guitar down, a speculative look on his face. "We are the only guests."

Olen sighed. "Just us? So, there's only one fair maiden for three single men. Shall we arm wrestle for her?"

My gaze flicked to Beck, and she winked at me, holding a finger to her lips. I grinned. "She's a beauty, but I'm not wrestling either of you."

Talbot smirked. "*You* may have to resort to brute strength, Olen Ash, but I use charm and talent to win over a lady."

"You can both go fly a kite," said Beck.

I chuckled as identical guilty expressions crossed their faces, but they each recovered quickly.

"My lady," said Talbot.

"I'll fly anything you'd like," said Olen, his brows wiggling.

Beck tugged on her lip. "I like the arm-wrestling idea."

Olen and Talbot stared at each other.

"Sure," said Olen, rolling up his sleeve. "Thanks for telling us Beck was here, Matthew."

I chuckled. "All for one."

"Move," Beck said to Talbot, kicking his chair leg.

Talbot scrambled to his feet, pulling the chair out for her, and Beck sat down, rolling her sleeve up. "What do I get if I win?"

Olen gaped at her while Talbot chuckled and folded his arms.

Beck raised her gaze to Talbot. "Don't get too smug, pretty boy. You're next," she said, her arm rippling with muscle.

CHAPTER THIRTY-SIX

Mama's voice boomed through the common room. "Don't you dare scratch that!"

Charcoal and I both froze. We hadn't finished our noon meal, a rich, garlic-laden vegetable stew, but the itch in my leg had become maddening.

"The two of you." Mama laughed. "You're peas in a pod."

Charcoal shook, looking smug, and I grinned. "He's the brains."

"I know." She bent over Charcoal and evaluated his shoulder. "Your leg itches too?"

I hoisted my heel onto the bench, nodding. I'd been dying to unwrap the bandages and examine what the maggots had done. For the last three nights, I'd woken from nightmares about Akiko and then lay awake in the dark, imagining I could hear the larvae, their tiny fangs squeaking as they chewed my flesh.

Mama squeezed my calf near the wound. "There's more seepage than I would have liked."

My gut clenched. If this didn't work and my leg didn't heal, how would I search for Akiko? Gunther had forecast the storm would blow itself out soon, and I wanted to resume my search as soon as I could. With luck, the storm had forced Pritchard to hole up too, so he may not have gotten much of a start on me. "It's not normal?"

Mama wiped her hands on a towel. "Some is. Maggots secrete an enzyme to help break down the dead tissue. This much seepage shows your wound was worse than we knew."

"They never stop wriggling." I shuddered.

Mama laughed. "They're growing larger. Let's remove them and evaluate their progress."

Queasy, I followed her into the kitchen and waited for her to toss a coarsely woven linen over the table.

When I swung my leg up, she unwrapped the leg and clucked her tongue twice. "Oh."

My head whipped around as my chest tightened. "Is something wrong?" Even if this didn't work, I would resume my search tomorrow.

Mama smiled. "They've finished. Let me get a bowl and tweezers. They have gotten so big Gunther can use them for bait."

Shudders ran up my spine.

Talbot stuck his head into the kitchen. "Oh, you're busy."

I waved him in. "I need a distraction."

Talbot glanced at my leg, grimacing. "It's worse."

I searched his face. "My leg?"

Talbot closed his eyes. "The maggots."

"Quit talking about me, Minstrel," said Olen, following Beck into the kitchen.

Unlike Olen, Beck avoided looking at my leg. "Mama, I'm rowing over to get supplies. Do you have a list for me?"

Mama glanced at us. "How long are you all staying?"

Talbot shrugged, but Olen said, "I'm heading out with

Beck, but I'll be back if I can convince Aurora's animal healer to evaluate Charcoal."

I winced as Mama dug into the mass of maggots. "I need to get back to the mainland to sort out a few things, but I'd rather return here than stay in Potter's cottage for now, if you have room for me."

Mama nodded. "If Beck makes a second crossing later today, you can go, but bring Akiko back, too. Becks, we'll need more root vegetables. Potatoes, beets, carrots—whatever you can find."

"Sure. Anything else?"

Mama plucked another maggot from my leg. "Artist, I'll make you an apple pie if you sit still."

I stopped squirming. "Deal."

Talbot laughed and looked at Beck. "Need help?"

She patted his cheek. "I'm a big girl."

I tried to keep still as Mama finished with my leg, but it tickled, and my nervous giggles elicited chuckles from the others.

Mama dropped the last maggot into the bowl with a flourish. "Done. Get you gone girl, or we'll be eating bass with a side of bass for dinner."

Beck saluted. "Yes, Mama."

Mama covered the bowl with a towel and patted Talbot's shoulder. "Make sure he doesn't move. I'll take these to Gunther and come back with a poultice."

As soon as the door closed behind Mama, Olen helped Beck shrug on her waterproof coat and waved at us as he followed her out the door. Talbot watched them through the window, his gaze wistful.

Maggot free, my mood improved. "Can't win them all."

Talbot shrugged. "First time for everything."

I stared at him. "This can't be the first time a lady has chosen a different dancing partner."

Talbot raised his eyebrow. "Dancing partner?"

My cheeks flushed, and I flipped through the blank pages in my sketchbook, searching for a message from Akiko.

Nothing.

Pritchard must have confiscated her pad and pencil. I couldn't let myself consider the darker alternatives swirling across my mind's canvas.

Talbot crossed his arms. "Listen, I've had an idea."

"Oh?" My wound itched as if Mama had missed a maggot, so I bent forward to inspect it.

"If Mama releases you, we should attend the revival."

My head snapped up. "Here? A revival in Toronto Depot?"

Talbot's eyebrow lifted. "Yes, tomorrow morning. Keep your voice down."

Charcoal scratched at his bandages, groaning.

"Charcoal, quit." I chewed on my lip. "What would I do at a revival?"

He frowned. "You'd *do* nothing."

I peered into my wound again. "Then why go?"

"Because I need to go for information and to be seen. Your interest would solidify my cover, since they're hoping you will join us. They're aware you're an artist, but not who you are, so we could hide you in plain sight."

I stared at Talbot. "Why would they believe I'd be open to joining them?"

"A ministry is better than the Avalon Society."

I blinked. "Why?"

Talbot peered at me. "Are you joking? I can't tell if you're joking."

Akiko eventually needed a stable home. She had already

survived one set of traveling, neglectful parents, and I didn't want to be another. "I've considered their offers."

He sighed. "If you want to settle, pick a community who *needs* your help. Don't be another conquest for them."

"Why don't you like the Avalon Society?"

"I've seen what happens to the people they reject," Talbot said.

His words were like a cold-water dousing. "Is that where they come from?"

"Who?"

Memories of the battle in Wakefield flashed before my eyes. "The revivalists."

Talbot shrugged. "Sometimes. We attract all kinds: discarded society hopefuls, people uninterested in contributing their skills or labor—people who don't *fit*."

Cara's face appeared on my mind's canvas. "And true believers."

He cleared his throat. "A few, but they are useful. Their passion makes believers of many."

Passion leading to purpose. Cara had tried to connect me to her truth. It hadn't worked, but I understood how a genuine believer could inspire individuals searching for a place in the world.

Talbot crossed the kitchen. "Also, of course, if Pritchard is working with Reverend Carter, there's a chance Akiko will be at the revival meeting."

"What?" I gaped at him. "You should have started with that."

"I'd have thought it was obvious."

Perhaps he was right. My mind was reeling now. "Talbot, how are preachers recruited?"

He filled a glass at the sink. "I apprenticed with Gabriel, a minstrel, much the same as anyone else... other than artists, I suppose."

I watched sunlight refract through his glass, sending rainbow reflections skittering across the table and up the wall until a cloud passed over the sun. "Were you on the road during your apprenticeship? Minstrels don't stay in one place long unless they're part of the Avalon Society."

Talbot tapped the side of his nose.

My eyes widened. "You apprenticed in the Avalon Society?"

He nodded.

"Do you dislike them because they didn't offer you a position?"

Talbot's laugh sounded like a bark. "No, they did."

I knit my brows, studying his face. "Why didn't you accept?"

His lips twitched. "It wasn't the plan—"

Olen burst into the kitchen, smelling of rain. "Beck said the water is still too rough for a passenger, so I have to go on the next trip with you, maggot man. What are we talking about?"

Talbot raised an eyebrow. "I've talked Matthew into attending a revival with me."

Olen snorted as he shrugged off his dripping raincoat. "Why?"

Before I could stop him, Talbot said, "In case they're holding Akiko."

Olen stared at me. "Holding? You said you'd left her with someone on purpose."

"I did, but he works for Reverend Carter." I squirmed. "We were searching for them, but then the storm hit."

Mama's return to the kitchen prevented Olen from asking follow-up questions. "I have what I need to make the poultice," she said, as she shook a fistful of wet herbs. "After we've dressed your leg, we'll let it set a spell, and then you can ring the bell for Beck."

I nodded, but she'd already turned toward Olen. "Mind yourself, lad. We had a clear view of the dock from the herb garden and Gunther will unzip you from crotch to neck with my blessing if you mess with our girl. *But,* if this is more than a passing fancy, he's waiting in the boathouse for a private word."

Olen's tanned face paled, and he seemed to waver before squaring his shoulders and shrugging his wet coat back on. "It's early days, but I'm drawn to Beck in a way I've never experienced."

He turned to leave but stopped and leaned toward me, speaking in a low voice. "The bond between father and daughter is precious and to be protected, no matter the cost. I'll help in any way I can."

CHAPTER THIRTY-SEVEN

By design, Talbot and I arrived at the revival between the shows, with plenty of time to take stock of the situation. I had spotted no children in the crowd, dashing my hopes that Akiko was there. After a rousing show filled with tales, songs, and an impassioned speech, which left the crowd breathless and tearful, they released us to socialize.

Talbot had left me here at the edge of a revival tent as bait, hoping my presence would attract a big fish, but no one appeared to take any interest or notice in me. The waiting left me twitchy and restless, so when a voice I didn't recognize addressed me, I flinched and shaded my eyes, squinting at the back-lit silhouette.

"Master Sugiyama?"

"Yes?"

"I'm honored to meet you, sir! I've heard so much about Popham Abbey."

My eyes watered. "Have you? Can you sit down?"

A waft of perfumed soap covered me as a chubby boy sat next to me, his freckled face shining. He was unlikely to know much, but no one else had approached, and I wanted informa-tion. "Have we met?"

"No, but I love listening to stories about Popham. I'm from Erie Abbey."

Stories about Popham?

I blinked. "I visited Erie Abbey."

The boy's eyes shone. "You did?"

"When did you leave?"

He sighed. "Soon after the snows melted. We didn't all leave together, though."

My breathing shallowed. Answers, *finally*. "Oh?"

The boy shook his head. "No, only twelve of us left with Master Hooper."

I raked through my memory but couldn't place the name. "You didn't want to graduate?"

He hung his head. "I guess it would be hard for you to understand because you went to Popham."

Any tidbit of information could be useful, so I took a deep breath and willed myself to be patient. "You have me at a loss. You are?"

"Oh! Begging your pardon, Master Sugiyama. I'm Dennis Filmer of Erie Abbey. Wait, can I still claim to be from an abbey?"

I raised my eyebrow.

Filmer swallowed. "I suppose I'm Dennis Filmer of Welland Island now. Or... I will be once they've finished building the seminary."

"Well met, Dennis Filmer of—the world."

"Well met, Master Sugiyama, and please remember me on your travels."

My lips twitched. "I wasn't planning on leaving yet."

Filmer thumped his fist into his forehead. "What a dolt I am. I didn't mean to imply otherwise."

This could go on all day. "It's fine. Why did you leave with Master Hoobler?"

"Hooper." Filmer squirmed. "Well, graduation was *so* far off..."

I waited.

His words tumbled over each other. "I'm fourteen, so the idea of restoring paintings for another four to six years was too much. I want to see more of the world!"

"Yes, I see." I scanned the crowd milling around the striped tents but didn't spot Talbot.

Filmer's head bobbed. "You've been to Erie Abbey, so you know. It's in the middle of nowhere. No one visits and living there is deadly dull. I don't know why the rest of them stayed."

The rest of them? "How many students stayed behind?"

"About sixty... plus the masters. I wonder if they even noticed our leaving."

With that, my hopes fell, and I scanned the crowd again. The boy didn't even know they'd abandoned Erie Abbey. "What's Master Hooper like? Is he here?"

Filmer shrugged. "He's like... any master and only talks about perspective and shadows. 'Get it right, Filmer! You *must* anchor your art!' Like nothing else matters."

I remembered those admonishments too well. "What are your plans now?"

Filmer brightened. "We're illustrating the war."

The skin on my neck prickled. "The war?"

He nodded. "Are you helping too? Isn't it exciting? Our mural space is enormous!"

What did he mean by *war*? "I've only assisted on one mural but found it difficult to work on my tiny portion of the whole." I smiled to encourage him to keep talking. "It helps when someone directs the illustration."

"That's what Master Hooper said! Master Pritchard would

have orchestrated the effort, but Reverend Carter sent him on an errand."

"You've met Carter?" I asked, trying to sound impressed.

Filmer frowned. "Not really. He spoke to us as a group."

"How many will work on your mural?"

"We're hoping for forty. They've gridded out the wall into four hundred squares, so forty of us would mean we'd each be responsible for ten. I'm nervous!"

Forty artists. "You'll be fine, Dennis, as long as you don't forget to anchor your art."

He smiled, but leaned closer and lowered his voice. "I'm worried about having enough time."

Time?

I nodded like I understood. "It often comes down to time, doesn't it?"

Filmer glanced around before continuing. "I hope I'm fast enough to keep up with the story. I'm slower than the others."

"The story," I repeated.

He nodded. "We'll illustrate the mural in real-time as they tell the story. Do you think it's already written? Or will they make it up as we paint?"

My stomach twisted. "Whatever happens, I'm sure the finished mural will be marvelous."

He grinned. "I keep imagining what the seminary will be like with the murals done."

Murals. Plural.

Cold sweat ran down my spine.

His eyes shone. "If I do well enough, they may let me help with the cathedral. What about you, sir?"

I shrugged, reaching for a neutral response. "I don't know where I fit yet."

Filmer brightened. "You'll like the seminary, and we should

finish the compound before the feast. The food is great, and it's weird to live with women, but nice, too."

Could this be where Pritchard had taken Akiko? "Is it crowded?"

He shrugged. "When we first got to the island, we lived in tents while the masters sculpted the seminary, but after they finished the dormitories, lots of people moved in. The kids running through the halls are noisy, but anything is better than the dusty quiet of Erie Abbey."

Kids.

"Lots of kids?" I asked, trying to sound casual.

"Sure," he said, picking at a loose thread.

I needed to reengage the boy. "I'm eager to visit."

"Yes, it sounds marvelous," said Talbot.

Engrossed in our conversation, I hadn't noticed Talbot join us.

Filmer's gaze flicked between us until Talbot introduced himself. "Preacher Talbot, well met young man. You've met my cousin."

Filmer brightened. "Well met. Has anyone mentioned how similar you look?"

To Talbot's credit, he didn't scold the boy for his artlessness. "Yes, several have noticed."

Filmer leaned forward, his face eager. "Are you coming to the island too?"

"They've asked me to give Master Sugiyama a tour of Welland Island," said Talbot, nodding.

My pulse jumped. If Talbot had scored us an invitation to the island, I could search it for Akiko.

"Will you come to the opening feast?" Filmer asked me.

I stood. "Yes, you've helped convince me."

He scrambled to his feet, bowing. "Wonderful, thank you."

Talbot clapped my shoulder, his hand heavier than it should be. "We should go."

Eager to know what Talbot had learned, I stood. "Farewell Filmore."

"Remember me in your travels," Filmer said, blushing.

I scanned the people chattering in the festive atmosphere as we left. The tents were a merry touch, their crowning flags snapping in the wind. "These people seem so *normal*."

Talbot's forehead wrinkled. "Rudy was an aberration, not the rule. Listen, Akiko may be on the island."

We passed beneath metal towers dripping with wires, their arms twisted and scratching at the sky, then turned north.

"I think so too—Filmer mentioned kids on the island." My stomach fluttered with anticipation. "When is the ceremony?"

"Two days, which doesn't give us much time. Here," he said, handing me a sandwich wrapped in waxed linen.

To me, two days seemed an eternity, but I chose not to argue the point. "Thanks." I unwrapped the sandwich and spread the corners of the bread. Cheese. The spicy brown mustard oozed onto the corner of my mouth and I licked it, my tongue curling at the sour tang.

Talbot stopped to point at a crumbled brick building. "Look."

On the seventh floor, someone had crudely drawn a small symbol on the sash of the third window.

"A fish?" I mumbled through a mouthful of sandwich. I tore off a corner to toss to Charcoal, then remembered I'd left him on the island.

Talbot glanced at me. "Ichthys."

I finished my sandwich, wiping my mouth with my sleeve. "What does it mean?"

"Early Christians used it as a code."

"Early Christians? From *Before*?"

"Mm." Talbot glanced behind us.

I stared at the fish. "What was the code for?"

Talbot pointed. "See how it's composed of two overlapping arcs?"

I nodded, squinting through the midday light bouncing off the sea.

Talbot drew an imaginary arc with his toe. "Upon meeting a stranger, the Christian would draw one arc. If the stranger drew the other, completing the ichthys, they'd both know they were believers. Today, we use the symbol to alert followers where they can find fellow believers."

"How?"

"The symbol was on the seventh floor—"

"And on the third window," I interrupted.

Talbot smiled. "Yes. To find the symbol maker, travel seven blocks north and go to the third door."

I blinked. "That's it?"

Talbot laughed. "Sometimes a simple plan is the best kind. Come, let's ring the bell for Beck."

Although I checked my sketchbook frequently, its pages remained stubbornly blank, so I'd covered the page with vignettes of Akiko. I'd drawn her happy and laughing, running down corridors pell-mell with a group of children, quietly reading in a cozy nook, and eating a cookie—her face lit with a delighted smile. I hoped she was happy.

"Did I miss dinner?" Olen drawled.

I scanned him. "I didn't hear the bell but welcome back. Dinner is around seven after Gunther returns."

Olen glanced at my sketchbook. "What are you working on?"

I set down my pencil and stretched my hand. "Doodles. Will the healer work with Charcoal?"

"Yes, but he'd prefer to do it here, rather than in Aurora. He'll be here the day after tomorrow." Olen dropped into a chair and sighed. "You're happier. Did you find her?"

"We believe so, but we'll find out tomorrow," said Talbot, glancing up from his book.

Olen frowned. "Tomorrow? Why not today? How long has she been missing?"

Too long.

To diffuse the rising tension, I kept my expression neutral. "Nearly a week."

Talbot sighed. "Matthew wanted to storm in right away, but I counseled patience."

"Why?" asked Olen, sounding incredulous

Talbot returned to his book. "Because they've *invited us* to visit tomorrow, which will give us a way on and off the island."

We'd argued about it all day, but in my heart, I knew Talbot was right. Finding Akiko with no way to spirit her off the island would be almost as bad as not finding her.

"Oh." Olen pulled out a chair and sat backward, his chin on the backrest. "Where is she?"

The pencil rolled down the table as I closed my sketchbook. "She might be in the seminary on Welland Island."

"Seminary?" Olen whistled. "Bold move."

I straightened. "Why? What's a seminary?"

Olen retrieved my wayward pencil, handing it to me. "A type of college from *Before*. Students attended to become religious leaders—priests, ministers, or rabbis."

"Then Reverend Carter is no longer trying to hide what he's doing on Welland Island," said Talbot.

Talbot's quiet, reserved tone alarmed me more than his message.

"Is it safe to go?" asked Olen.

My gaze slid sideways. "Talbot doesn't think so."

Talbot snapped his book shut. "It would be safer if I went alone, and I'd raise less suspicion than you."

"Don't worry, I can be covert," I said, raising my chin.

They snorted in unison.

Ignoring the twinge in my leg, I stalked to the hearth and threw another log on the fire. Sparks exploded from the coals with a *snap-pop*, several landing on my pants. The scent of scorched wool rose around me, and I swore as I brushed embers from my legs. Even though it was summer, Gunther had asked us to maintain the fire to prevent the dampness from taking hold.

Talbot and Olen ignored me, continuing their conversation as I glared at them. It was *my* daughter they discussed, and I needed to be the one to rescue her—to atone for my parental failures.

My failures, not theirs.

My shoulders drooped as I returned to the table. They were only trying to help. "Talbot, if I'm not there, I'm afraid Akiko will hide from you. She knows you through stories, none of which are good."

Talbot's squirming somewhat lifted my mood.

Olen studied me. "What if I join you tomorrow?"

With the three of us, we stood a better chance of finding and sneaking Akiko away. "Can you get an invitation for Olen, too?" I asked Talbot.

He shrugged, nodding. "The celebration is partly to gain community support."

Olen grinned. "I can be community-minded."

"Regular community," said Talbot dryly. "Not society community."

Olen plucked at my tunic. "Then I'll ask if Gunther has more homespun to lend."

Moved by their support, I swallowed to clear the lump growing in my throat. "Be sure you understand what you're in for," I said, as I smoothed my palms across my borrowed trousers.

Olen arched his brow. "I can handle myself, Artist."

I rose, gathering my things. "You misunderstood me. Homespun *itches*."

CHAPTER THIRTY-EIGHT

The predawn sky brightened while I waited for my friends to finish eating. "Ready?" I asked, bouncing on the balls of my feet. Not even the twinge in my leg could dampen my mood.

Talbot peered at me over his mug.

"No," grumbled Olen through a mouthful of food, shooting me a dirty look.

I sat opposite Talbot, folding my arms. My nerves had woken me hours earlier, so I had bathed, groomed, and dressed before any in the household stirred. Since I knew Mama wouldn't appreciate me attempting to make breakfast, I stoked the fire in the stove and chopped kindling while I waited for everyone else to rouse.

Despite my efforts, no one else caught my eagerness. Olen continued to eat with mechanical motions, and Talbot sipped his tea serenely. My nerves jangled as I waited, my leg bouncing and twitching beneath the table. Wide awake, I was ready to face the Reverend Carter's congregation, find Akiko, and rescue her from them. After today, I'd never let the kid out of my sight again.

Charcoal slid his nose into my hands, and I stroked his soft ears.

Talbot's composure slid toward torpor as he stared blankly at the wall. I cleared my throat, and he shuddered, raising his mug. "Get any sleep?"

Pleased, I nodded. It had been my first night unplagued by nightmares. I stretched my left leg, accidentally kicking Olen.

His fork clattered against his plate. "Watch it."

"Sorry," I lied. Olen was a morning malcontent, and it wasn't worth arguing with him until he'd eaten himself awake.

"Bacon," said Mama, setting a fresh platter down. The scent teased my nose, but I wanted to leave.

Olen's hand shot out and grabbed three slices, stuffing all three into his mouth at once. Talbot shook his head, eyeing Olen.

While they were distracted, I whisked their plates to the sink before they could protest. "Thank you, Mama."

She patted my cheek. "Good luck today. I hope we'll have the little one here for dinner."

"Morning, all," said Beck, kissing the top of Olen's head. Ever since Olen's talk with Gunther, the intimacy between the couple had grown. Beck set a mug on the table and grabbed a piece of bacon. "I'll row you boys over as soon as Gunther finishes loading my boat."

◄━━━━━━━

THE PREDAWN CHILL INVADED MY BORROWED CLOTHES, and I shivered as Beck rowed us across the glassy bay, each pull of oars bringing me closer to Akiko.

Once on shore, Talbot led the way toward the revival with

his loose, swinging stride. Olen stalked next to him, muscled and watchful. I followed, watching their body language. Although they still didn't like each other, the tension between them had calmed. Perhaps they were near syncing, or maybe because they had agreed to work together. Either way, I was glad for the reprieve.

As we passed the dilapidated brick building, my eyes easily found the ichthys symbol. Who lived seven blocks north and three doors in? Maybe I'd take Akiko to find out.

Despite the early hour, the crowds thickened as we walked toward the tents. I flowed along with everyone, losing Talbot and Olen in the river of people. No matter—we were all going the same way.

The festival atmosphere heightened as we got closer to the striped tents. People handed out candies and honey pouches as we passed, and I caught a piece of taffy tossed by a blonde. She winked, and I laughed, my heart floating.

The sweet peppermint reminded me of the taffy I'd eaten with Akiko and Charcoal on the pier. I smiled at the memory, sun-drenched and gilded with joy. I caught and pocketed several more pieces of candy to share with Akiko later. The candy wouldn't buy her forgiveness, but perhaps it would smooth the path forward, and I'd be a much better father in the future.

The crowd streamed toward the left tent, and I craned my neck, searching for Talbot and Olen.

"Matthew!"

I rose onto my tiptoes, trying to locate the voice.

"Over here," said Olen, waving.

I made my way toward him, mumbling apologies as I pushed through the crowd. "There you are."

Talbot's smile flashed. "Come, we're allowed in the other tent." As he walked forward, the crowd parted easily for him, and we followed, nodding at the people who'd made space for us.

In the second tent, the mood was softer, and the people chatted quietly. In contrast, the people in the first tent continued their boisterous conversations, their manners and clothing florid. While I fit into the first tent in my borrowed homespun, here in the second, I was shabby and underdressed. Why hadn't I worn my own clothes? I tugged at the tunic and straightened my trousers, unused to feeling out of place. The rough cloth scratched, leaving my skin sensitive and unsettled.

"Don't worry about it," murmured Olen. "I borrowed Gunther's clothing, too."

"We don't fit."

"Not here, but we will with them," said Olen, lifting his chin at the people in the other tent.

"Quiet," said Talbot. "It's starting."

From somewhere, a violin played a single note. It quavered, thin and mournful.

Both crowds hushed.

The violin played again, accompanied this time by an oboe. As instrument after instrument joined, the music swelled. I named each instrument until the harmonies grew so lush I could no longer distinguish one from another. The crowd in our tent parted as the violinist walked through, followed by the other musicians. After they passed through our tent, silence descended as the crowd waited, calm and expectant.

"Peace be with you," boomed a voice.

"And also with you," the crowd replied in unison, their eyes shining.

"Welcome, friends. Come through, and let's raise our voices in praise!"

Olen's eyes remained watchful and alert, but Talbot's smile flashed as he shook hands with people.

Someone raised the lakeside tent flaps, and the crowd surged forward. The sun broke over the horizon as we stepped from the tent, and I raised my hand to cover my eyes. Once again, the music swelled as the sun's golden image reflected on the sea.

My eyes watered. "Theatrical."

Four flat boats bobbed at the lake's edge, and smiling people dressed in blue directed us to the first. A man stood on the boat's ramp, speaking with each group. He turned several groups away, but seeing Talbot, he stepped aside to let us pass. Soon after we boarded, our boat launched, steam hissing as it billowed from a pipe. I leaned on the railing and watched the crowds mill around the remaining three boats.

"Too many people or too few boats?" I asked, as the giant paddlewheel pushed us from the shore.

"The revival was open to all, but they only invited the chosen to visit the seminary," replied Talbot, his smile hard. "Blessings to us all."

My stomach fluttered, and I finally understood Talbot's hesitance in letting me come. If things went badly on the island, I'd be trapped with no means of escape. My tongue soured, but I pushed my worries aside. Done was done, and there was no sense in fretting about it now.

THE BOAT RIDE TOOK FAR LONGER THAN I'D EXPECTED. We'd steamed across the endless sea for hours before I'd caught my first glimpse of the island. The others marveled at its size, impressed by how it towered over the water's surface. Though it fooled the others, to me it had an artificial, stretched appearance and I studied its contours, scanning for evidence of art.

On one side of the boat, Olen held an audience of well-dressed women in thrall. As if on cue, they tittered at something he said, several leaning forward to touch him.

I snorted. "What a flirt."

Talbot followed my gaze. "He could probably teach you if you asked."

I pretended to misunderstand. "Teach me what?"

"How to talk to women."

I pulled on my tunic, its collar chafing against my neck. "I talk to women."

"Not well," Talbot said, a smile tugging at his lips.

Our boat docked with a gentle *thump*, and my stomach rumbled as I followed Talbot onto the pier. "Hope we don't have to wait long for the feast. I'm hungry now."

"No surprise, it's nearly noon," said Talbot, glancing at the sky.

The cliff wall stretched several hundred meters above us. Near the top, they'd merged the seminary's stone walls seamlessly into the natural rock. Brightly colored flags snapped along the pier as we walked toward the cliff.

The island's scope daunted me. It loomed above us larger than I'd expected, which would make finding Akiko more difficult. We were scheduled to return to the mainland this evening, so I wouldn't have much time to search.

They directed us through an arched doorway into the base of the cliff, the heavy door dark and forbidding. I hesitated, but there was nowhere else to go—my choices limited to remaining on the dock or stepping through the doorway.

"We're here with you," murmured Olen.

His support provided the push I needed, and swallowing, I stepped forward.

The low passageway ended at a curved staircase, ascending into the dark. Shudders rippled along my spine as I climbed. The curving stairs were only lit by flickering torchlight, giving the impression we were climbing the inside of a chimney. Without windows or any way to mark our progress, I became disoriented. They'd provided no handrail or wall to prevent a climber from falling through the center void, so I sidled toward the outer wall, away from the center drop. As I climbed, I dragged my fingertips over the rough stones, fighting my welling panic. I'd been so focused on reaching the island and finding Akiko, I hadn't considered how trapped I would feel. By the time we arrived on the flat landing, I gasped from the combination of fear and exertion.

"Through here," wheezed Olen, tugging on a door.

Light flooded over us, and I squinted as I followed the others into a sun-drenched courtyard.

"Out of their gloom and darkness, the eyes of the blind will see," Talbot murmured.

"What?"

"More theater," he replied, as the door slammed shut behind him.

I whirled, tugging at the door handle, but it didn't budge. "It's locked," I muttered, pulling harder.

"Doesn't matter," said Talbot.

We'd exited the staircase onto a wide terrace constructed of interlocking stones. A low wall ran along the edge of the terrace, framing the view. Far below, the boats on the pier appeared tiny as we watched the next arrival.

When the heavy door swung open again, another group of people passed through it, squinting and gasping. "What an entrance," said Talbot. "Come, let's explore."

We followed him across the terrace and through an arched doorway, stepping into something from a storybook.

The ceiling soared thirty meters above us, culminating in a pointed arch. Massive stone columns supported the roof and created a gallery-like passage. The light filtering through an enormous, colored-glass window at the far end flooded the room with warm red, purple, and pink hues. Long, wooden benches faced the window and an elevated stage.

Dwarfed by the grandeur and scope of the room, I swallowed, tugging on the neck of my tunic. As we walked farther into the immense room, sounds died, reminding me of the hush I'd found walking between giant trees in the forest. Awestruck, I turned a slow circle, drinking in the details. I'd never felt smaller and less significant whilst simultaneously so inspired.

"They've built a cathedral," said Olen, his voice subdued.

A giggle floated through the building.

I spun, my eyes raking across the rows of wooden benches. When a curly, blonde head popped up, my heart sank. A small, red-haired boy dashed around the nearest column, laughing as he followed the girl. He skipped around us and ran down the aisle toward the blonde child. To avoid him, I stepped to the side, into the path of another child.

She collided against me, but continued without stopping. "Sorry, sir!"

I stared at the back of her head, my mouth opening and closing without a sound. She'd nearly rounded the column at the end of the aisle before I found my voice. "Akiko?"

The dark head disappeared.

I held my breath, my heart thrumming.

Akiko's face popped back around the column, her eyes widening.

I bolted toward her, my arms wide as she squealed and raced toward me.

CHAPTER THIRTY-NINE

My arms tightened around Akiko as I fought to catch my breath. In the cathedral's chill, she burned like an ember.

"I missed you, but you're squishing me," she complained.

My eyes stung as I breathed in the scent of her hair. After a week of worry, here she was, whole, healthy—and squirming. With reluctance, I released her but kneeled to search her face. "How are you?"

Her eyes slid sideways toward Talbot, but brightened at seeing Olen. "I know you!"

He grinned at her. "I know you too."

I led her to a wooden bench, drinking in the sight of her. "Tell me everything. What's happened?"

Akiko scooted next to me, swinging her feet as she ticked her fingers. "I got to watch them art this ceiling, I made a friend, and I won a cookie-eating contest."

Her eyes were clear and tone carefree. Whatever Pritchard's faults, he hadn't mistreated or frightened her.

She peered around me. "Where's Charcoal?"

I hesitated. How much should I share? "He's keeping Mama company."

Akiko leaned closer, watching as Talbot and Olen moved toward the exterior doors, arguing about something.

"He is different," she said. "More blue than orange."

I surveyed them. "Talbot?"

She nodded. "Did you sync?"

"Yup." I tickled her until she giggled. "You seem happy."

She beamed. "It's fun here."

She doesn't know.

While I'd been chastising myself for putting her in danger, she'd spent our time apart making friends and having fun. Telling her now would only taint her happy memories, so I kept my tone light. "If I'd been here, I would have given you serious competition in the cookie-eating contest. I'm glad you've enjoyed yourself so much, but I've missed you. You haven't even sent me any notes."

Akiko pouted. "After sploring the marsh, we came straight here, and I'd left my sketchbook at Master Pritchard's. He gave me chalk and slate to practice lettering, though." She searched my face, her eyes clouding. "You got the message Master Pritchard sent you, right? They had an art emergency and needed him to help finish the island in time for today."

"Why else would I be here?" I lied.

"I'm glad you are." She hugged my hand, resting her cheek against it.

The lump in my throat tightened. "What type of cookies?"

Her face lit up. "All kinds. Hazelnut, maple, and apple. Some were crispy with nothing in them. I ate a lot of those."

I brushed the bangs back from her face. "Save any for me?"

She patted my flat belly. "You can have one today, if you're good."

My stomach rumbled, and she giggled before glancing at her friends. "I should go. I'm *it* right now."

Before I could manufacture a reason to keep her near me, she skipped down the gallery toward the other children. "Mouse?"

She turned, raising her palms.

"Meet me for lunch?"

She nodded and waved, trotting after her friends. They shrieked as they chased each other from the room.

Talbot slid into the bench in front of me. "What happened?"

I shrugged. "She didn't know I'd been searching for her."

"Did you tell her?" asked Olen. When I shook my head, he sighed, dropping onto the bench beside me.

"What now?" I asked. "Do we collect her and go?"

"Could we actually leave?" asked Olen.

Talbot nodded, frowning. "Good question. I've seen no exit other than the locked door we came through. Even if we made it to the water, we wouldn't have any way to leave the island."

My gut tightened. "We're trapped?"

"Temporarily," Talbot said, his tone mild.

Olen jabbed my shoulder. "They weren't expecting any of us to stay overnight, so we'll slip out when the crowd leaves. What's today's agenda?"

Talbot shrugged. "They scheduled opening remarks after the last boat docks, followed by a tour of the grounds. They're serving a banquet lunch on the terrace, and they scheduled several of us to perform this afternoon."

Although I wanted to flee with Akiko now, Olen was right. It would be safer to slip away with the crowds. "Then we'll wait until our scheduled departure time. Anything else will draw too much attention."

Throughout the day, I did my best to blend into the crowds

and avoid notice. The shabby clothes Olen and I had borrowed from Gunther were helpful; no one seemed interested in conversing with us. Even without my fine clothes, Pritchard or Dennis Filmer could recognize me, but luckily, I spotted neither of them.

Akiko's tray clattered on the table as she clambered onto the bench beside me at lunch. "Split pea and ham," she said happily.

I'd piled my plate with fruit, cured meats, and cheeses. "It's too warm today for soup, but I haven't had split pea since we were in Newfane," I said, tickling her.

She squirmed, giggling. "Me either."

I lowered my voice. "We're leaving this afternoon with everyone, all right?"

Her eyes remained fixed on her food as she gnawed on her bread. "Aren't we still waiting for Ben and the others?"

"Yes." I set my fork down, studying her.

Her spoon traced figure eights through her soup. "Then can I stay here while we wait?"

My stomach sank, and the cheese turned bitter in my mouth. "You don't want to come with me?"

Her eyes slid sideways. "It's fun here. I have friends and I'm caught up in lessons."

My throat tightened, and I moved a strawberry from my plate to hers as a tiny bribe. If Akiko threw a tantrum, she'd draw attention to us. "It's better if we leave together today, but perhaps we'll come back and visit."

Akiko nodded. "That's what I was afraid of."

Her sad expression tugged at my heart. "I've been staying on Hanlan's Island, so it won't be just us. Beck misses you too."

Akiko brightened. "Maybe I can learn to fly my *own* kite! I miss my stuff."

A second pang of guilt snaked through me as I shoved a forkful of salty, cured meat into my mouth. I'd tell her about our bags later.

We enjoyed the afternoon of songs and stories. Talbot opened with a silly song requiring our participation, and Akiko chortled as she sang along with the nonsense lyrics. I relaxed too, the sound of her laughing soothing the hurt, raw part of me.

None of the minstrel songs or stories struck me as religious, but I watched Olen to gauge his reactions. He appeared to enjoy the afternoon's entertainment as much as the rest of the crowd, but as the afternoon festivities ended, his eyes sharpened.

This was it.

Olen and I waited near the largest group, with Akiko between us. She'd wanted to find her friends to say goodbye, but I'd talked her out of it. While attempting to convey boredom, I scanned the area for Talbot.

"There he is," said Olen in a low voice, raising his hand.

Talbot nodded, working his way toward us.

"What now?" I asked, after he joined us.

As usual, Talbot appeared calm and unruffled. "The reverse of this morning. They'll send out four groups of thirty, with each boat leaving prior to the next group descending."

"Let's be in the first group," said Olen.

I nodded; the larger the crowd, the more chance we'd have of slipping away unnoticed.

We waited, and when the crowd drifted toward the door, we moved with them. I kept my head down, positioning myself behind Olen and distracting Akiko by encouraging her to describe the surrounding people in terms of shapes.

My nerves buzzed when someone finally opened the door

leading to the unending staircase. The crowd moved in unison toward the entrance, and I shuffled with them, gripping Akiko's hand.

We'd almost reached the threshold when someone called Talbot's name.

He tensed, then turned.

"Brother Talbot, we need a word," said the man.

Talbot remained outwardly calm. "Now? I must get back."

Pritchard rounded a corner, heading toward us.

My mouth dry, I dropped Akiko's hand to slide farther behind Olen. "It's Pritchard," I muttered.

Akiko twirled, spinning lightly as she danced toward the edge of the crowd.

"Akiko," I hissed.

Her arms extended, she continued to whirl.

The insistent man tried again. "Preacher Talbot, we'll get you onto a later boat."

My alarm spiked as Pritchard spotted Akiko. "Dear child, I believe Jenny is searching for you! She and the others are baking miniature spice cakes. Come with me." He held out his hand, his face kind.

Akiko took it, glancing back at me as he led her away.

A roar filled my ears. If I shouted for her, I'd draw Pritchard's attention.

Talbot squeezed my forearm. "I'll keep her safe," he said. "I swear."

The crowd continued toward the terrible stairs, pulling me with it.

Heart galloping, I fumbled to pull my small sketch pad and pencil from an inner pocket. "Give these to her when no one is around," I said, pressing them into Talbot's hand.

He nodded, turning away.

"We need to go," Olen muttered.

I hesitated. Maybe I should stay too. Talbot and I could come up with some excuse, couldn't we?

"We need to go *now*," Olen repeated, dragging me toward the door.

Pritchard turned and scanned the crowd, his eyes hard.

My heart screamed as I ducked through the doorway with Olen close behind. My sun-bright eyes were useless on the dim staircase, and I tripped and stumbled my way down it as I tried to manufacture a plausible reason to stay.

Too soon, we reached the bottom, where smiling people in matching uniforms directed us onto a boat.

Shattered, I boarded with the others. The boat lurched as the paddle engaged, the hiss of steam drowning the cheerful voices of those waving from the dock.

I stared at Welland Island as we steamed west, my mind unable to fathom my failure. Not only hadn't we rescued Akiko, but we'd also lost Talbot.

Olen's words grated in my ears. "Don't worry, Talbot will protect her."

I nodded, struggling to remain impassive. What had I done? How could I have left her behind?

Olen continued, his voice gentle, "We could do nothing else, so our quiet departure was the best way to keep them safe."

"I hope you're right." My voice sounded normal, betraying none of the emotion swirling within me. As I studied the island, my vision narrowed. It was a fortress, built to be unassailable, impenetrable by men, but what about an artist? Could I use my skills to tear down Carter's defenses?

"We'll regroup once we're at Mama's," Olen said, his tone encouraging.

I shook my head as my eyes raked over the cliffs. "No. First, I'm visiting the warehouse for supplies."

CHAPTER FORTY

Drowsy from the afternoon sun streaming through the open window, I doodled, my mind unfocused and far away. Despite nearly filling my new sketchbook with vignettes and drawings, I hadn't landed on a plan to rescue Akiko and Talbot.

"A little help, boys?" called Mama.

On the pier, Gunther clomped toward the inn while wheeling a cart. I followed Mama out of the inn to help unload Gunther's catch, Olen ambling after me.

Mama pointed to a stack of crates. "Head to tail, please." She inspected the cart, then turned to Gunther. "Hullo, love, good catch today. This may about get us through dinner."

Gunther grinned, his skin reddening beneath his beard.

My eyes widened as I filled a second crate with fish and passed it to Olen. "All this just for dinner?"

Mama, hands on hips, gestured toward the guest dock. "We have a boatload of people to feed, literally."

I glanced past them and was sprinting toward Beck's boat

before Olen could shout my name. Too late, I skidded on the wet wood, nearly running off the end.

Ben grabbed my arm in time and swung me around, laughing. "How about a hug before you bathe, my friend?" He thumped his hand on my back hard enough to jar my teeth before setting me down to help Josephine disembark.

I caught my breath—somehow, I'd forgotten the magnitude and impact of the scars distorting Josephine's face. I clutched her to me, burying my face in her hair. She smelled of sun and dust, and my heart swelled as she nestled into me.

"Howdy, handsome," said Bowman, slinging his arm around my shoulder. I hugged him and turned in time to watch Ben pull Earl onto the dock.

She smiled at me, and suddenly shy, I grinned back. Had she always been this lovely? My groin tightened, and instantly, I was back at Popham Abbey—eleven and humiliated by my mutinous body. My heart raced, and I swallowed several times, my mouth impossibly dry.

"Matthew."

"Earl." With luck, I sounded more casual than I felt.

Genevie dashed my hopes, snickering as she tossed bags from the boat. "One of you grinning fools want to help shift this stuff?"

Our stasis broke, and we grabbed luggage, everyone laughing and chattering as if we'd never parted. My smile nearly split my face as my friends lined up for introductions, but before I could start, Mama shooed us out of her kitchen with the promise of sun-steeped tea and fresh cookies.

"When did you arrive?" I asked, as they dropped into chairs.

Josephine squeezed my knee before perching next to Ben. "Hours only. We found livery for the horses, then asked after you."

"You made a tall impression on a very short man," said Genevie, her eyes dancing. She looked like herself, tanned and fit from traveling—no longer drowning in sorrow.

"Where's Akiko?" asked Josephine.

My face fell. "With Talbot."

"What?" they yelled in unison.

I brought them up to speed, leaving nothing out, and ending with how I'd failed to bring her home from Welland Island yesterday. I glanced at Olen in case he had more to add, but caught him staring at Earl, a smile playing on his lips.

My chest tightened. He'd already won Beck and better not fancy Earl, too. I pushed away my thoughts to focus on my friends. "Tell me everything."

Ben smiled. "First, we met friends of yours on the way here."

Genevie patted my shoulder. "An Eliot, a Bert, and a gaggle of mini-Berts."

The grin split my face as my shoulders relaxed. "They made it to Wakefield in that old, squealing wagon?"

Josephine appeared puzzled and shook her head. "We encountered them about a week outside Wakefield, but they rode matching bicycles. It was a peculiar sight, and why we stopped to converse. It was fortuitous, as they advised us to avoid Whitehall."

I snickered, imagining Eliot Tuckett on a bright-pink bike. "Akiko chose the color. She'll be thrilled to hear they made it to Wakefield safely. What else?"

Josephine recounted their trip to Warwick, playing with Ben's fingers as she talked. They relaxed into each other, their speech and actions choreographed. When Genevie caught my unasked question and nodded, I couldn't stop smiling. They made a handsome couple.

Josephine paused as Beck and Mama entered the common

room. Mama set down a large pitcher. "Let's meet your friends, Artist."

"Mama, this is Josephine, a scholar, and Ben, an engineer. Genevie is a blacksmith, Earl is a butcher, and Bowman is another engineer. Everyone, this is Mama Rebecca, Beck, and Olen. Gunther is stomping around here somewhere, too."

Mama passed out glasses of tea. "Welcome. You're all staying, correct?" When everyone nodded, my heart lightened, and Mama beamed. "Lovely. Two engineers, a butcher, a blacksmith, an artist, and two scholars."

"Two scholars?" asked Josephine.

Olen raised his hand. "Me."

Josephine inclined her head. "Well met."

"We'll sort out rooms when Gunther returns," said Mama.

"What's cooking?" asked Olen, draping himself across an armchair.

Mama surveyed us. "Let's have a fry up. Fish and chips if volunteers will peel potatoes."

When Ben and Earl rose to follow Mama into the kitchen, I ached to go too, but everyone here knew I couldn't cook. Before leaving the room, Earl turned, her gaze flickering over me. My heart raced as a flush crept up my neck. What was it about this woman?

Bowman leaned forward. "How's the flier? If I never sit in a saddle again, it will be too soon."

I slapped my forehead. "It's gone too."

Genevie chuckled. "You lost your flier, you lost your bags, you lost your kid."

"And your dog," said Josephine. "Where is Charcoal?"

I hung my head. "We had an accident, so he's rehabbing nearby."

"He's fine," said Olen, sliding onto the sofa next to me.

"Mama patched him up, and he'll be good as new soon. What's this about a flier?"

Bowman scowled. "She was a thing of beauty. Gentle as a kitten and as docile as a lamb."

"A kitten with claws," I muttered.

Olen leaned back with his hands behind his head. "There's a flier in Aurora."

I shoved his shoulder. "The Avalon Society stole my flier?"

"My flier," said Bowman.

Genevie chuckled, patting Bowman's hand.

Olen pulled a face. "Found, not stole."

To stumble upon a flier I'd *hidden* was a stretch, but I didn't want to argue in front of everyone. I compressed my lips; Olen was getting on my nerves.

Gunther popped his head through the door. "We've got rooms sorted out. Grab your bags and follow me."

Their departure gave me a moment to retrieve my sketchbook, but I accidentally poked my finger with the graphite pencil as I tried to shove it into my pocket. I sucked on my injured finger and flipped the sketchbook open to send a quick message to Akiko, but found she'd written to me.

"Were fine. Thenx fur the pensill."

After I got her back, spelling would be a top priority. Beneath Akiko's message, I drew a cartoon of everyone standing together, waving, with a speech bubble above our heads. Inside it, I lettered 'HERE!'. I waited, but no answering message returned.

DESPITE THE EVER-PRESENT ACHE INSIDE ME, DINNER WAS a marvel. Mama produced platters of sizzling fish and potato sticks fried a crisp gold, beaming at our appreciative exclamations.

The rich fish and crispy potatoes were delicious, adding to the joy of our reunion. The room stank of the cider vinegar we sprinkled onto the fried food. We ate and talked and laughed, our energies in perfect sync. I even forgot my earlier irritation with Olen, who dovetailed neatly into the group. Emotions swirled through me as I gazed at their faces. Though thankful they'd arrived, their presence highlighted the absences of Akiko, Charcoal, and Talbot.

As dinner wound down, my thoughts returned to Akiko, and I lost the thread of discussion, but when their voices quieted, my head snapped up. "What did I miss?"

Ben cleared his throat. "We asked for your plan."

I blinked. *My plan?* My stomach sank at their identical, expectant expressions and the silence deepened. Finally, I admitted, "I don't have one," my words a rush. I plastered on a rueful smile and waited for someone to suggest something.

Although my strategy had worked before, it didn't work now. Ben folded his arms, and Genevie leaned back in her chair. Olen's gaze flicked from one face to another, a smile tugging at his lips.

I turned to Josephine, my expression pleading for her to say something. She'd come through for me before, but this time, she smiled as though encouraging me to share my thoughts.

It's up to me.

Though daunted, I straightened, my brain buzzing as I organized my ideas. "First, Talbot and Akiko are on the island together, and we've developed a rudimentary way of communicating." My fingers drummed on the table. "I've replaced my art supplies, but I've lost everything else. The painting, my sword, even Akiko's clothes."

"We brought some of your things," said Earl.

She was right; I'd forgotten we'd carried only the essentials on the flier. My heart lightened. "Thank you."

"Where is this island?" asked Josephine.

"Great question." A map was something I knew how to do. "Let me show you." I flipped the sketchbook to a new page, drawing the sea's shoreline from memory and labeling Toronto Depot.

Olen leaned forward to watch. "It took us a little over two hours to sail to Welland Island."

I nodded, sketching in the approximate location of Welland Island. I added Niagara Abbey, frowning. Why hadn't I noticed before how close it was to Welland Island?

Genevie sighed as she studied my drawing. "We can't approach the island without being seen."

"No," I said. "And worse, they've altered the land, so the seminary is several hundred meters above the water."

"What do we know about this Reverend Carter?" asked Bowman.

I slumped. "Not much. Talbot told me Carter was behind the revival meetings and is gathering crusaders."

"Crusaders?" Josephine frowned. "Sounds ominous."

I tapped the pencil on the map. "Why?"

She sipped her water. "The crusades were a series of religious wars occurring about a thousand years *Before* the world died."

"Eight hundred to a thousand years," corrected Olen, his eyes narrowing.

Josephine continued as though Olen hadn't spoken. "The Pope, a type of religious king, and the Christians of Western Europe traveled east to recapture the holy lands."

Crossed his arms, Olen continued the lesson. "The holy lands had fallen under Muslim—a competing religious group— control. They had great wealth and a vast empire. There were six successful crusades and a seventh failed attempt to capture Egypt."

"Why did people join the wars?" I asked.

Josephine and Olen simultaneously drew breaths, then froze. After a pause, Josephine's mouth thinned, but she motioned for Olen to continue.

Olen's answers crackled with intensity. "Nobles went for conquest—wealth, glory, lands, and slaves. The ordinary people went with the promise of salvation, for the pope had promised forgiveness for past sins and guaranteed entrance to heaven for those who died while on crusade. Many serfs fought and died for the promise of freedom."

"Charming," said Earl, pulling her hair back.

I wasn't sure if Earl meant the crusades or something else, but the muscle flickering in Josephine's jaw told me we should change the subject.

"You believe this Carter is recruiting religious soldiers?" asked Bowman, his brow furrowed.

"Yes," said Olen.

"No," said Josephine at the same time.

They locked eyes.

"Why?" I asked.

Olen squared his shoulders. "You've seen the seminary; it's a fortress. Why build a fortress if you're not planning a war?"

I studied Josephine. "You don't agree?"

She tugged on her lower lip. "Who would Carter war *with*? There are no other religious groups to fight or fend off and no pope to promise eternal salvation. We have enough food and supplies for many future generations, so what's the purpose of an army?"

Both points sounded valid. Carter *had* altered Welland Island into a fortress, but with so much surplus, what was there to fight for?

"It's late, and I ate too much," said Genevie. She dropped her hand on the table with a *thud*. "Let's pick this up in the morning."

Olen rose, pulling out Earl's chair for her. He said something in a low voice, and she laughed in response. Before I could find a plausible reason to ask her to stay, they left together.

"He moves fast," said Bowman in a sing-song tone.

My head whipped around. "What?"

"And he's too handsome for his own good," said Bowman, sighing.

Had everyone noticed? "I'm sorry about your flier, Bowman."

He clapped my shoulder. "It sounds safe enough, but I'd like to visit it."

I patted his hand. "Will the society let you in?"

Bowman grinned. "I'm an engineer, son. I'll engineer a way."

The notion made me laugh. "Then they don't stand a chance."

"You monitor my girl while I'm gone, you hear?" Bowman stretched, grunting as his neck popped.

I nodded, my groin tightening even as I tried to stop from imagining Earl undressing above us. "I'll do my best."

Bowman rolled his shoulders. "I believe in you, Artist. So does she."

My stomach fluttered as I attempted to decipher his message. Was he talking about my chance at succeeding with Earl, or the likelihood I'd organize a rescue plan?

CHAPTER FORTY-ONE

The sensation of wind blowing across my face lessened, and above me, the sails dropped even though we'd only sailed an hour this morning. "Gunther, why have we stopped?"

"We're fishing today, aren't we?" he asked, securing the canvas sail. "The fish won't leap into the hold themselves, so we must work to put them there."

I reddened. Because I needed an excuse to study the island, Mama had talked Gunther into letting us fish with him. I'd jumped at the chance, believing the hours stuck on the boat would let me spend time with Earl. Instead, Olen had monopolized her time, leaving me with no opportunity to impress her. "Yes. What should we do?"

Gunther heaved a bucket onto the deck. "We bait seven long lines with alewife."

The sloshing bucket of dead fish released a murky, oily odor. "Shouldn't that be alewives?"

Gunther ignored my joke, asking, "Ready to work?" as he stared at me.

My quip didn't elicit even so much as a smirk from

Genevie, Ben, or Josephine. Either my timing was off, or my jokes were bad. Perhaps both. Gunther glared, waiting, so I nodded, compressing my lips.

He picked up a fish. "These are juveniles, and we'll use them whole. Insert the hook into their mouths, then poke it through the gills."

The boat pitched, and I staggered, bumping into Genevie.

She gave me a look, then muttered. "Alewives!"

I grinned. "Good to have a genuine friend around again."

Josephine glared at us with her hands on her hips. "I'm trying to learn this."

"Shhh," Genevie and I said in unison.

Even Gunther's whiskers frowned as he folded his arms. "Your turn."

I swallowed, thrusting my hand into the bait bucket. The fish were cold and slippery when I tried to grasp them.

Ben shouldered me aside and dipped his massive hand into the bucket. He successfully pulled a fish out, but his triumphant smirk dropped as the fish popped out of his hand and slithered across the deck. He chased after it, staggering as the *Marybelle* rolled in the waves. Josephine clamped her lips together, but her shoulders shook with suppressed laughter.

Gunther stomped to the aft deck, muttering, leaving us to sort ourselves out. Genevie was the first to bait a fish, but eventually, we all figured out how to handle the slippery juveniles without sticking ourselves on the wicked barbs.

Gunther waited until we had three lines strung before returning and calmed after inspecting our work. "Pull up the mainsail, lad."

Eager to prove myself, I tried, but my hands, slimy with fish goo, struggled for purchase on the rope.

Genevie pushed me out of the way. "Take a break, me pretty." She hauled the sail up and fastened the rope as if she'd been born on a boat.

Gunther twisted the wheel, turning the bow into the wind. "Aye, lass, you're a good'un. Coming about!"

We ducked as the boom swung above our heads.

Gunther shouted, "Batten the mainsail, lass!"

Genevie gave Gunther a mock salute and lashed the rope to a cleat on the deck. The rope creaked as the sail filled. The schooner picked up speed, but before we'd resumed our previous pace, Gunther adjusted our course, allowing the sail to luff.

Puzzled, I watched him fix the rudder in place. "Why aren't we using a full sail?"

"If our bait swims faster than our prey, we go home empty-handed. Besides, you wanted extra time to peer at yonder rock." Gunther pointed.

I squinted into the sun. Welland Island loomed on the horizon, its shape hazy and indistinct through the mists which hadn't fully burned away.

Gunther coiled the first of the baited lines. "We'll work our way back and forth all day. The longer we fish, the less they'll take notice."

"Smart," rumbled Ben. He caught Josephine as she stumbled past, pulling her against his chest. She tilted her head back, smiling at him.

A lump grew in my throat, and my gaze flicked from them to the bow. Earl laughed at something Olen said and flames licked across my chest.

"I stink like a chum bucket," Genevie said, wiping her hands on her trousers.

I dragged my eyes away from them. "None of us will smell good except Olen and Earl. They didn't help with the bait."

Genevie glanced at the bow. "They get on well."

I crossed my arms. With luck, Gunther had another disgusting task for Olen. "What now?" I asked.

A smile split Gunther's face. "The best part of fishing." He dragged a wooden chest forward and cracked the lid. After handing around cups, he opened a small cask, pouring brown liquid into each cup. Curious, I sniffed it, wincing as it stung my nose.

"Your health," said Gunther, tipping his cup back.

The liquid burned, bitter and astringent, when I swallowed. It ignited a fire as it slid down my throat, making me cough and choke.

Genevie's eyes danced as she watched me splutter. She downed her glass and even set it on the deck before her coughing fit hit. Ben fared no better; tears rolled down his eyes as he sneezed repeatedly.

Josephine drank hers without incident but wrinkled her nose. "What is this?"

"Bourbon." Gunther refilled his own glass a third time and capped the cask. "The lads and I have been working on a special blend. It's primarily corn, with some rye. Wheat and barley, if we can get it, but the bakers get the first pick of those."

Genevie's breath hissed between her teeth, but she tossed back the rest of her bourbon and held her glass out for more. "I miss the fool. This tastes like I won't be fishing later."

Gunther filled it halfway, but Genevie shook her head. Shrugging, he filled it to the brim, then menaced the rest of us with his cask.

The boat rocked, and Ben caught Josephine as she stumbled. "Let's sit." They took the single bench. Gunther sat on his wooden chest, and Genevie grunted, sinking into a large coil of rope.

I cast around, but the deck had nothing else to sit on besides the bait bucket. I perched on it, the thin metal biting into the back of my thighs as I stole another glance at the bow. The conversation between Earl and Olen had turned serious, and he leaned toward her, appearing to hang on each word.

I snorted and raised my cup. This time, the alcohol was smoother, and I didn't cough, but the bourbon smoldered in my stomach as I stared at them.

Above us, the slap of the sails lessened, and Gunther grunted from atop his wooden chest. "Wind shifted."

I glanced at the island, but though closer, it wasn't yet distinct enough to capture in my sketchbook.

Gunther reached over and tightened a rope, which had gone slack. "Mind your lips, we're coming about."

Before my liquor-addled brain could put together the meaning of Gunther's words, the boat shuddered and my bucket skidded sideways, sliding several meters before it struck a deck cleat. It stopped but I, unfortunately, did not and sprawled across the deck in an icy slurry of dead fish, blood, and lake water.

The cold sharpened my bourbon-pickled mind in time to notice Earl glance my way. My face flamed as her cool, green eyes raked over me before she burst out laughing. I drank in the music of her laughter, the sound almost worth making a clown of myself.

"Charming," said Genevie.

"Mm." I rolled over, soaking my back.

Gunther squinted at me. "You're squishing me bait," he said, refilling his glass.

I sat up and pulled a flattened fish from beneath my right buttock, then waved it at Gunther. "Maybe we should use this one next."

Josephine's shoulders shook, and Ben peered around her. "You sitting in fish juice all day?"

I flapped my fish at him. "What else is there to do?"

Ben nodded at the island. "Aren't we here for information?"

My head swam. The island loomed over us, its rocky walls sharply defined. Had it floated toward us? My eyes juddered as I tried to focus on it. "Gunther, I'm cutting myself off from the bourbon."

"More for me and my first mate," he said, refilling Genevie's cup. They clinked glasses and downed their contents.

Genevie's face was rosy as she held out her cup for more.

Gunther obliged. "Pick up the bait, Artist. It won't smell better if left to rot in the sun."

Genevie shot a pointed glance in Earl's direction. "You best deal with your alewives if you want any kind of shot."

I sighed, my shoulder slumping. What did it matter? If Olen pursued Earl, he'd win her attention. Even Talbot's smooth charms hadn't beaten Olen's wit, looks, or confidence. Unless Earl preferred men with no romantic experience and no notion of how to flirt with women, I couldn't compete with Olen. In contrast to his rugged masculinity and charming banter, I wore borrowed clothes and rolled around in dead fish.

At least I'd made her laugh.

"We are here for information," I said, my tongue thick as I attempted to focus on Ben. "But I'm not sure I'd trust my sketching right now." I dropped the flattened fish into the empty pail. It landed with a *splat-thud.*

Gunther pulled on his beard, then spoke slowly, as if to a small child. "Artist. Refill the bucket first, or the dead fish will swim away when you do."

The island bounced as I turned my head.

Refill the bucket?

With my luck, I'd fall into the lake while attempting to finish the task. My words slurred as I asked, "What's the lowest point of the boat?"

Gunther and Genevie squinted at me in unison.

I pantomimed leaning over a rail to scoop water into the bucket.

Gunther sucked in his lower lip, finishing his bourbon.

The flattened fish slid from side to side as I swung the bucket, waiting for an answer. Though willing to be Earl's fool, I would not play the clown for the rest of them.

Genevie clambered to her feet. "Give it here, pretty boy." She tied a thin rope onto the handle and lowered the bucket over the side of the boat. With a jerk, she pulled it back up, setting it on the deck. Without a word, she took a swig straight from Gunther's jug.

"Good," he said.

"Good," she replied.

I dumped the bucket of water over my head, and the flattened fish slid down my face before landing on my boot.

CHAPTER FORTY-TWO

Tension filled the room as thick as smoke. I froze at the door, but Ben shrugged and waved me in. Sunlight streamed through the eastern windows, but the morning bird-song jarred against the angry energy filling the room.

Josephine glared at Olen. "Stuff it."

My eyes flicked from Josephine, pink-cheeked and hard-eyed, to Olen, whose jaw flexed in sync with his fists. I needed them to get along. It was Josephine's plan that had allowed us to win the battle in Wakefield, and if Olen had a similarly strategic mind, they could accomplish far more together than either would on their own. The trip to the island had convinced me I needed help in coming up with a rescue plan, and these two were my best shot.

"What's the problem now?" I asked Genevie in a low voice.

"We're enjoying another round of 'whose brain is bigger?' this morning," she muttered.

After witnessing the competition between Olen and Talbot, I should have expected this. The trouble was Josephine and Olen were too evenly matched—though Olen believed his inclusion in the society gave him an advantage.

I perched on the arm of her chair. "Ah. And the correct answer is?"

Genevie pointed at herself.

I grinned. "Want to see my finished map?" During our 'fishing' trip, I'd observed Welland Island from the east, west, and north sides. Though the water south of the island appeared open, Gunther had warned it was a marsh rather than a lake.

Ben joined us, frowning as he studied the map. "We'll have no cover, and no way to approach unseen from any angle."

I chewed on my lip. "Then unless we try for a moonless night, we'll need more than stealth."

Olen uncrossed his arms and shook out his shoulders. "You captured a lot of information yesterday."

To avoid watching Earl fall for him, I'd focused on my task —as soon as I'd sobered enough to draw. My lips tightened when Olen stepped toward me. Josephine wasn't the only one Olen was bothering.

"Move your papers," ordered Mama. She held the kitchen door for Gunther and Beck, who each carried enormous platters.

Gunther glanced at the map before I folded it. "Welland Island 'twas once part of the mainland."

Ben stopped spooning the fluffy, yellow-orange eggs onto his plate. "If it was, could we get most of the way there under the cover of the forest?"

When Genevie passed the pancake platter in the wrong direction, I considered stealing one from her plate. "We could check for records at the warehouse. Perhaps an old map will show potential routes to get us close."

"I'll go," said Josephine and Olen simultaneously. The air

between them rippled as they glared at each other. In unison, they turned to me, both hard-eyed.

I blinked, a sausage halfway to my mouth. The others were busy eating, their eyes locked on their plates.

Great.

"I'll go too, for supplies." I smiled, but neither scholar softened. "Can we walk together?"

Josephine snorted, and Olen rolled his eyes, but the conversation resumed. The escalation of animosity between Olen and Josephine worried me. Not only because I needed them to work together, but also because this wasn't the first time Josephine hadn't gotten along with someone in our party. She'd disliked Cara from the start, and I'd assumed it was because I was infatuated with Cara. But Josephine had been right to mistrust her, so was she correct about Olen too?

When the pancakes finally reached me, I filled my plate, but now the syrup was on the wrong side of the table. I sighed, spearing another sausage. The salt-fat flavors washed over my tongue, and I closed my eyes, chewing slowly.

When I opened them, Earl watched me with a ghost of a smile. She leaned forward. "What do you taste?"

My heart fluttered. "The sage and pepper come through first. There's a hint of sweetness and something more herbal... parsley?"

Her eyes crinkled. "Very good. You missed the ground mustard seed, but I used very little."

"They're marvelous."

Earl's eyes were a depthless green, like the plunge pool at the base of the giant waterfall. What pigments would I use to paint them? I had emerald in a tube, but I could mix a closer shade using phthalo green and a hint of Hansa yellow light. The transparent and opaque whites would create an intense, sunny color, filling her eyes with her intelligence and fire.

Someone cleared their throat, and I flinched as Genevie snickered. My flush deepened when Genevie fanned herself, so I shoved an enormous bite of dry pancake into my mouth, chewing furiously.

"When should we leave for the warehouse?" asked Beck.

"After Matthew drops his trousers for me," said Mama.

Pancake exploded from my mouth.

Mama smirked. "We should change your poultice before you go."

I nodded, wiping my mouth with the back of my arm.

"If there's room, I want to cross to the mainland too," said Ben, pushing his plate back. "We've been talking about the tower for weeks."

Bowman brightened. "Can I join you?"

Beck stretched. "Two scholars, two engineers, and an artist in my boat at once. Fancy. Are you coming too?"

Earl shook her head, and my heart fell. "No, I'm helping Mama clean and fillet the fish."

Mama beamed at Earl. "Your knife skills put mine to shame, and I've been cleaning fish my whole life."

Earl smiled, her eyes sliding back toward me.

Josephine rose and stacked the plates. "Mama, which librarian should I work with?"

"I like Freddy Garcia," said Olen, frowning.

Mama nodded. "Freddy is a good egg, but for land records, you couldn't do better than Antonia Frisk. She's older than dirt, but knows everything about this area."

"Antonia is older than dirt, all right," said Olen. "Wicked sharp, though."

Josephine glared at him. "Antonia sounds perfect."

"Freddy will be better at finding information about the crusades," said Olen, his eyes glinting.

Josephine's chin raised. "Good, then you'll be busy elsewhere."

Olen's eyes tightened as his lips compressed. "I'm heading back to Aurora anyway, so you'll have the warehouse all to yourself."

Bowman raised his head. "If you don't mind, I'd like to go with you. I want to check on my flier."

Guilt curdled in my stomach, and I stood in a hurry, accidentally knocking over my water glass. "Blast. Sorry, Mama."

"Leave it for Beck and come with me. Ben, a hand?"

We followed her into the kitchen.

"Trousers down, butt on table," said Mama, filling a large, metal bowl from the kettle. She brought the bowl and a clean towel to the table, then removed my dressing. "Clean out the wound while I collect the poultice herbs. Don't let him squirm out of it."

Ben nodded, his face serious, but as soon as Mama left, he snapped the towel at my face.

I jerked backward. "Hey!"

"Hey yourself." He inspected the cut, wrinkling his nose. "Don't squirm."

"You try," I grumbled, as Ben dabbed at the wound. "Do you like Olen?"

Ben nodded, rinsing the towel. "He's arrogant, but most society folks are."

"It's not like it was with Cara?"

Ben raised his eyes. "How do you mean?"

"Ouch, watch it." I scowled at my leg. Would it ever return to normal? "Josephine doesn't like him."

"Josephine doesn't *know* Olen. You could ease the situation."

"Why me?"

"They're trying to impress you," Ben said.

I blinked. Impress *me?* Their cooperation would impress me more than the sniping.

Mama bustled into the kitchen and inspected my leg. "Good work."

"He squirmed very little," said Ben, as he rinsed the bowl in the sink.

Rat.

The scents of basil and mint filled the kitchen as Mama mashed the herbs with a mortar and pestle. The green paste turned brown as she added red petals into the mix.

"Roses?" I asked.

Mama nodded, wiping her forehead with the back of her arm. "They're antibacterial and antiseptic. We've debrided the dead flesh but need to keep the rest pink and healthy. Hold still."

The poultice stung as Mama packed it into the wound, hot and cold at once, but the burn mellowed as she wrapped my calf with linen and secured the bandage with ribbon.

I rotated my leg, admiring her work. Akiko would love the festive wrapping. "Done?"

She nodded. "Try not to bump it today."

I grinned and slid off the table, testing my weight on the leg, the chill from the herbs already gone. "Thanks, Mama."

"Pull up your pants if you want to go to town, Artist," she said, wiping down the table.

I snorted, but obeyed. "Easy peasy."

Ben opened the door and jerked his chin to where Josephine and Olen glowered at each other from opposite sides of the room. "And them? I'm not sure Olen's temporary absence will ease things between them if you don't step in."

Although Josephine could be touchy and prickly, I trusted her motivations, so it was time to talk to Olen. I sighed and motioned to him. "Olen, a word?"

CHAPTER FORTY-THREE

A crack of thunder jolted me awake as the mainland bell clanged. The storm had blown in last night, just as we were returning from the third day of digging through records at the warehouse. A lightning flash briefly illuminated my room, casting stark shadows. The hairs on my arm stood when electricity crackled through the air—the strike very close.

The bell clanged again.

Someone wanted to cross the water... *now?*

Through the rain-streaked window, a blurred figure stumbled down the steps toward the dock in the predawn gloom. I wiped the window in time to watch Beck stagger sideways, her long hair swirling around her as the wind ripped her rain hood back.

Between the storm and my curiosity, there was no chance of returning to sleep now. I pulled on my trousers and pattered down the kitchen steps barefoot, buttoning my shirt.

"Morning," said Mama, from the table where she kneaded dough, elbow deep in flour.

I pulled my hair back, tying the lace. "Morning. Was that the bell?"

Mama snorted. "Fools all. Them who want a lift and her who rushed to row them."

Rain pelted the windows as the wind shifted. The yellow boat had reached the midpoint, even though waves crested and crashed against it. Thankful I'd filled the wood box last night, I opened the stove door, poking at the fire. "You're not worried?"

Mama continued to pummel the dough. "Beck knows what she can handle. If you want sticky buns for breakfast, don't feed the stove. I need warm, not hot, for this dough to rise."

My stomach rumbled even as Whistler's smiling face flashed upon my mind's canvas.

Mama stopped kneading, brushing an escaped curl back from her face. "The last time I made a man look so sad was when I told Gunther I'd marry him."

I grinned, closing the oven door, and wiping my hands. "Do tell."

The kitchen door blew open with a gust and spray of rain, and Mama chuckled. "Speak of the devil."

Gunther clumped across the kitchen and pulled a mug from the shelf. "Is the water hot? I have time for a slurp. Our fool girl reached the mainland."

I crossed my arms, leaning against the wall. "Why did proposing to Mama make you sad?"

Gunther snorted and lifted his eyebrows as he filled his mug. "Because she said no."

Mama lifted the smooth dough into a bowl and covered it with a linen towel. "I was *busy* delivering my Rebecca."

I glanced from her to Gunther. "You proposed during childbirth?"

Gunther shrugged, sipping his tea. "Thought 'twould give me the edge."

I picked up the kettle and refilled it, setting it back on the stove. "Mama, why did you say yes?"

Mama dried her hands while gazing at Gunther. "His face when he held my squalling girl. The expression of wonder on this old, bearded bass—I couldn't resist it."

Gunther snorted but kissed her cheek before shrugging on his raincoat.

While we waited, I sat down and flipped through my sketchbook. Akiko had replied to my drawing with a sketch of a smiling frog wearing a top hat.

"Brace yourself," murmured Mama, jerking her chin at the window.

Before I could rise, the door burst open and a blur streaked across the kitchen, launching into my stomach. I fell backward off the bench, cracking my head against the stone floor. Gasping, I tried to protect my face from Charcoal's furious kisses. His feet pummeled me, and I yelped in protest as I tried to wrap my arms around him. "Charcoal, quit."

With a sigh, he stretched out on top of me, his chin on my collar bones... until Ben and Josephine entered the kitchen.

Charcoal flew to them, wiggling and crying. Josephine squealed, dropping to her knees to hug the wet dog.

Genevie appeared behind them, yawning, her brown hair wild. "How's a gal supposed to sleep through this racket?"

Bowman stepped through the kitchen door and raised his hand, spraying the floor with rainwater. Olen and Beck followed him in and shed their dripping raincoats, radiant smiles on their wet faces.

"Hullo, chap," said Earl, from behind me.

I scrambled to sit up, but Charcoal bowled me over again in his haste to reach Earl. He sat, backing into her legs, gazing up at her with an enormous smile.

Olen hauled me to my feet as I rubbed the sore spot on the back of my head. "Why did you brave this storm?"

Olen beamed, pulling Beck to him. "Didn't want to miss Mama's breakfast, plus if we hadn't crossed, Charcoal might have tried swimming to the inn."

Bowman cleared his throat. "The wind helped push us here faster than expected."

My eyes widened. "You flew in this weather?"

Bowman shook his head. "It was calm when we left last night, and we hoped we'd make it back before dinner, but the storm's advancing wind pushed us to the north side of the depot, so we pedaled the flier over the ground."

"Took us all night," Olen agreed.

"If you want breakfast, I need my kitchen back," said Mama.

Ben made a shooing motion. "Out, out."

"Aren't you coming?" asked Josephine, her gaze flicking toward Olen.

Ben shook his head. "I'm on kitchen duty this morning."

Mama flapped her towel at us. "The rolls go into the oven in an hour, so you have plenty of time for chatter. Go on."

◆

AFTER THE WARMTH OF THE KITCHEN, THE CHILL IN THE common room made me shiver, especially after Charcoal jumped onto the padded bench and rested his wet head on my thigh.

Bowman squatted to rebuild the fire. "As advertised, Aurora was delightful. Someone had brought the flier to trade for membership in the community, but they saw through him. After Olen explained I'd engineered the flier, they offered me residency and invited us to visit."

"All of us?" asked Josephine, her voice uncertain.

Olen nodded, pulling Beck onto a loveseat with him. "We told them what we've learned about the Reverend Carter. They're concerned and sent us straight back to convey it."

My heart jumped. I'd hoped Aurora would extend an invitation—the opportunity would allow me to ask for help. "Will they help us rescue Akiko and Talbot?"

Genevie sighed. "This is Wakefield and Newfane all over again."

Josephine bit her lip. "I don't enjoy asking the Avalon Society for help."

Beck leaned into Olen's chest. "Why? We enjoy a cordial relationship with Aurora."

I smiled at her. "Let me guess, dragons fly at Aurora's festivals?" The Avalon Society only wanted the best—and her kites were exquisite.

Beck grinned. "You bet."

I wanted to ask more, but Gunther pushed through the swinging door, and Beck shook her head, her eyes flicking to him. Mint and hyssops perfumed the air as he delivered the mugs of tea.

Charcoal snored beside me, his eyelids flickering and paws twitching. The fur around his wound was growing back, the white line a reminder of how close I'd come to losing him. How close I still was to losing Akiko. If there was any possibility of help from Aurora, I needed to plead my case.

A boom of thunder startled me, and tea leaped from my mug into my lap. I sprang up, trying to pull the hot, wet trousers from my body. "We need help."

"With laundry?" asked Genevie.

I fanned my groin, my face red. "If Aurora is willing, let's invite them to come and discuss the options."

Olen shook his head. "They won't come here. You'll have to go there."

Josephine frowned. "Why should we?"

Bowman poked the fire. "They're a large community. It makes more sense to go there."

"How long will it take to get there?" asked Genevie.

Olen shrugged. "Walking? A full day, each way."

"That's too long," argued Josephine. "We need to stay here, closer to Akiko."

I wanted to stay too. "The weather is horrible, but some of us should go."

Josephine crossed her arms. "Then send the others. What if something on Welland Island changes, or Talbot slips away and you're not here?"

Olen cleared his throat. "They want Matthew to come."

"You have responsibilities, Matthew." Josephine's eyes tightened. "We can ask for help from the folks here in Toronto Depot."

"Yes, but I can't do both at once," I said. "I'll go there first since they've invited me."

She glared at me. "So, you're abandoning Akiko to play with the Avalon Society?"

My gut clenched, and I stiffened. "Unfair and uncalled for, Josephine."

Olen's eyes flicked between us. "If you're sure, we should go today."

"After breakfast," said Ben, entering the common room. "Where are we going?"

Rain pelted the window as another gust of wind hit the inn.

"Aurora, but I'm staying here if you don't mind," answered Bowman. He groaned as he stood. "I'm not cut out for traveling, but I'll speak with the librarians on your behalf, if it's helpful."

"Thank you. We need everyone's support." I scrutinized Josephine, waiting.

She sighed. "I'll go to the warehouse with Bowman, but I'm doing so under protest."

I nodded, trying not to let my relief show. It would be easier to ask Aurora for help without her scowling at them. Besides, a few days apart might smooth the friction between her and Olen.

"I'll visit Aurora too," said Genevie. "Earl?"

My belly fluttered while I waited for Earl's decision.

Her face straight, she said, "Stay here... and miss the chance to trudge through the rain all day? I'll join the expedition."

My cheeks warmed as I fought to keep my smile from splitting my face. "Road trip."

CHAPTER FORTY-FOUR

The long walk and heavy clouds obscured my sense of time, but my stomach rumbles told me we were at, or had passed, suppertime as we crowded onto the covered porch. We waited as Olen knocked, huddled close to escape the driving rain.

"Heya, Ash, back so soon?" asked a woman I couldn't see. Her voice snaked through the sodden air like velvet sheets on a summer's night.

Olen laughed, shaking like a wet dog. "Can't keep me away. Besides, even in this weather, I wanted to show Aurora off to my friends. Everyone, meet Bernice Böse, our administrator."

When he moved to the side, I caught my first glimpse of the administrator. She had silky, dark hair framing an oval face with a widow's peak.

Bernice stepped onto the porch as I tugged my hood back. "Matthew Sugiyama. Well met, Bernice."

Bernice smiled slowly, her full lips curving into a heart-shaped smile as she scanned me. "Very nice."

"Thank you?" My voice cracked, and I tried not to cringe. This wasn't the auspicious start I'd hoped for.

Without warning, she slunk toward me with the grace of a predator. "Bernice, please. Let's be friends."

Her words were cordial, but her sexual energy whipped toward me like a tentacle, and sandwiched between Genevie and Earl, I had nowhere to run. I cleared my throat, fumbling through the introductions. "Genevie Canning and Earl... Earl—"

"Kildare," said Earl. She stepped forward, extending her hand. "Earl Kildare, Butcher."

"I'll watch my fingers *and* my lambs," said Bernice. Though she kept her tone light, her eyes narrowed.

"Blacksmith," said Genevie, thrusting her hand forward.

While Bernice was distracted, I slid behind them, a frightened rabbit hiding from a wolf. Charcoal eyed me before shaking off, spraying my trousers with muddy water.

Bernice's lips curved again as she peeked at him from between the girls. "Hullo, little man. Looks like you need a good rubdown." Her eyes flicked to my face. "Why don't you come inside?"

"Lead on," answered Genevie.

Bernice ignored Genevie and turned to Ben. "My, you are one big hunk of man."

Ben's face purpled. "Ben Hensly, Engineer. Well met, Administrator."

Olen held the carved wooden door open. "Are we early enough for dinner?"

Bernice paused at the threshold. "We'd feed you even if you weren't Olen Ash. I can't abide an unsatisfied man." Her statement made, she swept through the open door, her throaty chuckles and musky scent trailing her.

Ben and I hung back, so the women followed Bernice first.

"Why didn't you warn me?" I muttered to Olen.

"Warn *us*," said Ben, his voice nearly indistinct. "I mean, Bernice is, well..."

Olen's teeth flashed as he followed us inside. "Warn you how? *Beware the interest of our beautiful administrator—you* would've ignored me. Besides, the girls seem intent on protecting you."

He was right. Genevie and Earl had stopped shoulder to shoulder—a human wall shielding us from Bernice.

Bernice appeared amused as she gestured toward the large table in the middle of the room. "Please sit. I'll round up the elders and organize a meal."

Ornately carved hobnail furniture upholstered with burgundy leather filled the handsome room. My feet hurt, but my clothes were wet and muddy, leaving me nowhere to sit.

I followed Charcoal toward a massive stone fireplace at the far end of the room. The fire crackled with intensity, knots popping, scattering sparks and ash. The size of the hearth and the sweet scent of applewood reminded me of Popham. I turned my back to warm it, surveying the room.

The central table, approximately two meters wide and four meters long, dominated the room. Ten heavy chairs flanked either side of the table. Smaller, round tables ringed the central table, each set with five chairs.

A mirrored wall opposite the fireplace provided an illusion of depth, making the table appear even more massive. Rain pelted the series of arched windows on my left. Beneath the windows ran a long bench covered with potted plants. The plants glowed vibrant green, providing a lively contrast to the dark furniture.

Bookshelves spanned the wall opposite the windows. Even from here, the leather-bound books were in marvelous condition, their gilt titles easy to read.

Josephine would be sorry to have missed this.

At Popham Abbey, books had filled Headmaster Sinclair's office, but their covers had faded, the printing long obscured. I stepped closer to the shelves. "Are these books new?"

Olen nodded. "Aurora is famous for its bookbinding."

I scanned the titles, but none were familiar. "Are these reprints? Restored stories from *Before*?"

Olen dropped into a chair, sighing. "Some, but others are new. We have many writers in the society."

Charcoal jumped onto a large, square cushion near the windows, turning several circles before sinking into it. He grumbled and closed his eyes, sighing.

I snapped my fingers to order him off, but Olen waved his hand. "It's a dog bed. Bernice had it made, since several members here have dogs."

Genevie scanned the books with an expression akin to thirst. "Do the writers supply your minstrels with fresh stories?"

"Only if we can't spin a yarn of our own," rumbled a sonorous voice. "Olen, you've brought me a crowd new to my tales."

Olen chuckled. "Everyone, this is Cedrick Jacobson, minstrel. Cedrick, this is Matthew, Genevie, Ben, Earl, and Charcoal over on the bed."

"Well met, everyone." Cedrick stooped to pet the dozing dog, his hand avoiding the healing wound. "Hullo Charcoal." Cedrick glanced at me. "This little chap has a few tales of his own to tell."

I winced. "Yes, and I'm afraid I'm the villain in some of his stories."

Cedrick chuckled, gesturing at the table. "Please, come sit."

Before I could protest my wet clothes, the door to the porch opened, and three more people stepped inside. The tallest man had a ruddy complexion and a magnificent beard that shone in the lamplight. He smoothed it like one petted a cat and pulled out the seat next to Olen, tossing his dripping coat over the back of the chair. "Brother," he said, nudging my friend.

Olen grinned. "This is Jon Velde, one of our writers."

Genevie leaned forward. "What types of stories do you write?"

Jon stroked his beard. "I'm partial to tales of dragons and elves."

"Fantasy," said Genevie, leaning back. "I love fantasy. I partly apprenticed as a blacksmith to learn swordcraft."

"A blacksmith," said Jon, his eyebrows rising. "I like a woman who plays with fire. Perhaps we could trade. I have several tales you might like."

"As do I," said Cedrick, sitting next to Jon.

Genevie grinned and patted the chair next to her for me. "How interesting."

I hadn't seen this playful side of Genevie since Whistler's death, and it warmed me more than the fire. A trace of a smile played on Earl's face as Genevie flirted with the storytellers, so I wasn't the only one who'd noticed.

Both people who'd arrived with Jon reappeared carrying trays. The first, a portly man with spiky, white hair; the second, a blonde woman with knife-sharp features. My eyes widened as she set her tray down, and beside me, Ben's chair creaked.

Bernice wasn't the only woman Olen had failed to warn us about.

The blonde had masses of curly hair and the most enormous breasts I'd ever seen. Her frame was so slight that I caught my breath, sure she'd topple over. "Weather like this calls for a cocktail," she announced. "I'm making martinis."

I didn't know what a martini was, but nodded, anyway.

Olen winked at me, his eyes flashing with mirth. "This is Marcy, our keeper. She makes a mean cocktail."

Dry-mouthed, I watched Marcy pour a clear liquid into a shiny metal cup. She covered it with a second metal cup and raised her arms as if poised for supplication. Without warning, she shook the cups, her breasts bouncing and shuddering.

Face burning, I fixed my eyes on the table in an attempt not to watch her. After the shaking noises stopped, my eyes slid to Earl. Her smile was wicked as she stared at Ben's slack face.

"Close your mouth," I muttered.

Ben flushed and cleared his throat before gluing his eyes to the tabletop.

Bernice reentered the room. "Martinis, Marcy? How delightful."

Marcy chuckled and poured the liquid into sparkling glasses. "The company warrants it."

Bernice pulled out the chair next to Jon, staring at me as she sat. "Indubitably. What's for dinner?"

Marcy's smile widened. "Tenderloin."

Ben made a choking noise.

Marcy set stemmed glasses in front of Cedrick, Jon, Earl, and Olen, then stacked the remaining glasses on the tray. It took everything I had not to watch her round the table toward us. When she set the glass in front of me, the side of her bosom brushed my arm, and I almost forgot to breathe. I shifted, my groin hard and tight. With luck, I wouldn't need to stand for a while.

"Cheers," murmured Bernice, her dark eyes boring into me.

I lifted my glass in imitation of the others, then gulped my drink. The alcohol stung, bitter with a piney flavor, reminding me of turpentine. The martini ignited an icy fire in my throat, and I leaned forward, coughing.

Genevie slapped my back hard and chuckled. "This one has seen little of the world yet."

"So I see," said Bernice, her smile dangerous. "If you choose to stay, we have much, much more to teach you."

"Stay?" I asked, my voice a raw whisper.

Marcy, all breasts and teeth, refilled my glass. "If you drink like this, I better hurry the meal."

Bernice sipped her martini. "Olen said you wanted our help to rescue your daughter and cousin from Reverend Carter."

Akiko and Talbot.

Their faces popped onto my mind's canvas, grounding me. My head cleared, and I set my glass down. "Yes. Carter has turned Welland Island into a fortress."

Bernice's brow furrowed. "What do you have in mind?"

I studied their faces, trying to read if they'd already made their decision. This meeting hadn't gone as I'd envisioned, and I hadn't made the best impression so far. Not only had I injured my dog, I'd lost my daughter and cousin too. If I couldn't impress them, they might choose to remain neutral, but without their help, we'd have to stretch our limited resources further, so I opted for complete honesty. "Nothing definite yet. It depends on who will help us."

Jon frowned. "A successful plan will rest on who this Carter is. Risto, you've met the man. What's his game?"

The portly man rubbed his spiky hair. "Good question. He's accustomed to being in charge. When he arrived in Toronto Depot, he already had an entourage of acolytes doing his bidding."

"Why did you meet him?" I asked, sipping my martini. It burned, but its icy fire had tempered, leaving my limbs floating.

Risto finished his drink and smacked his lips. "They referred him to me for pressure in his chest."

"You're a healer?" asked Ben.

Risto nodded. "I found Carter to be an unpleasant man, arrogant without warrant. I advised him to improve his health through diet and exercise, but he took offense."

"His expulsion offended him too, but he wasn't society material. Now *you*" –Bernice paused, her gaze pinning me to my seat– "are."

If there was ever a time I'd welcome Olen pulling female attention from me, it was now. I gulped, only breathing when Bernice turned her focus to Ben. "As are you. How did you both slip our net?"

Olen's eyebrows raised. "Ben too?"

Genevie chuckled. "And me, ages ago."

What did it mean that the Avalon Society had invited so many of my closest friends to join them? I turned toward Genevie. "You've said nothing."

She shrugged. "Whistler."

Whistler.

Proof the society wasn't infallible. Whistler was—*had been* —a marvelous baker and would have improved any community. But... if my friends were a measure of the caliber of people the society invited, perhaps I should reconsider their offers after I found my answers. Akiko and I would need to settle somewhere. My heart wrenched, and I pushed away the martini, refocusing my hazy thoughts. "So now what?"

Jon stroked his beard, looking thoughtful. "It depends on which community you want to join. Aurora is charming, but we have others that may suit you better. Either way, your choice will affect who we ask to assist with the rescue."

His words were a punch to my gut. "You won't help unless I agree to join you?"

Astonishment flashed across their faces, as if my membership had never been in question.

Spots floated in front of my eyes. If I accepted their offer, I couldn't search for my birth family, but if I didn't agree, they wouldn't help. What had gone wrong? Olen had been sure Aurora would help me. I eyed him, hoping he'd provide the voice of reason and convince them to help us without strings or promises.

Olen's eyes were warm and full of compassion. "This is how the world works, Matthew. We each have something the other wants, so let's strike a bargain."

CHAPTER FORTY-FIVE

Someone knocked on my door.

I froze, willing the knocker to leave, waiting for their footsteps to fade away. Even though the scent of bacon had crept up the stairs, I'd skipped breakfast to avoid another encounter with Bernice.

The knocker tried again, sending shivers down my spine.

"Matthew," Ben whispered.

My breathing slowed. "Ben? Are you alone?"

"Yes," he said, "but let me in before I'm not." There was a desperation in Ben's voice I fully understood.

I cracked the door and peered into the hallway before yanking him inside. I shut the door softly, wincing at the click of the latch, and twisted the lock.

Ben chuckled. "Which woman are *you* avoiding?"

I sagged against the door frame. "Does it matter? They're both terrifying."

Charcoal rolled over, exposing his belly as Ben sat on the bed. He rubbed the dog's stomach. "How are you doing, little man?"

Charcoal licked Ben's hand once in response.

Ben glanced at the door. "How long will you hide in your room?"

I rubbed the back of my head and shrugged. "I'm not hiding. Well, I'm not *only* hiding."

It was true. I'd been trying to think my way around the problem. If I couldn't convince Aurora to help us—without strings attached—the situation would force me to make an impossible decision. So far, I had come up with nothing, discarding each bad idea in turn.

Ben swung his legs onto the bed, nudging Charcoal aside. The dog grumbled but moved over, settling his head on Ben's chest.

I peered out of the window and watched Marcy flounce past, her hair gleaming in the morning's sun. After the dinner in the pub, I'd done my best to avoid the buxom keeper. "Marcy just left. Think it's safe to go downstairs?"

Ben ducked his head. "Not if Bernice is still there."

He was right. Of the two women, Bernice was the more dangerous. Could I throw myself on her mercy? How far would I have to go?

Artist, stop.

I pinched the bridge of my nose, trying to clear the lurid images dancing across my mind's canvas. "You should have convinced Josephine to come."

Ben groaned, flopping backward on the bed. "Can you imagine? She's already touchy about the society's elitism."

"Why do you think they didn't invite her?"

Outside, Genevie rounded the corner, deep in conversation with Jon. She looked like her old self, crackling with wit and humor.

Ben cracked an eye. "I don't think Josephine applied."

Applied? I hadn't applied, but I hadn't considered how the society typically recruited their members. "Did you apply?"

Ben shook his head. "No, but my grandfather was a member, so I grew up within the society."

"Oh?" I perched on the edge of the chair, keeping half an eye on the comings and goings of the people of Aurora. Try as I might, I couldn't remember much about Ben's family. "Your parents weren't members?"

Ben cleared his throat. "They died when I was seven. Afterward, I was on the road with my grandfather."

"On the road? Your grandfather was a minstrel?"

Ben nodded. "Yes, and we traveled around New England, visiting the society's smaller communities throughout my childhood. I didn't live in a community for longer than a winter until it was time to apprentice. Still, after I picked engineering, they offered me membership."

Ben's skill at storytelling had taken me by surprise when I'd met him at Rochester Depot. Funny, I hadn't put it together before. "Where is your grandfather now?"

"He died right before I accepted the temporary billet in Rochester Depot."

I gazed at him. "Where I messed up your invitation to settle in Newfane?"

Ben shrugged, playing with Charcoal's ears. "Even if I had settled, I don't think I would have improved my life much. And then I met you and Josephine."

"Do you have siblings?"

Ben shook his head. "No, just me and my grandfather, so I'm another orphan for your crew."

Ben's words struck a chord. I was effectively an orphan, abandoned into the abbey system. Akiko's parents were dead, and Josephine had no relationship with her family, their bonds shattered by their shared trauma. Genevie's mother was still alive but had moved so far south that they hadn't seen each other in years. Even my friend Sally Park had been an orphan, raised by her uncle.

Ben's eyebrow rose. "You're smiling."

I grinned. "Thinking about Sally."

Ben chuckled. "Demented infidel basher, what will you do about Aurora's ultimatum?" he asked in falsetto.

I snorted. "Good one."

"Seriously, have you decided?" Ben rolled to his side and propped his head up with his hand.

Charcoal stretched, his hind legs kicking.

I summoned my inner Sally. "Bickering pig troughs, Hensly, it's *not* that easy."

The corners of Ben's eyes crinkled. "If it were, you wouldn't be hiding."

"I'm not—oh all right. I'm hiding." My shoulders drooped.

"And…?"

I pulled the leather lace from my hair and shook it out. After yesterday's march through the rainstorm, a knot had snarled my hair at the nape of my neck. I needed a bath but, naked in a tub, I'd be easy prey. My nostrils flared. "Why should the Avalon Society's desires trump those of the rest of the world?"

Ben sat up. "The world's… or yours?"

I frowned. "Okay, mine too. I want their help, but I don't want to settle here—or anywhere—until I find my birth family."

His brows furrowed. "You don't think they are here in Toronto Depot?"

I shook my head, my ears burning from the admission. Before leaving Wakefield, I'd been so sure I'd find my family in the depot. Because of my certainty, my friends had traveled for *weeks* to meet me here. "Akiko and I searched for days, trying to find a location that worked with the perspective of the painting, but if I captured the image correctly, it can't depict this depot. Coming here was a mistake."

Unable to face Ben, I wandered to the dresser, randomly opening drawers.

The silence deepened, increasing the pressure in my head, but Ben's voice didn't sound angry when he finally spoke. "If they're not here, what will you do?"

I sagged against the dresser, turning to face him. "I don't know, but if I accept Aurora's offer, I fear they won't release me."

"Release you?"

"Typically, artists agree to a commission of three to five years and then reevaluate. Do you think the society would let me leave after five years?"

"Doubtful."

"Exactly, so if I agree, I may lose the chance to find my parents. Plus, what about Akiko, and—"

Ben smirked as he waited for me to finish my sentence. "And?"

Earl's face filled my mind's canvas. If she wasn't Avalon Society material, would they make an exception... assuming she wasn't planning to return home to Star Creek? And what about when Akiko came of age? The society's exclusivity meant they even evicted their *children* if they found the young people lacking after they completed their apprenticeships. How could I build a life for Akiko with this hanging over us? Even if I abandoned my quest for answers, Aurora's offer troubled me.

I scratched at my beard. "If I don't agree to join them, I don't think they'll help."

"Truth."

I sighed. "I hoped you'd say something different."

Ben swung his legs off the bed and leaned forward, searching my face. "Do you have any kind of plan?"

I said nothing, but my face betrayed me.

Ben sighed. "So even with help..." He stood, stretching. "Assuming you had as many people as you needed, how would you go about getting her back?"

"Hypothetically?" I pictured the island's sheer cliffs. "To storm the seminary, we'd need ropes or ladders for people to climb to the terrace. We could also come in from the top with the flier."

"How many people live in the seminary?"

"Fifty? Sixty?" I shrugged. "Though many of them were women or children."

Ben frowned. "The women who attacked Wakefield were as dangerous as the men."

"Truth." I stared out the window again. If I had grabbed Akiko when I had the chance, none of this would be happening now. "I don't want to fight around the children, so I'd rather sneak into the compound."

Ben's chin lifted. "Interesting. We wouldn't need as many people, either."

Could we sneak in? If so, I could leave my decision about the society until later.

Outside, Bernice rounded the corner of the guildhall toward the inn, and I shrank back from the window frame. "Bernice."

"The women here." Ben shook his head. "Marcy is *something*."

My eyes widened. "Have you ever seen—"

Ben's eyes danced as he shook his head. "No."

Footsteps approached the door, and we froze. Someone knocked sharply, but instead of answering, I raised my finger to my lips. Ben nodded, his eyes wide as the person outside the door rapped on the door again, then tried the knob. It rotated halfway before the lock caught. Soon after, the footsteps stamped away.

"Could have been Earl," said Ben, his voice low.

My heart leaped at the idea of Earl at my door. Not for the first time, I wished I'd found my parents in Toronto Depot, but now besides answers, I also wanted resolution. Without questions about my past dragging me backward, perhaps I could focus on the next step in my life. But I hadn't found my family, and if I accepted Bernice's offer, I might never get the answers I needed. Would not knowing leave me stuck, stranded in the limbo space between being a youth and a man?

My breath caught. If I never found out where I came from, I may never learn who I could be. Even if it meant Aurora wouldn't help, I couldn't accept their offer right now. With luck, Josephine and Bowman would have good news to share from the warehouse, and we'd find another way to rescue Akiko and Talbot.

As Bernice stepped into view on the street below, I shrank back, sure she could peer through the wooden siding and walls. "Bernice spooks me."

Ben's teeth flashed. "A woman like her could eat someone like you for breakfast and still prowl for a snack."

As though she'd heard us, Bernice threw her hands up and whirled, slinking away from the inn.

My shoulders relaxed as I exhaled. "She's pretty, though."

"Gorgeous, and way too much for you to handle."

"Agreed." I glanced at him, a smile twisting the corner of my mouth. "You and Josephine."

"Uh-huh." Ben's face purpled.

"I like the two of you together."

He cleared his throat. "Me too."

"Have you—"

"Not with Josephine... not yet. We had no privacy while

traveling, and by the time we got here—" Ben shrugged, then raised his eyebrow. "Have you?"

My toes curled in my boots as I shook my head. "No. Do you think it's too late to learn?"

In response, Ben roared, slapping his thigh, tears streaming from his eyes. My heart hammered as I stared at him, trying to decipher his mirth. Was that a yes?

CHAPTER FORTY-SIX

A stack of books staggered along the depot's cracked pavement, their shadow stark in the midday sun. Though the books obscured their bearer, my heart lifted.

Josephine.

I snatched a book out of the air as it slipped from the towering pile. "Did you take *all* the books?"

Josephine beamed as I lifted some books from her arms. "I'm so glad you're back, because I have good news for you."

After we failed in Aurora, I needed good news. I still didn't know how to approach Welland Island unseen, and although I'd sent several doodles to Akiko, she hadn't responded. Each time I tried to plan, I spent the time worrying about her—if she ate enough, if she still enjoyed the time with her peers, if she washed her teeth, and whether she had practiced her reading. The longer she spent on the island, the more afraid I was they would discover her impossible talent.

I bent to kiss Josephine's cheek. "What?"

Her eyes shone. "A boat steams to Welland Island twice a week with new recruits."

Ben wrapped his arms around Josephine and kissed the top of her head, lifting the remaining books off her arms. "Says who?"

She snuggled back into him, rubbing her arms. "The harbormaster. Apparently, he's not a fan of Reverend Carter."

If people were regularly traveling to the island, could we slip our own recruits in with the reverend's people? "Are many aboard?"

She clapped her hands. "Yes, twenty to twenty-five."

We'd estimated fifty to seventy people within the seminary walls, but if forty to fifty recruits arrived on the island each week, the estimates were worthless.

My face must have betrayed my dismay because Josephine's smile turned anxious. "I'm sorry. I thought this was helpful."

I shook my head. "It is good information. Look, here comes Beck."

Ben caught Beck's bowline and secured the boat, then took the rest of Josephine's books from me. "Can you find the others?"

I whistled for Charcoal and hurried to collect Genevie and Earl from the market. "Boat's here," I said, when I found them.

Earl, surrounded by paper-wrapped parcels, smiled at me. "Perfect timing. I needed another hand."

"Or a mule," said Genevie, twisting toward me. The surrounding people jumped out of the way of the long metal bars she held.

Earl ignored her. "Hold out your arms."

I obeyed, flinching as Earl loaded parcels into my arms. They emitted an odd, metallic scent.

"What?" she asked, pausing.

I lifted my chin, ignoring the growing ache. "They're cold."

Earl's smile widened. "Frozen beef."

Teeth gritted, I tried to keep my arms from shaking under the weight. "In July?"

"Mmm, stored in an ice hauler's hold. There, the last one. Let's go."

I staggered after them, trying to balance the parcels, but when we reached Beck's dock, the yellow boat was halfway to the island. Genevie and Earl set down their supplies, but I didn't want to drop anything and said nothing.

Charcoal circled me like a shark, his quivering nose high in the air.

By the time Beck returned, my arms trembled, rubber-like. Genevie gave me a strange look as she and Earl transferred their cargo into the boat. When they'd removed half of the load from me, I lowered my arms to ease the strain. The pile wobbled, and a package slid toward the edge of the stack. Without a free hand, I had no way to stop it and tried to catch it on my right thigh, which proved a mistake. I lost my balance and crumpled to the dock; parcels rained down around me with a *clunk-thunk.* "Sorry," I muttered, my face flaming.

Charcoal snatched a paper-wrapped package and sprinted to the end of the dock.

"Get back here," I growled. "Give!"

"Let him have it," said Earl.

I shook my head, glaring at the dog, who stared back at me, holding his parcel. "No, it sets a precedent."

She lay her icy hand on my shoulder. "They're his."

Distracted by her hand, I glanced at her. "What?"

"It's organ meat for him," said Earl.

Genevie snickered. "Dog food, Matthew."

I blinked. "He could have helped me carry it."

"Looks like he is," said Beck merrily. "Let's go, little man."

Charcoal trotted to the boat and jumped in, still holding his parcel.

Genevie and Beck chortled at the spectacle I made scrambling after the frozen meat I'd dropped, and I fought the urge to pelt the boat with the remaining parcels as I gathered them.

"If the meat wasn't mostly frozen, you'd have resembled Carter's recruits," said Beck, pulling on the oars.

I glanced at the bloodstains on my tunic and trousers. "They wear red?"

Beck nodded, whistling as she rowed us toward the island. "It's gotten so many in the depot look busy when they see a person dressed in red come by for goods or services. I'm hearing stories of mounting debts."

As I stared at my clothes, an idea ignited, so when the boat hit the dock, I leaped out and raced toward the inn with Charcoal on my heels. "Ben!"

Ben's gaze raked over me. "Are you bleeding?"

I glanced down. "No, it's dog food. Listen, I have a *plan*."

"You left them to carry everything?" asked Josephine, peering out the window.

"What?" I glanced outside to where Beck, Genevie, and Earl were wrestling the cargo out of the boat. "Blast. Come on."

When we reached them, I tried to apologize. "Sorry, I—"

"Give us a hand this time?" interrupted Genevie.

Under Beck's direction, we transported the meat to Mama's cellar. When finished, Ben studied me and grimaced. "Laundry time."

Impatient to share my idea, I ignored him. "I know how to approach the island," I said. "Two boats of recruits steam out to the island each week."

Genevie crossed her arms. "But they know what you look like."

I nodded. "Yes, but if we dress like recruits and fill our decoy boat with similarly dressed men, I can blend with them and sneak into the compound as part of a larger group."

"A second boat?" asked Josephine, her eyes brightening. "Aurora agreed to help?"

I shook my head. "Long story."

"A boat will get you to the island, but how will you reach the seminary up top?" asked Beck.

"Distraction," I said, beaming. "Here's what we will do..."

CHAPTER FORTY-SEVEN

My heart thumped as our counterfeit boat approached Welland Island.

"Steady, Matthew," Ben murmured.

I ducked my head, bowing it like the other recruits on the boat, hoping no one had seen me break from the prayer. The preacher had droned on for almost an hour, but by the stomach rumblings of the surrounding people, not everyone was in peaceful repose. I was hungry, too; I'd been too keyed up this morning to eat breakfast. Although the sun was high overhead, this time, I didn't expect the seminary to welcome or serve us lunch.

No matter. We'd feast tonight after we'd brought Akiko back to Mama's. With luck, we'd liberate Talbot too. "Cover me," I muttered.

Ben nodded, moving between me and the others. As soon as he'd blocked me from view, I dropped to one knee, pulling my sketchbook from my pocket. The "recruits" we'd sent to the island earlier had attached short segments of rope over the edge of the terrace wall, and I used the ropes as a starting point, lengthening them so they reached the base of the island, accessible from the dock. The air hung heavy and humid, the fetid water mingling with the mineral, mildewed scent of the granite cliffs.

To make sure I'd forgotten nothing, I stared at my sketch, examining the drawing for weaknesses.

"Here we go," Ben murmured.

Our boat was a few hundred meters from the dock, slowing as the pilot prepared to bring us alongside. By the time the vessel bumped the dock with a *thud-squeak*, I was scarcely breathing.

As planned, we tumbled from the boat onto the bobbing dock, shouting and cheering when the heavy cliff door opened. Several preachers stepped onto the dock. Their eyes widened, one man moving to stop the first of the recruits who'd reached the door.

"What's wrong?" asked the recruit.

"There are too many of you," said the preacher.

"I'm sure I don't know what you mean," replied another recruit in an excited voice.

I hid my smile; wearing homespun, red garments, no one would recognize him as the stonemason from Aurora. Even though I hadn't agreed to join them, some of Aurora's members had come with us to get a closer look at Welland Island.

"Let us through!" shouted voices from behind me.

The preachers exchanged glances.

Ben nudged me, and my heart thrilled as I peeked at the cliff near the south end of the dock. The confusion our crowd had created had given our four climbers a chance to shed their red clothing for tan-gray uniforms. I'd painted the clothing to blend with the cliff's stone. Two of the climbers were already fifty meters up, while high above the island, the flier circled.

The other boat neared the dock and its captain blared a

horn, adding to the confusion. Although I couldn't spot them, our kayakers would be paddling toward the island; we'd set the sound of the horn as the signal to approach.

"Let us through!" someone cried.

The preachers stepped aside, and the crowd surged forward. Ben and I moved with them, keeping our eyes locked on the cliff door. As we shuffled toward it, I scanned over my shoulder. The kayakers were barely visible as they paddled low against the water.

The crowd moved forward again, and Ben and I stepped nearer to the entrance, the crush of bodies intensifying as we all squeezed toward the narrow doorway.

Six meters.

The preachers huddled together, whispering and gesturing. While they were distracted, I peered up at the flier.

Five meters.

One wing dipped, and my heart stopped as the wings wobbled. Nausea rose in me as the machine appeared to slip sideways, near stalling.

Four meters.

When the flier dropped from the air, sliding out of view above the island, a buzzing filled my ears. I tried to swallow and reached out to tug on Ben's tunic.

Three meters.

A scream, followed by a sickening *thud,* made the people around me turn toward the south end of the dock. A climber had fallen and lay lifeless and bloody on the dock.

The preachers shouted, trying to push through the crush of people, as the three remaining climbers raced up their ropes. Although they climbed faster, they continued to lose altitude, sinking toward the ground.

"The ropes are stretching," said Ben.

Mouth dry, I shook my head. "They're not stretching;

they're lengthening." I glanced at the door, just two meters ahead.

The primary knot of preachers had spotted the kayaks, and one man waded through the crowd toward the climbers who were nearly back on the dock. The distractions meant I could slip past the remaining preachers and through the door, but by now, the seminary would be on high alert. Even if I got into the compound, I wouldn't be able to slip back out.

Time for Plan B.

I muttered our code word, "omega," and we eased our way backward through the crowd of men. Because we didn't turn away from the door, no one noticed we retreated, the illusion helped by the actual recruits still pushing forward to enter the cliff. When we'd broken free, we re-boarded our counterfeit ship and pushed off. The three remaining climbers bolted past an astonished preacher and leaped onto our boat.

Waves of despair washed over me as we pulled away. Wrapping my arms around myself, I sank to my knees. Our departure signaled the kayakers, who turned as a single pod, heading south toward the tree line.

Nauseous and shaking, I watched the island recede.

I'd failed again.

A litany of what had gone wrong tumbled through my mind. Not only hadn't I rescued Akiko and Talbot, I'd trapped several of our decoy recruits on the island. Worse, one of our climbers had fallen and died. And Bowman—my breath caught, and I sank to my knees, my grip tight on the iron railing. Bowman had crashed the flier. How would I face Earl? With luck, our decoys would pass as genuine recruits until we could regroup, but their fates, like Bowman's, were unknown.

In theory, the plan had been simple. Swelling the number of recruits as cover to sneak inside and find Akiko and Talbot. We'd theorized Reverend Carter would have us all thrown out rather than interrogate us one by one, and as a unit, we'd leave, spiriting Akiko and Talbot away. Instead, we'd left worse than empty-handed.

"What happened?" asked Ben, dropping to one knee beside me.

I blinked, my jaw working. "Carter was ready for us."

Ben's eyes darkened. "How? I don't understand how everything went wrong. The flier, the climbers..."

I could barely meet Ben's eyes as the island shrank in the distance. My gorge rose, and bile flooded my mouth—thick, bitter, and sour. "Carter has weaponized *art*."

CHAPTER FORTY-EIGHT

The wind's violence matched my mood, and in response, my small boat leaped across the churning water. Storm clouds gathered on the eastern horizon, a bulbous raw umber with Mars violet and green-gold undertones.

No matter. I'd deal with the coming weather later.

Eyes narrowed, I focused on the spot I wanted to beach. Glancing at the wind indicator on the mast, I shoved the rudder, ducking as the boom swung overhead. The wind filled the sail with a *crack*, and the little sailboat flew toward the abbey, a fine mist spraying my windburned face. As I hauled up the daggerboard to prepare for beaching, the boys on the bluff above abandoned their afternoon lesson, dancing and pointing at my boat. A hundred meters from the shore, I dropped the sail, letting the boat slow, and crouched, ready for impact.

The boat hit the sandy gravel with a *thud-crunch*, catapulting me onto the beach. Fueled by rage, my mind burned sharp, slowing time as I flew. I landed on my feet, flinging the bowline to the first, wide-eyed boy who'd reached the beach.

"Tie it off," I ordered, striding up the hill toward the abbey. As I crested the hill, I allowed my fury to ignite into a molten mass.

The young master who'd been instructing the class on the lawn bowed. "Master Sugiyama."

My eyes smoldered. "Where's Headmaster McCully?"

He blanched, licking his lips. "His office?"

I pointed at the nearest boy. "Take me there."

The boy trotted to the headmaster's office without a word. When we reached the door, I pounded on it with the side of my fist, each *thud* harder. By the time Headmaster McCully opened it, I was nearly incandescent.

McCully paled, stepping backward. "Matthew—"

I swept past him without waiting for an invitation and stalked to the windows. Whirling, I faced him, my hands flexing. To protect the abbey, I needed him to understand the danger Carter posed. "I've found the missing artists."

The headmaster blinked, excused my escort, and shut the door. His voice was quiet. "Missing artists?"

I ground my teeth, my breath coming in gasps. "From Erie Abbey. Unless you're *also* missing artists from here?"

McCully shook his head, sinking into an armchair. He gestured toward the other chair, but I ignored him, pacing. "They're on Welland Island, in the Reverend Carter's seminary."

"Seminary?" Headmaster McCully rubbed his jaw, his brow furrowed as though I'd jabbered in an unfamiliar language. "What does it have to do with us? Please, sit."

I ached to shake the man. Artists in the abbey system tended toward insularity—focused on their craft rather than engaging with the greater world—but to ignore what happened outside the abbey walls was foolish. Worse, with this kind of threat to the abbey, it was dangerous and shortsighted.

A cloud of dust erupted as I flung myself into the empty

armchair, a part of me enjoying the expression of annoyance crossing McCully's face. "The artists from Erie Abbey work for Reverend Carter," I repeated. To slow my message, I drew my words out, enunciating each.

McCully's outward appearance remained placid. Why hadn't he leaped forward with alarm and outrage? Carter's representatives could *already* be on their way here to Niagara Abbey.

If I'd told Headmaster Sinclair this news, he'd have jumped to his feet, shouting orders to fortify Popham as he strode down the stone hallways, flexing his sword arm.

I snapped forward, and McCully flinched, recoiling backward. He recovered quickly, settling back as if preparing for a long conversation, but his drumming fingers gave him away. He wasn't as serene as he pretended, and somehow, this small tic soothed my anger. "What will you do about it?"

He cleared his throat. "Why don't I call a meeting of the masters?"

A meeting?

My fingernails dug into my palms, but I hid my frustration, nodding once.

McCully released a breath and rose, smoothing his palms over his robes as he flashed me a small smile. Moving to the door, he pulled a thick, braided cord hanging on the wall. The faded gold of the cord matched the dust motes swirling in the sunlight.

We waited, his silence contemplative, mine masking the cauldron of emotions boiling within me. Even the familiar scents of books and stone didn't comfort me.

McCully brightened at a soft knock, his face animating. "Come in."

Master Bower stepped inside, his eyes widening. "It *was* you, in the boat."

My eyes tightened. "It was."

"Please assemble the masters in the dining hall." McCully's voice was even, but his body was too still. Perhaps my warning had affected him after all.

Bower nodded but didn't move, as though waiting for more.

"Now," I said, my single-word demand ringing in the quiet room.

McCully's jaw clenched, but he nodded. "Now."

"Certainly." Bower paused before saying, "Welcome back, Sugiyama," in a quiet voice.

Headmaster McCully stood to shut the door behind Bower, but I shook my head. "Let's go, too."

STILL SILENT, McCULLY LED ME TO THE DINING HALL. The cavernous room was empty, but groups of students huddled on the lawn, whispering and gesturing.

"You've upset our routine," said McCully.

His bland reproval unnerved me. I'd come to warn them— to create a stir—nothing I should apologize for. To rein in my frustration, I focused on the masters entering the dining hall in twos and threes. Bower was the last to arrive, closing the doors behind him. I nodded to those I recognized, counting heads.

Eighteen.

It wasn't much, but I needed every artist I could gather.

Headmaster McCully's chin lifted as he squared his shoulders. "Thank you for coming, masters. Even if you didn't meet Master Sugiyama the last time he visited, you've seen the watercolor he painted while he was here."

Several of the men nodded, their gazes curious and frank.

"And now," said McCully, "he's brought news of Erie Abbey's artists."

The energy level of the room jumped as everyone stilled and focused on me.

This was it.

If I didn't convince them to help, there was no way I could meet, let alone beat, the power Reverend Carter had amassed. "Thank you, Headmaster. When I was last here, you asked me to explore Erie Abbey to determine why they'd stopped communicating. I found Erie abandoned—no artists, no answers."

They waited, nodding.

"While staying in Toronto Depot, I had the occasion to meet a former Erie Abbey student. He confirmed he left with eleven classmates to follow Master Hooper from Erie Abbey to the seminary on Welland Island." I paused, studying their faces, trying to gauge the effect of my words. "A seminary is a type of religious college from *Before*."

The men murmured, glancing at each other, as Tom Staker gaped at me.

I raised my palms. "Welland Island is now a fortress, approachable via a single point."

The men appeared confused, exchanging puzzled glances, but Bower's mouth hardened as though he understood the implication of my message. "Go on," he said.

I nodded. "The boy said he left with the others to improve Welland Island and its seminary. He told me about plans to live-paint several large murals."

Headmaster McCully sank to a bench, staring vacantly toward the ceiling.

"Why?" someone asked.

Why *indeed*? I stood straighter. "He told me they would illustrate a war."

Headmaster McCully snorted. "Sugiyama, this is preposterous conjecture. Surely you didn't come to alarm us needlessly?"

Men nodded, relaxing.

I stared at them. Where was their anger, their fury? They waited, curious but not alarmed. My hands balled as I turned to Bower. Surely a man protective of dead artists' *paintbrushes* would rally the others to protect the abbey.

But instead of anger, Bower smiled. "Sugiyama entertains us, brothers. Not only is he a talented artist, but he has developed his storytelling skills while on the road. I hope you don't expect more art supplies in trade."

Men chuckled, further dissipating the energy in the room.

I could lose them.

Tom Staker raised his hand, and I focused on him. "Staker?"

He sighed, shuffling his feet. "Which boy did you speak to?"

The boy's face materialized on my mind's canvas. "Dennis Filmer."

One master sat up straighter. "A dumpy boy with straw-blond hair?"

Several masters leaned forward, their eyes sharp and interested as the smiles fell from their lips.

I nodded. "A chubby, freckled boy who struggled to anchor his art."

Robbert spoke in a quiet voice, "I remember him. Not a brilliant talent."

Now the men exchanged troubled glances.

Bolstered by the shifting mood, I stood. My boat wasn't large enough to take them to the island, but I could show them what I'd seen. "Can someone bring a canvas and easel?"

A gray-haired master with sharp features nodded and

opened a closet I hadn't noticed. He set up an easel and canvas, then stepped back, his eyes watchful.

The act of pulling my sketching pencils from my rucksack helped center me. With rapid, sure strokes, I sketched the outline of the island from memory, glancing up when Staker cleared his throat.

Staker rubbed his jaw. "Filmer said they left voluntarily?"

The pencil scratched against the canvas with rhythmic *snick-snick* sounds as I shaded the folds and curves of rock. "Yes, after the snows melted. Thirteen boys left with Hooper, but based on what Filmer described, Carter plans for at least forty artists to collaborate on the mural. Filmer said their goal was to illustrate the war. He believed it an attempt to capture what happened during an event from *Before*."

"You don't?" someone asked.

I shook my head without looking up. "I think Carter plans to use artists in battle... soon."

The men muttered, shifting, restless in their seats. In ones and twos, they drifted behind me to observe what I drew.

I'd nearly reproduced the island on my sketch, but it wasn't until I drew tiny figures on the water-side dock that the masters understood the *scale* of what Carter had built. Their gasps brought McCully out of his stupor, but he looked unconcerned as he walked around the easel to view my work.

To observe his reaction, I backed away from my sketch.

His expression didn't change until he leaned in closer, peering at the tiny figures of people and the paddle-driven barges docked at the island's base. "It's a fortress," he said, in a shrill, breathy voice, his face conveying alarm.

Finally.

I nodded, glancing at the surrounding men. "Yes."

"What for?" asked Robbert.

Their expressions ranged from blank to troubled, so I chose

my words carefully. "Last year, people following the directions of a man who worked for Carter attacked a community I stayed in."

Bower's chin jutted, his eyes narrowing. "Attacked? Violently?"

Sprays of blood and Whistler's split skull splattered onto my mind's canvas, anguished cries ringing in my memory. "Very. They killed at least ninety-five souls between three communities. Twenty fell during the attack on Wakefield alone."

Bower stared at my drawing. "Have you met Reverend Carter?"

My unfinished drawing had done its intended job, but the artist in me yearned to finish what I'd started. Fighting the urge to step forward and complete the sketch, I twirled the pencil in my hand. "No, but if he's preparing for a war using artists, don't we have a duty to respond? At the least, to secure Niagara Abbey?"

Bower's face hardened. "How do you know Carter will use artists?"

Hope glimmered in McCully's eyes. "Yes, perhaps you're mistaken and jumping to conclusions."

The other masters wavered, wanting to believe anything but the grim warning I'd delivered.

It was now or never. I drew a deep breath and opened my energy. It was an unthinkable breach of etiquette and it swirled as it surrounded them, allowing them to experience the truth of my words. "I know, Headmaster, because I witnessed them kill a man with art."

CHAPTER FORTY-NINE

The cramp in my hand had gotten worse, and even shaking it out wasn't helping. Following the meeting in the dining hall, I'd passed the time in my room drawing, partly because I needed something to do while I waited for dinner and partly because I'd seen how useful my sketch had been in convincing the masters to heed my warnings. Since only Olen and I had seen the compound, I'd drawn as much of the seminary's layout as I could remember from our visit.

I paced the room shaking my hand, then crossed to the window and flung it open. The viscous air was grassy and herbaceous, tinged with a floral sweetness. Though the storm clouds had moved closer, sunlight drenched the grassy bluff. A *clang* split the air, followed by a grunt. I craned my neck but couldn't find the source.

"Good lad, again!" called someone. Several more metallic clashes happened in quick succession, followed by cheering.

This was what I needed.

Tossing the pencil onto the drafting desk, I pulled off my borrowed robes and outer tunic. Skipping down the stone steps,

I pulled my linen undertunic from my waistband and retied the leather lace holding my hair back.

I squinted against the sunlight skipping off the crashing waves as I crossed the lawn. "Hullo, Staker. Are the masters done with their deliberations?"

The boys he'd been instructing stopped drilling, lowering their blades as I approached.

"Master Sugiyama," he said, shrugging. "They dismissed all but the senior masters."

Interesting.

I gestured toward the rack of swords. "May I join you?"

Staker grinned. "How good was the sword master at Popham?"

I raised my eyebrow. "Let's find out, shall we?"

Staker called for a student to bring me a sword while he pulled off his robes and unbuttoned his outer tunic. "We're using fencing blades today, Sugiyama."

The sword brought to me was light and flexed when I pressed it. I wrapped my fingers through the knuckle-bow and slipped my pointer finger into the pas d'âne, taking a few practice swipes.

The boys grinned and backed up, their faces eager.

"Now, boys," said Staker, "whenever you face a new opponent, try not to forget the basics. How do we hold our swords?"

"Like a bird," answered a ginger-haired boy.

"That's right," said Staker, circling me. "And why do we hold them lightly?"

He lunged at me, but prepared, I sidestepped, parrying his steel.

"To keep the flexibility in our wrists," said another boy.

"Correct," said Staker, lunging again. This time, he feinted to his right and tried to swipe at my leg.

I blocked his sword and stepped into him, knocking him

backward with a blow from my forearm.

Staker's eyes widened, but he grinned. "When you spar with your partners, safety is paramount, so we maintain distance, we communicate by holding eye contact, and we reveal our intentions through the beginning stance of our swing."

He motioned for me to attack, so I slowly lunged, as they had taught me in fencing class, maintaining eye contact, and flicking my sword as though to dislodge a fly clinging to the tip. Staker easily parried, then spun and knocked into my bad calf with his shin. Stung, I went over backward, landing hard.

The boys cheered, and Staker bowed. "However, in a proper fight, you use everything you can against your opponent. You must fight as though there are no rules. Your lives may depend on it."

He extended his hand, and I gripped it. Without warning, I yanked back hard, flipping him over me. Tucking his head, he somersaulted, then sprang to his feet. We crouched, circling each other. I watched his face and his eyes for tells, but both remained expressionless as he thrust at me.

I blocked his attack, then counterattacked, our steels crashing and clanging. We broke apart and circled again. The sounds of the wind and the waves and the cheering boys fell away, leaving only the vibration of our swords. His breathing, my grunts. Sweat ran in rivulets down my face, stinging my eyes as I swung and parried. We fought—knocking each other down and slashing with the lightweight swords—as though only one of us could survive.

Our sparring carried us toward the edge of the lawn. As he circled me, I knew he'd force me into the shrubbery if I gave him the chance. I sidestepped and hit his back hard as he rushed past me, but he ducked and spun, using my hip thrust against me. I backed away, moving to my left.

We circled, breathing hard, assessing each other. Before he attacked, his left hand twitched. Forewarned, I dropped my right hip, bringing the sword in an arc and stopping it just below his navel. He jumped backward and nearly went over the bluff's edge, his arms flailing, so I released my sword to grab a fistful of his undertunic and yanked him forward. He dropped his sword as he somersaulted over me and came up, wiping the sweat from his brow with the back of his arm.

"You're an excellent swordsman," I said, panting. I bent and retrieved the weapons. "Did you learn here?"

He clapped me on the back and took both blades from me. "My father was the sword master here before me, but I've never fought someone like you before. You're classically trained, but there's something else in the way you fight."

"The sword master at Popham was a stickler."

Even though I kept my words light, I knew Staker was right. I'd learned what real fighting was during the battle in Wakefield. There, I'd learned to conserve my energy, hide my moves, and attack whenever I had the slightest advantage—very different from the poised stances and mannerly conduct they'd taught me at Popham.

My willingness to fight dirty was the reason I'd survived. If a fight came... I hoped these boys would take Staker's words to heart. Pushing away grim visions, I sighed. "Thank you for this. I needed the exertion, both mental and physical."

He tossed me a towel, wiping his face on another. "We fight to win many kinds of peace. Boys, what are you waiting for?"

The lads returned to their sparring, and I watched, thinking about Staker's words. Fighting was one way to win peace, but it wasn't the only way.

Tom stepped closer. "They appear to be ready for you."

Five men, including Headmaster McCully and Bower,

waited on the veranda. My stomach tightened, and I took my time wiping my face. "Dinner?"

Staker nodded. "Good luck."

I slung the towel around my neck and jogged up the steps to the veranda.

"Pleasant day for a sparring match," said a master.

I nodded at him and turned to McCully. "Sir?"

Headmaster McCully cleared his throat, my stomach sinking at the sound. "We'd like to offer a permanent position here for you and your ward."

My eyebrows shot up, and I licked my lips, tasting salt. "A position?"

Bower nodded, frowning. "We've agreed you'd be an asset to Niagara Abbey. It's possible your entering the abbey system will also smooth the tension between Reverend Carter and the rest of us. We are so few... engaging in caustic maneuvers against Carter's followers cannot be good practice."

McCully glared at Bower. "What Bower *meant* to say was we invite you to join us as a senior master and hope you'll accept. We believe your acceptance will further remove you from Reverend Carter's notice, easing the tensions for everyone."

I blinked at McCully, unable to speak. My highest hope had been they'd join me against Reverend Carter, but I'd have settled for them making preparations to defend themselves. I'd never imagined they'd offer me a position, and to offer a spot to Akiko—this surprised me most.

Headmaster McCully cleared his throat. "To your point about the outside world, we agree. We've allowed ourselves to become too isolated, so we'd like to establish a cooperative community here, operating independently from the abbey while supporting us and our work. We'd do the same, exchanging our resources for theirs."

My chest caught. "It's how Popham worked."

McCully's eyes were warm as he stepped closer. "Yes, and as a senior master, you'd have the option of residing in either the abbey or in the community. Should you choose to stay, we'll help you negotiate for Akiko's release."

A band tightened across my chest as I stared at the sea.

Negotiate?

I hadn't even considered negotiation. Their solution had merit and with the abbey's support, it wouldn't take much to establish a cooperative community. Cooperative communities were highly desirable and attracted good people, so many would flock to apply. The location worked too; the abbey was near enough to Toronto Depot, and far enough from Welland Island, so with a good dock, we could easily establish ourselves on the lake's trading routes.

As a minstrel, Talbot was unlikely to settle anywhere, but would everyone else consider settling with us? Alone, I had struggled to parent Akiko, but this could be an answer. Akiko clearly longed for stability, and if I accepted the abbey's offer, she would have structure, guidance from the masters, a chance to catch up on her schooling, and the opportunity to make lasting friendships. If needed, I could work with her on her art secretly, but negotiate for her to attend classes on composition, portraiture, and working with different media like any other student.

The resolve I'd found in Aurora wavered. Although I didn't know the cost of giving up on my quest to find my birth family, the price of losing a friend was steep. Even now, Bowman's fate was undetermined. But if I settled at the abbey, would Reverend Carter agree to leave us be? I turned to the masters and scanned their hopeful faces. "Can I think about it?"

Headmaster McCully's eyes dimmed, but he nodded. "For as long as it takes. Be certain of your decision, Sugiyama."

CHAPTER FIFTY

Hands swollen from the spray, I hiked—shifting my weight over the side of the boat—as the boom flew over my head. The boat shuddered as it fought the wind, and I tightened my chapped hands on the rudder and mainsail line. No wonder Gunther's hands rasped like sandpaper.

The wind changed again, and the sail luffed. The boat settled deeper into the water as it slowed, drenching me when waves crested the bow. After loosening the mainsail line, I ducked, the boom swinging over me, but I sat up before tightening the line, and the boom swung back, striking me across my crown.

Stars exploded in my eyes as pain cascaded down my skull like shooting tendrils of ice. I retched, belly crawling to the edge of the deck. Gasping, I hung my head over the side and stared unseeing at the steely gray water, blood thick and bitter in my mouth.

Tiny fish, nearly translucent, darted in my wavering reflection.

The wooziness had lessened when a wave smashed into the

port side of my boat, pushing the starboard edge toward the water. As the next wave broke over my face, I reflexively swallowed the musty water. The boat rocked back to center, pulling me—gagging and retching—out of the water in time to snatch a breath before another wave swamped me. Flopping onto my back, I gasped, waiting for the spinning to stop.

Fractured clouds scooted across the granite-gray sky, the lower clouds moving faster than the painted feathers higher up. Storm clouds billowed to the east. Already, the storm-pushed winds were fierce—if I didn't make it back to Toronto Depot before the full storm hit, I could be in trouble.

My boat was three meters long, with a shallow dish in the center. Without a cabin, it provided no cover. Gunther had warned me boats like this were built for skipping across a bay on a sunny day, but not in weather of any kind. In hindsight, I should have improved the vessel, but I'd been too angry after my failure on Welland Island. Instead, I'd headed directly to Niagara Abbey to warn them, and then in too much of a hurry to return to the depot to pay attention to the small boat.

Although steel shards stabbed my skull, I sat up, hauling in the mainsail line. As soon as I tightened it, the boom swung, and the sail filled. The boat picked up speed, and I watched the wind indicator, tacking to catch the next gust before losing momentum.

Over the next hour, I danced across the waves, bending and turning just before losing the wind. The little boat skimmed the fractured lake surface, skipping through the growing chop. The eastern sky had darkened, so when the air temperature fell, my heart sank. I wouldn't make it back to Mama's before the storm hit.

To beat the storm, I'd chosen the direct route across the middle of the lake. The northern shore was invisible, but I could make out where the southern shore broke the horizon. Toronto Depot lay somewhere in the invisible west.

If I turned south, it would take longer to get to the shelter of the depot and could bring me too close to Welland Island. But if I stayed in the open water, I risked a rough ride. A sudden wind overwhelmed my already-full sail, and the boat leaned farther than I believed possible, exposing its hull. Heart in my throat, I hiked my full weight out over the higher side. The deck lines I'd slid my feet through bit into my shins as my body bowed with the strain. If the boat went over, it would either catapult me into the roiling chop or snap me in two.

The wind luffed, and the boat heeled in my direction too quickly. In a blink, it slammed into the water, submerging me from head to waist. When it rocked back, I broke the surface of the water, gasping. Shaking the water from my eyes, I shoved the rudder away from me and pulled my feet from the straps. If it came to it, I'd prefer to take my chances in the water than break on top of it.

Turn south, Artist.

Before I could set a new heading, the sail filled with a *snap* as the boat turned; the boom swinging with lethal force. I ducked in time and scanned the southern shore, trying to pick a landmark to work toward, but the skies opened with a crack. The force of the sudden deluge caught my breath and obscured the shoreline, leaving me at the mercy of the sea.

The sail filled with a jerk, and the boat slid through the water, plowing through the larger waves. As it picked up speed, it rose onto the wave tips, and the ride smoothed out. I squinted at the wind indicator while icy pellets stung my face.

The boat shuddered as the sail caught too much wind, and we leaned again. This time, I fell forward, scrabbling on the slick deck for something to hang onto. Without my feet secured in the straps, I had nothing to brace against. I hung onto the rudder and mainsail line as the little boat heeled to its starboard side.

Before the boat could right, a wave hit the exposed hull, and I struggled to breathe as the tip of the mast kissed the water. As it broke the water's surface, the boat's axis rotated, allowing the mast to slide into the water like a knife through a cake.

We capsized before I could process what was happening. Tremendous pressure pinned me against the submerged deck. I blinked when the water switched from dark to light, as if the storm overhead had stopped. For a moment, the water was as brightly lit as a sunny day, and I watched the submerged mainsail luff gently, its ropes snaking away toward the deep dark. My chest heaved when the water went dark, and I pushed away from the boat, kicking free of the ropes sinuously winding against my leg.

I broke the water's surface in time to watch another fork of lightning smash into the roiling surface. The storm's roar disoriented me as I bobbed in a trough between fractured waves.

Now what?

The hull of my boat was already two troughs over and moving away from me, caught in a separate current. As I swam toward it, waves broke over me rhythmically, each trying to drag me down toward the deep dark. My shoulders ached from the effort as I focused on the boat, but I had no choice—I needed to reach the boat before I exhausted my strength. Despite my focus, the waves pulled me backward every time I reached toward the hull, making the next reach harder. As another wave swelled beneath me, I kicked with all the strength I had left, determined to slide down the boat's side of the wave and not backward again. I caught the crest as the wave broke beneath me, slamming me against the boat. The pain stunned me, but I scrabbled against the slick hull, searching for anything to grasp. When my left pointer finger hooked into the dagger-board channel, I relaxed, waiting for the next swell to lift us. As it released us, I squirmed my way onto the hull, dragging myself inch by inch onto its slick, curved surface.

The afternoon sky was as dark as night, the air saturated and impenetrable. Wind battered my back as I lay limply across the sailboat's hull, my calves and feet floating in the water. I wasn't beaten, but I was spent, and until the storm passed, I could do nothing. A strange peace descended upon me, a weary acceptance of who and where I was. As hard as I tried, some things were simply beyond my control.

As I sprawled across the bobbing hull, I focused on Akiko. When I'd left Niagara Abbey this morning, there had been no news in my sketchbook. I had to believe Talbot would have found a way to get word to us if anything had changed, so the best I could hope for was the status quo. My arms were too tired to check if I'd lost my sketchbook during my swim and I snorted as a wave tasting of minerals and algae drenched my face.

Now what?

Even if the storm stopped before night fell, I didn't know how to right the boat, but with luck, I'd be near a shoreline and could wait for rescue. Once again, I'd put myself squarely in the path of danger. While seeking my family, I'd found myself in trouble on the road, in the air, on the water, and now *in* the water. Perhaps it was time to admit I was not a good traveler... and settle. Besides, Niagara Abbey's offer created exciting possibilities, like a blank canvas waiting for art. If my friends were also ready to settle, we could establish the community with a scholar, engineer, blacksmith, and maybe even a butcher... if Earl could forgive me.

My stomach clenched. What *had* happened to Bowman? At best, Bowman had landed and talked his way to safety. Only

Akiko knew who Bowman was, so he had a chance. At worst... I couldn't let myself think about it.

If we opened negotiations for Akiko's return with Reverend Carter, it risked alerting him of her importance to me... but who was I to Carter? My parents had attempted to hide me from him, but if I didn't understand why, he might not either. Besides, what did it matter if Carter attempted to establish a sanctuary to practice religion in peace? If his followers were content to let us live as we wished, why not return the favor?

A wave broke against the boat, and I sneezed, my nose filling with water. Wet and storm-tumbled, a life of peace now seemed a worthy goal. Besides, if I was honest with myself, did my birth family matter more than my friends? Whoever my parents were, they'd chosen to leave me in the abbey system. Chosen to remain silent when I graduated. In contrast, Josephine, Ben, and Genevie had battled weather, hunger, and crazed fanatics with me. Even Earl and Bowman had helped me more than my parents by loaning us the flier.

So, what was wrong with abandoning my quest to find my birth family and live with my *chosen* family?

When a shrill, squealing noise rang across the waves, I picked up my head, scanning the gray water. I squinted into the wind-driven rain, expecting a hapless bird or rubbing debris.

Nothing.

The shriek came again, and I glanced over my left shoulder, my neck and back protesting as I turned my head. A pile of debris floated on the water but disappeared behind a wave. Eyes narrowed, I watched the waves heave, waiting for the debris to reappear.

The squeal came again to the right this time, and my eyes widened as a man appeared between the waves, clutching a plank. He disappeared between the troughs, then reappeared on the next wave over. He blew his whistle again and again as he slid down the backside of the wave.

I let go of the boat with my right arm and reached for him as he crested the wave. He slid out of reach, so we waited for the next swell. This time, our fingers touched, and he kicked harder, releasing the plank. My grip tightened as the wave tried to suck him away, but I hung on, the fingers of my left hand clinging to the hull.

"Thanks," he gasped, as I pulled him against my boat, the whistle floating in the water between us. When the next swell lifted us, we squirmed onto the hull and lay on our bellies, facing each other.

The man chuckled.

I was too tired to join him, but my cheek squeaked against the hull as I smiled. "Matthew."

"Bryer."

I'd run out of words, but he appeared to be waiting for me to say something. "Well met?"

Bryer chortled, then turned his head and spat. "I've drunk more water today than is good for a person."

I closed my eyes, but they popped open as the whistle shrieked. "Is someone else in the water?"

Bryer grinned with the whistle clamped between his teeth. "Sure hope so or we'll be here a while."

My heart lifted. "Do you know where we are?"

"We're in the lake, my friend," he replied.

Though Bryer continued to blow his whistle and the capsized boat pitched and rolled, I dozed, my mind rousing occasionally before falling toward slumber again until the whistle's tone sharpened, spiking my adrenaline. Bryer's eyes gleamed, and his face was nearly crimson as he puffed enthusiastically, so I lifted my chin and followed his focus until I saw a boat.

A boat.

"Hey, hey!" I shouted, waving my left arm above me. "Over here!" I pounded the hull with my free arm as Bryer's whistle screamed.

The boat turned slowly toward us, its wooden prow crashing through the waves. Through the rain, I caught glimpses of the crew rushing across the storm-beaten deck. One moved toward the railing, carrying a heavy coiled rope. As the boat neared, I chanced to look up at our rescuers, and my heart stopped as I drowned in Earl's fathomless, green eyes.

CHAPTER FIFTY-ONE

The sailboat's hull shuddered under the weight of the next crashing wave. I ducked my head, wincing as the chilly water washed over me.

No matter, rescue was here.

But when I looked back up, Earl was gone, and Gunther stood in her place. Even his whiskers scowled. "Fools find each other," he muttered.

"What?" I asked, blinking. Had I hallucinated Earl?

Olen's face popped over the railing. "Who's your friend?"

I glanced at Bryer, then back at Gunther. "Permission to come aboard, Captain?"

Gunther's weathered face scrunched into a smile, eyes crinkling and mustache curving. "Aye. Come aboard, lad."

They threw the knotted rope net over the side, and Bryer struggled to pull himself up, his arms shaking from the effort.

Without help, he'd never make it up, so I slipped backward off the sailboat's hull and swam behind him. Once I was in position, he put his foot on my shoulder and pushed up. I lost my grip and slid underwater, spluttering as I came up for air. Bryer crawled up the knotted rope, inches at a time.

"Matthew, come on!" Olen shouted.

I held up a finger, taking a deep breath. The sounds of the storm muted as I sank beneath the surface and swam to the submerged mast. The knots I'd tied were stuck—the rope swollen—and my chest heaved as I struggled with them. Slowly, they released, freeing the canvas bag of art supplies I'd lashed to the mast. Bag in hand, I kicked backward, struggling to reach the surface. When I broke through to the air, my lungs were on fire.

Olen, halfway down the rope netting, whooped. "Idiot! I nearly jumped in after you."

"Here," I said, shoving the sodden bag at him.

He hooked it with a grunt, climbing toward the railing.

Using the motion of the waves, I hauled myself back on top of the submerged hull and caught the rope netting. The rope twisted around my hand painfully as my momentum swung me around. My back slammed into the side of the *Marybelle* with a wet *slap*, jarring my vision. I twisted, pulling my knees beneath me, then tried to stand on the hull of my capsized boat. The hull bucked, and without my grip on the netting, I would have gone over backward.

"Better climb, Artist," called Gunther, squinting behind me.

On instinct, I sprang from my boat's hull as a broad wave slammed into it. The wave shoved my boat against Gunther's with a sickening grinding sound, and when they separated, my overturned sailboat rotated away into the storm.

My arms were rubbery by the time Olen helped haul me over the side. I lay on the deck, gasping, staring up into the storm clouds. Several lightning strikes happened in quick succession, the water around us turning a ghostly cadmium green. This struck me as funny, and I chuckled.

Bryer giggled in response, and soon we howled with tears streaming down our faces, wet with our good fortune and the rain.

"How did you find us?" I asked, gasping for breath.

Gunther jerked his chin at Olen. "He was sure you'd try to ride the storm front, and convinced me to depart before it hit the depot. But 'tis luck yon tweeter has a hearty set of lungs."

Bryer put the whistle in his mouth and gave it a short toot.

"The girls are below with hot drinks and towels," Gunther said, squinting into the driving rain. "Get below, fools."

Girls.

So, I hadn't imagined Earl. Olen reached his hand out for me, and I took it, pulling myself onto my feet. The deck pitched and rolled in the storm, and I staggered and lurched after them, clutching my sodden bag. Halfway down the ladder, I dropped the bag. It hit the gleaming wooden floor with a wet *thud*.

Even so, Beck beamed when I reached the bottom. "We laid out dry clothes and towels in the front cabin. Leave your things, and we'll deal with them later."

We filed into the cabin, stripping off our clothing. I toweled off shivering, pulling on a pair of dry trousers and a thick knitted tunic. "You have a terrible bruise," I said.

Bryer twisted to examine his right shoulder. "My foot caught in a line as I fell overboard, and I hit the hull."

Olen shook his head. "You're both blasted lucky. Matthew, you'll be a rainbow of bruises tomorrow too."

I chuckled. "I feel great right now."

"Dry clothes and a couple of pretty faces," agreed Bryer. "I'm happy myself."

Olen grinned. "I'll tell Gunther you think he's pretty."

Our hearts light, we tottered back into the galley where Earl passed out steaming mugs. When I took mine, our fingers touched, hers lingering before releasing the cup. The brief contact set off lightning strikes within me and, flustered, I took a sip of tea, spluttering as molten mint seared my tongue.

"Hullo," she said.

"Hot." I could have kicked myself when she turned away without responding. I ran the tip of my tongue against the roof of my mouth, wincing.

Gunther clomped down the ladder, shaking his head like a wet dog. "Ach, 'tis dampish."

Spots floated in front of my eyes as my chest squeezed, leaving me breathless. "Who's steering the boat?"

"Relax, Artist," said Beck. "We use a storm anchor to true ourselves. Want to introduce your friend?"

"I'm Bryer," he said, introducing himself.

Olen sighed, leaning back on the bench. "What were you doing in the water?"

Bryer finished his mug before saying, "Sailing."

I chuckled. "More like floating."

"And a bit of clinging," said Bryer, agreeing. "I'm Old Joe's replacement."

Gunther's eyes lit up. "Do you have news?"

"A mail craft is drifting in the Ontario Sea. Reward. Spread the word," said Bryer, raising his mug.

"Mail craft? Isn't that what you do?" I asked Gunther.

He nodded. "But only between the friendlier folk. Old Joe also stopped at the filling stations with the cranky and the curmudgeonly."

Olen and I snorted simultaneously, earning a glare from Gunther. "I storm watch from the flybridge, but holler if you need me," he said.

Bryer set his mug down. "I'm sacked."

Olen slipped his arm around Beck, yawning. "Take the hammock in the bow cabin. We're crashing in the aft."

Rain burst through the hatch, soaking my head and shoulders as I fastened it behind Gunther, but after I finished, Earl tossed me a towel. My nerves jumped and danced as I dried my hair, the schooner's galley impossibly snug now it was just the two of us. When I finished, I folded the towel and picked up my mug, careful to keep space between us.

"I won't bite," she said.

My quick laugh was shrill until my fingers spasmed and I dropped the mug. It caught the edge of the counter, splashing the dregs of the lukewarm tea across my groin. I studied my sodden trousers with my face flaming.

Earl chuckled and slipped into the booth. "Sit, Sailor." She settled back as if to wait for me to speak.

When my eyes flicked toward the aft cabin, her lips curved into her lopsided smile, so I took a deep breath. "I thought you and Olen..."

Earl raised one eyebrow. "Really?"

I stared at my fingers, then nodded. "When we were out fishing, you looked like—" I stopped, rethinking my words. "You looked... friendly."

Her eyes twinkled. "He asked for advice about Beck."

I straightened. "Beck? What about her?"

Ear tilted her head. "Do you really want to talk about Olen and Beck?"

What I *wanted* was to paint her exactly as she appeared now, illuminated by the soft light coming from the oil lamps. I wanted to watch her face solidify on a canvas, where I could stroke the curve of her cheek to life with my brushes, and... I pressed my lips together. "Yes?"

Earl toyed with her mug. "Okay, I'll play along. Olen has a dilemma. He wants a future with Beck but doesn't know if he should leave Aurora or talk her into moving there."

My eyes traced Earl's cheek, stopping at her lips. Which pigments would I use to capture them on canvas? Earl's lips were more luminous than opera rose, but more delicate than rose madder.

"Artist?" Earl's grin turned wicked. Had she read my mind?

I dropped my eyes as a flush crept up my neck. "Aurora invited her to join them an age ago."

Laughter bubbled in her voice when she said, "He knows, but doesn't want to come between her and her family. Plus, his brother is in Toronto Depot."

The scarred keeper's face chased Earl off my mind's canvas. "Right, Aya."

Earl nodded. "Family is tough."

A pang stabbed me, but I pushed it away, focusing on her. "Where is your family? Star Creek?"

She shook her head. "Someone left me at the filling station, so I grew up there. I don't know who my parents were. All I know is they didn't want me."

Stunned by her statement, I stared at her. Why hadn't something this foundational—something we *shared*—come up before this? "Same here."

Her green eyes danced. "I know."

As much as I wanted to explore what else we had in common, I needed to say something first. "I'm sorry about Bowman."

Her face turned serious, and a distance opened between us. Her eyes shuttered, and my heart cried out as the energy flowing from her stopped. "Me too, but I have to hope he survived the fall."

Our moment passed, but I ached to have it back. I sat back, sighing. "I need to try harder to keep us all out of trouble."

Earl's gaze flattened. "Your friends are adults. You haven't made them do anything."

I gestured at the galley. "You're here in this storm because of me."

She shrugged. "Maybe we seized on an opportunity for adventure and excitement."

I studied her. "This *adventure* got Genevie's husband killed—that's too much excitement. What if my next plan splits Ben and Josephine, or Olen and Beck?"

"Genevie told me about Whistler and about how you changed their lives when you arrived in their community," Earl said, twirling her right braid.

I snorted. "Are you sure she didn't say 'wrecked' their lives?"

Earl's lips tightened, and she dropped her braid. "We make our own choices, Artist." She crossed her arms. "To insist you're responsible for our decisions is patronizing."

Though softly uttered, her words echoed in my ears, lancing my core. Earl was right; my self-centered lens was ludicrous, as ridiculous as suggesting I'd capsized my sailboat so I could rescue Bryer. My friends had helped because of their characters, not mine. Because they loved Akiko and loved me.

The truth of Earl's words crashed over me like storm-driven waves and when my thoughts quieted, I saw Earl anew—my eyes washed free of the doubts clouding my vision and judgment.

Akiko was my priority.

The admission released me, leaving my heart buoyant. I would accept Niagara Abbey's offer and move forward with negotiations for Akiko's return. With luck, my friends would join me in the community I'd build, but if they wanted to continue their adventures, I'd wish them the best.

Shivers raced up my spine as our energies brushed against each other, sparking like minute explosions. "Thank you. I needed to hear that."

Earl's lips curved. "Happy to be your storm anchor, Artist."

CHAPTER FIFTY-TWO

I nearly yelped as Josephine's hug crushed me. As Olen had predicted, my skin was a rainbow of purple, blue, and green bruises, but she didn't notice my reaction, continuing to squeeze me as she chattered.

The weak morning sun struggled to break through the heavy clouds left behind by the storm, but the air was alive with the excited shrieking of gulls wheeling and screeching overhead.

I let her words flow over me until she mentioned Carter. "Wait, what?"

Josephine turned, narrowing her eyes. "Which part?"

"What about Reverend Carter?" I set down my soggy canvas bag, bending to pet Charcoal. He pranced around me, wiggling, swiping at my face with his tongue.

Josephine tilted my chin up. "He's holding an open meeting here the day after tomorrow."

Olen whistled. "Does Aurora know?"

Ben nodded, picking up my bag. "We sent a runner to inform them."

Olen grinned, helping Beck onto the dock. "We'll have to wiggle our way in."

Gunther grunted, tossing our discarded clothes down to me. Wet trousers landed on Charcoal, who sighed. My body ached as I picked up the clothes. "I need to wash these before I can go anywhere."

Earl hopped off the rope ladder, the corners of her mouth drooping. "It's not only your clothes that need washing, so see you when you smell better," she called over her shoulder.

Genevie chuckled. "They'll write legends about your skill with women, Artist."

"Doubtless," I said, as Bryer clambered down the rope. "This is Bryer. We found him out there."

Genevie narrowed her eyes. "We've met."

Bryer brightened. "Gen?"

Genevie wrapped her arms around the man and lifted him, shaking him up and down as she chuckled. We stared at the strange pair, exchanging glances.

Josephine crossed her arms. "Explanation, please."

Genevie tossed her arm over Bryer's shoulder. "Bryer was the ferryman in Portland Depot when Whistler and I went to the coast last year."

Bryer grinned. "Where is the bald man?"

"Dead." Genevie punched him lightly on the shoulder. "Come, I'll catch you up."

Genevie's matter-of-fact tone caught me by surprise, and my breath hitched as she and Bryer headed up the pier.

Josephine patted my cheek. "Grief ends."

"Mm," agreed Ben. "Especially when suitors call."

I followed them toward the inn. "Suitors, plural?"

Ben chuckled. "Jon Velde and Cedrick Jacobson have each visited."

I snickered. "Busy lady."

Josephine flashed me a look. "Just because you're hopeless doesn't require Genevie to remain celibate."

My face burned, but before I could retort, I tripped on a dragging trouser leg. They continued up the pier without me as I squatted on the pier to fold the sodden clothes.

"Aye, 'tis the most sense I've seen from you yet, Artist," said Gunther, as he clumped past me, whistling.

"I'm getting it from all sides, aren't I?" I asked Charcoal, folding the last tunic.

He licked my face in sympathy.

It was clear they planned to attend Carter's meeting. As his people hadn't seen my friends, they'd have a better chance of blending with the crowd without me. Besides, if Carter and his top people were in Toronto Depot, there'd be fewer on the island.

Maybe almost no one.

A chill ran up my spine. This could be the break I'd been waiting for. By myself, I might slip into the compound unnoticed. "I'll need a boat," I said out loud.

Charcoal huffed, turning to glare at me.

"The last boat was too small to bring you, and you're lucky I didn't. But you have a point." If I was successful, I'd be rescuing Akiko, Talbot, and maybe even Bowman. The sailboat I'd lost had been too small to transport more than me. Frankly, it had been too small for me too, given the storm.

I turned, appraising Gunther's schooner. Though he could sail it himself, it took skill to handle such a large craft. I either needed something smaller or to find someone to help me sail.

WHEN I REACHED THE INN, I POKED MY HEAD INTO THE kitchen. "Where do I wash laundry?" Mama held out her arms, but I shook my head. "It's time I started cleaning up my messes."

She crossed the kitchen to kiss my cheek. "I'm glad you're back, safe and whole. The laundry kettle is under a shed roof tacked to the end of Gunther's shop."

I turned to leave, but stopped as the memory of Gunther striding across the storm-lashed deck flashed onto my mind's canvas. "He was magnificent in the storm, and I'd like to thank him. Does he need anything?"

Mama's eyes crinkled. "He's set, still chuffed with the skylights you added. As long as he has a place to fiddle about and his precious boat, he's a contented man."

I winked at her. "I think you play a role there, too."

Hands on her hips, she clucked her tongue. "So, thicken the walls between the bedrooms."

I fled with Mama's laughter ringing in my ears, my face beet red. But when I reached the shed, I stopped, perplexed. How was laundry "done"? A large kettle burbled, its tone menacing, so I set the sodden clothing down on the wooden bench to assess.

Gunther poked his head out of the shop. "Oh, 'tis you," he said. "I fancied Mama had come to do the washing."

I squinted at the kettle, shaking my head. "Just me. I'm doing laundry... I think."

Gunther snorted. "Check your pockets before dumping the duds in the suds."

I snickered, but obeyed and found my sketchbook in my tunic pocket. "You're smarter than you look, my friend."

Gunther pulled out his pipe and leaned against the wall. "Aye."

"You were right about the sailboat, too." Once I'd checked the rest of the clothes, I dropped them into the kettle, stirring the mass with a flat, wooden paddle. I poked at the floating clothing, but the water had gone cold.

"It was too little," I admitted, while rebuilding the fire.

"Aye." Gunther chuckled and drew on his pipe. Fragrant smoke curled toward me.

While the kettle warmed, I watched the Cassel-brown waves stroke the shore. "Out of curiosity, how big of a boat would you use to skip back and forth to Niagara Abbey?"

Gunther squinted at the sea. "How many folks?"

Bubbles formed around the edges of the kettle, releasing lye-scented steam and coating my tongue with a slippery, bitter film. I poked the clothing again. "Good question. Maybe six, plus gear?"

"Just to ferry back and forth?"

I nodded, fishing out a tunic with the blade of the paddle.

Gunther pointed at the second, half-filled tub, and I plunged the tunic into it.

"What now?"

His eyes crinkled as he pointed at a ridged, metal board hung on the post nearest the tub. "Scrub."

When I set the board in the tub, it fell in, submerging beneath the murky, gray-tinted water. I tried propping it against the side, but it slid down again. Sighing, I pulled it from the tub, it off, and opened my sketch pad. The paper was damp but workable, so I drew the tub and washboard with light strokes, then added a hooked edge to the board. I tested it, but the tub's lip was too wide, and the board rocked against it. Shrugging, I altered the tub, squaring one end. This time, the washboard snapped onto the tub's edge, the fit sure and snug.

"Better," I said, rubbing the tunic over the metal ribs. When I was reasonably sure it was clean, I rinsed it in the third tub. Two more tunics and three pairs of trousers left to go. I sighed, my back already sore. "How tall is Mama?"

Gunther squinted, gauging me. "A half-meter shorter than you."

I altered the tub again, adding four sturdy legs to raise it so I could scrub while standing. My pencil was getting shorter than I liked, so I made a mental note to replace it. The tub was still a little short for me, but I didn't want it to be too tall for Mama. "Much better," I said after I finished the second tunic.

Gunther shook his head. "I'll never get used to watching you bend the world to your will."

I grinned. "At least I have one useful skill."

"Two skills. You're a dab hand at laundry, son." Gunther crossed one leg over the other. "Seven."

I stopped scrubbing, confused. "Seven what?"

"Seven to seven and a half meters. The boat," Gunther said, watching the waves again.

I returned to the laundry, a sailboat crossing my mind's canvas. "Right. That's large enough to incorporate a cabin?"

He grunted. "Aye."

I gazed past him to the schooner moored at the end of the pier. "How big is the *Marybelle*?"

Gunther shifted his gaze, his eyes softening. "Fifteen meters from bow to stern."

"Marybelle is a pretty name. Why don't you have one of those chesty gals on the front?" As soon as I'd asked, Aurora's keeper—*Marcy*—flashed onto my mind's canvas. I scrubbed the trousers vigorously, trying to wash my canvas clean.

"I don't hold with water tarts." Gunther chuckled and straightened, rapping his pipe out against the kettle before turning to go. "Besides, Mama would flog my hide. But if I had enough to trade and time enough to wait, I'd put a dragon like Beck's queen on her prow."

After I'd wrung and hung the clothes, I rested on the shore, tossing a stick for Charcoal. As I'd said to Mama, it was time for me to clean up my messes. While my friends were occupied at Carter's meeting, I would retrieve Akiko from Welland Island, but first I needed a seven-meter boat... or any boat I could improve.

I tossed the stick again, and Charcoal took off like a shot. Bryer stood at the end of the pier, his shoulders slumped, staring east. We both wanted something out of reach, so perhaps we could help each other. If he would sail the sea again, and I found a boat. And if I could convince him *without* alerting Genevie.

Charcoal splashed through the shallows to bring the stick back. He dropped it and shook, spraying me with lake water before settling himself along my leg to gnaw on the stick.

"More laundry, and a lot of ifs," I said, gazing east across the water.

CHAPTER FIFTY-THREE

Bryer and I arrived before sunrise and moored along the tree line, waiting for Carter and his entourage to depart Welland Island. As the day dawned, I held my breath, hoping for the drawn, cloudy weather Bryer had predicted. If the sun rose and the skies blued, our kayak, boat, and sail would stand out conspicuously against blue-hued water.

By seven o'clock, I knew we'd be fine. Out of nowhere, Baudelaire's L'Étranger popped into my mind. "J'aime les nuages... les merveilleux nuages!"

Bryer blinked at me.

I clapped him on the back. "You were right about the clouds."

After Carter's ships departed, we readied our equipment. Although the ships were still visible on the western horizon, I nodded, and without words, we launched the kayak; the water rippling as I slid into the boat.

Charcoal watched, his dark eyes wary, but made no noise and didn't move to follow.

The kayak slipped through the still water, nearly noiseless.

I'd done my best to hide our presence by altering everything into the peculiar, gray-brown-green color the water adopted on overcast days. Even our clothes were the same color, and I had spare clothes similarly hued to disguise Bowman, Talbot, and Akiko.

When my kayak bumped softly against the dock, I slid from the low seat onto the wooden structure. My heart pounded as I lashed the boat and retrieved my pack. Flat against the cliff wall, I crept to the cliff-side door, pressing my ear against it when I reached it.

Nothing.

My nerves screamed, but I drew a deep breath and tugged on the door. Though I'd expected it to be locked, the door swung open. I clamped my lips and poked my head inside, but the entryway was vacant. Only the stone steps, spiraling up into the dark, were visible. This would make things easier; if I'd found it locked, I'd planned to climb the cliff like I had the wall of marble in Rochester Depot. Rochester Depot now felt like a lifetime ago.

Still, I hesitated, glancing at the end of the dock. The kayak rode so low it wasn't visible, and even though I knew where we'd anchored, I couldn't make out the shape of our boat against the tree line.

Time to go.

After shutting the door behind me, I waited for my eyes to adjust to the dim light. The staircase waited, silent and empty, and remembering the dizzying drop in the middle, I kept to the outside edge, running my fingertips against the rough stone as I climbed.

Each time a torch guttered, I froze, expecting a burst of light from either above or below. When none came, I climbed on. My rubbery legs burned when I reached a landing. The last time I'd visited, the spiral staircase had ended at the door exiting to the courtyard. This time, there was no exit door. Instead, two staircases, one leading left and one leading right, continued up.

Any changes they'd made to the interior of the compound would increase the difficulty of my task. Stymied, I studied each staircase. Which was correct? From here, I couldn't spot any differences.

I waited in the dim light for several heartbeats, then turned left.

My pulse pounded as I resumed my climb. I kept my footfalls light, but my ragged breathing sounded like a roar in my ears. The stairway ended at a wooden door, outlined by a faint light. I'd chosen correctly; this door would take me to the courtyard, or at least open to an outdoor area.

Again, I set my ear against the door and listened, but heard nothing. The door emitted a faint squeal as I eased it open, and I flinched. Squinted through the crack, I half-expected to find armed men standing on the other side. If caught, I had a prepared explanation, but to my relief, there was no one present. A good thing too, as I no longer had my sword and the excuse I'd come up with was flimsy.

Instead of the outdoor courtyard, the door opened into the empty cathedral. Light streamed through skylights in the graceful ceiling, and surprised, I nearly let the door shut behind me. Because the previous courtyard door had locked behind us, this time, I'd come prepared with wadding. Before the heavy door could latch, I jammed my fingertips into the gap, wincing as it pinched my fingers. My heart thudded as I eased it open enough to stuff wadding into the latch.

I let the door close, then pulled it open again to make sure the wadding had worked. My escape route set, I examined the cathedral. The last time I'd been here, children had raced through the grand space playing hide-and-seek. My heart ached for the sounds of small, racing feet, but the room's hush remained.

The children had run from the courtyard toward an interior door. Glancing at the doors leading toward the courtyard, I slipped toward the far end of the cathedral and through an interior door leading to a short hallway. Four doors faced me: two on the left, one on the right, and one at the end of the hallway.

I pressed my ear to the first door, the smooth wood cold against my cheek. The door vibrated, a muffled whirring behind it. I couldn't hear anything through the other three doors. My mind raced as I weighed the three silent doors, and I squeezed my eyes shut when I pulled on the single door across from me. From this side, I couldn't find a locking mechanism, but the door didn't budge. I crossed the hall and pulled on the next door, which was also locked.

All I had left to try was the door emitting the faint noise or the door at the end of the hall. While weighing my options, something moved in the cathedral. I froze, straining to make sense of the sound.

Footsteps.

I sprinted toward the last door and pulled on it. It opened, but through the crack, I couldn't see more than a curved stone wall.

The footsteps approached.

I slipped through the door, easing it closed before the footsteps rounded the corner. My eyebrows rose as I evaluated the room. It was round, with a series of tiny windows, each less than a half-meter square, set near the ceiling, over twenty meters up. A rectangular opening roughly a meter by a meter-and-a-half in the center of the flat ceiling provided illumination, and through it, the heavy clouds scudded past. Other than a wooden chair, the room was entirely empty and smelled of stone and lake water.

The footsteps stopped outside the door.

My mouth dry and bitter, I moved away from it, putting the wooden chair between the door and myself. It wasn't much of a weapon, but it would be better than nothing if it came down to combat.

The silence stretched, my nerves jangling. Barely breathing, I waited, every muscle tense as I tried to discern the meaning of the faint scraping and ticking noises coming from the hallway. The sound gradually faded, and I relaxed, leaning on the back of the chair.

I watched the light from the ceiling's opening move across the curved stone walls until I grew weary of waiting. If I waited too long, I risked leaving the compound just as Reverend Carter returned. I crossed the room and pressed my ear to the door.

Nothing.

Despite my flipping stomach, I cracked the door, then yanked it open. My heart pounded when instead of the hallway, I stared at a stone wall assembled between the door and the hallway. I patted the stones, then shoved at them, expecting them to slide, but they were as solid as the rest of the room. A howling filled my ears as I hurled myself against them. This wasn't a room.

It was a cell.

CHAPTER FIFTY-FOUR

Over the first hours, I yelled myself hoarse, but no one came. Slumped on the floor, I leaned against the stone wall, glaring at the smug wooden chair sitting in the center of the room, but it remained unfazed.

The sun set, shrouding the cell in darkness. To keep the circling despair at bay, I made a wager with myself. If I saw the moon through the hole in the ceiling, I'd find a way to escape. I circled the room, desperate for a glimpse of the orb, but it remained stubbornly out of frame.

A mantle of exhaustion fell over me as I slumped to the floor. The damp air had steadily cooled, and I shivered, pulling my knees to my chest. All I'd brought in my pack were the spare clothes and a small bag of taffy. I retrieved the pack, setting the candy—a gift for Akiko—on the offensive chair before draping the extra clothing over me. I dozed, but each time I moved, the clothes slid off me. Chilled, I slumped against the wall, waking again and again, until my brain was as thick and solid as the stones imprisoning me. In moments of wakefulness, I wondered what Bryer and Charcoal were doing. Certain my plan would work, I hadn't organized a backup or contingency plan, but I'd left a note in my room, so my friends would now know where I'd gone.

When dawn brought enough light to draw, I pulled out my sketchbook and pencil, shaking my head at the stub. I'd forgotten to replace it, and there wasn't much left of it.

With care, I drew the door and the wall beyond it, stopping frequently to count the courses of stone, to ensure my drawing was as accurate as possible. As needed, I sharpened the pencil by rubbing it across a rough-edged stone. Each time I did, it shrank more, becoming increasingly difficult to hold.

When the drawing was ready, I considered the changes I could make. "Keep it simple," I muttered to myself.

I closed my eyes and visualized the stone wall before me. In it, I imagined an arched opening, leaving an inset stone door jamb against the wooden frame to anchor the perspective. I imagined the stones no wider than the ones framing the tiny square windows above me, and the smell of minerals and mortar filled the room as I worked, my fingers tingling.

When I'd finished, I looked up at the graceful, arched opening inset into the wall exactly as I'd imagined... but beyond the new opening was another wall.

Like Fortunato, they had walled me behind unknowable courses of stone.

Bellowing, I threw my sketchbook and pencil across the room. "Let me out! Release me!" My throat burned like I'd gargled fire, but I continued to yell and scream until no further sound came. In a huff, I piled the clothes and dropped onto the pitiful cushion. My stomach grumbled, but I ignored the taffy, concentrating on the doorway. I could try again, but what if they'd filled the *entire* hallway with stone?

I crawled to the other side of the room to retrieve my sketchbook and pencil. The tip had broken, so I spent more time resharpening it. It had grown so short I had to pinch it between my thumb, pointer, and middle fingers to hold it, and my hand cramped before I'd drawn anything. As I massaged it, I stared at the wall. While I had nothing but time, the pencil wouldn't hold out indefinitely, so every move I made from now on needed to be deliberate.

Flames of fear licked at my mind's canvas, but I shoved them away and prowled the circular room. If Reverend Carter was hungry for artists, he wouldn't want to waste my talents, so someone would come. My stomach growled, but what I really wanted was water. I clapped my hands, again and again, hoping to attract someone's attention, but no one came. What would happen to Akiko if I didn't escape?

I spent the next hours inspecting the stone walls, searching for any irregularity, but if this room had ever had another exit, I couldn't find it. Exhausted, I lay on the floor, staring at the rectangular opening in the ceiling. It was the only exit, but even if I climbed the smooth stones, the opening was two and a half meters from the wall. Maybe Ben could climb a horizontal surface, but I didn't know how. And if I tried and fell, the twenty-meter drop could be the end of me. I considered trying to enlarge the opening, bringing it nearer to the wall, but I couldn't see what might be above the solid parts of the ceiling.

When night fell, I gave in, flooded with shame as I opened the bag of taffy. Tears tracked down my cheeks when I popped the first piece into my mouth, but the sweet ignited my thirst, tightening my already raw throat. I'd never been lower as I made a pillow from the clothes and lay under the ceiling's opening. Hours later, my eyes flew open when something punched my gut.

"Matthew?" whispered a voice from above.

My breath expelled in a wheeze as hope jolted through me. "Here," I rasped.

Talbot's voice was tight and thin as he kneeled over the ceiling's opening. "I only have moments—*he's* coming. Listen, we're leaving tomorrow."

"We are?" I whispered.

Talbot's silhouette moved from side to side. "No, *we* are. The reverend is abandoning Welland Island."

"Why?"

Talbot muttered something, and I covered my face as small stones skittered into my cell. I scrambled to my feet and moved to the side of the room. "Talbot? Get me out of here!"

Nothing.

"Talbot!" I clapped my hands, then relaxed as his shape again blocked the stars.

"Sorry, I couldn't risk a lookout. Listen, I'll take her with me and try to get you word once I know where we're going." The shape shifted again.

My legs shook. "Help me get out of here!"

"I don't know how." He sighed. "They walled you in, and there's nothing here, no ropes or ladders or anything. I'm sorry."

The stars glimmered as his shape disappeared.

Cold snaked through my veins as I waited, my ears straining for the scrape of a foot against the stone. Hours passed, but when the faint shuffling came again, I asked, "Is the boat still near the woods? We had ropes on it."

A shape blocked the starlight again, and my heart lifted until a voice like obsidian spoke.

"Mr. Sugiyama, thank you for joining us."

Mouth dry, I stared at the silhouette. "Reverend Carter?"

The dark shape shifted. "Why, you're *not* as thick as reported."

Slivers of ice ran down my spine. Where was Talbot? "Why am I here? What do you want?"

Carter sounded amused, but his words froze my heart.

"Want? You artists are all insufferable, but your scheming has made staying here near Toronto Depot untenable."

"I'm sorry." As soon as I'd uttered the words, I wanted to take them back, but I needed to show him I could be contrite, helpful even. He needed crusaders, and given the chance, I could show my usefulness.

Carter chuckled. "You will be, and so will your parents. I know where they are and have quite an ending planned for them. Before they go, I'll tell them of the crows waiting to take you apart here in the sepulchre I had built for you. Farewell, little artist."

My eyes tightened as a hissing roar filled my ears, and he didn't even give me a chance to reply before he withdrew.

"Carter!" I shouted. The poisonous, black rage welling inside me lent me a voice that echoed from the stones.

No answer.

"Carter!" I screamed again before my voice failed. I crossed the room and slammed the wooden door again and again until it splintered in its jamb.

Carter's words sank into me, sapping the last of my strength. I meant nothing to him. He had sprung this trap to remove a pest, to swat me away like an irritating fly. For hours I stared at the ceiling, waiting. Even when I dozed, I woke each time my brain registered a noise to stare at the opening. Each time, hope fluttered in my chest, only to shrivel when no one came.

The next time I awoke, the sun streamed through the opening. If they had departed at dawn, I hadn't heard them. My stomach twisted as Carter's words echoed through my mind until my eyes rested on an unfamiliar knapsack.

The memory of something pummeling my stomach flashed through my mind as I crawled toward it. Talbot had filled the knapsack with two canteens, a loaf of bread, and four apples.

My hands shook as I opened the first canteen, drinking eagerly, but stopped after three large swallows, remembering too much water could cause stomach cramps and nausea. I dug through the knapsack but found nothing else—no art supplies, rope, or pickax.

At least I wouldn't starve. I picked up an apple, sighing. As I turned it in my hands, the memory of the day I'd won the Head Boy competition surfaced. I'd won after completing an improvement on a scale never imagined by a student—the repair of a lighthouse from *Before*.

This room reminded me of the lighthouse—both were round stone towers. The lighthouse I'd repaired had a spiraling staircase winding up its outer walls, but they wouldn't work here because I couldn't reach the center opening from them.

Could I draw a staircase in the middle of the room?

The room was too narrow, approximately five meters wide and twenty meters high, and because all I had available to improve was stone, the stairs would have to self-support. I scrambled through memories of the stone staircases I'd seen, trying to picture one which could support a twenty-meter rise with this narrow of a footprint, but every staircase I envisioned reached its maximum height two-thirds of the way to the ceiling, leaving a gap of five to eight meters. Still, it moved me fifteen meters closer to my goal.

My heart lifted, and I bit into the apple. The sensation of sinking my teeth into the crisp flesh freed a part of my soul and I delighted in the crunch, the bitter leather of its skin, and its sweetness. Its summer-fresh scent flooded the room, setting my senses swooning. I ate the entire fruit, including the core, as I circled the room, picturing the staircase.

CHAPTER FIFTY-FIVE

With meticulous precision, I drew for hours, stopping only when the light faded. In the deepening gloom, I devoured the bread before catching myself; I'd need something in the morning to fuel my improvements. I set the rest aside, knowing if I didn't escape the cell tomorrow, I'd regret my gluttony.

The remaining light faded as I sat motionless, thinking about the staircase I'd construct. As the dark deepened, I mentally rotated the staircase and sharpened what I had left of my pencil. Without care, I'd run out of graphite before I finished my stairs—even now it barely protruded from between my fingers. If only we artists could improve our art supplies!

The stars emerged, their light cold and sharp. Were Akiko and the others seeing them? By now, surely Bryer had returned to Hanlan's Island, but then why hadn't Ben and the others come? Since Carter and his followers had abandoned the seminary, nothing prevented my friends from entering... unless something had happened. My gut tightened as I struggled to catch my breath, picturing the worst. For all

I knew, Carter had reduced Toronto Depot to smoking rubble.

Like Brookfield.

Familiar hurts welled, but I sighed as I watched the stars glimmer. That I'd trapped *myself* was the most bitter truth to swallow. Not only had Carter's people known I'd come to the island, they'd known I'd do so alone. It rankled me I had entered my cell and waited placidly for Carter's artists to entomb me. My capture hadn't merited a single, villainous laugh, and other than Carter's brief visit, they hadn't acknowledged their victory at all.

I snorted as Earl's words echoed through my memories. Even in defeat, I was over-inflating my importance. I wasn't a handsome prince rescuing Princess Mouse. Instead, I was the damsel in distress, and I'd locked myself into my own blasted tower, then set a dangerous man after my parents. I groaned, slapping the palm of my hand against my forehead.

Life was not like winning a school prize, and no amount of effort on my part could guarantee me the outcome I wanted. Why had it taken so long for me to understand this?

If I escaped this cell, I would make changes.

No.

I shook my head. "*When* I escape."

The stars twinkled in agreement.

Dawn arrived wet and greasy. The misting rain falling through the ceiling's opening startled me awake, and I rolled toward the wall, desperate to keep my sketchbook dry. When my pulse slowed, I sat up.

It was time.

By now, I'd imagined the spiraling staircase so often I didn't need to cement the vision before touching pencil to paper. As I built the staircase, stone by stone, a pillar appeared before me, with steps carved from the outer edges, working their way toward the middle. It looked more like the tip of a freshly sharpened pencil than a staircase, but it was the best I could imagine. Though I'd made each pass as narrow as workable, the stairs ended two meters from the ceiling, with the last tread a scant quarter-meter wide. I stood on the precarious top step, which was barely wide enough to support both of my feet, and tried a tentative jump. My fingertips barely brushed the ceiling as my fears soared higher than my feet. I caught myself and wobbled at the top of the stairs, terrified I'd tumble down the steep, pyramidal sides and crash into the floor.

My legs shook as I circled the stairs, considering my options. There was little left of my pencil, so if I made the wrong choice, I might not get another chance to escape.

Again and again, I'd assumed I could succeed if *I* tried harder, but could I instead lean on the abilities of my friends? Josephine had a talent for strategy and thinking through the big picture, but her fault was timidity, and without urging, she'd never set her plans in motion. Genevie had a knack for forging relationships as strong as the metal crafts she manufactured, and Ben's mind incorporated creativity, strategy, and physical strength, but even he would struggle to find a way out of my predicament. I didn't know Bowman like the others, but like Ben, even the cleverest engineer couldn't solve a problem with no materials on hand.

I discounted Olen's charm, Beck's kites, Gunther's sailing, and Mama's nurturing. Earl's face on my mind's canvas made me even more determined to escape. Though I didn't know what the future held, I wanted the chance to find out.

The only one who could manufacture materials was *Akiko*. She could create from nothing, and if she were here, she could draw anything—a pole, a ladder... or a *rope*. But could she create from wherever she was? With everything happening, we'd never tested the limits of her creativity.

My skin buzzed as I turned to a blank page and pinched the pencil. I needed to ask for help without alarming her, so I drew a cartoon version of myself standing next to a tree, holding a short length of rope, looking plaintively at a bag of candy stuck on an out-of-reach branch. To convey urgency, I drew a lumbering cartoon bear approaching me as he tied a bib around his neck. To highlight my ask, I drew several arrows pointing to the rope.

My hand shook as I drew a frame around the image, then turned the frame into a book, adding a caricature of her reading the book.

I stared at the drawing for a long time. What if she didn't understand, or couldn't sneak away to draw in secret, or... wasn't *capable* of sending me a rope?

To distract myself, I ate the rest of my bread and one of the remaining apples. My stomach cried for more when I'd finished, and I glanced at the bags of candy sitting on the stupid wooden chair.

Two bags.

My heart thumped as I approached the chair. Akiko had closed the new bag with a length of thin cord, curled around the bag like a pig's tail. My fingers shook as I untied the candy and unfurled the cord. It was a meter long and too thin, but it was enough. I hummed as I improved the cord, thickening it and lengthening it to over twenty meters. When I'd finished, my pencil was barely large enough to pinch.

I raced up the steps and stopped at the top with the rope in my hands. The opening was overhead, but with nothing to tie to, I'd need to weigh down the end of the rope. My meager possessions included the pack of spare clothes, the knapsack Talbot had dropped, two canteens—one empty, and two bags of taffy. Even together, it wasn't heavy enough to counter my weight.

I picked up the sack from Akiko and unwrapped a piece of taffy as my gaze slid to the wooden chair I'd refused to sit on, then flicked to the opening in the ceiling. With luck, the chair would fit through, but was it sturdy enough to hold me? I moved the candy and sat gingerly on the chair.

Nothing happened.

I wiggled back and forth, but the chair, unimpressed, remained a chair. For a long while, I sat and ate candy. When I'd stalled long enough, I stowed the rest of my items into the pack and strapped it to the seat of the chair. I wound the rope through the slats on the chair's back and then under the seat, securing it with a double bowline knot Ben had taught me in Rochester Depot.

My legs shook as I carried the chair up the stairs. At the top, I paused, doubt lancing through me as I tried to judge the size of the chair in relation to the opening. This would never work—either the chair had grown, or the opening had shrunk.

I squeezed my eyes shut and calmed myself by listing the many reasons I needed to leave the cell. Akiko, Charcoal, Earl —my parents. When centered, I drew a long breath, crouched, and heaved the chair at the opening. Ready to duck if the chair came crashing back down on top of me, I watched, dry-mouthed, as the chair flew through the opening, rotated, and landed with a *thud,* spanning the edge of the short side of the opening.

I blinked, expecting the chair to slide back through the ceiling, but it didn't move even when I tugged the rope. As I pulled, I waited for the inevitable cracking of wood.

Nothing.

"Now or never, Artist."

I took a last glance around the room. The chair held as I climbed, my arms and shoulders straining as I squeezed past the chair. When I reached the edge, I hauled myself up with the last of my strength, then rolled onto my back, gasping. Crows exploded from the ledge where they'd perched, their metallic caws shredding my nerves as the memory of Carter's speech echoed through my mind.

The air was fresher, fragrant with the scent of cedar, a welcome change from the damp granite of the cell. Gratitude welled inside me as the rain washed my face, and I allowed myself one sobbing gasp before sitting up to examine my surroundings. They had built the circular tower on the edge of the cliff. On one side, a metal ladder descended onto the roof of a shorter building.

Even from this vantage, I couldn't find where Bryer and I had moored the boat, and a wave of vertigo swept over me as I peered down to see if the kayak was still lashed to the dock. I jerked back, swallowing rapidly, and pulled my pack from the chair.

Undaunted by the rain, Carter's chair waited.

My top lip curled as I flung it from the tower, smirking as it smashed into kindling on the rocks below.

CHAPTER FIFTY-SIX

Even before my toes contacted the courtyard, I knew jumping had been a mistake, but Carter had removed the ladder he and Talbot must have used to access the lower roof. The drop was farther than I'd expected, and my left leg crumpled upon impact. I bellowed as my leg split open.

Rolling over, I dragged my trouser leg up, scowling at the blood running down my calf. I tore the tunic I'd brought for Akiko, wrapping it around my leg before knotting it tightly. The fall had pulverized the last apple, so I heaved the mush at a wall in a fit of pique. Calming, I stood to test my leg, wincing as I hopped in a circle.

Good enough.

I trotted to the cathedral door, trying not to drag my foot. I expected the door to be locked, but it opened easily, so I crossed the sanctuary to the door leading to the staircase. Because of the wadding I'd stuffed in the latch, this door opened too, but the passage behind was gone, a stone wall in its place.

My stomach lurched. The stairway was the only way to reach the lake's surface.

I sprinted across the courtyard to open the door we'd left through last time, but again, faced a stone wall.

"No!" I howled at the rain. Even though I'd made it out of my cell, I was still trapped in this horrible place. When I glanced over the edge of the courtyard's wall, the far-below docks swam in my blurred vision. My shoulders slumped, my breath coming in gasps.

Maybe there was another way down.

I surveyed the courtyard. They'd filled the hallway beyond the sanctuary and the exit stairs, so the cathedral was a dead end. To my left was the assembly room. The room was empty, but I crossed it to the door on the far side. I hesitated, afraid I'd find yet another stone wall, but it opened onto a hallway. My heart racing, I trotted down the passage, opening doors to peer into chambers along the way. Near the end, I found the mural room and stopped, curious about what they'd painted.

As expected, Carter's artists had painted the scene from our second rescue attempt where the climbers had tried to reach the courtyard, and the flier had fallen.

The flier.

Was it here? Was it operable?

Before leaving, I paused at a disturbing image. A flat barge, filled with crying children, floated on choppy waves. The expression of terror on their faces made my skin crawl.

I backed away from the unpleasant scene and left through the far door. It led to a second hallway, providing access to numerous bedchambers. Some were set up dormitory-style with rows of bunks, and some with single beds. I opened each door, scanning the contents, searching for anything I could use to get off the island.

Someone occupied the last room, and I smelled the blood before I recognized Bowman. Tears welled in my eyes as I gazed at his broken body. "I'm sorry, my friend."

Bowman's eyes opened, and I leaped back in fright.

"Matthew. You came." His eyes closed.

"Bowman? Bowman!" I fumbled through my pack, but all I had left was candy and a half-filled canteen. My fingers shook as I unscrewed the canteen's cap. "Here, drink," I said, carefully dribbling a little water onto his chapped lips.

He swallowed, opening his eyes again.

"What happened?" I rasped.

His voice shook as he answered. "They erased the canard, and the flier stalled."

Erased?

Artists didn't erase. I closed my eyes, my fury growing. "I'm sorry."

He nodded, shifting as blood leaked from the corner of his mouth. "Are they gone?"

I ripped another strip from Akiko's tunic to dab his lip. "Yes, but they blocked the stairways."

Bowman coughed, the sound wet and phlegmy. "Find my flier."

His words sparked like lightning through me. "Can I repair it?"

"Think so. Come for me when you find it," he said, his voice weaker.

I bit my lip, loathe to leave him, but unequipped to help him. I needed to get him to Mama. "Have some more water first."

"No time." He shook his head. "I have no time."

My eyes welled. "I'll hurry, Bowman. You hang on."

I raced through the compound, searching with panic-blurred eyes. I checked all the larger buildings surrounding the courtyard, but found nothing.

What if they'd erased the whole machine?

I pushed my fears away. "You're not *that* important," I

whispered, as I turned a slow circle to survey the courtyard. What would *I* do if a man had fallen from the sky? I'd have pushed the machine out of the way and thrown a tarpaulin over it.

My eyes widened—I'd seen a tarpaulin in a storage building. My leg protested as I retraced my steps across the courtyard. When I reached the building, I pulled open its wide doors. They'd stacked large wooden crates in haphazard piles in front of a tarpaulin-covered mass. I shifted two of the crates, giving me a chance to pull back the tarpaulin. The gossamer wing shimmered in the pearlescent light.

It was here.

I shifted the crates, then pulled the rest of the tarpaulin off the flier. Once I'd pedaled it into the courtyard, I inspected the frame. One corner of the wing was bent, and there was a small rent in the aft side of the left wing, but otherwise, it appeared sound, apart from the missing canard.

I raced back to Bowman's room. "I found it," I rasped, relieved his chest continued to rise and fall.

"Take me," he said, his voice a whisper.

Doubt cascaded over me as I studied him. Even uninjured, he wasn't a small man. How could I move him without hurting him more? "I can't carry you, but I could drag you."

He closed his eyes. "Hurry."

I retrieved the tarpaulin, then carefully pulled Bowman from the bed, laying him on the canvas. He groaned, the sound twisting my gut. "I'm sorry, so sorry," I said, as I pulled him through the hallways. Mama could help him, so I kept my eyes forward, ignoring the pain in my leg.

Bowman barely moved as I pulled the tarpaulin into the rain. "Will it fly?"

He didn't open his eyes but said, "If you rebuild the canard."

I'd spent so much time in the flier I could easily picture it, the graceful prong and tiny shovel-headed wing protruding from the front of the flier. But when I pulled out my sketchbook, the pencil stub wasn't with it. I patted my pockets frantically, then dug through my pack.

Blood dribbled from the corner of Bowman's mouth as he labored to breathe. He didn't have time for me to retrace my steps to search for it, but when I reached down to wipe the blood from his mouth, I froze.

Blood.

My lips compressed as I yanked up my trouser leg and untied the tourniquet. Blood welled from the split skin, and I dabbed my finger in it, painting the flier onto the last page of my sketchbook, using my fingernail like a palette knife.

Bowman moaned when he saw what I was doing, but I continued to work feverishly, ignoring his disgust. When I finished, I clambered to my feet and retied the bandage. Woozy, I wobbled around the flier, testing the new canard. It appeared sturdy, but when I surveyed the courtyard, my stomach plummeted. Though wide, the courtyard wasn't long enough to launch the flier. Even with a good headwind, I'd need another thirty meters to launch the flier.

To escape, I'd have to launch into the abyss. Dizzy, I walked to the edge of the courtyard, glancing over the edge. My stomach lurched, but I returned to my sketchbook and untied the bandage around my leg.

When I'd made an opening in the wall wide enough for the flier to pass through, I retied the bandage, slumping against the wall. What were the chances I'd survive this flight? Even if I'd drawn the canard correctly, I couldn't be sure the damage to the flier's frame wasn't catastrophic.

I cleared my throat and ran my fingers through my hair as I

glanced from the flier to the gap in the courtyard's wall. I circled the flier again, scanning for anything I'd missed.

"Matthew," Bowman said.

I kneeled by him, taking his hand. "I'm here," I whispered.

"Take me with you." Beads of sweat sprang onto his forehead, but his eyes pleaded with me.

"Yes, of course." I swallowed my nausea, dragging him to the flier. We groaned in unison when I wrestled him from the ground and strapped him to the back seat. He whimpered while I worked, and tears flowed down my face as I buckled the last straps. When I slid into the pilot's seat, my hands shook, making it difficult to fasten my harness. I stared at the sky through the missing section of wall, my heart galloping in my chest. Fear filled my mouth with copper and my eyes blurred as I gripped the handlebars with shaking hands. "Bowman—"

He made a clucking sound. "Let's go. One. Last. Flight."

The flier lunged forward and tears blurred my vision, but I pedaled with all my strength, gasping from fear and the exertion as the courtyard's edge rolled toward us. I closed my eyes as I pedaled us over it, but when the flier's nose tilted toward the water, they popped open.

We plummeted toward the rocks at the cliff's base. I pedaled as fast as I could, screaming, wrenching the handlebars toward me with all my strength. Behind me, Bowman roared.

My stomach dropped as the wings caught, the nose rising.

"Yes, boy, yes!" Bowman bellowed.

By meters, we rose. I sat back, drenched with sweat, my lungs straining for air as I pedaled, my feet a blur. "We did it, Bowman," I hollered, the wild exultation giving me a voice. I trimmed the wings and turned us toward Toronto Depot, relishing the drizzle's chill. I laughed again, settling back.

Bowman said nothing.

"I wasn't sure we'd make it, but you built her to last." I

shook my head. "She's a marvel." I glanced down, noticing my spreading bloodstain. I must have lost the bandage during our drop. "Bowman?"

There was no answer.

The flier wobbled as I twisted. Bowman sat slumped forward, his head hanging.

"Bowman?" Tears welled in my eyes as I scanned the shoreline. There was nowhere to land, but even if there was, I knew it was too late.

The lump in my throat grew as I pedaled west. Beneath us, boats crowded the lake, more than I'd ever seen before. I watched them sail back and forth as Toronto Depot's ruined skyline sharpened. Dizzy, I allowed the flier to sink toward the water, my trouser leg red to the knee.

We circled Hanlan's Island. The *Marybelle* wasn't in her slip, and the pier was empty, but was it long enough to land on? We circled again, and my vision grayed.

It was time to land.

Carefully, I lined the flier up with the dock and let it sink, pedaling only enough to keep us aloft as the dock slid toward us. The flier crabbed sideways as a gust hit us, but I glanced at Beck's flying queen, using it as a guide to correct our path.

The flier's wheels hit the wooden dock with a thud, and we rolled smoothly down its length, the wheels clicking with a *thud-thump* as we crossed each board. Tears streamed from my eyes as Charcoal raced down the length of the pier toward me, Akiko sprinting behind him.

CHAPTER FIFTY-SEVEN

Genevie assumed command, crackling with energy as she dispatched Akiko to get help. Time blurred as Ben and Josephine helped me to the inn under the steel-gray skies, but when they brought Bowman's body into the inn, I broke down, shuddering as I wept. To give me time to collect myself, Mama shooed everyone but Akiko from the kitchen, then bustled around preparing her suturing materials and gathering herbs.

"Was there really a bear?" asked Akiko in a low voice. "You missed lunch."

I shook my head slightly, a small smile on my face. "There's taffy in my bag," I rasped.

Akiko retrieved both bags and unwrapped a piece from each. "Looks like taffy," she said, squinting at the candy.

Mama set a bowl of warm water on the table and laid her hand on my thigh. "I hope this is the last time we do this, Artist."

I patted her hand. "Me too."

Akiko bit the piece of peppermint candy in two and tossed half to Charcoal. "To establish my baseline."

I snorted and averted my eyes as Mama cut away the trouser leg.

"Yuck," said Akiko, peering over Mama's arm. "Your leg will never win a contest."

I drank in the sight of her, healthy and whole. "There are leg contests?"

Akiko glanced at me with pity written across her face. "Not for you."

Mama frowned at me as she cleaned my leg. "You've reopened two of the old wounds *and* created a new one."

My eyes roved around Mama's cheerful kitchen, comforted by the familiar objects and scents.

"It bled a good deal," I said. They didn't need to know how I'd used the blood.

Mama studied me. "Your color isn't good, but to heal this leg, we must build you back up."

Akiko bit the strawberry taffy in two, tossing half to Charcoal. "Mmm, this is good."

My heart lifted, and I grinned at the dog, who smacked the candy happily. "Can I have one?"

Akiko eyed my leg. "Free pass until Mama rebuilds you." She unwrapped a candy and shoved it in my mouth, her breath sweet against my face. "Want one, Mama?"

Mama's eyes crinkled. "Oh, why not? What are my choices?"

"Peppermint, Strawberry, or Strawberry-Mint."

I arched my brow, memorizing Akiko's face. "Strawberry-Mint? You didn't offer me one."

Akiko looked smug. "You're being built back up, not spoiled."

The room swam as Mama cleaned the wounds, but I concentrated on the strawberry flavor of the sticky candy. "Where's Gunther?"

Akiko bounced in her chair. "Can I tell him?"

Mama patted my leg dry. "Yes, keep him distracted."

"Check." Akiko's eyes glowed. "Reverend Carter marooned the other kids on a boat and hid them on the lake, so Gunther, Olen, and Beck took the pirate ship to hunt the kids."

"To *look for* the kids," corrected Mama, chuckling. "For once, the people of Toronto Depot pulled together and everyone with a boat headed out to search for the mites." Mama shook her head. "The man is a monster."

"How are *you* here?" I asked Akiko.

She lifted her chin. "I got lost on purpose." Glancing at Mama, she asked. "Does he need more distracting?"

Mama nodded as she threaded a curved needle. "This is the worst part."

She was right, and I squeaked as the needle bit into my skin. "Worth another taffy?"

Akiko tore her eyes from Mama's sewing. "One more," she said, handing me a peppermint taffy.

The minty candy soothed my raw throat but did nothing to distract me from Mama's work. Pushing it into my cheek, I asked. "Where is Carter now? Did Talbot bring you here?"

Akiko's face darkened. "I *told* you, I got lost on purpose."

I picked up her hand and shook it. "Well, Matthew," I squeaked in falsetto, "let me tell you the *entire* story."

Akiko giggled. "Fine. Reverend Carter left the island with the other old people. He had two boats and I accidentally-on-purpose was on the second boat."

"Were the other kids there too?"

Akiko shook her head. "No, but I saw the rough-in on the wall at the seminary, so I knew I shouldn't go with the other kids." She bit her lip. "I felt bad though."

"Were you tempted to stay with your friends?" She had

been so happy on the island, and a part of me had wondered, given the chance, if she'd stay with them.

Akiko cackled, like I had made a joke. "You're silly. Besides, you said family sticks together."

A lump swelled in my throat, but I nodded. "Why didn't they notice you on the grownup boat?"

She shrugged. "I wore black robes and stood next to the artists. Grownups don't look too hard."

I pictured the sailboat I'd disguised to blend with the water. "Smart plan."

"When the boats docked, I got lost and came here, but Ben was rowing, not Beck." Akiko pursed her lips. "He's slower, and he shoves the boat along instead of letting the water do it."

I glanced at Mama. "Do you know what happened at the meeting?"

"I went, but I'm not sure I understand what happened." Mama tied a knot, then snipped the thread. "We assumed Carter called the meeting to negotiate and settle his many outstanding debts. Here child, take this bowl to the sink."

Mama threaded the needle again. "But after we'd settled in to listen, he thundered on about how we were godless and unsavable. At the conclusion of his admonishments, he told us he'd left the children floating on a barge by themselves. Later, we learned he'd held the meeting as a distraction while his people raided the warehouse. By the time the dock administrators and harbormaster had organized search parties, Carter and his people had gone."

I blinked. "They just... left?"

Mama nodded and resumed her sewing. "They ransacked the warehouse and our seed library on their way out, but yes, they left."

A rush of heat swamped me as the needle pierced my skin, but I shook it off, focusing on Akiko. "Talbot?"

She nodded. "He went with them. Will we go too?"

Puzzled, my brows knit. "Why?"

Akiko shrugged. "The other artists went; Master Hooper and Pritchard and Bower."

Bower?

My pulse jumped. "Master Bower was on the boat?"

"They were all there."

None of this made any sense. "Who else?"

Akiko sighed. "Everyone."

I winced as Mama's needle hit the thinner skin along my shin. What did *everyone* mean?

"It's why I could be on a boat with the others," Akiko continued. She unwrapped another candy and pretended to toss it, trying to fake out Charcoal.

I propped myself up on my elbows. "Others?"

She rolled her eyes. "Other art students."

My pulse leaped. "How many?"

Akiko shrugged. "A hundred? More?"

Sweat broke out along my upper lip. "A hundred? That's more than was at Erie Abbey."

"Duh."

My ears buzzed. "Duh?"

"It means I know," Akiko said, as she watched Mama snip the thread. "Last one?"

Mama nodded. "One more, then we put the herb paste on and wrap the dressing."

"Your leg is like a roasting chicken," said Akiko, her eyes dancing.

"Duh," I said.

Akiko cackled. "The only one who wasn't there was Master Staker."

I blinked. "He's at Niagara Abbey."

Akiko shook her head. "It's empty."

Sweat sprang out along my spine. "Erie is the abandoned abbey."

Akiko compressed her lips, her eyes sliding toward the common room. "Want me to get Josephine?"

The candy curdled in my stomach; the sweetness turning sour in my mouth. "Why?"

"You'll believe *her*." Akiko rolled her eyes.

I lay back, resting my right arm on my forehead. "I believe you." My head swam, and my temples pounded as I fought to sort through the information.

Mama paused her sewing. "Are you feeling faint?"

"Matthew is fainting?" chirped Akiko.

"Hush, child. Go get Ben."

The common room door swiveled and, moments later, swiveled again.

"Mama?" asked Ben, his voice full of gravel.

Mama snipped a thread. "After we get Matthew to bed, will you row me over? I need supplies."

Ben set his hand, heavy and warm, on my shoulder. "Do you want me to go for you so you can watch him?"

"No," she said. "I'm leaving Akiko in charge."

"We're rebuilding him," said Akiko.

I opened my eyes. "I'm still here."

"Prepare to be chicken-fied," said Akiko, as Mama spread a cool paste over my leg.

I glanced at Ben. "Akiko said there were artists with Reverend Carter?"

Ben nodded. "A fair number of them attended the meeting, and a man called McCully led the group that ransacked the warehouse."

"Headmaster McCully," I said automatically. My heart hammered as I sat up. "Headmaster McCully was with Reverend Carter?"

Akiko twirled on her stool. "Told you."

My mind spun as Mama wound gauze around my leg and Carter's words reverberated in my memory: *"I know where they are, and I have quite an ending planned for them."*

If Headmaster McCully worked for Reverend Carter, I needed to get back to Niagara Abbey. Without Talbot, the abbey was the only place I would find answers.

Akiko bent over me, her face inches from mine.

"What?" I asked, staring up at her.

She squinted one eye. "I'm trying to decide what color you should be."

My stomach clenched. "Don't you dare."

Mama chuckled. "He'll turn the right color on his own, child."

"Too bad," said Akiko, sighing.

CHAPTER FIFTY-EIGHT

The morning sun sparkled on the waves while we waited for Beck to row the dinghy to shore a second time. She landed the small craft, and we helped her pull it farther onto the beach, the hull grinding and scraping along the sandy, shell-strewn surface. I helped Josephine down from the dinghy, waving at Gunther, who waved back from the *Marybelle's* deck.

"He's not coming?" Akiko asked, tossing a pebble into the water.

Charcoal splashed into the shallows to investigate.

Beck shook her head, hopping from the dinghy. "He said he wanted to fish."

Olen grinned. "What, is his little, brown jug full again?"

Beck snorted. "Probably." She studied the trail. "Shall we?"

"Let's go." I led the way up the trail to the bluff, pausing at the base of the lawns to observe the abbey's lakefront face. The windows were dark, and no smoke rose from the chimneys. Akiko was right; they had abandoned the building.

Genevie tossed her arm over my shoulder. "Is this shack like the one you grew up in?"

I grinned. "Nope, this one is much smaller. Come on." I crossed the lawn, wincing as I climbed the shallow steps to the veranda, Akiko on my heels, and Earl climbing after her.

The others hung back, gazing at the building.

From the top of the steps, I beckoned to them. "Really, it's okay. If anyone was here, they'd already have come out."

Akiko skipped around us. "Last one inside is a smelly bear," she taunted.

Olen sprinted toward the veranda. "Not it!"

Genevie pushed Ben backward before bounding up the stairs and Josephine giggled as she trotted after her. Ben and Beck, the last two left on the lawn, eyed each other before sprinting toward us.

We burst into the dining hall, bright-eyed and smiling, while Charcoal barked and cavorted around us. Earl laughed, clapping. This was the first time I'd seen her smile since I'd brought Bowman's body back to Mama's, and it gladdened my heart.

"Phew," said Akiko, pinching her nose. "Smelly bears, all of you."

I glanced around the cavernous dining hall, remembering the last time I'd been here. "If you want a tour, Akiko can show you around better than I can."

"What are we searching for?" asked Ben.

I shrugged. "I need answers. The last time I was here, Headmaster McCully offered me a position and the opportunity to create a symbiotic community."

Josephine crossed her arms. "It makes little sense."

"Agreed." I turned to Akiko. "How much of the abbey did you explore last time?"

Akiko evaded my eyes and stared at the floor.

I chuckled. "Good. Can you take us to the headmaster's office first?"

She grinned. "Right this way."

Olen and Josephine's eyes lit up when they spotted the books in the headmaster's office.

I crossed to the desk and rifled through the piles of papers. With luck, the answers I needed were here, somewhere. How Carter had forced two abbeys into service, perhaps even information about me or my family. "Do you want to sort through this?"

Josephine nodded, her face eager.

Olen hesitated before asking, "Mind if I help?"

Josephine gazed at him, but after a blue aura shimmered between them, nodded her head. Olen beamed in response.

Akiko and I stared at each other, wide-eyed, but none of the others appeared to notice.

"What next?" asked Akiko.

I rubbed my jaw. "When I explored Erie Abbey, I found rooms with mechanical equipment. A sort of metal tower. Did you find anything like that here? Maybe Ben can make sense of it."

Akiko brightened. "Yup. Room with lots of buttons and ear warmers. Come on."

Olen and Josephine barely looked up as we left.

Akiko skipped down the hallway. We followed, peering into the rooms we passed. She led us to a dark hallway and stopped to push on the wall.

Ben whistled as the wall swung inward. He stepped into the room, shaking his head. "I think this is radio equipment."

The word was unfamiliar. "Radio?"

He nodded, a faraway look in his eyes. "If I can find the power source, I'll see if there's anyone on the line."

I glanced at the others, but they shrugged.

"What next?" asked Akiko.

"We need art supplies," I said. "Bower called it the vault when he took me."

"The locked room! This way." Akiko led us to the subbasement and stopped before the familiar door. "I couldn't figure out how to get in."

I tugged on the door, but it didn't open.

"Let me look." Genevie bent and inspected the lock. She straightened, winked at me, and reached above the door frame. She pulled down a brass key, grinning. "Good thing you had a blacksmith with you."

Akiko giggled, taking the key from Genevie. After unlocking the door, she struggled to pull it open and slipped through the narrow gap. "Wow!"

I pulled the door the rest of the way open and followed the women inside. As before, the weight of the room, the air heavy with sorrow and turpentine, pressed against me. The history behind the carefully stored belongings a solemn reminder.

Akiko spun, her eyes roving over the shelves of supplies

"Please organize two full sets, Akiko."

She turned. "Two?"

We locked eyes, and I nodded. "Two. While you're busy, we're going to explore."

Akiko turned back to the shelves, running her fingers lightly over the lines of brushes. "Find you later."

Earl, Genevie, Beck, and I wandered through the subbasement, poking our heads into dim rooms. Most had little illumination other than the narrow windows filthy with grime near the ceilings.

After climbing a cramped set of stone steps, we found ourselves in a narrow hallway. The first two rooms were empty, but the third door opened onto a gallery. The line of windows stretched as far as we could see, their window frames burnished and gleaming in the sun. Paintings spanned the length of the gallery along the inner wall. We wandered down the sunlit room, stopping frequently to inspect the artwork.

"What is it?" asked Beck.

My eyes tightened. "They called this style of art iconography. It typically depicts religious scenes."

Genevie shivered as she studied a painting. A naked man floating above waves was attempting to protect a terrified, naked baby from another man with eyes having no iris or pupils. The man with unseeing eyes was trying to escape a flame but was shackled to the ground. In the background, the sun rose, chasing the night.

Earl tilted her head and narrowed her eyes. "Are these old or new?"

I studied the painting. "This is old, from *Before,* though it might have been old even before the world died." I glanced at the next painting, shaking my head. "This one is new."

In it, a pale, bearded man with an oval-shaped face held an open book in his left hand, his right hand gesturing as though explaining the text. A red sunburst adorned with Greek characters encircled his head.

"Charming," said Beck, two paintings down. She stepped backward, revulsion on her face.

The painting depicted a naked man being tortured as a crowd watched, entertained. They had chained the figure to a gridiron set over a fire, and a man with scorn written across his face held a chain attached to the victim's ankles. Three men stoked the fire, and a fourth speared the victim under his right arm.

"The Blessed Saint Lawrence," read Earl. She wrinkled her nose. "Was this the type of art you studied?"

"Certainly not. We studied iconography as a style and subgenre of art, but not to replicate it." I examined the painting.

Though well composed, I didn't understand why the artist had taken such pains to illustrate the grisly scene.

"Why are there so many?" asked Genevie, wandering down the line.

I shrugged. "Maybe this was Headmaster McCully's private collection."

Genevie frowned. "Suggesting he worked with Reverend Carter long before you met him."

I stared at her. "He probably also knew what happened to Erie Abbey before he sent me there."

"Matthew!" Charcoal and Akiko burst into the gallery. "There you are. Come on!" She turned, sprinting from the gallery.

We followed, exchanging glances.

Akiko waited at the staircase, frantically waving. "Hurry!" She led us through a maze of hallways, arriving before an iron door. It shrieked as she pushed it wider.

I squinted into the gloom. "What am I looking at?"

Akiko heaved an exaggerated sigh. "Your eyes are old. Here, wait."

She disappeared into the gloom, then emerged, thrusting a canvas at me.

I gazed at it, my mouth tasting of ashes.

"The headmaster was a thief." Akiko lifted her chin, daring me to argue.

I studied the painting. *Home.* "What a rascal. Is the rest of our stuff here?"

She bobbed her head. "*Even* my dirty socks from Master Pritchard's cottage. *Everything* is here."

My mind wobbled as the implication hit me. Not only had Pritchard set me up, he'd been working with Niagara Abbey and, likely, Erie Abbey too.

The abbeys were complicit with the rise of religion in the region.

What of the other abbeys? Which of them was a part of Carter's larger plan? My stomach churned, nauseous with betrayal.

Earl slipped her arm around my waist, leaning her head against my shoulder while Beck and Genevie helped Akiko gather our things. Earl's warmth comforted me, my heart lifting at our contact until Genevie thrust a canvas bag at me, laying my sword on top.

Bruised and reeling, I followed them out of the dark.

CHAPTER FIFTY-NINE

When we reached the dining hall, I dumped our things onto the nearest table. My sword clattered onto the surface and lay there, gleaming and lethal against the dark, burnished wood. Seeing it reminded me of Staker. Akiko hadn't seen him on the boat with the others, and I couldn't imagine him complicit in McCully's betrayal.

"Now what?" asked Akiko.

"Lunch," said Genevie. "Can you go tell Ben? Fetch Olen and Josephine, too."

Akiko giggled and barked before crying, "Fetch!" She scampered out of the hall, Charcoal on her heels.

My nerves jangled, and I itched to draw, to lose myself in the soothing ritual of art. While my friends repacked our things, I opened the demonstration closet and rummaged through it, pulling out an easel and a blank canvas. My pencils were still in the felted pouch I'd left Popham Abbey with. I stared at them, hoping zealots hadn't infiltrated Popham, too.

Akiko popped her head into the dining hall. "Woof, woof," she said. Then, waving, she trotted off again.

Josephine spotted me and crossed the hall. "We've found some correspondence, but nothing concrete yet. I want to keep digging after lunch."

I nodded, sharpening a pencil. "Niagara Abbey has been working with Reverend Carter for quite a while."

Josephine's brow furrowed. "What did you find?"

"Religious art," said Genevie, joining us. "And stolen bags."

Josephine glanced at the bags on the table. "They had your things? Even your painting?"

I nodded, the increasingly familiar embers in my gut igniting. With a sweeping stroke, I started my drawing, setting the horizon first.

Akiko pulled Ben into the dining hall. "See? We found everything—*even* my dirty socks."

Ben put his hands on his hips. "They didn't wash them? Rude."

Akiko giggled. "So rude." Kneeling on the bench, she unzipped a bag. "I hope I didn't leave a sandwich in here."

"If you did, you can eat it for lunch," said Ben.

Akiko pretended to gag, then noticed me and wandered over to examine the canvas. "Are you improving?"

"Yes?"

She patted my hand. "I didn't want to live here, anyway. Oh, look, Gunther's coming." She whistled for Charcoal and ran across the lawn toward the trail.

Ben and Earl organized lunch, and from the corner of my eye, I watched Earl show Akiko how to core strawberries with a short paring knife.

"See how the whole middle comes out?" said Earl, demonstrating on another berry.

Akiko took the knife and held it gingerly, scanning Earl for approval. Earl handed her a strawberry, then watched her cut the top off and remove the core.

"Perfect," said Earl, her lips curving.

Akiko brightened and reached for another berry. "I'll try again."

Ben winked at Earl. "Try on each one, please."

I continued to draw as they prepared the meal, the mechanics of my work calming my mind and bringing me back to my center.

Gunther clomped over and whistled. "*Marybelle* looks mighty fine."

"She's an excellent subject," I said, capturing a fluttering ribbon near the wind indicator.

Gunther watched, his face slack. "Can I have the drawing when you're done with it?"

His request extinguished the corrosive heat licking at my core. My eyes crinkled, and I wished I'd painted it in color instead of sketching. "It's yours, my friend."

Earl unrolled a leather parcel, removing a sharpening steel and long carving knife. She set the tip of the sharpening steel on the tabletop, pulling the carving knife across it, toward her, the blade moving across the steel with a melodic *zing*. After repeating the movement a dozen times, she switched the carving knife to her left hand to repeat the process.

Like me, she had a ritual. When finished, she carved the rind from the roasted beef and tossed it to Charcoal before proceeding to slice the meat into translucent slivers.

Josephine rubbed her hand across the middle of my back. "A master at work."

I nodded, dragging my eyes from Earl.

Josephine smiled at my drawing. "That is how I feel when I watch you change the world."

I'd nearly captured the scene—the shore, the water's movement, and *Marybelle* floating proudly on its sparkling surface.

Josephine's voice was soft as she asked, "How are you dealing with everything?"

I sighed, setting my pencil on the easel's ledge before slumping against the window frame. "In truth, I'm so blasted angry, it's hard to see straight. I don't even trust my memories of Popham and am questioning everything I knew about the abbey system."

It was worse than that—now there was no way I could trust anyone in an abbey with Akiko in case they were a part of Carter's organization. The betrayal also meant there would be no cooperative community in our future—that dream had died when Akiko had emerged from the gloom with *Home* in her hands.

I swallowed as Genevie joined us. "It's as though someone knocked down the place I grew up in, so I can't go home again."

"I know what you mean," said Genevie, pulling Josephine against her. "It hurts, but it also means you're not obligated to return, and it's freeing to make your own choices. Come, lunch is ready."

Ben glanced at us. "Where shall we sit?"

I needed to be anywhere but *here*. "Outside? It's a beautiful view."

"Picnic," Akiko squealed, running to open the door.

ONCE OUTSIDE, I SANK ONTO THE SUN-WARMED VERANDA steps and bit into my sandwich. I hadn't thought I could eat, but they had piled the roasted beef onto chewy rolls with sliced tomato and sharp cheddar, and I chewed with enjoyment. Beside me, Charcoal wolfed his cubes of beef, cheddar, and bread. He burped, his eyes fastened on my food.

"No," I said. "Mine."

He sighed, laying his chin on his paws, but his eyes continued to trace the sandwich as I moved it back and forth until I handed the rest to him. He wolfed it down, then raced to join Akiko. I picked up my bowl of salad, listening to the bees buzz from the azaleas sprawling along one edge of the veranda.

Genevie dropped onto the step next to me, setting down her bowl. "Do you think she'll come with us?"

I followed her gaze to where Earl chatted with Ben and Josephine. "I hope so."

"Me too. She's a good egg." Genevie laughed when Charcoal abandoned Akiko and made a beeline for Josephine, who hadn't finished eating.

I picked through my salad, chasing down the fragrant strawberries and chunks of cheese. "Did you know Earl is an orphan? They left her at a filling station when she was an infant."

"Really?" Genevie tipped her ransacked salad bowl toward me. "She belongs with us then."

With us.

A family crafted by love and sacrifice, a family which had stood many tests. A family who would stick together. I bumped Genevie's shoulder with mine.

"Another sandwich?" asked Ben, carrying the platter. He eyed our bowls. "The lettuce is edible too."

"Prove it," said Genevie.

Ben set the platter down next to her, waving off Charcoal, and dropped onto the step below us. "I didn't eat mine either."

"Didn't eat what?" asked Josephine, as she and Earl wandered toward us. They took seats next to Ben and stretched out like two graceful cats flanking a bear.

"Lettuce," we said in unison.

Josephine tipped her bowl. "Me neither."

Akiko led the others to where we'd gathered and squeezed

between me and Genevie. She picked up my bowl, stuffing lettuce into her mouth until Genevie slid her bowl over too, and everyone chuckled. Fragrant smoke drifted from Gunther's pipe, and I took a deep breath as the tension inside me uncoiled.

"I'm sleepy," said Beck. "Let's stay here forever."

Gunther chuckled. "We'll have to decide if we're staying the night or heading back. Either is fine, but if we go back, I've got fish for Mama to fry."

"Head back," mumbled Akiko, her cheeks bulging with lettuce.

"We leave in an hour then," said Gunther, as smoke trickled from his nose.

I glanced at him. "Gunther, do you mind if I alter *Marybelle*?"

Gunther squinted at his boat. "I trust ye, Artist."

After reviewing my sketch, I took a deep breath to center myself and visualized the change I'd been considering since Gunther had rescued me from the storm. When ready, my eyes snapped open and my fingers tingled as I elongated the prow, then carved a dragon figurehead into the front of the ship. The timbers on the schooner groaned as I mimicked Beck's queen, crafting a snarling dragon with a thin snout, broad forehead, and sharp teeth. Under my pencil, the dragon's wings unfurled alongside the bow until she was a part of the boat instead of attached to the front.

When I finished, Gunther openly wept.

Beck rose, wrapping her arms around me. "Thank you," she whispered before pulling back and asking, "When are you leaving?"

"Leaving?" Akiko squinted at us.

Genevie chuckled and pulled the child closer. "You didn't

think we'd sit on these steps until you were an old lady, did you?"

Ben cleared his throat. "The question is, where do we go next?"

I bit my lip. Before Carter had threatened my parents, my plan had been to settle *here* to provide a stable, structured life for Akiko. But now, even though saying goodbye to Mama, Gunther, Beck, and Olen would hurt, I didn't want to settle near Toronto Depot. Besides, Akiko deserved to be raised in a united, cooperative community, and I couldn't imagine a more allied community than the family we had created.

Chills ran up my arms. Akiko didn't need me to be the *best* father. She needed me to be a father who kept her with her family.

Josephine leaned against Ben. "Does Talbot need our help?"

I stretched, shrugging. I didn't want to discuss what Carter had threatened in front of Akiko. "Talbot can take care of himself, and I'd rather not put us in front of Carter again if I can help it. I don't know what the artists will do, but if we can avoid trouble, we should."

Akiko squirmed out of Genevie's grip. "*Home* might point the way." She disappeared inside and returned, studying the painting.

"Can we all see?" asked Ben.

Akiko rolled her eyes, but turned the painting toward us.

Olen straightened, frowning. "That's the stolen painting?"

My gaze raked over the familiar canvas as I nodded. "Someone said it depicted the CN Tower in Toronto Depot."

"Why?" asked Beck, glancing at Olen. "Is there another tower like it?"

Olen let out a whistling breath. "Sure is. It looks like the Strat in Las Vegas Depot."

"Goody," said Akiko. "We're going to the land of painted horses and cowboys."

"To painted cowboys on horses," said Genevie, lifting her glass.

"To sandstone and cactus," said Josephine, her voice eager.

Earl stood and raised her glass, her smile hesitant. "To buffalo and antelope."

Ben's eyes crinkled as he lifted his glass. "To going together."

My breath caught as they turned toward me. They planned to continue this quest with me, to travel thousands of kilometers into the unknown, based only on Olen's recognition of a skyline I'd painted from *visions*. That I could rely on their support, that I'd known they would continue with me—*with us*—spoke volumes.

This was my genuine family—the family I would protect at all costs, but if we made it to Las Vegas Depot before Reverend Carter, we could also warn my birth parents. Depending on what they were like, perhaps, we'd even choose to settle near them.

My heart full, I raised my glass. "To each of you, and to traveling to Las Vegas Depot, together."

AUTHOR'S NOTE

As many of you know, the story kernel of the Elemental Artist series sprouted while I was attending the 2016 Womxn's March in Seattle. As we shuffled through the streets, I wondered about a world without politics, money, power, religion, or greed, but I didn't yet know *who* I'd be writing about.

Matthew was neither inspired by a specific person, nor did he appear to me as a fully fleshed character. In early drafts, he was reserved and unflappable, hiding his trauma and angst. It was clear he was driven to find answers, but I assumed he was a loner, drifting through the post-apocalyptic world without the benefit of technology to help him reach his goal. But as I continued to revise the story, he opened up, and I came to understand him better. Still, imagine my surprise when he decided to adopt a kid in his typically naïve, bumbling way. But once he had committed himself to parenting Akiko in Oil and Dust, I knew I wanted to further explore their relationship in Graphite and Turbulence.

The modern father-child relationship fascinates me. I'm endlessly charmed watching fathers who play with their children without letting gender stereotypes get in the way. The father in Spain who dresses himself and his tiny daughter in costumes to take out the garbage enchanted me—Google it and see if you don't melt too!

My father and I didn't get along when I was a child. He was born and raised in Japan, and his ideas of what the parent-child relationship should be didn't mesh well with my Americanized opinions. That we are similar in nature and character didn't help! It wasn't until we were at a dance lesson practicing for my wedding that I realized how wide of a cultural gap we'd been bridging. When our Georgian dance instructor scolded him for not looking at me while we danced, my father objected, saying it was rude to look someone in the eyes. It floored me—even though I'd grown up in the limbo space between my eastern and western heritages, there were *still* cultural gulfs I was unaware of.

As adults, he's become one of my best friends. He's much more of a "girl dad" now than he was as a young father, and I'm better equipped to appreciate him for who he is. My childhood memories, the many modern fathers who are redefining fatherhood (search YouTube for a channel called *How To Dad*), and the relationship I have with my dad now, all inspired Matthew and Akiko's relationship.

Regarding the geography the characters encountered in Graphite and Turbulence, I unabashedly admit I took certain liberties, as novelists are wont to do. My choices to make Niagara Falls taller than it currently is and to call Lake Ontario the Ontario Sea exasperated my Canadian copy editor. In my defense, Matthew's world is several hundred years in the future, and I had a ball imagining what changes might happen to the natural world without man's interference.

For example, I assumed the dams and locks along the Niagara River failed, allowing the water to pour forth without restraint and would thus boost the overall volume at Niagara Falls. This would allow the river to carve the rock, lengthening its total plunge. The drowned lands were similarly how I envisioned nature taking back the built environment. Without intervention, I imagined sewer and storm water systems clogging and failing. With so much impervious surface, I pictured the water pooling and ponding over the acres of concrete and asphalt. Over time, muck would accumulate, providing a substrate for marsh plants and animals to take hold and thrive.

Regarding Lake Ontario, according to NOAA, the difference between an ocean and a sea is size. They say a sea is smaller than an ocean and partially enclosed by land. Since you can sail from Lake Ontario to the Atlantic Ocean (via the Saint Lawrence Seaway's locks), I would posit man's intervention transformed Lake Ontario into a freshwater sea. Plus, if the ocean levels continue to rise because of climate change, the Atlantic could push further toward the lake. And, frankly, the Ontario Sea sounds infinitely more romantic than Lake Ontario, so I hope my Canadian readers will forgive my imagination's alterations of their geography.

Thank you so much for reading Graphite and Turbulence! I hope you enjoyed reading it as much as I enjoyed writing it. Please consider reviewing it on Amazon, Goodreads, or any other book site. Reviews help so much to bring a book to a reader's attention. As a bonus, reviews provide motivation to writers, too, so by writing reviews, you are enabling the creation of new books. Matthew's story will continue in Charcoal and Smoke, Book 3 in the Elemental Artist series.

ABOUT THE AUTHOR

Thank you for reading Graphite and Turbulence. I hope you enjoyed the journey.

Please leave a review to help other readers find the book. Your review really helps me out!

Want a free, signed book plate for your book? Post a picture of the book on your socials! Don't forget to tag and follow me so I can DM you for your mailing address.

Jami Fairleigh is a biracial, Japanese-American writer, urban planner, and hobby collector from Washington. She shares her life with a husband, a trio of well-mannered horses, a pair of dubiously behaved parrots, and one neurotic dog. Her writing has been published by Terror House Magazine, Horror Tree, Defenestration, and Amsterdam Quarterly. She is currently working on the third novel in the Elemental Artist fantasy series. You can find her and more information about her writing at jamifairleigh.com.

THE ELEMENTAL ARTIST

Matthew's origin story is available for free when you sign up for my email newsletter and updates on my books and other fiction at:

What would you paint if you could change the physical world with your art?

Seventeen-year-old art student Matthew Sugiyama has his heart set on winning the coveted position of Head Boy, but so have the other thirteenth-grade boys in the abbey.

Winning the spot will secure his future after graduation, but is his art magic strong enough to win?

THE ELEMENTAL ARTIST SERIES
READING ORDER

A Garland of Cedar and Snow
Oil and Dust
Graphite and Turbulence
Charcoal and Smoke (Spring 2023)

ACKNOWLEDGMENTS

The creation of a novel is an alchemical process wherein the writer's imagination is crafted by many hands, minds, and hearts into an *experience*, and with luck, a memory. The art begins when the writer imagines a world or person or event that *could* be.

Through drafts and revisions, a team works together to refine the writer's vision into a book ready for consumption. Once published, readers focus the story through the lenses of their own experiences. The act of reading is the final, essential spark needed to bring the characters to life. With this in mind, I'd like to acknowledge the people who helped bring Graphite and Turbulence into being.

Thank you to the writers and organizers of the Rainforest Writing Retreat for providing the time and space for me to draft the last quarter of this story. Picking up a dropped story thread is difficult, but the craft talks I attended at the virtual 2021 Rainforest Writing Retreat provided much-needed inspiration. The shared, silent writing sessions and word-count competition provided oodles of motivation. I'd also like to thank my critique partners Jami Sheets and Jamie Sogn, who cheered me on through the revision process. A double thanks to Jamie Sogn, who promoted Oil and Dust during her Pitchwars Instagram takeover day.

My production team included many amazing people. First, I'd like to thank my beta readers, Erik Shimizu for his many, many questions and parenting insight, Doug Fairleigh for being a supportive spouse and providing feedback on the relationships Matthew builds, and Richard Odey for his invaluable comments and insights into the pacing and plot, as well as his opinions on how to write a male character.

Next, I'd like to thank my editors; Charlie Knight (CKnightWrites) for ensuring the tone and style of Graphite and Turbulence meshed with what we'd established in Oil and Dust and for providing priceless notes about the emotional impacts of scenes, Warren Layberry (Dark Water Editing) for tightening my prose, catching factual errors, and immeasurably helpful comments about the geography of Matthew's world, and Hyper-Speller at (https://www.wordrefiner.com) for your lightning-fast capture of typos, homonyms, and homophones... and for helping to wrangle the ever-pesky commas littering this text.

Thank you also to Andrew and Rebecca Brown (Design for Writers) for another beautiful cover.

For inspiration, I follow several amazing graphite artists on Instagram. Thank you Jono Dry @jonodry, Fabrice Goosens @fabricetheartist, Stephanie Bower @stephanieabower, Armin Mersmann @arminmersmann, and @my_life_works for sharing your work.

I'd again like to thank the tool makers behind Scrivener, Fictionary, ProWritingAid, BookFunnel, reMarkable, Publisher Rocket, BookSirens, NetGalley, and Vellum. Without your products and platforms, it would be much, much more difficult to be an independent author. I'd also like to thank the #WritingCommunity on Twitter. Your humor, humanity, and encouragement mean a great deal.

Thank you also to Annie Carl at The Neverending Bookshop for putting Oil and Dust on your shelves. All, please support your local indie bookstores!

Next, I'd like to thank all the ARC readers who read and reviewed Oil and Dust. Thank you authors Rebecca Demarest and Helen Garraway. Rebecca, your feedback, advice, and friendship have improved my writing experience. Helen, I *so* appreciate your many mentions of Oil and Dust on both Instagram and Twitter. I'm forever grateful to both of you!

BookSirens ARC readers: Thank you Michelle, Jenny, Anna, Jeanette, Ralph, and Lauren. Special thanks to Lauren de Ford for splashing Oil and Dust all over Facebook. I can't wait to meet you at a future 20Books Vegas conference!

NetGalley ARC readers: Thank you Lori, Jodie C, Paul V, Danny F, Reviewer 492564, Educator 816933, Kayla P, Brittney G, Christine J, Books By Your Bedside, and Victoria B.

For every reader who has left (or will leave) a review, thank you, thank you, thank you. I so appreciate your wonderful, kind, and thoughtful words. They provide me with motivation to finish this series.

Last, I'd like to thank Dave Correia, who made my week when he called to ask for an advanced copy of this book to take it on vacation with him.